...never stopp... ...rene... ...service for more than th... ...f... ...nurse and a health visitor. Scar... ...public health and lives on the West Coast of Scotland with her fiancé and their two sons. Writing medical romances and contemporary romances is a dream come true for her.

Born in the UK, **Becky Wicks** has suffered interminable wanderlust from an early age. She's lived and worked all over the world, from London to Dubai, Sydney, Bali, NYC and Amsterdam. She's written for the likes of *GQ*, *Hello!*, *Fabulous* and *Time Out*, a host of YA romance, plus three travel memoirs—*Burqalicious*, *Balilicious* and *Latinalicious* (HarperCollins, Australia). Now she blends travel with romance for Mills & Boon and loves every minute! Tweet her @bex_wicks and subscribe at beckywicks.com.

A DADDY
FOR HER TWINS

SCARLET WILSON

FINDING FOREVER
WITH THE
SINGLE DAD

BECKY WICKS

MILLS & BOON

First published in Great Britain 2023
by Mills & Boon, an imprint of HarperCollins*Publishers* Ltd,
1 London Bridge Street, London, SE1 9GF

www.harpercollins.co.uk

HarperCollins*Publishers* Macken House, 39/40 Mayor Street Upper,
Dublin 1, D01 C9W8, Ireland

A Daddy for Her Twins © 2023 Scarlet Wilson

Finding Forever with the Single Dad © 2023 Becky Wicks

ISBN: 978-0-263-30614-9

08/23

A DADDY
FOR HER TWINS

SCARLET WILSON

MILLS & BOON

This book is dedicated to the fabulous vaccination team staff I work with, some of whom gave me tips about Singapore! Thank you, Elaine. x

CHAPTER ONE

ARTHUR FLETCHER WAS TIRED. More than tired. And it was all entirely his own fault. He'd landed at Singapore Changi airport, remembered he'd been told it was the finest in the world, and lost himself in the dazzling array of butterfly gardens, canopy park, waterfall fountains, not to mention the delicious eateries and shopping opportunities.

He'd been warned of course. But Arthur had decided—instead of immediately grabbing his suitcase and leaving the airport as he'd done on every other occasion in cities all around the world—he would take some time to enjoy the experience.

If everything worked out the way it should, it would likely be two years before he was back at Changi airport and moving on to a new post. St David's Children's Hospital—where he'd landed his latest paediatrician post—was only five years old and was already developing an illustrious reputation around the world. Set in one of Singapore's busiest districts, it rarely had empty beds, and the teaching and learning opportunities were vast. The chance of the promotion had appealed, as had the chance to go back to Singapore—a place he'd loved and worked in before.

Everything would have been great if he'd actually managed to collect the keys to his apartment and move in as planned. But it seemed that life had decided to throw him a few spanners and he'd unexpectedly ended up in a hotel overnight. He was just hoping he could get things sorted out quickly.

He tugged at the collar of his short-sleeved shirt, trying to adjust to the warmer climate again. His appointment as a paediatric consultant who would be involved with the doctors' training programme at St David's had gone smoothly. He'd worked previously in Singapore after qualifying as a doctor, and after taking an appointment in the US, and then in Germany, he'd been pleasantly surprised to be headhunted for the new role.

His official meeting and tour of the hospital wasn't until ten o'clock, but his late-night ventures at Changi airport had made him edgy about oversleeping, meaning he hadn't really slept at all. He'd finally got dressed just after seven, and was now sitting in the main entrance-way of the hospital, in the visitors' café.

Even though it was early, the streets of Singapore had been bustling, and the hospital foyer was entirely the same. He knew there was a shift change, with staff leaving and entering in a whole rainbow variety of scrubs. Scrub colour was usually dependent on role, and there were a few he hadn't yet identified.

His phone buzzed and he had a quick check. He gave a sigh and sent a text back. Lisa. He also noticed a message from Jess. He sent her a message back too. Both ex-girlfriends. Fletch had a habit of being a serial dater who could never last longer than six months. He was always up front about it. He had no plans to settle down in the near future, and when any relationship he was in reached that 'next stage' point, he always had the hard conversation and walked away amicably.

He'd lived all his adult life like this. While he'd like eventually to have a family of his own, he just didn't feel ready yet—likely because of his own upbringing as a child. His mother had dated a few men after his father had left, always saying she was 'trying before buying'. It had taken her a while to finally meet his stepfather and settle down. And the behaviour had kind of imprinted on Fletch.

Most of his exes had moved on successfully with no hard feelings. He was lucky like that. But they all kept telling him one day he would meet 'the one'. Fletch gave a smile and put his phone back in his pocket. Maybe in a few years.

As he sipped his coffee, he could feel the buzz through his body. He was excited about this new job. Excited about moving back to Singapore for a spell. He'd always loved this country, with its pleasant climate, friendly people and world of opportunities.

He watched as there was some jostling near the main entrance. A woman had her hands full, holding the hand of one young child, the other, grasped in her arms was clearly having a bad day, and she was struggling with a stroller and several bags.

He stood up without thinking and automatically walked over. 'You've got your hands full, let me help you.'

She blinked as she blew a wayward strand of hair out of her eyes. Fletch was always cautious when offering to assist, knowing that some people didn't appreciate it, but this lady was different.

'Brilliant,' she said, placing her squirming child in his arms. 'Meet Mr Cranky, also known as Justin.' She rejigged her bags, organising them on her stroller, and nodded to the young girl beside her. 'This is Mia.' She wrinkled her nose as she kept walking, now keeping the stroller under control. 'I'm Madison, I don't think we've met before.'

She was wearing a pair of navy scrubs, her light brown hair tied up in a ponytail and he could see freckles on her nose. She also had a hint of an accent. Scottish? Irish? He wasn't sure.

'Arthur Fletcher,' he said, walking alongside. Mr Cranky was looking at him suspiciously, but hadn't yet objected to being held by a stranger. 'I'm starting as a paediatrician this morning.'

Her footsteps slowed for a second and she gave him a broad smile. 'You are? That's fantastic. You'll love it here,' she said without hesitation, and then looked a bit thoughtful. 'I'll see you, then.' She glanced down at her scrubs. 'I'm one of the physios and part of my role is rehab, so I'm sometimes on the children's unit.' She looked over at Justin and gave a sigh.

'I don't know what's going on with my boy these last few days. He's been cranky and irritable.' She held up a hand and laughed before Fletch could speak. 'No, I'm not asking you to look at him. He's just out of sorts. Nothing serious.'

Fletch smiled. 'So, I'm Arthur Fletcher. But call me Fletch. The only person who calls me Arthur is my grandad.'

Madison's eyes twinkled. 'Named after him?' There was something about those eyes...

He nodded. 'You got it.'

They reached the elevators and she pressed a button. 'We're heading to the crèche. Have you been shown around yet?'

He shook his head. 'Well, allow me.' She smiled. 'You might as well know where the crèche is, as they'll hold some of your potential clientele.'

He nodded as the elevator rose, trying not to notice the shadows under Madison's eyes, or the paleness of her skin. She was clearly tired. But he didn't want to ask intrusive questions.

'I love your accent,' he said.

She laughed. 'Scots. But I'm not really sure why. My mum and dad are both from Scotland, but Dad was part of the British Consulate so I've lived all over the world.'

'You have?' He adjusted Justin, letting the little guy fold into his neck.

'Germany, Italy.' She nodded her head. 'We were in Singapore twice. I did most of my high school time here and always knew I wanted to come back.'

'So, you live here for good now?'

She nodded towards her children. 'Family ties. I love it here.'

He looked again. Her children clearly had some Asian heritage and his eyes went immediately to her hand. No ring. But he assumed nothing. He knew better than to do that.

The elevator doors pinged open and she led him down the corridor to a brightly coloured room, where children were clearly separated by age. The crèche was well staffed and children were signed in and out. A staff member came over with her arms outstretched to take Justin. 'How's my favourite?' she said to him as Madison's daughter skipped off to play with some friends. 'Did they have a good time in Scotland with your parents?' she asked Madison.

'They loved it,' she replied quickly. 'But getting them back into a routine is proving a challenge. This is Jen,' said Madison, 'and this is Fletch, one of the new children's doctors who was gracious enough to help me.'

Jen's eyes flicked over to Fletch with a hint of curiosity. 'Nice to meet you,' she said as she stroked Justin's hair. She glanced back to Madison. 'Still feeling a bit off?'

Madison nodded and took a deep breath. 'He didn't sleep well last night—well, none of us did. But he was just unsettled. I honestly wonder if he's a bit jet-lagged. They've only been back three days. No temperature, no cough. Just…irritable.'

Jen gave a brief nod. 'Don't worry, I'll keep him close, and call you if I'm worried at all. You okay if I let him sleep today?'

'Of course,' said Madison. She watched as Jen walked away with Justin, talking gently in his ear. Fletch could see the strain on her face.

Like any mother she was clearly worried. He knew it was none of his business, but did she have any help? And why was he even wondering? He hadn't even met this woman for more than five minutes and he had the weirdest feeling around her—almost as if she were pulling him in, and making him curious.

His phone buzzed as they walked back down the corridor. 'Where are you headed?' she asked as the elevator doors opened again.

He glanced at his phone. 'Finally, keys for my apartment.'

She raised her eyebrows. 'You haven't moved in already?'

'No, there was a bit of a hiccup and I stayed in a hotel last night.'

She folded her arms, looking amused. He was almost relieved to see the worry lines disappear from her face. 'That sounds like a story.'

'It is.' He turned his phone around and showed her the apartment.

'Wow.' She took the phone from his hand and started swiping through the photos, then gave a shudder and laughed. She handed the phone back. 'Too much glass for a mother of two three-year-olds.'

Fletch gave a conciliatory nod. 'You're right. I'll spend two years trying not to touch it at all. But I'm happy with the amenities. There's a gym, a swimming pool and a garden.' He rolled his eyes. 'All I really needed was the keys.'

'So, what happened, then?'

'The agent got delayed. His flight got cancelled and his partner's father was sick.' He held up his hands. 'I wasn't going to go to another hospital to harass someone for keys when their father was sick, so I said I'd book into a hotel for a night or so.'

'So, you get your keys today?'

'Thankfully, yes. I'll need to do some shopping. Get a few bits and pieces, and some food.' He paused for a second, and then just asked. 'Would you be able to point me in the right direction? I've been to Singapore before, but stayed in a different part, so I'm not as familiar with the shops and markets near where I'm staying.'

She waved her hand as the elevator doors opened, depositing them at the paediatric unit. 'Absolutely no problem. Give me a shout before you finish today and I'll give you a list of where, and when, to shop.'

He opened his mouth to ask what she meant, but she winked at him and disappeared into another room.

Fletch gave an amused laugh and walked down the corridor, shaking his head, not quite sure what to make of Madison.

She was friendly, obviously had her hands full, but there was something else about her. He was intrigued. He wanted to ask questions. But could well be reading things that weren't there at all. Maybe he was still jet-lagged? Yes, that was it. Once he'd given himself a few days to meet people, and see around the city again, he might finally get his head on straight.

A woman appeared in front of him, with a steely demeanour. She looked him up and down, and he re-alised instantly he hadn't collected his ID badge yet. 'Dr Fletcher,' he said, holding out his hand. 'I'm the new pae-diatrician, and Madison—' he gave a sideways glance to see if she was anywhere in sight, '—had started to show me round.'

The woman's nose wrinkled for a second as she clearly decided if she was on board or not. 'Rui Lee,' she said quickly, 'Sister of the Paediatric Unit. Come with me, Dr Fletcher. I think you have a meeting in a few hours.'

He held in a grimace and followed the fleet-footed woman down the corridor. As he looked out over the city landscape he couldn't help but smile. From the mo-ment he'd set foot in St David's this morning he'd had a good feeling. A vibe. Something that was hard to explain. But he could see it in the faces around him. Staff wanted to be here. People wanted to work here. There was no drama. No chaos or rush. Everything seemed controlled. Parents were at the sides of the beds with children. Staff were intermingled amongst them. He could hear short bursts of childhood laughter, and low voices murmuring around him.

Inquisitive medical students, clearly wearing new white coats, were gathered around a whiteboard in a room as a pharmacist was going through the chemistry aspect of medications. In another room, he saw some student nurses in mid-discussion with a tutor about childhood vaccinations. Teaching sessions weren't confined to universities or lecture halls. Teaching was happening directly on the wards. This was the reason he'd come here. This was part of the programme he was to lead, and he could already see the benefits before his eyes.

The good feeling kept rolling through his body as Sister Lee took him along the corridor towards the management offices. 'Settled in?' she asked over her shoulder.

He was slightly surprised at the social question. She'd seemed the tiniest bit hostile. 'Eh, almost,' he said. 'I had a bit of an issue getting access to the apartment I've rented. But hopefully that's solved now. I spent last night in a hotel, but I couldn't really sleep, so I arrived here early and had a coffee.'

She gave him a curious glance. 'So, you don't already know Madison Koh?'

Ah, so this was why she was being sociable. He shook his head. 'I met her downstairs for the first time.' He gave a soft laugh. 'She seemed to have her hands full so I offered to help.'

This time the glance he was shot was careful. 'Madison is one of our best physios. She does have her hands full. It's such a shame that she lost her husband a few years ago.'

His footsteps faltered but he quickly recovered. His brain automatically going into backwards mode, making sure he hadn't blundered unintentionally when talking to Madison. He didn't think so.

'That's such a shame. She seems a very nice woman. I'm looking forward to working with her.'

Rui's eyes were steady. 'She is a very nice woman. Her husband was a radiologist here. He's missed. We're all lucky in a way, because we get to see their children every day. I can see elements of Jason in each of his children.'

'That's nice.' Fletch meant that sincerely. 'I'm glad you mentioned it,' he added. 'I would have hated to put my foot in it around Madison.' His steps slowed as they reached the management offices.

'I'll leave you here,' said Rui. 'It was nice to meet you. I'll go over some procedures and electronic systems with you later.' She gave him a half-smile. 'Hope you get your apartment situation sorted out.'

She left him next to an unusual arched window that gave a spectacular view of the city landscape. He stood for a few moments, his head full of what he'd just heard. Madison seemed nice. Now he understood why she looked so tired. She was on her own.

He knew it shouldn't matter. But she was a colleague, so it did. He made a note to be mindful where he could when working together. For the second time today it struck him how curious he was about her, and he shook his head as he tried to imagine why he was drawn to this new colleague. A pull. That was all he could describe it as.

Smiling to himself, with one more glance at Singapore, his new home, he knocked on the door.

Madison finished typing up her notes and checked her emails for new referrals. Her hair had escaped from its too-loose hair scrunchie again and she attempted to tame it back into some kind of submission. A text appeared on the watch on her wrist and she had a quick glance. It was the crèche, reassuring her that Justin had settled. Thank goodness.

It was odd. She couldn't quite put her finger on what was wrong with her son, she just knew he wasn't himself. There wasn't anything to scare her, or to make her rush to her own paediatrician. There was just…something.

He was irritable. He was restless, and, even though he was clearly tired at times, he didn't sleep well—which then meant that no one slept well. She'd checked all the usual things. His temperature was fine. He was eating and drinking. Peeing and pooing. He had no unusual rashes. He was up to date with his vaccinations. And there were no outbreaks of any normal childhood diseases that she knew about. She'd even sounded his chest. But still, there was nothing to explain why her boy wasn't his usual self.

Madison had worked hard at keeping a happy work-life balance since the death of her husband. She was careful to give equal attention to her children, and happily had the ongoing help from her in-laws. She used the crèche while at work, and the twins were enrolled for nursery and due to start soon.

But the sleepless nights were getting to her. She'd thankfully accepted the offer from her in-laws to have

Justin and Mia overnight. The whole family had shared her devastation when Jason had been killed in a cycling accident, a few months after their children had arrived. Her parents had arrived from Scotland, and Jason's sister and parents had flocked around her, helping her keep things together and continue to function.

Her parents had finally needed to return to Scotland, but continued to visit and had even taken their grandchildren back to Scotland for a few holidays to help Madison out with childcare when necessary. The kids were just back from a fortnight with her mum and dad in the Scottish Highlands. Her in-laws were also there on a weekly basis, always only a telephone call away. She was lucky. She knew that. But learning to adjust to life without Jason had taken some time.

Now, she was getting there. The perpetual sadness had started to lift. She was determined to not miss out on the joy of her children and making memories with them. It helped she'd continued to work in the same place. There were no awkward questions from her colleagues. They knew her circumstances. They accepted her and her children with open arms and she was eternally grateful.

She lifted one of the nearby slimline tablets, logged in, and pulled up the referrals. Two from Paediatrics and two from the adult rehab ward. She already had ten patients on her list, but she could cope with four new referrals. She might even have time to grab a snack today. She took off her watch and tucked it into her pocket alongside the tablet, heading down to the wards.

By the time she'd finished her adult patients, the lack of sleep from last night was starting to hit her in all the worst ways. She hurried into Paeds and gave Rui a wave before ducking into the staffroom to heat up some soup. The staffroom was filled with comfortable sofas, a sink, microwave, and coffee machine. Madison set the timer for two minutes and sat down on a bright red sofa, considering the box of snacks in the middle of the table. The staffroom was empty. Most staff had already had their lunch by now and she was running late.

A hand touched her shoulder and she bolted to her feet, eyes wide, head going from side to side.

'Sorry.' Fletch was standing behind her, looking sheepish. He'd changed into a set of green scrubs and had his hospital ID clipped to his uniform now and his name badge on his chest.

For a few seconds her brain tried to compute. She recognised him, of course. But he looked different in his doctor scrubs than he had in his shirt and suit trousers. Scrubs seemed to reveal more. Whether anyone wanted them to or not.

Fletch had a broad frame, defined shoulders and muscular arms. He worked out. There was no flab. This guy worked out. With the v in his scrubs she could see a peek of chest hair and alongside a hint of a tan. Did he work out with nothing on? And why were the only words that would register in her brain 'work out'?

Madison gave herself a jolt, as her brain tried to settle. She couldn't remember the last time she'd let her thoughts linger on the physical attributes of a male colleague. What was wrong with her?

He remained apologetic. 'I didn't mean to wake you.'

Heat flooded her body and she could feel it in her cheeks. She was embarrassed. Of course, she was. She'd never fallen asleep at work before. That was disgraceful.

She was on duty. She was supposed to be seeing patients. And this guy was brand new—what on earth would he think of her?

'I wasn't sleeping,' she said automatically without thinking. Denial seeming like the best defence.

He winced. 'You were snoring.'

The heat in her cheeks multiplied and she could feel tears brimming in her eyes. She'd worked so hard to keep her reputation impeccable at work, especially because her colleagues knew everything she'd gone through. The last thing she wanted anyone to think was that she couldn't cope being a single parent, or that she wasn't doing the best job possible for her and Jason's kids. Even the thought of that made her heart ache.

Somehow, falling asleep at work seemed to fit in the category of not coping.

'I don't snore!' she snapped.

Fletch jerked backwards as if he'd been stung. She could almost see a shield forming in front of him as he straightened. 'Of course, no problem. I'll leave you to it.' He turned and walked out of the room without another word and Madison cringed.

Her stomach growled as she stepped over to the microwave, her appetite gone. She stared at the soup for two minutes and then poured it down the sink, putting the carton in the bin.

She closed her hands over her face for a few minutes and took a few deep breaths.

Get it together, she told herself.

She tried to be rational. Okay, so she'd now just snapped at—and likely offended—the new doctor, who, from this morning's meeting, had seemed like a perfectly nice bloke. He was going to think—she couldn't even imagine what he might think, but this was someone she wanted to have a professional, respectful relationship with. She didn't want awkwardness, or tension. She certainly didn't want him to write her off as either someone to feel sorry for, or someone who might be unreliable because he'd caught her sleeping at work.

She sat back down and leaned her head forward into her hands. She was tired. She was overtired and, hopefully, that would be sorted for her tonight, thanks to her in-laws.

Her stomach growled and she absent-mindedly opened the biscuit box and took one. The very last thing she needed to happen was to go back to work and start to be light-headed because she hadn't eaten.

The biscuit was gone in two bites and she stood up, brushed her uniform down and washed her hands.

She took herself back out onto the ward. Rui Lee was discussing a patient with another member of staff, and Madison gathered some equipment to assess her two new patients. By the time she'd gathered what she needed, Rui was finished.

'I'm going to do the two new assessments.' She took a breath and tilted her chin. 'Is Dr Fletcher still around? I wondered if he might want to observe as part of his orientation?'

Rui gave her a careful look. 'He's gone down to Radiology. He wants another set of films on a child and wanted to see if they could be shot another way.'

Her eyes were steady on Madison. It made her feel as if Rui were steadily unpeeling her skin like an onion. She'd taken other new employees with her as part of their orientation, so it wasn't that unusual for her to show someone around. 'No problem,' she said with a forced cheeriness she didn't normally have to use at work. Again—what was wrong with her?

She was aware she'd been feeling restless lately—wondering if it was time to start thinking of herself as a woman again, and not just a mother. Her thoughts always went back to one thing—was she ready? It was hard to know, but her mind was starting to go places it hadn't in the last few years, maybe her brain was trying to tell her something?

She disappeared to assess her patients, concentrating only on work for the next few hours. The words about Fletch going down to Radiology made her the tiniest bit uncomfortable and it was utterly ridiculous. Radiology was where her husband, Jason, had worked. She could imagine them both meeting. Discussing the possibility of different films to get a better view of the issue. Jason would have bent over backwards to ensure his service assisted in the best possible way for a patient's outcome.

She swallowed, a lump in her throat. She'd tried hard over the last two years to keep those kinds of thoughts in a careful place. The first time she'd walked back into work after Jason's death had been like a throat punch. She'd almost turned around and walked back out. But she couldn't do that. She had a family to support. Children to bring up. A life to lead.

Her workmates had all been a great help. And, in Madison's head, she still just took things a day at a time.

She had moved on. She didn't spend all day thinking about Jason. Sometimes, when one of the kids did something, she saw a glint of Jason in them. It was amazing the mannerisms that seemed to be inbuilt—the twins had been too small to have any real memories of their father—but occasionally one, or both, of them would do something that really reminded her of Jason. It gave her comfort. It reassured her that she still had a little part of him.

The first few times it broke her heart. But now, the pain wasn't raw. He would always hold a piece of her heart. But she couldn't spend the rest of her life grieving. She was happy to be settled with the children and getting on with her life. If only she could get to the bottom of what was going on with Justin.

CHAPTER TWO

MADISON HAD BEEN partly relieved she hadn't seen Fletch for a few days. But it was clear he was certainly making waves—of the good kind.

Everywhere she went, someone mentioned the handsome, friendly paediatrician who was making friends throughout the hospital.

'He doesn't really know anyone here yet,' she heard one of the nurses on the rehab unit say.

'Didn't he work in Singapore before?' asked another.

Madison hid her smile. It was clear that word was getting around about the new doc. It was always interesting watching the hospital grapevine from the sidelines rather than actually being part of it.

'I'm sure he did,' said the original nurse. 'But it was another hospital in another part of the city. I think he knows some of the consultants though.'

Madison held up her tablet. 'I have a patient to see, and he's one of Fletch's. Does anyone know where he is? This is a new referral and I'd like to get a bit of background before I start.'

'He's just gone to the cafeteria,' said a passing support worker. 'I passed him on the stairs.'

Madison glanced at her watch. She could do with a coffee, having missed breakfast this morning, and although she would usually just grab one in the staffroom, she was more anxious to have a chat about this patient.

'I'll go and find him,' she said with a wave of her hand and made her way out of the ward and down the stairs. As she entered the cafeteria, Fletch was exchanging pleasantries with another of the consultants and she wondered if she could interrupt, or if this was work talk. But Fletch caught her gaze and waved her over. He didn't exactly look delighted to see her—maybe her slightly snarky behaviour before had created a bad impression. Darn it. Not exactly ideal when she had to work with this guy—as well as muddle through her feelings.

She gave both doctors a beaming smile as she grabbed a croissant and a coffee, determined to give him a new perspective of her. 'Hi, Fletch, I wanted to catch you about the new patient you referred. Is now a good time, or will I see you back on the ward?'

'No problem,' Fletch said immediately as the other doc's page sounded and he headed off. 'Let's grab a table.'

She sat down opposite him and put some jam on her croissant, hoping for a quick burst of energy from the calories. He had a big pile of muesli and some bacon on a side plate.

His phone buzzed as he sat it on the table and he looked, but ignored it. He took a few spoonfuls of muesli. 'So, what kind of regime would you normally put Adrian on?'

Madison took a sip of her coffee. Straight to the patient, part of her liked that, and part of her wondered if he didn't want to do niceties with her because of her previous snarkiness. She took a breath and started succinctly.

'It's difficult. I checked his records but can't find a history of where he's been treated before. Cystic fibrosis is a difficult disease and it's always tougher when a child moves into your area and you can't get a realistic picture of the history of the disease for your patient.'

He nodded in agreement. 'His parents were staying in Italy, so I think it will be some time before we get to see his records, and we'll need them translated too. I took a verbal history from them—' he spun around a notebook he'd taken from his pocket '—and will be the first to admit that I don't know the standards for treatment for CF in that country. I'm going to have to hope it's based on the same worldwide information that we know.'

Madison gave a nod as his phone beeped again. 'I'll check his films before I start chest physio this morning. And I'll go easy to begin with.'

'I'll maybe come along. His chest is very congested.' He picked up his phone and sighed.

'You're popular.' She smiled.

He gave a rueful smile. 'This is what happens when you're an eternal bachelor and stay friends with all your exes.'

Madison was a little taken aback and started laughing. 'You stay friends with them all?' This information should currently make her run for the hills. If she was going to be attracted to anyone again—the last thing she'd pick was an eternal bachelor.

He nodded. 'Mainly.' He put a hand on his chest. 'I treat women well. I just don't go the final distance. And I always try and keep things friendly.' He tapped a few keys, clearly answering one of the messages.

'Doesn't that get a little messy?' She took a bite of her croissant, hating the fact she was getting drawn in.

'Only if you let it,' he said breezily. She was getting a whole new picture of this doctor, and it was…interesting.

'Have they all moved on?'

He nodded as he chewed. 'Most of them.'

'So, you're the one that got away?' she teased.

He blinked, and his face broke into a smile, then he shook his head. 'I hope not. I hope I'm the one that…' he was clearly thinking about it '…prepared them to meet the love of their life.'

'Ahh…' Madison smiled. 'So, they all go on to get engaged or married after they leave you?'

'Quite a few have.'

Her brain was teasing her for being so straightforward with this new doctor that she barely knew. But he seemed to have invited this chat, and she was keen to ease things and have a smooth working relationship between them both.

'Maybe you're just a good luck charm for them.'

He kept smiling. 'Now, that sounds better than *the one that got away*. That's kind of foreboding. Like the kind of guy you see in all those comedy films, and I don't mean the hero.'

Madison could feel herself start to relax a little. This was getting easier than she'd thought it would be. Maybe he'd just written off her snappiness the other day as exactly what it had been, horror and embarrassment. If he had, that was a relief.

'You mean like the one they all either laugh at, or when he's the actual baddie?'

Fletch's eyebrows shot upwards and he laughed. 'Baddie? Love it. Is it Scottish? Or is it just because we work in a world of kids?'

Madison shrugged. 'Bit of both, probably.' She bit the inside of her cheek and then asked, 'So, you see your job in life as to prepare whoever is the current girlfriend for the man who comes after you?'

Fletch had the grace to look a bit sheepish. 'I like women. I do. I like dating. I like having a relationship, I'm just not ready for marriage and families.' He said the words and then cringed, lifting one hand. 'Sorry, I didn't mean it to sound like that.' He took a deep breath. 'I heard about your husband. I'm very sorry.'

Madison wasn't upset. She was used to people saying things around her that some might consider thoughtless. But she'd moved past that. She nodded in acknowledgement. 'Thank you. You might hear people around here mention him. Jason worked in Radiology. The twins were very young when he died, so they don't remember him.' She steadied herself for a second. 'But I have videos, I have photos of us all together, and I have them up around the house. They know about their dad, and they know he died in an accident. I have good support from my hospital colleagues, and from Jason's family—they might be at the other side of the city but they help as much as they can, so we do okay.'

She got the usual sense of awkwardness that she always recognised when she spoke about her bereavement. But it was much better to get this over now, rather than have it as the elephant in the room, with a new workmate. She understood he would already have heard about her circumstances from someone else around here.

She licked her lips and looked out across the cafeteria,

being hit by a wave of melancholy. 'Was Jason the love of my life? I'd like to think so.' She gave a soft smile. 'Will I become the female version of the eternal bachelor? Probably not. I'd like to think I'd meet someone else at some point.'

The expression on his face had changed from a bit awkward, to a hint of sympathy. She wasn't sure if she was grateful or offended. 'Do you get lonely?' he asked.

Her skin prickled as if the wind had just blown past them both. The palm of her hand automatically started rubbing up and down one of her arms and she gulped. She was sitting across from a really handsome man. She was trying to make the part of her brain that noticed the colour of his eyes and slight dimple in one cheek switch off.

He'd just told her he was an eternal bachelor and always bailed on a relationship before it got serious. He was the opposite type of partner than she would ever look for—when she ever decided she was ready to do that.

She closed her eyes for a second. 'I get lonely when one of the twins is upset and I can't attend to them both at once. I get lonely late at night when I can't fall asleep and my brain works overtime. I get lonely when the kids are sleeping and I'm lying on the sofa myself watching the TV. I get lonely when one of the kids does something great, that makes my heart swell, and I don't have anyone to share it with.'

She took a thoughtful pause and added, 'But loneliness isn't just for people who are single. Sometimes people in relationships feel lonely too.' She opened her eyes and locked them on his. She could see the surprise on his face, and he must be wishing he hadn't asked the initial question. She wasn't quite sure where all that had come from, it just seemed to bubble up from deep inside. 'I'm lonely when I don't have someone to ask, does my bum look big in this?'

He laughed, and she could feel the small wave of relief from them both. 'Sorry,' she said quietly. 'No one has really asked me that.'

She looked around the cafeteria and he followed her gaze, even though it didn't focus on anyone in particular.

He gave a slow nod. 'I guess most of your colleagues still have you in their head as being Jason's wife.'

She knew he was right. It was natural. 'They do.'

There was silence for a few seconds and she didn't want any more awkwardness to descend between them. She pushed her coffee cup away. 'Are you finished?'

He nodded, and she wondered if he was relieved. 'Will we go up and see what we can do for Adrian?'

She cleared their dishes onto her tray and stood up, giving a nod. And as he followed her, she tried to make sense of the deeply personal conversation she'd just had. She wasn't quite sure why she'd opened up to Fletch. Maybe it was because he was a stranger. Maybe it was because he hadn't known Jason and didn't have memories stuck in his head. But somehow, she wasn't quite sure how to make sense of all this.

Fletch was having a strange old day. He was happy to work steadily with Madison. She was conscientious and he stepped back to allow her to assess her patient. As he watched her every move, he could see how sensitive she was towards Adrian's mother, who was clearly anxious. But there was something else. He could almost feel it in the air. Every now and then, their gazes connected and

Fletch could swear he felt a buzz. A hint of something between them. Of course, he ignored it, just as he suspected she was doing. Because they had a child to focus on. But it was still…there.

Adrian had been booked today as a new patient, with a chronic condition. It was common to see a new child with a chronic condition when they moved into the area. It was important that a child's care was as coordinated as possible. But when Fletch had first met Adrian and his mother this morning, he'd realised that Adrian likely had a chest infection and needed treatment. That was why he'd referred Adrian on to Madison for some specialist physio assistance.

She was professional, and her knowledge and experience shone through. When Adrian's chest film was available, they could see the damage in his lungs and subsequent chest infection. Fletch prescribed IV antibiotics, which the nurses set up and administered. Once they were completed, Madison started her physio. The massage had to be vigorous to help the sticky mucus in Adrian's lungs, but Madison was clearly used to adapting her skills for children and took the lead from Adrian's mother.

Fletch had worked with a whole range of professionals in his life. Most of them skilled and hard-working. But there was something about Madison that drew his attention. Her calm manner, her sweetness. There was something about her aura. He felt a little spellbound seeing in action something he'd definitely never experienced at work. The glimmer of attraction was absolutely there, but he tried his best to push it away. They'd already had that slightly awkward conversation downstairs where he'd declared himself as the eternal bachelor—without revealing the probably imprinted behaviours of his mother. That seemed like a ridiculous excuse now, and he wondered why he'd always chalked his behaviour up to that without examining it any further.

His attraction to Madison struck him as odd. Of course, he'd dated work colleagues in the past. But Madison was a person he'd never date. She had been widowed for only a few years, and had two young kids, her hands were clearly full. It wasn't that he hadn't dated women with children before. He had. But he was conscious of the fact he didn't want to play with children's emotions and become part of their lives when he knew deep down he would walk away. As a kid, he'd liked some of the guys his mum had dated. Some of them had been kind and considerate to him, taken an interest in his academics or sports interests. Then, in a flash, they'd been gone. Fletch had never wanted to do that to a kid.

He was guessing that Madison was either his age, or slightly older. Her brown hair had always been in a ponytail when he'd seen her. She had tiny lines around her eyes, and her skin was pale with a few freckles. He blinked as he realised just how much detail he'd noticed about Madison.

There had been that awkward meeting in the staffroom, where she definitely had been sleeping, and snoring just a little. But he cringed as he remembered how clearly embarrassed and upset she'd been, and wished he'd handled things a bit differently.

Their conversation downstairs earlier had been illuminating, and he got the impression she'd told him things she wouldn't normally say. Maybe he felt responsible now.

He'd almost let her admit something that she might have wanted to for a long time.

And the words resonated in his brain. In the blink of an eye, he'd imagined her lying awake at night, and on the sofa. He'd imagined that space in someone's heart when their child did something, and the other parent would never see that.

And even though he knew he shouldn't be having these thoughts, or taking in her shape in her uniform, or how dark brown her eyes were, he knew it was happening.

Once she'd finished with Adrian, he spent some time with the boy's mother, persuading her that Adrian should stay in overnight for some more IV antibiotics.

He moved around the ward, and went down to do an outpatient clinic, enjoying spending time meeting more patients and their families. He would be here for two years—it was important to try and build relationships.

By the time he went back up to the ward later he had a few more patients to see. As he approached the nurses' station to update some charts he could see Madison frowning. One of the nursing staff was clearly relaying a message from the phone to her.

'There's been an accident on the MRT, so they're delayed. They think it will be an hour before they get here.'

The MRT was the Mass Rapid Transit system and was Singapore's railway. It was usually very reliable and this was unusual. Madison glanced at her watch, and he saw her wince. 'What's up?' He couldn't help but ask, even though it was none of his business.

She pressed her lips together, and looked rueful. 'This is a child who lost their leg a few years ago. They are coming for a review of their new prosthesis. There have been issues and I really need time to work with the team to ensure the best fit and make sure there are no balance issues.' She looked up at the main clock on the wall. 'The crèche closes at six. I have to pick the kids up. I can't short-change this family. I need to spend time with them.'

He could see the pain on her face. And he understood. He had patients he would go above and beyond for too. 'They can't reschedule?'

She took a deep breath. 'They are about to go on holiday for six weeks. They're going to Australia and New Zealand—it's their first holiday since the accident and I don't want Hope's mobility to be compromised while she's away.' Madison gave a sigh. 'I want her to have the time of her life.'

'I'll help.' The words were out before he'd even thought about them.

'What?' Her head turned in surprise, and he was conscious of a few other heads turning too.

He shrugged. Help out a colleague, for a professional reason? Of course, he would. 'I have no plans. I can help with the children.'

She blinked and opened her mouth, but the words didn't come out. He felt a small flare of panic. Maybe she didn't want him to look after her kids?

'I mean, I'm a paediatrician. Of course, I can entertain your children for an hour or two if it will help you out.'

Everyone was looking at him now. 'Madison?' he prompted.

'Thank you,' she said, clearly stunned. Then it was as if her brain kicked into gear. She nodded to the nurse on the phone. 'Let the family know I'll meet them in the rehab suite.' She turned to Fletch. 'Do you mind if we go down so you can meet Mia and Justin? I want them to know that we are…friends. I also need to introduce you to the crèche staff again and let them know I'm happy for you to look after the children.' She bit her lip. 'Where will you take them?'

'Do you have a preference?'

He wondered if she wanted him to bring her children up to the ward area. But she took a breath. 'There's a children's playground in the hospital grounds. How do you feel about that?'

He smiled. 'I can do a children's playground. Point me in the right direction.'

She nodded gratefully.

It didn't take long to organise things. Mia looked at him with a mix of disinterest and amusement, Justin looked at him with caution. They were still engaged in activities with their crèche workers and Fletch promised to come back at six.

'Are you sure about this?' Madison asked as they walked down the corridor.

'No problem,' he said casually. It didn't feel like a big deal to him. He knew she was widowed. She'd told him her in-laws were on the other side of the city.

She looked a bit hesitant. 'I'm going to head down to the rehab suite and prepare things for my patient. Will I just come to the playground after we finish?'

He pulled his phone from his pocket. 'Better swap numbers just in case I have to move about.'

'Wh-where would you move to?'

He raised his eyebrows. 'You have three-year-olds. We both know that they're going to be in charge. If they need the toilet or some food, I'll do exactly what they tell me to do.'

He saw her tense shoulders relax back down. She pulled out her phone. 'I'm not sure I want to be one of the women in your phone,' she joked.

'Consider it an honorary position,' he countered. 'If I put you in a room with all my exes, I'm sure you'd tell me I had impeccable taste.'

This time it was Madison's eyebrows that rose, but she still swapped numbers with him before hurrying off.

It was almost six before he knew it and he hurried down to the crèche where the staff had Justin and Mia ready and waiting. Both had their jackets and small backpacks on their shoulders. He knelt down. 'Hi, guys, I'm Fletch. Remember?'

There was the smallest of nods of the head. 'So, we're going to the playground to wait for Mummy like she said, okay?'

Both nodded and he held out his hands. Mia slotted her little hand into his without a moment's thought. Justin was more wary. His hand took a few seconds to come up. Fletch led them through the corridors, to the elevators and down to the main entrance. The playground was only a few minutes away.

He asked some questions but only Mia answered. Her speech was clear and to the point. Her sentence construction was good. He couldn't really judge with Justin because he seemed lost in a little world of his own, just padding along beside them.

When they reached the playground, Mia was quick to shrug off her jacket and backpack and dump them on the bench with Fletch before running off to climb the slide. He waited for Justin to do the same. But instead, after he'd taken off his jacket, Justin sat up on the bench alongside Fletch.

'Don't you want to go play?' Fletch asked.

Justin shook his head. Fletch did his best to try and engage him in conversation, conscious that Justin might just be shy. He'd met lots of kids, was well aware they all developed at different paces, and all had individual personalities.

But Justin gave the bare minimum of answers. Fletch could tell that Justin understood him, comprehension didn't seem to be an issue, but even when Mia came over and tugged at his arm to join her, he refused. After a few minutes, he leaned in towards Fletch.

Fletch put his arm around the three-year-old. 'Are you tired, buddy?'

Justin gave a nod and closed his eyes. The climate in Singapore was warm and Justin's skin felt comfortable, so Fletch wasn't concerned he was sick, or had a fever. Some kids did exhaust themselves at day care, and he was just here to keep an eye on them, and make sure they were safe, he shouldn't pry.

Mia had befriended all the other kids in the playground and was quite the boss, taking charge and telling them what to do even though some were twice her height.

After a while, he pulled Justin up onto his lap, and let him cuddle in against his chest. He sat there, feeling the rise and fall of the small chest against his. It was nice.

During his training, he'd spent many a night shift in the various neonatal units he'd covered in. Fletch had never been averse to letting a small baby sleep against him to let their mother or father have a break. He'd also spent time with kids who'd been sick overnight, and ended up staying with them until they were eventually settled.

He'd always pictured in his head that eventually he would do this, once he was a father. Everything up until that point was just him in training. But before, being a father had seemed so far off. He'd imagined he'd be in his late thirties, maybe married, and working as a consultant in a permanent place. All of a sudden, he realised he wasn't a million miles off any of those things. He was at the start of his thirties, and he'd landed a job he'd really wanted. Two years was something. But he hoped the opportunity could become permanent. The future he'd imagined had started to sneak up on him, and he hadn't even noticed.

He glanced down at Justin again. While he had multiple memories of holding kids through the night, he couldn't recall ever doing this. Being in the daylight was different. He could see people passing, glancing in his direction. Would people assume these were his children?

Mia occasionally came over and dug into her backpack either for some grapes, or for a drink of water. Justin kept sleeping.

He hadn't even realised how much time had passed when his phone chirped. He glanced at the screen.

Where are you guys? Everything okay?

He typed a reply.

Still at the playground. All good.

After a few minutes Madison arrived. She seemed a bit out of breath, as if she'd rushed to get there.

He watched as her eyes instantly found Mia, who waved over from where she was playing on the slide. A frown creased her brow as she sat next to Fletch and instantly put her hand on Justin's forehead, checking his temperature.

'He's been sleeping the whole time,' said Fletch. 'He hasn't played at all. Mia, meantime, is queen of the playground.'

He could see the mixed emotions on Madison's face. She stroked Justin's hair. 'He's been doing this. He seems so tired all the time. But he never sleeps well at night. He's just irritated.'

Now it was Fletch's turn to frown. 'Have you had his bloods checked? Does any kind of anaemia run in the family?'

She sighed, and he was sorry he'd said it, as he could see the guilt flush over her face. 'Not yet,' she said. 'I wonder if he's having a growth spurt. Or, if he's just getting overwhelmed with things at the crèche.'

Their glances locked and he didn't look away. He didn't want to. They might be discussing her child, but there was still something else, something in the air. He was determined not to look away and eventually Madison gave a small sigh and looked down towards her lap.

Fletch knew he had to tread carefully. He barely knew these kids. And Madison was a new colleague. He'd already offended her once. Last thing he wanted to do was do it again. Particularly when he couldn't work out what was going on between them. Was he reading this wrong?

He took a breath. 'Sorry, it's not my place to say anything. But, if you want me to have a look sometime, we can have a chat, and see if we can come up with something.'

It was Fletch's way. Even though he was a paediatric consultant with a wealth of training, he was crucially aware that parents always had to be his partner when it came to kids. Nobody knew their kids better than their caregiver.

She gave him a sideways glance and he could tell she was thinking. After a few moments she gave a nod of her head. 'I'll have a think about it. Sometimes I think that because we see so much in the hospital, it can give us the tendency to blow things out of proportion and imagine worst-case scenarios.' She held up her hands. 'Maybe I just have a kid that's not going to be a good sleeper. It happens.'

He adjusted Justin on his lap. 'You're right. It does. But know, if you want me to have a look, I will.'

She reached over and put her hand on his arm. 'Thanks, I appreciate that.'

He couldn't help but let his eyes go down to where she had her fingers on his skin. He was feeling sensations that he shouldn't be. Not at all. He swallowed as the warm little body against his chest shuffled to get more comfortable.

'No problem,' he mumbled, not making eye contact with her, and immediately feeling stupid.

He lifted his head as she moved her hand away. 'Do you live near here? Do you need a hand getting home?'

He could tell she was instinctively programmed to say no. 'I don't mind,' he added quickly. He stood up, still holding sleeping Justin.

'Do you want me to wake him?'

She shook her head. 'No, don't. He'll just be grumpy.'
She looked around. 'Actually, I live about a ten-minute
walk from here. Would you mind? The children and I
walk in, and back, every day. I've just stopped bringing
the double stroller as I thought they were getting too big
for it. And it's not the easiest thing to manoeuvre when
the streets are busy.' She gestured towards Justin. 'But I
hadn't figured on him sleeping.'

Fletch gathered up his things and waited while Madison collected a reluctant Mia, who was still ruling the
playground.

The streets of Singapore were busy, with lots of people
who had clearly finished work, and were heading to the
many bars or restaurants in the area. The tantalising aro-
mas around them made his stomach growl in anticipation.

People smiled at them as they walked past, probably
assuming they were family. Normally, Fletch might have
felt a little uncomfortable, but this felt fine.

He instantly straightened his spine a bit more as the
feeling settled in his mind. Why wasn't he uncomfortable? Was it because of the thoughts he'd just been
having? Or was he really thinking about changing his
eternal-bachelor status?

He wasn't dating Madison. That wouldn't happen. They were just friends. So, what was it about this
woman that was making him question things? Sure, she
was pretty. Sure, she was good at her job. But there was
something else, something deep down at the pit of his
stomach that made him look at her in a way he knew he'd
never looked at anyone else.

He was curious about her husband. Everyone at work

spoke highly of him. He hadn't heard a single bad word. He wondered if they'd met at work, or at school. Had Madison dated yet since her husband died? Somehow, he suspected not, not for any reason other than how tired she'd looked the first time they'd met.

'Any plans this weekend?' he asked casually.

'Oh, yes.' She glanced over her shoulder and laughed as they dodged the people on the streets. 'Laundry. Laundry. And laundry. Or, as my gran used to call it "the washing".'

He smiled at the thick accent she dropped into. 'What? No space flight? No cruise ship?'

She signalled they were changing direction and they turned a corner towards a large central apartment block. 'I'll have you know I am the owner of multiple cruise ships and space rockets. Usually, I find them in the middle of the night when I try to visit the bathroom without turning on the lights. My feet have the scars.'

'Ouch.' Fletch winced at the thought of it.

He could tell she was getting more relaxed as they entered the building and she pressed for the elevator. 'You okay with this?'

'Sure,' he agreed as the doors slid open. It only took a few minutes to reach her apartment and as she opened the door, Mia ran on inside. Fletch could see a fairly large apartment with light floors and large windows. And there, on the wall opposite the entranceway, was a photo of Madison and—he guessed—her husband.

It was a snapshot, with Madison looking around ten years younger, and wearing a red dress. Jason had on jeans and a T-shirt, and had his arms wrapped around Madison's waist. They were looking at each other and laughing. Something tugged inside Fletch. They looked happy. As if they had the whole world at their feet.

They had no idea what would happen next.

Madison caught his gaze and gave a small smile and held out her hands for Justin. Her eyes drifted to the photo and there was a flash of sadness as she took Justin. 'I like my kids to see their dad every day,' she murmured. 'I want them to know he'll always love them.'

'Of course,' said Fletch as he tried to swallow the lump that had appeared in his throat.

There was a second of awkward silence. 'Thanks for today,' Madison said quietly.

'No problem. Maybe tomorrow you'll get a chance to tell me about your patient.'

'Sure.' She smiled.

He stepped back as she closed the door. Fletch headed back to the elevator. As he climbed back inside and pressed the button for the ground floor, his eyes were still fixed on her door.

And he couldn't quite say why.

CHAPTER THREE

MADISON HELPED THE young man to his feet and into his crutches. She had a strange role in the hospital, funded by two streams, Paeds and Rehab. But sometimes, like today, she was called to assist in other areas.

A colleague had phoned in sick due to their mother having a fall, and Madison was in the ER, this time helping a young man who'd just had a plaster put on his ankle learn to use his crutches.

She didn't mind this. It did mean she'd end up with a backlog of work for the next few days, but she could cope.

The emergency work just felt like an extension of her rehab role, and she was lucky within rehab she worked with both adults and children. Today had been mainly about assessing people after accidents or breaks to make sure they could go home safely. An eighty-nine-year-old man who'd damaged his knee had nipped up and down a flight of stairs with one crutch like an acrobat, while this teenager was definitely struggling. She took her time, giving him some more instructions, and demonstrating with a different set of crutches until finally she'd been satisfied he was safe to go home.

As she completed her electronic notes she heard a baby crying in one of the nearby cubicles. It was a horrible cry that sent a chill down her spine. Her natural instinct couldn't stop her and she moved over to the cubicle, seeing a pale-faced man clutching the baby.

'Is someone seeing to you?' she asked.

'The nurse has gone to page someone,' he said. She could see his hands shaking. The waves of exhaustion were emanating off him.

'Do you want me to take a turn?' she offered, holding out her hands.

She could tell he was torn. 'This is my sister's baby,' he said. 'Our father is sick, and she went to help. She's only been gone a day. I said I could help as I've looked after Jia many times before. But he's been really upset for the last few hours.'

'Let me help,' she said, taking Jia into her arms and taking a good look at the baby. Her skin chilled. As someone who'd spent a few years working in Paediatrics she had a horrible suspicion of what was wrong with the little one. His temperature was clearly high. She checked the chart the nurse had completed, ten minutes before, then rechecked with the digital ear thermometer again. She marked in the results and peered back out from the cubicle.

She couldn't see the nurse whose name was on the chart, and she wasn't sure which paediatrician was on call today. She didn't want to leave carrying Jia and it was clear his uncle was exhausted. She pulled her phone from her pocket and sent Fletch a text.

Who is on call today? I'm down in the ER and suspect a baby has meningitis.

Madison was well aware she was a physio. Her range of expertise was different from a doctor's and it wasn't for her to diagnose a baby with meningitis. But she'd learned over the years to trust her instincts and to voice them. The people working around any child should be a team, and the worst that could happen here was that she'd be wrong.

The nurse came back and did a quick double take at Madison, then gave a grateful nod. 'The paging system is down. I've phoned up to Paeds but they are looking for the on-call doctor.'

Madison pulled a face, 'I just texted Fletch to ask who was on call.' She was slightly worried the nurse might think she was overstepping.

'The new doc? Great, thanks. If we don't hear something in five minutes, I might go on up to the unit and grab someone. Would you be okay with that?' she asked Madison.

Madison nodded, knowing if it came to it, she would do that task instead. But a few seconds later, just as Jia's scream was getting more high pitched, Fletch appeared at the cubicle.

'Paging system is down,' he said quickly, 'and I'm not sure if Dr Zhang knows yet. But in the meantime, can I help?'

Both Madison and the nurse nodded at once, and Fletch stepped inside, introducing himself to the uncle and quickly taking a history. He laid Jia down on the trolley and did a quick but thorough examination, his face serious. Madison watched as, even though Jia was upset and screaming, Fletch kept his voice smooth, talking in a steady stream to the little one through the examination, and occasionally stroking his face.

Madison could see his notes.

No rash
High temperature
Colder hands and feet
Irritable
?bulging fontanelle

He asked Jia's uncle a few questions about the baby's feeding and nappies over the last few hours and gave a slow nod of his head.

'We're going to transfer you both upstairs to the paediatric unit. I suspect Jia has meningitis and there's a specific test we need to do. We will also put a small intravenous line in, to give him some antibiotics.' He took a breath. 'Can you call your sister? I would be happy to talk to her.'

Jia's uncle looked stunned and started to shake and cry, moving back over and gathering Jia up in his arms. 'I can stay,' said Madison quickly as she pulled over a chair and put her arm around his shoulders.

She might not be able to do the complicated procedures, but she could free up the nurses and Fletch's time to do what they needed to do to help Jia.

Within a few minutes they all headed up to the paediatric unit. Fletch had spoken to Jia's mum and reassured her of the best possible care. She was on her way back. Madison kept her arm around the uncle, who was starting to calm down now. She'd already told the ER staff where she'd be and that she'd stay to support the family member during the lumbar puncture.

The test could be difficult to perform, and caregivers could frequently be upset during it, so Madison was happy to offer to help.

By the time they were on the ward, the staff there had a bed ready, a trolley with the equipment for the lumbar puncture and another trolley prepared with the intravenous equipment and antibiotics. Madison knew, as soon as the call had been made upstairs, that the staff had gone into automatic pilot, knowing that time was of the essence.

Fletch remained the calmest man in the building. It was the aura he had about him. One of the more junior doctors came to observe and it was clear she was impressed too.

He slid the tiny needle into the base of Jia's spine while he was turned on his side. Madison ended up holding the baby as his uncle was too upset but the procedure was literally over in minutes. Fletch made the decision to start Jia on antibiotics as soon as the sample was sent to the lab and within forty minutes of the baby appearing in the ER, the IV was running.

The nurse who would lead Jia's care signalled to Madison to go and take a break, giving her arm a gentle squeeze. 'Good call. There's something in the breakroom for you and Fletch.'

Madison gave a sigh and a grateful nod. She waited for Fletch to speak to a few colleagues and write up his notes before heading to the staffroom.

The coffee machine was switched on and bubbling and two pieces of hazelnut chocolate cake were sliced and each covered with a napkin. She gave a broad smile. 'Someone's brought birthday cake in.'

Fletch poured coffee into two mugs and brought them over, sitting down beside her.

It had been a few weeks since that day he'd offered to look after the kids for her. Neither had acknowledged it, but it was as if something had changed in the air between them. There was a closeness that Madison wasn't sure she could acknowledge. Of course, they'd seen each other around the hospital in passing. But they hadn't actually sat down together and had a proper conversation, and she didn't want to admit that made her a little sad.

She enjoyed the happy-go-lucky aura Fletch often had about him. It kind of lifted her into another space, where she didn't want to think about sleepless nights, laundry and dishes. But she knew that, right now, what they both needed was a debrief.

She was conscious of how close they both were on the sofa. But it wasn't uncomfortable. It was…reassuring.

'Thanks for the text,' he said, lifting the napkin from the plate.

'Thanks for answering. I wasn't sure who was on call. Just had a feeling about the baby.'

He gave a nod. 'Dr Zhang has put a different system in place while the pagers get fixed. He was on the surgical ward doing a consult, so it's likely I would have come down anyhow.'

'How do you think Jia will do?' she asked nervously.

'I'm almost sure this is bacterial meningitis, and the waiting is always the hardest part now. We've got him before he became septicaemic, but that doesn't mean it won't still happen. The next few hours will be crucial.'

'Do you want me to stay to help with the uncle?'

He looked at her for the longest time. 'You've got the

kids to think of,' he said finally. 'And won't you end up with a whole backlog of work?'

The coffee she'd just sipped seemed to stick in her throat. Was he telling her he didn't want her around? Or was it something else?

She questioned the way her brain did this. And it only seemed to do it around Fletch. In other parts of life she took people as she found them, and was confident in herself and her abilities. But with Fletch, his mere presence had her second-guessing herself, in a way she wouldn't with someone else.

His phone sounded and he pulled it out of his pocket. His mood shifting and a smile spreading across his face.

'What is it?' she couldn't help but say, even though it was entirely none of her business. Her brain was still churning away. Maybe his other words had just been genuine concern for a colleague?

'Monique, one of my exes, has texted to say that she's expecting. I'm delighted for her. She always wanted a family, and she and her husband are over the moon.'

Madison thought for a minute. 'Doesn't it ever feel a bit odd that your exes text you stuff like that?'

He looked surprised. 'Not at all. I want to know she's happy. I want to know she's doing well. Same for all of them. And if any of them were ever in trouble, I'd help in a heartbeat. I think I might do the friend stuff better than I do the boyfriend stuff,' he said, then give a bit of a worried shrug as if he was thinking about all this.

7He looked up and met her gaze, the shrug continued and he pulled a face. 'I've gone to a few weddings, too.'

'Really?' She couldn't help but almost laugh. 'And the

grooms don't mind?' She took a bite of the hazelnut and chocolate cake.

He honestly looked surprised. 'Not that I've noticed.'

She shook her head. 'If Jason had wanted to invite one of his exes to our wedding, I'd have had questions.'

'But why?' He looked genuinely intrigued. 'All my exes have moved on. We're still friends, they are getting married, and they invite friends. Why is that wrong?'

Madison gave a shudder. 'It just seems...odd.'

He raised his eyebrows. 'My choices are odd? Maybe it's you. Did you finish with previous boyfriends with screaming and fire?'

She was thoughtful for a moment. 'Only one, but he cheated and that's different. The others...' Her voice trailed off and then she shuddered again. 'Some of them were bad choices in my teenage years or early twenties, and I might actually cross the street rather than be forced to say hello again.'

He laughed and ate more cake. 'That says more about you and bad choices.'

She knew he was teasing her.

'With the exception of your husband, of course,' he added quickly.

Those words kind of killed the humour in the room.

Madison pushed away the remainder of her cake and settled back in the sofa with her coffee, her shoulder brushing against Fletch's.

'I don't think you'll like this one either,' he murmured.

She turned her head, suddenly conscious of how close they were, and pulled back a little. 'What's the this one?'

'I'm godfather to one of their babies.'

She groaned.

He put his hand on his chest. 'And I don't want to blow my own trumpet, but I am the best godfather on the planet. Sonny is cute and cheeky, and will likely cause his parents a world of trouble. It just shines out of him. And I get to sit on the sidelines and be the all-knowing uncle.'

'What age is he?'

'Nine.' He shook his head. 'Just wait till those teenage years hit. I'll likely end up with him staying at mine for a bit. Viv has already threatened me with it.'

There was still lightness in his tone, but she caught something else. 'And you'd do it if she asked?'

He didn't hesitate. 'Absolutely.'

Madison set down her coffee cup and folded her arms. 'That's kind of nice. And exactly what someone who wasn't a full-time parent would say.'

He grinned. 'You've been talking to Viv, haven't you?'

She smiled too. 'Not yet. But we think the same way.'

He held up both hands. 'Hey, I just want to be everyone's friend. Is that a bad thing?' He shifted a little and then continued. 'I sometimes feel bad about ending things. I never want to give false expectations, but, you know, I still sometimes feel like I'm letting someone down. So, I do my best to end things well and stay friends. It's important to me, because I—' he held up his hands '—I like these women. They are good people. And I wish them well.'

Madison's stomach clenched. What was it about being around this guy that made her brain whirr, her skin tingle and her mouth sometimes say things she shouldn't?

'What happens when you decide you want more?'

His hands stayed in mid-air, sort of frozen, before descending slowly. He took a slow breath. 'I guess I've just not reached that stage in my life yet,' he said carefully.

Madison put her elbow on her knee, resting her chin on her hand. 'What happens if you reach that stage in your life and realise that one of your exes is likely the person you were supposed to live your life with?'

The expression on Fletch's face changed. For a moment, he was thoughtful. 'I have to be honest, I don't think that's likely to happen.'

'You won't ever meet the love of your life?' She couldn't hide her cynicism.

He shook his head. 'No, that I've met her yet. That I've let her slip away.' He took a few seconds. 'All my exes were lovely people—all very different and unique in their own way.' He put his hand on his chest. 'And I think if you had a realistic conversation with any of them, they'd say the same as me. It just didn't click. We had fun, we liked each other, we respected each other. I know that I loved some of them. But would that love have lasted for ever?' He was already shaking his head. 'I don't think so. Because I don't think I've met her yet.'

'Met who?' It was a silly question, but she was kind of mesmerised and disappointed by his words right now.

'My person,' he said without pause.

Their eyes locked. Madison's insides were not designed to twist and turn like this. He hadn't met his person. That was what his brain said.

And the ridiculous tiny voice in the back of her head was chanting, *But he has met you. You didn't even get considered.*

Honestly, was she some kind of teenager all over again? Where had that ridiculous thought even come from?

Seconds passed, and their gazes remained connected. He licked his lips and she had to tell herself not to lean forward. He'd said the words. He hadn't met his person yet. She just couldn't look away. And, apparently, neither could he.

But her brain wanted a different answer. One where she was at least considered—even for the briefest of milliseconds.

'Do you think you'll know right away?' she said, her words almost a whisper, still looking into those eyes.

His eyes were green. Pale green. That somehow looked good with his dark hair. She'd noticed them before, had tried not to look too closely. But from this position, it was impossible to miss.

His reply was throaty. 'I'm not sure. Should it be love at first sight? I'm not sure I believe in that. Do I believe in getting to know someone first?' He licked his lips. 'I guess I do.'

'I guess that means your person could be right around the corner,' she said, before she could stop herself.

'Or ten years away,' he countered.

Her skin chilled and she breathed, forcing her mouth into a smile. 'Or ten years away,' she repeated.

She shifted her position on the sofa, wishing she hadn't eaten that cake, and telling herself that was what was playing havoc with her insides.

'I guess I should get back to work,' she said, lifting her plate and cup and carrying them over to the sink. 'If you don't need any help, I'll go back to the ER to cover.' She turned towards the door.

Fletch moved next to her, bringing his own plate and

mug. She thought he was going to just agree and let them part company, but his words stopped her footsteps.

'When did you know?' There was an intensity in his eyes.

She spun back, 'What?'

'Your person. When did you know that Jason was your person?'

Madison bit her lip. It was an intensely personal question, but one she'd likely brought on herself. 'I knew within a few weeks of dating. We clicked. And everything else around us clicked. We both got jobs here. We found an apartment that we liked, things seemed to move quickly—but it didn't feel quick. It felt right.' She took a breath as she felt a tug at her heart. 'And I just knew.' The lump in her throat was real and she blinked back tears, spinning back around and walking out of the door before there were any more questions.

Guilt swamped her. She'd been sitting there, having different thoughts, stupid thoughts, about a guy she hardly knew, and who had helped her out once. He'd given her no real sign or indication that he gave her a passing thought. But even though she'd tried to fight it, and ignore it, she knew that he was stirring something in her that she hadn't felt in a long time.

Part of her was horrified. This wasn't Fletch's issue. This was hers. Maybe she was just reaching that stage— the one where she might consider moving on, trying to meet someone else. But even as the thought fully formed in her brain, she still felt weighed down with guilt. What if people thought three years wasn't long enough?

She didn't even know if it was. She just knew for the

first time in for ever she was attracted to someone again. There. She'd admitted it.

She laughed bitterly as she walked down the corridor as she tried to tug her untidy hair back into a ponytail again. She wasn't young. She wasn't thin. She wasn't pretty. She had twins. Would any man ever find her attractive?

Even if she wanted to think about moving on, she had so much more to consider. Her in-laws. Her own parents. Her workmates, and the most important people of all. The twins. How might they feel if she met someone, and decided it was time to introduce them to the twins? The last thing she would ever want was to have a line of perpetual boyfriends who would meet the children, decide this relationship wasn't for them, and walk away.

She could never do that. She could never line her kids up for any kind of hurt. Why was she even considering any of this?

It was too much hassle. Too complicated. She finally smoothed her hair down and rewrapped the ponytail band, taking a few breaths.

No. She would stop these thoughts. She would stop them right now.

Fletch would be pushed to the back of her thoughts completely.

She had to guard her children, and her heart.

Fletch was back on the ward, focusing on Jia. He'd prescribed some pain relief for the baby as well as the antibiotics, and between Jia's uncle holding him, and his lead nurse rocking him on her shoulder, Jia finally seemed less agitated. The lab phoned after checking the cerebrospinal fluid, confirming it was bacterial meningitis, which reassured him around not delaying commencing the antibiotics.

All the time he kept working his brain kept going back to one person. Madison.

He couldn't understand it. He'd met lots of women in his life. But for some reason, at this place, he'd met someone who he'd had one of the biggest conversations in his life with.

She put him on the spot. Held him to account in a way that was challenging, uncomfortable and definitely attractive.

She wasn't his type. He kept telling himself that. But his curiosity about this woman just grew and grew. He found himself looking for her, and drawn to her.

When she'd asked the question about his person, he'd been thrown. Lots of people had joked with Fletch that he would meet someone, settle down and have a couple of kids, and, truth be told, he'd always thought that would be in his distant plans.

He'd never felt ready before. He'd never had reason to be. Because he'd never met the person that conjured up this amount of feelings in him. This amount of turmoil. This amount of concern, and curiosity. But now, here he was, looking into a colleague's dark brown eyes and wondering if he could kiss her.

It was strange, the buzz he felt between them. He wasn't entirely sure that it was all just in his head. If it was, then thank goodness no one could hear his thoughts. But if it wasn't, and Madison recognised the buzz too, what then?

Did he really want to test a relationship with someone

who was widowed and had two young kids to take care of? It would be like no relationship he'd ever had before, and Fletch wasn't entirely sure he was unselfish enough to be that person.

The thoughts made him uncomfortable. If he couldn't be honest with himself, how could he hope to succeed in a relationship with someone else?

'Dr Fletcher, can you come and review a few patients, please?' It was one of the other staff and he immediately nodded and went to do his job.

Paediatrics had always been his thing. From the second he'd started working as a doctor, he'd known where his speciality would be. Others were obsessed with different kinds of surgery, or specific medical conditions. Fletch had known it would be Paediatrics. From that first moment he'd stepped onto a paediatric ward he could feel it in his blood. The chaos. The innocence. The beauty. He'd just gelled with the area as his speciality. And he hadn't changed his mind, not for a single second.

Children were honest. Children wore their hearts on their sleeves. And some of them didn't have the best start in life—through no fault of their own. Babies and toddlers often couldn't say what was wrong, and Fletch saw that as his job to find out.

He'd worked in several countries now. But Singapore had drawn him back. The healthcare system was better than in some other countries. The climate was good, life expectancy was good here too. For him, as a medic, job opportunities were good. Although the population was dense, he'd never felt crowded. He'd mastered some of the Malay language, and a smattering of Indian, which, alongside English, meant he could communicate with the majority of the people he came across. His contract was for two years. But, even before getting here, Fletch had been considering the fact he might want to stay.

It wasn't that he never wanted to work in the US again. He'd trained in Chicago and been brought up in the mid-west. But as a boy, he'd always wanted to travel the world. He'd worked in Germany, France, Australia and now back in Singapore for the second time.

His thoughts drifted back to Madison. She was Scottish, but was still here. It sounded as if she'd also decided to make Singapore her home in her early twenties. He couldn't help but notice the parallels in their lives that pulled them back here.

He wondered if she eventually might want to go home to Scotland where her parents were. He'd never commented on the fact she might need support, and he never would. Apparently, Jason's family helped her. Would they still help if Madison moved on and met someone else?

He gave himself a shake. Again, none of his business. Why did most of his thoughts focus on Madison?

He took a breath. Was he imagining that something was in the air between them? Was Madison the most beautiful woman in every room? Probably not. But she was the only woman that held his attention. He liked that her hair occasionally fell out of place. He liked the fact she offered to help with most situations, and had a real commitment to her work and her patients. He also admired the way she coped with her children on her own, alongside handling whatever was going on with Justin.

He could see a number of Madison's traits in Mia. The determination, and the leadership. Clearly, he hadn't known Jason, but he was sure he must be in there too.

Fletch wasn't sure what to do next. He felt as if this whole thing were like an elephant in the room. Was he brave enough to take the next step when he didn't know what on earth he was doing?

He kept asking himself the question as he worked for the rest of day, wishing someone would whisper the solution into his head.

CHAPTER FOUR

HE'D GONE FOR an early morning run, trying to sort his head out. He had run in Singapore previously, but this time his route took him mysteriously past both Madison's apartment and the hospital. He was approaching the entranceway to St David's when he caught sight of a familiar figure stretching a little way in front of him.

'Madison?'

She looked up, her hair in a ponytail on top of her head that obstructed her view. She flicked the hair away. For a second he wondered if she was embarrassed. After all, the black and red running clothes left nothing to the imagination. But then, his were much the same.

She straightened up. 'I didn't know you went running,' she said in surprise.

'Same.' He smiled. 'How did you manage to get away?'

She blinked, then must have realised he was talking about the kids. 'Oh, twice a week I drop them into the nursery then come for a run before I start work. It's the only way I can fit it in.'

He glanced at his watch. 'How about breakfast before we start the day?'

There was a café right on the street next to him, and he

saw her give a quick glance, bite her lip, then say, 'Sure. That would be nice.'

Fletch thanked the fact he had his debit card tucked into his waistband as they sat down at one of the outside tables. The waitress was out instantly taking their order.

The coffee appeared quickly and Madison took a sip and gave a long sigh. She glanced around. 'This is nice. Mornings are usually top speed for me. Taking a few minutes out is nice.'

Fletch smiled in agreement. It *was* nice to be able to take a breath. He could only imagine her normal morning routine—and that was before she hit work.

'Before you ask,' he said, 'I've already checked on Jia before I headed for my run. He's been stable overnight.'

'Good.' She nodded.

She relaxed back into her chair. And he found himself leaning towards her. 'So—not work—something else, if you had a whole day off, what would you do?'

Her brow crinkled in amusement. 'Okay, I'm assuming I'm not taking Justin and Mia with me?'

For a second, he wondered if he'd offended her. But Madison didn't look offended. She just smiled. 'I'd read a book, have a bath, go for a massage, lie in the park in the sun, maybe take in a movie, or get my hair done.'

She met his gaze and laughed. 'What? Too much? Or just said it all too quickly?'

He laughed. 'Well, you didn't need to think about that for long.'

She smiled in agreement. 'I know.' She blew a few strands of hair out of her face. 'I love my kids dearly, they are the best thing that ever happened to me. But do

I want some me time on occasion? Of course, I do. I'd be a fool if I didn't admit that.'

He liked that about her. She was honest. But she did it in a half-joking way. He didn't doubt for a second she loved her kids, but now she was striking his interest even more.

Her black T-shirt and black and red running leggings hugged every part of her. Madison wasn't stick-thin, like an athlete, she had curves. Ones he could notice and admire. But Fletch had never really been a guy solely attracted by looks; he was always drawn to a person. And even though he'd barely arrived in Singapore, it seemed that he'd already found someone who captured his attention.

As the waitress set down their breakfast dishes, and Madison started on her scrambled eggs, he started chatting again. 'Okay then, what book and what movie?'

She bit into some toast and thought for a few seconds. 'See, you probably think I'm going to say something like *Pride and Prejudice*, but nope, not for me. I want some sci-fi. Giant planet worlds, technology I've not even thought of, and an anti-hero like Darth Vader.'

He almost choked. 'You don't want much, do you?'

'You shouldn't ask questions if you don't like the answers,' she joked.

And just like that he knew. He knew at some point he'd like to ask this woman out.

It was too soon. He didn't know enough about her. She didn't know enough about him. But he was certainly keen to find out more.

'Who says I don't like the answers? Maybe I'm just a bit surprised. Go on, then, what's the movie?'

She shrugged. 'Depends entirely on my mood.' She gave him a mischievous glance. 'I'm a sucker for a Christmas film. But I swing between *White Christmas* and *Die Hard*. And I absolutely adore action movies. Fast cars, burning buildings, chases, explosions, space battles.'

'You're like every guy's dream date, then, aren't you?' he said before he had time to stop himself.

She raised her eyebrows and let out a laugh. 'Not sure I've ever been called that but—' she glanced at her watch '—for half seven on a Tuesday morning, I'll take it!'

He liked that she was neither offended nor shocked. His eyes were drawn to her clear skin and bright smile. Madison Koh was definitely pretty. But the biggest attraction was her easy manner. He wondered how he would feel if he were in her shoes—a single parent, widowed, with twins and full-time job. Would he be able to cope as well as she apparently did, and still make the time to have breakfast with a new colleague?

He could tiptoe around things. Try and find out if she was dating again—or if that was a possibility. Or he could just ask. But would that seem too forward?

They finished breakfast and both looked at their watches at the same time. 'No rest for the wicked,' said Madison brightly. 'I need to jump in the shower and get along to the ward.'

'Me too,' he agreed. 'But thanks for joining me for breakfast. It was...' he couldn't hide his broad smile '... nice.'

She shot him a cheeky glance. 'Nice? Wow. I'm bowled over with compliments here.' She gave him a wave. 'Gotta run, see you later.'

And she did run—or jog—over to the hospital and

disappear inside the main entrance. He did his best not to fixate on her figure, but failed miserably. His spirits were high. New job. New colleagues. New possibilities.

CHAPTER FIVE

FLETCH FINISHED HIS last set of notes and started walking through the hospital. Checking the ER, the rehab ward, and then hanging about the crèche. Madison appeared, rushing as usual, then her footsteps faltered as soon as she saw him.

'Something wrong with Jia?' she asked instantly.

He shook his head, and glanced over his shoulder. 'No, he's doing good. I thought we should talk.'

Madison looked confused, a frown creased her brow and he wondered if he was about to make the biggest fool of himself. 'About what?' she asked.

'Us,' he said without hesitation, figuring if he was going to make an idiot of himself, he might just do it straight away.

Her face straightened and he saw her taking a big gulp. 'Wh-what do you mean?'

'I feel as if you're stuck somewhere in my brain. I can't explain it. I can't make sense of it. And I figured I'd just ask you if I was going crazy, or if there is something in the air between us. I might be imagining this. And just tell me, and I'll go off into a corner and hide. I promise, I'll be entirely professional and won't mention any of this again.' He stopped babbling, and tried to read her face.

She looked stunned, and he hoped that wasn't because he'd just blindsided her with a whole heap of nonsense. 'Just tell me. Am I imagining things? Because it doesn't make sense.'

She blew out some air through her lips and set her bag on the floor, glancing towards the door of the crèche. There was no one else around. They were entirely alone.

'You're not imagining it,' she said. 'And I can't explain it either. I like you,' she said, and he could tell it took real bravery to say those words. 'But I don't know if I'm ready to like you,' she added, her voice a bit shaky.

He took a step closer, putting his hand on the sleeve of her jacket. 'Have you dated anyone since Jason died?' he asked, wondering if this was the road he should take.

She gave a sorry smile. 'I've been on one kind of date, that I didn't tell anyone about, and it didn't work out. I wasn't ready.'

'How long ago was that?'

'Two months,' she said with no hesitation.

There was silence between them for a few moments and Madison rested her head against the wall. 'You're a serial dater, Fletch. The actual opposite of the kind of guy I would look to date.'

He nodded. 'Oh, I know. And maybe this will earn me a slap, but I never figured I'd want to date someone who was a widow, with twins.'

He could see her hold her breath, and he wondered if he'd been too honest.

'You told me yourself you walk away if anything feels like it could be serious. I don't want to introduce my kids to someone who might only be in their lives for a few months. I'm not comfortable with that.'

She moved as another member of staff came down the corridor to collect their kids from the crèche. And he was conscious that she didn't really want other staff members to see them together.

'Okay,' he said carefully. 'So, do we ignore this? Pretend neither of us noticed and just get on with things? Do we avoid each other, or smile and play nice?' He shook his head. 'I've never been here before. I've never been attracted to a woman and not asked her out.' He gave a small laugh. 'But I've certainly never had the same conversations that I've had with you.'

'Ditto,' she said, and he looked up and caught her gaze. Those brown eyes again. Something sparked in her. 'You haven't actually asked me out.' Her lips turned upwards into a smile. 'Not that I'm nitpicking.'

And in that second, he just knew.

'Madison Koh, would you go on a date with me?'

She licked her lips and spoke quietly. 'I think you and I should set some ground rules.'

He nodded in agreement. 'Okay.'

'Don't be offended. But I'd rather keep this between ourselves.'

It wasn't the first thing he'd expected her to say, and he was a bit surprised. 'Okay, why?'

She held out her hands. 'I feel confused enough. Lots of the people around here knew Jason and were his friends. I'm not sure how the general news that I'm dating again will go down with some of them.'

'And it would be entirely none of their business,' said Fletch promptly.

She gave a rueful nod. 'And I know that.' She put her hand on her chest. 'But if I don't know how I feel about this, and if I'm ready or not, the last thing I want is everyone else wading in with their opinion.'

'So, you want to keep things secret?' He wasn't sure that he liked that, but he understood where she was coming from. Did he want to end up with a reputation as the hospital love rat who maybe broke a widow's heart?

Madison was looking at him intently. '*I* want to know how I feel. If I'm ready. If I can cope with dating again.' She paused and gulped. 'If I can feel again.' Her voice was shaky.

'You're scaring me, Maddie,' he said. 'We might go on a few dates, realise we're not a match, and have to give this up.'

She straightened her shoulders. 'Or, we might go on a few dates, decide that things between us are good, and then I can watch you run for the hills. I'm sticking my neck out here, Fletch. I feel as if all the risks are on my side. All I'm asking is that we keep things quiet for a while.'

He realised she was right. This was a much bigger deal for her than for him.

'But how can we work this out if you don't want me around the kids? Are you comfortable asking Jason's family to babysit if you're going on dates again? Do you know how they would react?'

She winced. 'I haven't had that conversation with them yet. But I know it will need to happen. To be honest, I think they might be all right. They take the twins overnight every second weekend—just for one night, and they generally juggle between when we are all working. They've done it since Justin and Mia were just over a year and I'd stopped breastfeeding. It's mainly been to give me a break and to give them some alone time with their grandkids. They really do dote on them.'

'So, that will work out as one date every two weeks?' he asked. He couldn't help but raise his eyebrows.

She gave him a smug smile. 'Maybe it's going to teach you to take things nice and slow. Get to know each other, so we can decide if the spark is real, or if we're just bouncing off each other.'

The eyebrows stayed up. 'Bouncing off each other.' He laughed and shook his head. 'You've no idea, the pictures in my head right now.'

'Stop it.' She gave him a strong nudge.

'So, what do you want to do? Dinner? Sightseeing? Movie?'

She leaned against the wall again. 'I haven't been to the pictures since before I was pregnant. But I'm not sure that's first on the list for me.'

'The pictures?' He was amused.

'That's what they call it in Scotland. I like it.'

'So, why didn't you go when you were pregnant?'

'Duh…because I didn't fit in the chair.' She laughed. 'And I was too uncomfortable, right from the beginning. So, it just wasn't a good idea. I have missed it,' she said thoughtfully. 'But no. Somehow, I don't think sitting in the dark for three hours, and in silence, will be the date of my dreams.'

'I'm moving up to the date of your dreams?' He smiled in pleasure, 'Pressure's on, then.'

She shook her head. 'Don't get cocky. No one likes a smart-arse.'

He grinned. 'So, when is our first date? When are the kids with their grandparents again?'

'Saturday,' she said. 'Two days.'

'So, I've got two days to plan the dream date?'

Her face broke into a smile, and for the first time she looked relaxed around him again. Something fizzed inside him. They were doing this. They were actually going to go on a date.

'So, we're on. Saturday. What time will I pick you up?'

She gave a smile. 'How about lunch time?' He didn't want to second-guess but he could swear that smile reached her eyes.

'Pick you up at one-thirty,' he said, and walked back down the corridor trying not to do a skip in his steps.

CHAPTER SIX

SLEEPLESS NIGHTS WERE a great leveller.

As Justin fretted on and off, Madison's brain worked overtime. Maybe she should just ask Fletch to have a look at him. She'd searched the Internet for everything, which didn't help, because all she came up with were tragic stories of some unheard-of disease or another.

Madison also didn't want to seem like either a helicopter parent, or a paranoid wreck. As a professional, she was used to dealing with both kinds of parent. The nurses on the ward joked that as their kids had all grown older, they'd all been bitter about the lack of sick days they'd managed to achieve throughout their school years. Nurses were quick to assess, and several admitted to being called by the school when their child—who'd felt a bit squeamish—had actually vomited at school.

As she lay on the sofa, with Justin sprawled across her, she spotted a red notebook that she'd picked up from a stall at the hospital advertising new kinds of pharmacy drugs. It was small enough to fit in her uniform pocket. Ideal. She'd start writing down Justin's symptoms, and even her panicky thoughts. It might help her put some context around things so she could decide if she wanted to ask Fletch to examine him or not.

The trouble was, it wasn't just Justin that was on her mind. Part of her was glad she'd had that honest conversation with Fletch before they'd considered moving forward.

She couldn't pretend she wasn't attracted to him, or deny there was a spark between them. But there were so many other influencing factors.

He wasn't her kind of guy. He wasn't. She'd never been the type to date the hospital Lothario. Her Jason would never have been labelled that way. Honest, fun, and with integrity was how he was best remembered.

And even though Fletch had numerous ex-girlfriends, she'd noticed things about him. He hadn't said a single bad word about anyone that he'd dated. The fact he'd remained friends with so many—and that was still a sticking point—surely showed that he'd treated these women with respect?

He'd seemed genuine when he said he wanted them all to be happy. But he'd also been honest with them all about not being ready to settle down.

And this was the part that made her stick the most.

She'd known him a month. A month at arm's length. How on earth could she know if he was the kind of person she might consider having a longer-term relationship with, or spending time around her kids?

Red flags were waving at the side of her eye right now.

Maybe he would just want to date for a few months and then let it come to a natural end. She hadn't properly dated since Jason had died. Could she cope with that? That feeling of rejection, and possibly a broken heart?

Justin squirmed in her arms and she moved like a contortionist trying to get back up from the sofa and take him through to his bed.

There was no way she was having a broken heart. She was smart enough for this. As soon as feelings started to get involved rather than naked attraction, she would reassess things.

The underlying question was still there—was she ready?

She moved over to the window to stare out over the night view of Singapore. Hotels and tower blocks were everywhere, with tiny lights in windows illuminating the dark sky. It made her feel so tiny in this world. One small person in a place with more than five million.

Madison rested her head against the cool glass. She knew what Jason would say, and what he would have wanted for her. He would have wanted her to be happy, just as she would have wanted the same for him had things been turned around.

She was lonely. She could admit it. She would love some adult company. A hand on her waist or round her shoulders. Lips at her ear, or on her neck. Fun, sexy texts. Someone to lie next to in bed and have ridiculous late-night conversations with.

She shivered and lifted her head. Yes, she was ready. Even if Fletch wasn't the right person, he was a good start. At some point she had to get back out there. Her work colleagues had to stop thinking of her as part of a pair, and start to see her as a living, breathing woman, who might want to date again.

It was time to set her life in motion again. Yes, Fletch might be a heartbreaker. But he was an honest heartbreaker. She knew what she was getting into. And he did too. Because she'd told him she wasn't sure about all this. At the very least, the man with a thousand exes could teach her how to date again.

She gave a small laugh to herself as she glanced at her sleeping children and walked back through to her own bedroom. Her wardrobe doors were open and for a moment she wondered what on earth she would wear for her date on Saturday. And then she started laughing again, the warm feeling spreading through her. Because Madison Koh couldn't remember the last time she'd thought about what to wear.

She might buy something new. Shoes used to be her thing. She'd loved stilettos and high heels. At the moment, they were only ever pulled out of the cupboard by Mia and Justin, who tried to totter around in them. Most were bashed beyond all recognition and she didn't mind that for a second.

But maybe it was time for a new pair. And a few other new things.

Life had been too busy for her to take time to focus on herself. She hadn't let herself slow down at all, in her haste to get back to normal life and create a new routine for herself and her children once Jason had died.

It would be nice to take a breath. To have some space.

As she climbed into bed and pulled the duvet over her, her thoughts had finally started to settle. The immediate panic was gone. This might be a good decision—if she let it be.

Fletch had spent the last few days imagining every date known to exist in Singapore. He wanted to do something special. He wanted to have time where he and Madison could chat, flirt, be comfortable around each other, and just enjoy each other's company.

He still didn't know enough about her. And he wanted to.

But he was so, so conscious that he had to tread carefully.

This wasn't like any of his previous relationships. He couldn't compare this to any of the women he'd casually dated. Everything about this was unusual for him, and the confidence he usually felt around women had dimmed. He wanted to get things right.

He reached her apartment right on time and she swung the door open before he even had a chance to knock.

'Wow,' was all he could say.

Madison was ready. Her hair was loose around her shoulders, she had on a red dress, belted at the waist, and a pair of red stiletto heels.

'Double wow,' he said, with a wide smile, pointing at her shoes.

She looked down. 'What?'

It was that second that he noticed her lipstick matched her dress and shoes. He took back previous thoughts. Madison was quite possibly the most beautiful, sassy and spectacular woman he'd ever seen.

'I like the shoes,' he started, then paused. 'No, I *love* the shoes. But we might be doing a bit of walking today.'

She stared him straight in the eye, clearly contemplating telling him she could walk a thousand miles in those shoes. And he would have believed her.

She had a slim tan bag over her shoulder and she bent down, took her shoes off and flung them in the bag. 'Hold this,' she said, disappearing back into her apartment and coming back with a pair of black Converse boots on her feet.

She pulled the apartment door closed and spun around, her hair brushing his nose and a waft of spicy amber and orange aroma hitting his senses. 'Just so we're clear,' she said, 'at some point today, I get to wear those shoes.'

'Your wish is my command,' he agreed. 'I for one will be very happy to see you in those shoes. But in the meantime, let's go.'

Fletch wasn't entirely sure what she'd think of his plans. He just hoped she wouldn't be disappointed. It didn't take them long to reach their destination.

As the green grass sprawled out before them she looked at him curiously. 'We're going to the Botanic Gardens?'

He nodded. 'When was the last time you came here?'

She wrinkled her nose. 'With Mia and Justin's play-group, while they were still babies. I tried baby yoga lessons too, they were at the gardens.'

His heart sank a little and he ignored it. 'So, the last few times you were at the gardens you were with the kids.'

She nodded.

He reached over and took her hand in his. 'So, this time, you're here as an adult. Our mission—if you choose to accept it...' he winked at her '...is to have a chance to wander and talk. We'll go see the orchids too—as long as you're not allergic and haven't told me.'

The edges of her lips turned upwards. 'I'm not allergic. And the orchid gardens will be lovely. It's a long time since I've been in there.' She gave him a nudge. 'And don't sell me short. We have to walk to the bandstand and take a moment to look at the view around.'

'And probably spoil five or six people's iconic camera shot?' he teased.

She shrugged. 'There's enough minutes in the day for us all.'

They stopped for coffee at one of the cafés near the park entrance, and Fletch took her hand back in his. She didn't object, and he gave her a smile as they started to stroll along one of the paths.

'So, your outfit. You knocked it out the park and put me to shame.' He glanced down at his white button-down short-sleeved shirt and khaki shorts. He looked appreciatively at the red dress again. 'Is it new?'

She gave a little tug at the belt with her hand holding the coffee. 'It is. When you asked me out, I realised it had been a long time since I'd bought something nice, you know, not just functional.' She narrowed her gaze. 'But you've ruined the shoe effect. I used to wear high heels all the time. Loved them. Could have run in them. Hurdled. Climbed a mountain. But I hadn't bought a pair since before I was pregnant, and the ones I have, the kids just play in them now. So, there was something kind of nice about buying a new pair.' She raised her eyebrows. 'And there was no doubt—no matter what colour the dress had been—the shoes would have had to be red.'

He laughed. 'Even if the dress was orange or pink?'

She threw back her head and laughed. 'Of course! You're so out of date, Fletch. Pink and red, or orange and red, it's a thing now.'

He shook his head. 'So, shoes is your thing, then?'

She took a breath before she spoke. 'They were. And I'd like them to be again. There hasn't been a lot of me time. And I get that,' she said quickly. 'That's the same for every parent.' She sighed. 'Is it wrong that sometimes I'd just like time to breathe?'

He gave her a thoughtful glance. 'An old friend of mine was a health visitor in England—kind of like a family health nurse in other parts of the world. Because she visited babies and children up to five, she thought when she had her own, she'd be fine.' He gave a rueful smile and said, 'She phoned me one night around dinner time as she'd had to put her two-year-old in his room, and was sitting on the floor holding the door handle.'

'Was he having the terrible twos and wrecking the place? I remember those days well.'

Fletch nodded. 'Oh, he was having the terrible twos—but he wasn't wrecking the place. She'd put him in his room because she said she was ready to kill him.'

Madison closed her eyes. 'I think every parent has had that moment at some point. It's awful. You feel so helpless—as if you're doing the worst job in the world.' She looked at him with interest. 'What did you do?'

'I told her to keep talking. So, she did. She sat on the floor and let it all out.' He shrugged. 'I knew the little guy was safe, and I could hear him through the door. His tantrum was spectacular. But having an adult chat to tell her she wasn't a bad parent, and literally no one has this down, seemed to help her.'

She gave him a suspicious stare. 'But you're not a parent. How do you get it?'

'Who says I do? I try to. That's what's important. Especially as a doctor. You know we both see things we have to question and we have to ensure every child is safe, but we also know that most parents do a good job, even against challenging circumstances. I try to always remember that.'

He swallowed, realising he might be getting too close to the truth for Madison. She'd been practically alone these last three years, there would have been lots of times she probably felt like pulling her hair out.

'How is your friend now?' she asked.

'Kelly's good and decided the terrible twos weren't so terrible after all. She's expecting again.'

While a smile appeared on Madison's face something flickered behind it. Was that a hint of sadness?

He moved on quickly. 'So, tell me, did you always want to be a physio?'

She laughed. 'Not at all. I kind of fell into it. I was one of those kids who finished school, taking very generic subjects because she wasn't sure what subject she wanted to apply for at university.'

'So, you just picked physio out of thin air?'

'Yes, and no. I went to some of the university open days. I looked at a variety of English courses, some computing, I flirted with the thought of working in film, but eventually met a woman who was manning one of the stands, she worked as a physio and explained her role, the science behind it, and how it often helped people regain their independence. I'd never really thought about the role before and it intrigued me.'

'And that was it? Four years later you qualified as a physio?'

'Yes, and the more I did the course and the placements, the more I loved it. It's the perfect job for me.' She turned her head towards him. 'What about you? A straight-A student and a walk right in to medicine?'

He pulled a face. 'Yes, and no. Yes, to the straight-A student. No, to walking right in. I had to wait two years. My father—who was also a doctor—had a stroke. Like most people it was right out of the blue and totally unexpected. He was fit, not overweight, no blood-pressure issues, but he'd had some strange viral infection that year, and it seemed to do some lasting damage to his systems.'

'So, you deferred your studies?'

'Yes. Dad needed a lot of assistance to begin with, but he started a rehab programme that really worked for him. It was slow, with small gains. He still doesn't have full use of his right arm, but for the most part, he's done well.'

'Did he get back to work?'

'He works a couple of days a week now, and seems to get on well.'

'You must have done a bit of physio yourself, then, if you were helping your dad with his programme?'

'Yeah, I did. I think it gave me the chance to appreciate the part everyone plays in a team—before I even started medical training.'

She smiled at him. 'Thank goodness.'

He looked amused though. 'You considered film?'

'Absolutely. Not to be an actress or anything like that, but to work behind the scenes. Never happened though and that's probably for the best. Who knows where I might have ended up?'

The park was tranquil, even if it was in one of the most populated cities in the world. There were plenty of other people strolling along the winding paths and letting the summer air surround them.

They reached the turnstiles for the National Orchid Garden and Fletch paid the small fee to get in. As soon as they crossed through, they were treated to the enchanting aroma of the variety of lilies. Colours were everywhere. Vibrant displays for red, pink, purple and white, each part leading into another that was even more spectacular.

'It's so beautiful, but I feel as if I should whisper,' said Madison. 'There's something so peaceful about this place.'

'It is peaceful,' Fletch agreed. As they wound through the paths, some parts were overshadowed with greenery and others in the brilliant sunshine. The climate in Singapore was perfect for the growth of the huge variety of specimens in front of them. 'One thousand types,' he murmured, 'and over two thousand in this garden alone. It's no wonder people get lost in here.'

She wrinkled her nose. 'I'm not sure I took you for a gardening type.'

'I'm not really. Dad had a greenhouse. It became quite central during his rehabilitation.' He gave her a wink. 'I can grow you a nice tomato, or green pea.'

'Hidden talents,' she joked. 'Don't let that bit of gossip get around the hospital. You'll be fighting them off.'

'I'm taken,' he said, without hesitation.

They'd moved past the fountain, the mist garden and walked through a dozen arches of multicoloured orchids by this point. She stopped walking and let her hand drop from his. 'This is our first outing. And we agreed we'd keep a low profile.'

He looked at her curiously. 'We did, and we will. But I don't date more than one person at a time. Do you?'

The words were like a challenge. 'Of course, I don't,' she said aghast. 'You know I've not dated for years. Can you let me get the hang of this again?'

'Oh, you can get the hang of it again, as long as you don't break the dating rules.'

He'd started walking again and she slowly joined him as they made their way out of the orchid garden, back into the main park and towards one of the cafés.

'What are the dating rules?' she immediately asked.

He couldn't help teasing. He wanted her to be relaxed around him. He understood dating again was a big deal and, while that also intimidated him, he was trying not to think of what it all could mean.

'The dating rules are simple. Always food in one form or another. Honesty as much as possible. Alternate picks for movie nights. No bad music, and...' he paused '... dancing at every opportunity.'

Madison's mouth fell half open. 'What?'

He pulled her into his arms and waltzed her around in a few circles. Her eyes were wide. But her body moved in tune with his. Her footsteps faltered and she laughed, looking down at her red dress and Converse boots. 'Shouldn't I have changed shoes for this?'

'You can if you want, but we might still have some walking to do.'

'Why, where are we heading next?'

'This is for amateurs. Let's show the world we're professionals.'

Her nose wrinkled but he could tell she was intrigued.

He still had one hand at her waist and his other in her hand, keeping her in the waltz position. Their bodies were only inches apart, noses only a little further. No one was bothering them. Fletch could notice a few glances in their directions.

He could kiss her. Right now, he could kiss her. But

they were supposed to be taking things slow. And even though she was right in front of him wearing a gorgeous, figure-hugging dress, the scent of her perfume catching his senses, her red lips still only a few millimetres from his... 'Come,' he said. 'Let's go to the place you made me promise I'd take you.'

It only took them ten minutes to reach the bandstand. The octagonal gazebo was surrounded by terraced flower beds, palms and a ring of yellow rain trees.

Madison's face lit up. 'There's no one there.' Her footsteps quickened. He understood her haste. The bandstand was rarely empty. It was one of the most popular photo spots in the whole park. It was also a renowned wedding photography spot, but fortunately it was late afternoon at this point, and most of the wedding pictures had likely been done.

He held her hand as he led her up the steps, and gave her a bow. 'Want to put your shoes on now?'

The converse were toed off and she opened her backpack to pull out her red shoes. It only took a second for her to slip them on and stand in front of him. 'You were saying?' she teased.

He held out his hand. 'Do you want some music?'

She was laughing as she slid her hand into his. 'I'm terrified to let you choose.'

'How about we play a game of chance? I'll put my phone on random and we'll dance to the first song that plays.'

She tilted her head as she thought about it. 'Give me a tiny clue of what's on there before I agree.'

He pretended to have to think about exactly what was on his phone. 'Some hard rock, some soul, some oldies, a few from the charts in the last few years, and some film soundtracks. Oh, and the odd Christmas album.'

She laughed out loud. 'So, it really is a lottery? We could be dancing to "I Wish It Could Be Christmas Every Day" in the middle of summer?'

'Shouldn't life be full of random chances?' He wanted to lean forward and push her hair away from her face. It was blowing in the wind, and blocking his view of those hypnotic brown eyes. She licked her red lips and he almost groaned at the world for playing with his body, mind and levels of testosterone.

'Go for it,' she joked.

He paused for a second to press a button on his phone then slid it into his back pocket. He didn't wait for fate to thwart him, and just took her into his arms again and started moving as the music started to surround them.

Both of them burst out laughing at the same time as Berlin's 'Take My Breath Away' started playing.

Fletch couldn't hide his delight and picked her up and swung her round.

'It's a fix.' She laughed as he set her back down and they began swaying against each other.

'I told you I had old movie tunes in there. It just so happened that someone was clearly smiling down on us today.'

'It is an old one,' she agreed. 'I wasn't even born when the original movie came out.'

'Neither was I.' He grinned. 'But we've both still seen it, and know the song. Isn't it weird how some things just last the test of time?'

He'd meant the words in an entirely different context, but wanted to bite them back as soon as he saw the fleeting emotion in her eyes. But she didn't fold to the feelings. She just dipped her head for a second, gave a tiny shudder and lifted her head to meet his gaze again.

In that tiny movement, he suddenly realised just how brave Madison Koh was.

He felt it.

And he also felt a bit terrified.

The last thing he wanted to do was lead this woman on a merry dance—metaphorically speaking, of course.

This wasn't normal for him. He couldn't remember *ever* feeling like this. That had to account for the terror. And the other overwhelming thought was that, right now, he didn't want to be anywhere else in the world but right here. With her.

He ignored the small lump that had definitely appeared in the back of his throat and just let her body move gently against his. 'I've got you,' he said.

Nothing more. And he meant it. He'd wondered if he—and this—would end up just being part of her journey of moving on and moving forward. He couldn't push himself to think long term yet. But what he also knew was that he was in exactly the place he wanted to be.

She gave him the smallest smile and he could feel the tension release from her muscles. He allowed himself to relax too, and smile at the music and dance their way around the bandstand.

He noticed a few people snapping pictures of them, and even though they were from a distance, he was conscious that sometimes people posted on social media spontaneously. He moved them, so that Madison's back was to the people. The last thing he wanted was a member of Jason's family or someone from the hospital seeing a private moment between them.

The music came to an end and he gave her a little bow, not drawing her attention to what he had noticed.

'Thank you for the dance.'

She turned and picked up her bag. 'Thank you for finally letting me put my shoes on. I bought them specially. Do you know how mad I'd have been if I hadn't had a chance to show them off?'

Fletch put his hand to his chest. 'As a guy with the odd female friend, I can safely say that's definitely not something I want to find out.'

She put the bag at her shoulder. 'The day is still young. What's next?'

He grinned. 'You know how I told you one of the dating rules involved food?'

She nodded and he could tell she was interested. 'I definitely like dating rules that revolve around food. I know it's only around five, but I have a favourite place that means we need to jump on the MRT. Are you up for it?'

She patted her stomach. 'I'm always up for some food. Lead the way.'

He took her hand again and they headed out to the nearby station, Fletch swiped for tickets at the machine and they jumped on the next train. The journey was pleasant. MRT was one of the most efficient transport systems, it had a reputation for being clean, safe and even had built-in Wi-Fi for those doing longer commutes. They exited at Downtown station and took the five-minute walk to Lau Pa Sat market.

Even this early in the evening the delicious smells and noise of crackling food pulled them in.

Her eyes were gleaming. 'I wondered where your favourite place was.' She looked around the busy market-
place. 'But which is your favourite seller?'

'I'm already hungry with just the smells,' Fletch admitted. 'But the best satay stalls won't be set up yet. How
do you feel about a drink?'

The air was warm and Madison pulled at her dress. 'A
drink would be good.'

'What do you normally drink?'

She wrinkled her brow. 'Usually wine, or a cocktail.'
Then she laughed. 'I say that as if I have managed to
find time to have a drink in the last few years. I think
I can count on one hand how many I've actually had.'
Her eyes kept drifting over the various beverage places
around them. One of them caught her attention. 'How
about a craft beer?'

Fletch couldn't help but let the biggest grin appear on
his face. 'Sounds like heaven.'

They walked over and perused the beers before finally
selecting one each and taking their tall glasses with the
chilled beer and having a seat at one of the nearby tables.
It was nice just chilling. 'I love people-watching.' Madison sighed, taking a sip of her beer.

'Do you ever make up stories about the people you
watch?'

She shook her head and looked amused. 'What do
you mean?'

'I had an auntie, and she used to try and entertain me
when we were waiting in line for something or were out
shopping, by making up stories about the people around
us.'

'Like what?'

Fletch scanned the people around them, thinking hard. 'Okay. See that man in the orange shirt?'

Madison saw him instantly. He wasn't hard to miss. Fletch leaned his elbows on the table. 'So, people won't realise, but that's his *lucky* shirt. He wore it to his first date with his latest girlfriend, he wore it to a job interview to get a job he really wanted, and—' he leaned forward conspiratorially '—and he's just about to buy a lottery ticket today, and guess what?'

She put her chin on her hand as she grinned at him. 'He wins?'

Fletch threw up his hands. 'He wins! Now, it's your turn.'

Madison tapped her other hand on the table and surveyed the crowds. It took her a few moments to pick someone. 'Okay, the older woman in the black skirt, beige shirt, with the hat and the pink bag.'

Fletch spent a few seconds before he spotted her. 'Okay, unusual bag colour, but carry on.'

Madison raised her eyebrows and looked mockingly serious. 'This is where it gets dark.'

Fletch started to laugh. He just couldn't help it. 'Okay, then.'

Madison licked her lips. 'So, this lady is not happy. She's found out her lover has been cheating on her. But this woman is no fool. She's like a modern-day Locusta— you know the professional poisoner of Ancient Rome? So, she's found a new untraceable poison and has laced it through his hair products, face cream and toothpaste. She's just left his luxury penthouse knowing that the next time she goes back, he'll likely be on the floor.'

Fletch opened his mouth. 'I'm shocked. Where did that

come from? You seem like such a good-hearted person.' He was shaking his head as he started laughing.

Madison was laughing too. 'What did you expect, a fairy-princess story? Because that's not me. Oh, no. I want the thriller, the mystery film or novel. The twisty plot with some characters having a spirit as black as coal.' She threw up her hands. 'That's when all the fun happens.'

Fletch took a long, slow sip of his beer. 'Shocked,' he said as he set it down. 'Shocked, I am.'

She leaned forward. 'Come on, let's do another.'

'You're scaring me now.'

She scanned again and nodded in the direction of a young woman, in a school uniform. She looked in her late teens. 'The other thing I like is some dark academia. So, this is Nora. Everyone thinks she's the school good girl. But Nora is *not* a good girl.' Another teenager, almost identical, emerged from the store that 'Nora' was standing outside. 'Here's where it gets interesting.' Madison beamed. 'That's Jules. Her best friend. But Jules has just won a scholarship to Oxford in England. Nora came second. So, they are just about to go on a school trip to Japan. And at Shibuya Crossing—the busiest crossing in the world—Jules doesn't know it, but she's about to meet a sticky end.'

Madison lifted her beer glass and clinked it against his. 'Cheers.' She sat back in her chair. 'I could do this storytelling stuff all day.'

He leaned back in wonder and kept shaking his head. 'Please tell me this is not the kind of storytelling you do with your kids.'

She pulled a face. 'Not yet. But I suspect Mia might

inherit some of her mother's tendencies. She loves attacking her play people with dinosaurs right now, and there are several heads and limbs missing.'

He couldn't help the low belly laugh. 'And you're proud, aren't you?' He held up his beer glass so she could clink it again.

She leaned forward and the clink resounded as she said the words, 'Immensely.'

Fletch leaned back and gave her an admiring glance. Madison Koh was one of the most interesting women he'd ever met. He was glad he'd trusted his gut. Even though his brain had tried to interfere, he couldn't pretend he wasn't interested in her, or deny that he thought she was gorgeous and sexy.

Vibes were there for a reason.

They didn't need to be a perfect match. It didn't need to be the perfect time. He just wanted a chance to see where this might go. And just as he'd realised as he'd been holding her, he'd never felt like this before—he also realised he'd never been prepared to take a chance like this either.

Of course, he couldn't say things would work out. He didn't know that. How could he? Because deep down, he still had doubts. These feelings were new to him. He still wanted to tread with caution.

He leaned across the table and threaded his fingers through hers. 'Are we going to do this all night?'

She gave him an astute look. 'Maybe,' she said decisively. 'Or at least until you can buy me the best chicken satay in the whole of Singapore.'

'Ah,' he said with interest. 'So, it's chicken satay that you want?'

'Doesn't everyone?'

He waggled his hand. 'I'm torn. There are also the prawn noodles.'

'Hmm…' said Madison, clearly contemplating the option. Then she shook her head. 'No. It's got to be the chicken satay.'

They moved along to her favourite stall and watched as the vendor freshly cooked two portions of chicken satay and loaded the steaming food into bowls for them both. They moved to the nearby tables and sat down to eat. Madison gave a grateful sigh. 'This is lovely,' she said. 'Most nights I have to concentrate on having a routine and getting the kids down. Can't tell you the last time I managed to get here after seven when the stalls were open.'

This time, instead of beer, Fletch grabbed them both bubble tea on Madison's instructions and sipped at the unusual concoction dubiously.

'It's more popular here than cola now,' she said, as she watched him.

He screwed up his nose. 'It's a bit sweet for me. But interesting.'

She grinned as she kept her gaze on him. 'You hate it, don't you?'

He pulled a face. 'Kinda…'

'Go get something else.' He didn't need to be told twice and came back moments later with a diet cola.

Madison finished her satay slowly, clearly savouring every bite, before lifting her hands above her head and stretching like a cat who'd just woken up.

'This has been lovely, thank you,' she said as she smiled and looked at the busy streets round about her. 'Makes me feel like I actually have a bit of a life again.'

He was about to ask her a question but she shook her

head and lifted one hand. 'Don't take that the wrong way. I love my kids. I love being their parent. But now and then, it's nice to be an adult again. And get to do adult things and have adult company.'

It took her a few moments to realise what she'd said. Fletch had already started laughing as her cheeks flushed. 'Oh, no.' She groaned and put her head down on the table. 'You know what I mean.'

They'd both finished now and Fletch stood up, extending his hand out towards her. 'I know what you mean,' he said genuinely.

She slid her hand into his and they walked back through the bustling crowds to the MRT. 'Want to do something else?' he asked. 'Want to go to a bar, or have you changed your mind, and want to find a film to watch?'

She shook her head and, in that moment, they strode into the stream of red and yellow lights from a nearby store. The lights reflected off Madison's loose brown hair and red dress, leaving him momentarily transfixed at the effect. It was like watching a movie star on the big screen. He didn't need to go to a cinema. He had his own right here.

She realised the lights were illuminating her and lifted her hands, giving a laugh. 'Ten seconds of stardom.'

He moved in front of her, joining her in the stream, and slid his arms around her waist, his face just above hers. 'Maybe it's just giving us the perfect moment.'

He wasn't asking the question out loud, but there was no doubt the question was there. They had been casually tactile with each other all day. He wasn't going to kiss her without knowing it was what she wanted.

He wondered if she would pause, if she would step

back, but he didn't have time to process those thoughts before she'd wrapped her arms around his neck and her lips were on his. At first it was the gentlest of brushes. But a few seconds later, the kiss was warm, tender, open-mouthed and inviting.

One of his hands slid up from her waist and into her hair, the silky strands falling through his fingers. The press of her body against his, and the sweet smell of her perfume, mixed with all the scents and noises around them. The world kept moving. But they stayed fixed in place.

For the first time since he'd been with Madison, his brain didn't allow for any second-guessing. This moment, this kiss, was meant to be. He believed that.

As they finally broke apart, he could feel the warm breath from her mouth landing on his cheek. 'Wow,' she whispered.

'Wow,' he repeated. He couldn't stop the broad smile on his face.

She reached up and touched his cheek. 'This has been a great day,' she said, her fingertips pressing lightly. He knew the but was coming. And it did. 'But it's time for me to go home.'

He could argue about how early it was. He could make a case for them spending the next few hours together. He could make a case of what exactly they could spend the next few hours doing. But he got the silent message. For now, this was as far as Madison was prepared to go. And he accepted that.

He gave a nod of his head, not letting himself speak. Again, he took her hand in his and they walked to the

MRT, jumping on the next train and heading back to Madison's district.

Of course, he wanted to walk her to the door. Of course, he would have loved to have gone back inside her apartment with her. But once they entered the main doors to her building she turned and kissed his cheek. 'Thank you, Fletch,' she said softly.

He stepped back. She turned and headed to the elevator and he waited until she'd stepped inside and turned back to face him.

'Till the next time,' she said with a smile, and as the doors slid closed he tried to pretend his heart wasn't secretly exploding with delight.

CHAPTER SEVEN

MADISON HAD FLOATED back up to her apartment and the smile had remained on her face while she dressed for bed and took off her make-up.

She hadn't really expected things to go so well. She hadn't really expected to feel so connected to the man she thought couldn't possibly be a match for her.

Was her judgement off? Had it been so long since she'd trod this path that her senses had died and tucked themselves off in a drawer somewhere?

At numerous points today her skin had tingled. Usually when their gazes had connected and she'd felt just… something. Her new dress and shoes were back in the wardrobe. But she could see them. They were half taunting her. Her dress had wrinkles at the waist due to wear, and the shoes had a tiny scuff.

It was almost as if they were sending her a message. *You did this.*

Madison wasn't some teenage girl. She couldn't possibly put a whole lot of stock in one good date. But she could keep it. She could keep the memory of it, and of that first kiss.

She was ashamed to admit she couldn't remember the first time Jason and she had kissed. She was sure she had known previously, but somehow it now just seemed mixed up in her head. It was a distant, hazy memory, whereas tonight's kiss was standing bright and under the spotlight.

She wrapped her arms around herself and smiled. She wasn't sorry to have called an end to the night. She knew what could have happened. It could very easily have happened.

But she wanted to take charge of the pace of things between them. It was easy to get swept away. Whatever happened, she had to work with Fletch for the next few years. It was important she didn't jump in too quickly.

As she sat on the sofa, her long blinds pulled back to let her gaze over the city, her fingers caught the soft notebook on the table beside her.

That brought her back to reality. Justin.

She was getting more and more worried. Vague things. No real, specific shout-out-loud-this-kid-needs-to-be-taken-to-the-doctor kind of things. She definitely couldn't put her finger on it. But something had changed in her little boy. She knew it in every fibre of her being.

She'd doubted herself before. But the last few days, she'd been noting things down. Every little thing.

She was well aware some people might think this was the diary of a hypochondriac mother. But the right person would listen to her, and take this seriously.

And all of a sudden, Madison had confidence in who the right person was. She picked up the notebook, flicked through, grabbed her pen, and started writing again.

'I've added someone onto your list,' said the secretary.

'No problem,' said Fletch as he reviewed some results. 'Who is it?'

The secretary looked over. 'It's the kid of one of the staff members. They asked if they could have an initial appointment to see you and discuss some concerns.'

He nodded. It was always a compliment when a colleague asked him to see one of their kids and he was happy to do it, conscious that in another ten years, he might want them to repay the compliment.

He didn't even glance at the name, so when Madison walked into his office a few hours later with Justin in her arms he could have—quite literally—fallen over.

His eyes automatically went to the screen. Sure enough, Justin Koh was in this appointment.

He walked around the table automatically, holding his arms out towards them both. 'Maddie? You don't need an appointment to ask me to see Justin. I'll see him any time. Hey, little guy.' He put his face down nearer to Justin and spoke to him directly. 'How are you doing? Remember me? I'm Fletch. One of your mummy's friends.'

Fletch didn't often wear a white coat. He preferred wearing normal clothes when dealing with children. So, he was frequently on the floor during consultations in order to assess a child properly.

Maddie seemed nervous. 'No, I know. But I wanted to make an appointment. I wanted this to be official.' She sat down in the chair opposite his, and arranged Justin on her lap. 'I wanted to discuss some things I've noticed with Justin.'

Fletch could tell she wanted to keep things formal, so he went with the flow. 'Tell me what you've noticed.'

She pulled a red notebook from her pocket. 'So, in the last four weeks I've noticed some changes in Justin.'

'Okay.' Fletch nodded. He always paid attention to

what a parent told him. He was also well aware that for some children their stage of development sometimes alerted parents to things that might have been there, right from the start.

'In the last four weeks, Justin has seemed unnaturally tired. At first, I thought it was a growth spurt. But his growth has been steady. Nothing to really draw any attention. And even though he's always tired, he doesn't sleep well at night. I've tried a whole host of different things, without any real success.' She gave a sigh. 'And, of course, I know the two are connected, but I've also noticed other things.'

Fletch was watching carefully. Justin was three. At three, most kids were attention-seeking. Happy to chat, wanting to be involved in whatever was going on. Curiosity would have brought many three-year-olds out of their mother's lap by now, and either exploring the box of toys in the room, or starting to touch all the things on Fletch's desk.

Justin was sitting. Clearly paying attention, but his eyelids did look a bit heavy.

'There are other random things. Sometimes he feels a bit sick and doesn't eat well—even when it's his favourite food. His concentration seems to be affected. Jigsaws he was completing a few weeks ago, now get flung to the floor in frustration. Now and then we get some outbursts, and he gets frustrated with Mia, and they fight. He's also had one or two dizzy spells. And he complains at night that his legs are sore.' Her voice started to crack and she automatically started rubbing Justin's back. 'It seems like a whole lot of nothing that I can't put my finger on. But I just know that there *is* something. And I feel a fool because this is my boy, and I can't work it out. I can't tell him what's wrong and make him feel better again.'

Fletch gave a slow nod. 'Madison, I'm going to help you with this. This could be easy, or it could be hard. We might have to do a whole host of tests to rule things out first, before we consider real possibilities. Are you okay with this?'

Her chin was trembling but she nodded. He pointed over to the examination trolley. 'Okay, so we start simple. Justin, Mummy's going to help you take off your T-shirt and trousers and I'm going to have a little look at you.'

Justin frowned but didn't seem annoyed. He let Maddie slip off his T-shirt and trousers, and sat up on the examination couch with her at one side and Fletch at the other.

A proper top-to-toe physical examination was crucial in assessing children. Fletch was glad that Justin wasn't actively unwell right now with a fever. That always made things worse. And while Justin glared at Fletch the whole time, he let him look in his ears, eyes, nose and throat, and sound his back and chest. He also didn't object when Fletch got him to stand straight to check his legs, spine, posture and muscle groups.

After about ten minutes, Fletch made a few notes and touched Madison's hand. 'Okay, nothing obvious. But I think you knew that. How do you feel about a urine specimen, a nose swab, and, if we put some numbing cream on his arm, some bloods?'

Madison flinched and pressed her lips together. She must have known this was coming, but she gave a nod and said, 'Can Roki do the bloods?'

'Absolutely,' Fletch agreed, knowing that Roki was one of the best phlebotomists on the unit. He handed her a specimen bottle. 'I'll go and speak to Roki while you try and persuade Justin to do a pee for us.'

An hour later, a much more disgruntled Justin was sipping a carton of orange juice and nibbing on a biscuit. The urine dipstick had been negative, but both the sample and the throat swab had been sent to the lab for analysis. The bloods had been expertly taken by Roki and would likely be back in a few hours.

Fletch sat down next to Madison. 'This is only the first few steps. Let's have a look at the overall picture, then sit down again and see if we can narrow down specifics.'

As the process had continued, he'd seen her get more tense, and he got it. She'd vocalised her fears that there could be something wrong with her child. That was terrifying enough.

Madison gave a tight nod and Fletch couldn't help himself. He reached over and squeezed her hand. 'We'll work this out.'

Right now, Fletch was unsure what could be wrong with Justin, but there was a whole host of possibilities that he would consider. He wanted Madison to have a little faith.

'Will we agree a time tomorrow to look at test results? You don't need to bring Justin. We'll look at what comes back and decide a plan.'

She nodded her head as she picked up Justin again. 'Okay, thanks, Fletch. Come on, gorgeous, let's get back to nursery.'

She disappeared out of the door and Fletch bit his lip.

He was glad she trusted him enough as a doctor to bring Justin to see him. He wished she'd had a chat with him beforehand, but maybe she'd been worried he might say no? Fletch would never have done that, but he couldn't help but wonder why she hadn't mentioned it.

This also muddied the waters between them. Before, they were purely colleagues. Now, she was officially the mother of one of his patients. If things continued to develop between them, depending on the results of the tests, it might reach a point that he'd have to hand Justin's care over to someone else.

Some others might rightly badge this as a conflict of interest.

But Fletch didn't think they were at that point yet. He'd know if they were. At least he hoped he would…

Madison's chest was tight as she delivered Justin back to the crèche and ducked into the nearby ladies to let the tears she'd been holding in flow unhindered behind a bathroom door.

She was shaking, even though she knew it wasn't rational. She'd said the words out loud and got a doctor to see her son. But she hadn't got any doctor—she'd asked Fletch.

His face had been shocked when she'd walked in. Part of her had hoped the secretary would have warned him, when she'd agreed to put Justin on the schedule this morning. But, for whatever reason, Fletch had clearly not realised Justin was on his list.

He'd been gracious and professional, and she was thankful for that.

But in the meantime, she had a whole lot of worry about what could be wrong with her little boy. She texted one of her friends, and contemplated phoning her mum back in Scotland. But if she told anyone else, she would likely only worry them too—and Madison didn't want to do that.

She wiped her face and blew her nose before coming out of the stall and washing her hands, not even bothering to glance at her own reflection. She still had a few patients to see before she finished tonight and wanted to get back to business.

Fletch stared at the swab result, urine results and blood levels, which told him very little at all. A small rise that could indicate an inflammatory response somewhere, or a start of an infection, but nothing major.

Madison appeared in the doorway looking jittery. He called her over and showed her the results on the screen. She was smart enough to understand them without much explanation and he could sense her wave of disappointment. He'd wanted to text her last night, or call her, but wasn't sure if that was an intrusion when he knew there was so much else going on in her life.

She sagged down in frustration next to him. 'Nothing really,' she said with a wave of her hand.

He nodded in agreement. 'Okay, I have a suggestion, but I'm not sure if you'll like it.'

Her brow creased and she looked at him. 'What?'

'I'd like to spend more time around Justin.'

She froze. He could see it in the tensing of her muscles and the way her mouth formed a small 'o'. 'What exactly do you mean?'

'I'd like to see what he's like at home, what he's like when it's bedtime, how he settles—or doesn't.'

'Y-you don't believe what I've told you?'

He put his hand over hers. 'I absolutely believe what

you've told me. But I need something else to work on. I could ask if we could admit him for a few days—'

'No.' The word was out of her mouth instantly.

He acknowledged it, and continued, 'Or, I can spend more time around him. In the park. In my office if you prefer. In the crèche—which I will probably do. But I also think seeing him in his own environment will probably be for the best.'

She swallowed and he could see her contemplating things. 'Would you do this for someone else's child?'

He thought about this honestly. 'Yes, and no. I've done this before when I sensed a diagnosis in a child was going to be tough.'

'Were you dating that mother?' was the rapid-fire question.

'No,' was his honest response.

He waited a moment then continued. 'I respect that you said you don't really want your children to meet someone you are dating. This is complicated. Physical examination was unremarkable for Justin, and his tests haven't specified anything for us. I want to get a better sense of him. I want to see the interactions with Mia, and if that influences him in any way. I want to see how he functions in his own world, his own safe place, rather than in a doctor's office or crèche with other children.'

He watched her breathe deeply. 'I understand what you're saying. I think you could be right. But what does this mean for us? I want there to be clear lines when it comes to my children. I don't want things to be blurred, and I don't see how this is anything *but* blurry.'

'Do you want us to draw a line under things? Do you want to forget about dating?' He was saying the words out loud because he thought he should—it was the respectable thing to do—but his heart was currently held in an invisible clamp.

'No.' Her answer was swift, and the clamp miraculously realised its tension.

Her hand went to her hair and she started fumbling with it, redoing her ponytail, which was absolutely fine.

He waited a moment and then spoke. 'Neither do I.'

She dropped her hands and met his gaze.

'So, how do we do this, Madison?'

'Come tonight,' she said, and he got the impression she was saying this before she changed her mind. 'Bring takeout. The kids like chicken noodles. You can watch him at dinner, see them play together and then you watch as I do their bedtime routine.'

Her movements were clearly unconscious, but she straightened her spine and dropped her tense shoulders. It was clear she'd made up her mind.

'What time?' he asked.

'Early—six p.m.?'

'How are you going to explain the fact I'm there?'

'Friend from work,' she said quickly. 'I'll tell the kids we have work things to talk about when they go to bed.'

He nodded. It was a sensible solution. It made sense. Even if he didn't want it to. Something panged deep down in his belly. This wasn't how he'd expected to feel. Never, in his eternal bachelor days, had he ever really wanted to ingratiate himself into the life of his girlfriend's children—particularly after one date!

He wasn't sure if he was more surprised or conflicted. Of course, he should know his own mind. And his mind right now was quite fixated on Madison. But she was a package deal. And that had to play a part in every move that he made. So, even though he was scared, and his brain screamed caution, he still wanted to pursue this.

'No problem, I'll see you then.'

Madison wasn't sure she'd made the right decision. Her brain had gone back and forth all day, and when she'd finally picked the kids up from the crèche she'd almost texted Fletch to cancel. But things got away from her. Justin was more cranky than usual, and Mia seemed to have had new batteries inserted and talked nineteen to the dozen. By the time she'd wrestled them out of day care, got home, dumped their stuff and finally stripped off her uniform it was almost exactly six.

She pulled back her wardrobe door and stared at her clothes. A green blouse, a pair of black jeans—or the black T-shirt with the sequin lightning flash? But no. She stopped herself, not wanting to draw any attention to what was about to happen. She grabbed the grey yoga pants she normally wore around the house and pulled on an old rock-band T-shirt. Fletch would just have to take her as he found her.

'Guys,' she said, as she steered them into the bathroom to wash their hands. 'Mum's work friend is bringing us dinner. He'll be here soon, so wash up.'

Mia, never one to miss anything, started asking questions. 'Is it Rui? What's she bringing? Is it ice cream?'

Madison sighed but smiled. 'No, it's not Rui. It's Fletch, the new doctor. He's bringing chicken noodles.'

'Ooh…' said Mia and jumped up at the table, obviously ready to start eating.

The knock at the door was perfect timing. Justin still

looked mopey, but moved over to the table as Madison went to answer the door.

Fletch had the food in his hands and gave her a nod, looking down to her legs. For a second she thought he was looking at the yoga pants, then she remembered he was more likely looking for the children.

She pulled the door open. 'Come in.'

He stepped inside and his footsteps faltered as he clearly caught sight of the children sitting at the table. Both of them had lifted their knife and fork in preparation for the food.

'Under pressure,' murmured Fletch and started humming the Queen tune as he made his way over to her kitchen. 'How do you want to do this? Put it all out at once?'

Madison opened the boxes, looked inside and inhaled deeply. 'Mmm…' She picked up one and took it over to the table and divided the contents between Mia's and Justin's bowls. 'Here we go, guys.'

She then found two large plates and opened the second container and divided between herself and Fletch. She nodded her head to the right. 'Bathroom's through there. Go and wash up and I'll get us some cutlery.'

She poured some soda for them and water for the kids and Fletch joined her at the table a few minutes later. 'Guys, you've met him before, but this is Dr Fletch.'

Mia was already eating. She chewed for a few seconds then looked at him as only a three-year-old could. 'Red or pink?'

'Pink,' he said without blinking.

'Puppies or kittens?'

'Puppies.'

'You lose!' declared Mia happily.

Fletch gave a look of fake horror. 'How did I lose? How can puppies ever be the wrong answer?'

'Because we're not allowed a puppy in here. We could only have a kitten—but Mummy doesn't want one.'

Mia side-eyed her mother, and Madison did her best to act as if she didn't notice.

She nudged Fletch and turned her attention to Justin. 'How are the noodles, honey?'

He was stirring them around his bowl, occasionally spearing a bit of chicken. 'Fine,' he mumbled.

Madison breathed. Maybe there was nothing wrong with Justin at all. Maybe he'd just aged into a teenager overnight, and the tiredness, lack of attention and one-word answers were just something she should get used to.

But Fletch seamlessly took over. 'I brought some dinosaurs with me. Do you both like dinosaurs?'

Two little heads looked at him, their attention instantly on him. 'Yes,' said Mia immediately.

'Yes,' said Justin in a low voice.

'Well, once we've finished dinner, and if it's okay with your mummy, I'll give you them.'

Two pairs of eyes turned on her. 'It's fine,' she said quickly.

Fletch was an easy dinner companion, and Madison ate the chicken noodles even though her stomach seemed to be somersaulting around. She was conscious of everything. Every glance, every look. Every time Justin yawned. Every time he was a bit distracted. Then she made herself stop.

She had to stop. She wasn't examining every little move or word of Mia. If she did, she would be exhausted.

Fletch asked both an easy stream of questions. Mia was fascinated with Fletch's accent, and tried to imitate it, making them all laugh.

Once Madison had cleared the dishes, she took out two wine glasses and poured some pinot grigio, handing one to Fletch as they sat down on the sofa. Fletch handed over his bag of goodies to the kids and the two settled on the floor in front of Madison and Fletch to play. Justin disappeared for a few moments and came back with a kit bag that was already full of dinosaurs, which he added to the rest.

Madison wondered how she was supposed to feel about all this. Having Fletch in her apartment and around the kids wasn't nearly as awkward as she'd feared it might have been.

She wondered why she'd built it up so much in her head. She knew the reason he was here. It was to assess Justin. And she could sense he was doing just that. They had the large-screen TV on in the background. It was playing an old nineties film and the children were completely ignoring it as they were definitely in dinosaur land. Petty fights and squabbles were happening as Mia tried to commandeer most of the new pieces, and Justin's little chin jutted out as he held his own against his sister.

He was moving position, occasionally rubbing his joints in a way a child shouldn't. After a while he started rubbing his eyes and getting snarly with his sister. Madison glanced at the clock. It was around forty-five minutes before she would normally get them ready for bed.

'I'm going to switch the shower on. Justin, you first.'

Mia gave a sideways glance of triumph that Madison clocked instantly. 'Actually, both just come together.'

Justin instantly started to make whining noises, throwing down his dinosaur toys and dragging his feet. Normal toddler tantrums actually didn't bother Madison that much. She hurried them both in the shower and had them dried and in pyjamas within ten minutes.

'Say goodnight to Dr Fletch and say thank you for the dinosaurs,' she prompted.

'I want to stay up,' said Mia.

Justin didn't make the same objections. He was tired. He wandered through to the main room and gave Fletch an interested look. 'Thanks for the rex,' he said. 'Night-night.' Then he turned, went to his own room, and climbed into his bed. 'Kiss, Mummy.'

Madison kissed her son, stroked his hair and murmured in his ear. 'Love you, darling.'

His eyes closed instantly, but Madison knew he wouldn't sleep right through. He hadn't in weeks.

Mia was more of a challenge. By the time Madison came back through she was sitting on the sofa next to Fletch with her favourite book in hand. Fletch was obediently reading to her, with a grin on his face.

'I do as I'm told,' he murmured as Madison sat down next to them both.

Her daughter was a feisty little character, and, while she would never let her be rude or overbearing, she didn't ever want to dampen her enthusiasm or curiosity. Somehow, she didn't think Mia would ever be anyone's fool.

Mia shot her mother a look and Madison nearly laughed out loud. Mia had got her own way. She made Fletch read her three different stories before Madison finally herded her off to bed.

When she came back through, she hesitated in the

doorway. Fletch was sitting comfortably on the sofa, wine glass in hand, watching the TV.

It caught her right in the gut.

This was the first time she'd had another guy back to her place—like this—since Jason had died.

Shouldn't she be crying right now? Regretting she'd asked him over? Because although it felt a little odd, it didn't feel wrong. Did that mean that she was ready to try something new?

There wasn't anyone to have this conversation with, or pose these questions to, so Madison went with her instincts.

She crossed back into the room, picked up her glass of wine and sat back down next to him. 'What do you think?'

Fletch looked thoughtful. 'I'm still in a process of elimination. I think we look at inflammatory responses next with a more specific blood test, or even a few simple scans. His joints bother him, that's clear. And the irritation—could that actually be an underlying mild inflammation in the cerebral tissues?'

Madison started and he reached over and touched her arm. 'Don't be alarmed. I have to think of everything.'

She nodded but couldn't help but be scared. The normal cause of that kind of thing was meningitis. 'He's had all his jabs,' she murmured. 'But that doesn't rule out viral meningitis.'

Fletch shook his head. 'His symptoms would be more acute if he had a viral strain of meningitis.'

'I guess so.' His hand was still on her arm and she looked down at it. The feel of his fingers on her skin was warm and comforting. It was also starting a series of tingles up the length of her arm.

He hadn't mentioned her sloppy, comfortable clothes. She wasn't sure he'd even noticed. They didn't seem to bother him, and that made her glad, because the girl in the uniform at work, the girl in the dress at the orchid garden, was—nine times out of ten—the girl in yoga pants at home.

She lifted her head and his pale green eyes met hers. 'The kids have gone to bed,' he whispered. 'Do you want me to go?'

Her reaction was instant and she shook her head. She really, really didn't want him to go.

But her nerves were honestly shredded. Before she had a chance to think, Fletch leaned forward until his lips were inches from hers and she could feel his warm breath. 'How about we relax and watch a movie? If Justin wakes up in the next few hours I'll be able to see what he's like.'

He hadn't asked if he could kiss her. But the closeness was invitation enough for Madison. Kissing him now would release the pent-up frustration in her stomach and mind, about wondering whether it might ever happen tonight or not.

She brushed her lips against his and he didn't hesitate to reciprocate. His hands were in her hair a few seconds later, then his lips were on her throat as her fingers ran along the stubble on his jaw. She could taste him, she could smell him. It was like dipping her toe in the waters of intimacy again, and every cell in her body was switched on. She wanted to laugh out loud that she still worked. She'd wanted to joke in the past that those parts of her had probably died, but it would have been so inappropriate to say those words out loud. So she'd only thought them, in her own head, in her own space, as part of her grieving process.

Her own fingers climbed up into his dark hair, and she resisted the urge to pull on it, instead taking a breath and separating her lips from his.

He rested his forehead against hers. He was smiling. She could see his lips and his teeth, and he was breathing hard.

She didn't need to say the rest. That she wasn't ready to go any further. That this wasn't the time and the place. Because Fletch just got that naturally.

He slung his arm around her shoulders, and relaxed as she snuggled in beside him, trying to still her thudding heart. She picked up the remote and scanned the movies available.

They both started laughing as *Top Gun* and its sequel appeared. 'We can't scroll on by,' said Fletch. 'Original, or new?'

'Let's go with something new,' she said. The words felt natural, and she closed her eyes for a second at the double meaning.

'Sure,' he said easily and selected the movie. Madison relaxed back and put her hand on his chest, letting the next few hours be full of supersonic speed, eye-watering manoeuvres and some iconic theme tunes.

CHAPTER EIGHT

FLETCH WAS STRANGELY comfortable in his skin. And that made him uncomfortable.

What made this worse was that he felt as if he was always pretty comfortable at the start of a relationship—when things were new, when the attraction sparked, and when his head was permanently full of the newest woman.

But that made his insides curl. Because, deep down, the feelings he had now didn't parallel how he'd felt around a woman before. This seemed…different.

And if you asked him to take a notebook and write down all the differences? He doubted he could.

That was what was so odd about everything. Last night, of course, he'd wanted to push things on. But he'd known Madison wanted to control the pace and he was fine with that.

And he wasn't an idiot. He didn't want either of Madison's children seeing something untoward. Children talked. And he wasn't sure if Madison had told them she might date other people—or how that would go down with her extended family.

Fletch had been in complicated relationships before,

and he'd always been happy to just go with the flow. This time? He was nervous in a way he hadn't been before.

So much confusion around all this.

And then there was Justin. It had been interesting watching him undisturbed in his natural habitat. It gave Fletch the chance to see all the little idiosyncrasies and how they affected the child.

He got what Madison was saying. He also understood why she was likely feeling paranoid about everything. It was such a collection of seemingly unconnected symptoms. Some paediatricians might think along neurodivergent lines, but Fletch wasn't convinced.

He sighed and pushed back from his chair, trying to concentrate on work. He had twenty patients to see as outpatients this afternoon and another seven to review on the ward.

As he walked out of his office and along the corridor, he heard Madison speaking to one of the junior doctors. Their voices were hushed.

'Anything I can help with?' he asked.

Madison was in her dark blue uniform, her hair pulled high in a ponytail. 'I think I'm just stepping on a few toes,' she said, clearly trying to keep her voice light.

'Do you have concerns about a patient?' asked Fletch reasonably.

She nodded. 'I've got a suspicion about a new admission.'

Fletch held out his hands for the notes and the other doctor started talking. 'Two years old with respiratory symptoms, some swelling and a cough.'

Madison added, 'The cough is like a bark, and there's definite stridor.' She leaned over him looking at the notes.

'Do we know the vaccination history of the child, and where they flew in from?'

Fletch met her gaze and knew what her suspicions were. 'Unusual,' he said to her.

'What?' asked the junior doctor.

'Let's go and see,' said Fletch. 'Come with us, Madison, if you don't mind.'

She gave a nod and followed them into the patient's single room. She gestured to the junior doctor to follow her lead, washing her hands and donning a plastic apron and face mask. Fletch was repeating the motions at another sink in the room.

He introduced himself to the parent, and started to examine the little girl. 'When did she start to become unwell?' he asked.

'A few days ago. It seemed like a cold, and she had a sore throat, but things have just got more severe since then.'

'Has she had her routine childhood immunisations?'

There was a few moments' silence and the man shook his head. 'No, we've moved about a lot and haven't managed to get them completed. We've been so busy.'

'Can you give me an idea of what countries you've been in?'

'India, Malaysia, Vietnam, Haiti, and Africa.'

Fletch gave a nod. 'I'm going to take a look at Rimi's throat.' He encouraged the child to open her throat and shone a pen torch inside. He caught a glimpse of something and gave Madison a knowing look. 'Dr Yan, can you see the unusual colouring?'

Dr Yan nodded. 'The membranes look grey.'

Fletch nodded and then started pressing his finger very

gently into Rimi's throat. 'You mentioned swelling, but this is unusual and is characteristic of a particular condition. This kind of swelling of the throat is called a bull neck.'

He turned to the parent. 'I'm going to do some blood work and some swabs, but most importantly Rimi's symptoms make me think she might have diphtheria. We're going to get her started on antibiotics right away. She'll need some inhalers and oxygen too.'

He turned to Sister Rui Lee, who had appeared at his side as if by some unknown antenna. 'I'll get a cardiac monitor and assign someone to monitor her closely,' she said, bustling away.

'Why does she need a cardiac monitor?' asked the parent. He was right next to Madison and she turned and spoke softly to him. 'Diphtheria can cause myocarditis—inflammation of the heart muscle— which can cause irregular heartbeats. That's why they'll put her on a cardiac monitor for now.'

Fletch gave her a nod, and also pointed to Rimi's throat. 'We have to keep a careful eye on the swelling of the throat. If it starts to obstruct Rimi's breathing, we'll have to talk again.'

He stayed there a few minutes longer, applying cream to allow the insertion of the cannula for the IV antibiotics, and talking through things with the parents, taking notes of all possible carriers and contacts.

As he walked back down the corridor, still making notes on the tablet, he gave a loud sigh. Madison followed him into the office and closed the door. 'I can't believe they didn't get their kid vaccinated. Don't they know diphtheria can kill?'

'Clearly not,' said Fletch, shaking his head. 'And I will have that conversation with them later. In the meantime I have to hope this isn't going to end up in a tracheostomy for this little girl—that would lead to permanent scarring.'

Madison's face was pale. He could tell she was thinking about her own kids. 'They moved about a bit and were just too busy to get the jabs done.' She blinked back tears as she murmured back the parent's words. 'I hope this doesn't have consequences they'll regret for the rest of their lives.'

Fletch took a deep breath. 'Vaccine is a choice, but it's difficult to understand why parents—if they do want to get their child vaccinated—just don't prioritise it, and take the fifteen minutes it takes to attend an appointment with their child. Most people think the diseases we vaccinate against are virtually non-existent now. They don't realise they can be fatal until something like this happens.' He leaned over and put his head in his hands. 'Rimi has severe throat swelling. I'm going to have to stay here tonight, in case her throat obstructs.'

'Are you on call?'

He nodded. 'And usually I go home, and just come in if required. But not tonight.' He shook his head. 'I can't take that risk. If Rimi deteriorates I want to be here.' He took a breath. 'I also want to be here to support Dr Yan. Can you imagine being the junior doctor on duty with a child like that on the ward overnight?' He shook his head. 'It will be a learning experience, but I'm going to make sure I'm right here on his shoulder if he needs me.'

'And I'm sure he'll appreciate it.'

Fletch looked around her and glanced at the closed

door, before leaning forward and taking her hand. 'I was going to ask you if we could take the kids to the play park for an hour—just so I could watch them again.'

'Watch them, or watch me?' she asked, with a half-smile. She was only teasing, and he knew it. But she was closer to the mark than she thought.

'Definitely both, but I'm sorry. Not this evening.'

'Where will you sleep?' she asked him.

He was aware that although some physios in some departments—like ICU—would be on call overnight, Madison didn't have that kind of role.

'There's a room for the junior doctor just outside the ward area, and there's a room for the on-call consultant on the next floor. Believe me, I've slept in worse.'

'I'm just glad you're happy to do it.' Madison smiled. 'Makes me know I've picked the right doctor for my kid.'

His heart gave a little jump. Yes, this was a compliment. And that was the way it was meant. But it was also a reminder to him about treating the child of a friend. And he didn't think of Madison as a friend. He thought of her as, potentially, so much more.

She moved over and gave him a quick hug. 'I have to get back to work. Text me later if you want.'

'Hold on.' He scribbled something on a prescription pad. 'I talked Rimi's parents through the fact they'll need to take a course of antibiotics. Can you ask them to go and get these at the hospital pharmacy, and start them straight away?'

'Absolutely.' She disappeared out of the office and left Fletch considering what next. He reviewed Rimi for the next few hours. But also spent some time considering

Justin. He ordered a few tests on the blood sample already taken. He'd take more bloods if he really had to.

He also ordered a simple ultrasound of Justin's joints. It wasn't invasive, only required gel, and a probe, and chances were Madison would actually be able to read the results herself straight away. If anything, it might give her reassurance.

But cases like these could be difficult. There was always the chance of ruling out just about every possible considered diagnosis, and still being no further forward. Frustrating for doctor, parent and sometimes the patient. For a second he thought about what that might do to his relationship with Maddie, before instantly pushing it away.

He was too thorough, too ethical to even consider that thought. So, he continued to consider other options, sporadically going out and discussing Rimi with Dr Yan, checking her swelling, monitoring her heart rate and administration of intravenous antibiotics and overseeing some steroids too, anything to try and delay the consequences of the disease.

He knew he was being ultra-cautious, and also that he had to have some faith in his junior doctor, so he made his way up to the sleeping quarters. It was comfortable enough, with a single bed, a desk, a chair, a TV and a separate shower room and bathroom. But it was what was sitting in the middle of the bed that stopped him. Normally, the hospital housekeeping staff would make the bed and leave fresh scrubs and towels. This time there was also a little basket with a pile of goodies.

He moved forward, his eyes scanning the basket.

Crisps, chocolate, biscuits, a peach, some jellies and a little note.

Something to see you through the night. M

Something washed over him as he sat on the edge of the bed. It was like a tidal wave of warmth, and part of him told him that he shouldn't be feeling this.

He'd only been with her a few times. What if he changed his mind later? What if this was all just the normal rush of first meeting someone—when you wanted to spend every second with them?

But everything about this made him scared. That was what was different here. Because he liked her. He really liked her. And liking her meant he was moving away from who he was, and who he'd ever been. Fletch, the serial dater. Fletch, 'not the next stage'. Fletch, the man who'd managed to stay on good terms with all exes, because they knew exactly who he was.

But what would happen if he wasn't that person any more?

Madison was trying to find her new normal. As Jason's parents collected the kids for their overnight stay, she waved them off, and wondered if Mia or Justin would mention Fletch.

She had told them that she'd asked the new doctor to try and help her get to the bottom of why her son was so irritable and tired these days. She'd also been truthful and said he'd spent some time with the kids, trying to assess Justin. It wasn't a lie at all. It just wasn't the complete truth. And that didn't sit well with Madison. Because she loved Jason's parents dearly. They were important people who she would always want to feature in her life.

Fletch had sent her a message telling her to dress up and wear her favourite high heels. She was excited. She liked being a grown-up again.

This time she was wearing a green dress, and a spectacular pair of multicoloured heels. She'd dried her hair with some curls and was ready to go as soon as Fletch appeared at the door.

He was more formally dressed than last time, wearing a pair of trousers and shoes and a short-sleeved shirt and jacket. She tipped her head. 'You scrub up well,' she said, unable to stop smiling.

Fletch let out a low wolf whistle. 'Loving the shoes,' he said admiringly.

Madison tilted them from side to side. 'As my gran in Scotland would say, they're a pair of wee crackers!'

Fletch laughed at her thick Scottish accent and held out his elbow to her. 'Are we ready to go?'

She nodded and enjoyed their walk along the streets and on to the MRT, even though she had no idea where they were going.

'Is this going to be the thing for us?' she asked.

'What?'

'That you whisk me onto the MRT and I never know where we're heading.'

He gave her a playful look. 'Would you like a hint?'

She held up her fingers. 'Just a tiny one.'

He leaned over, his nose brushing against her cheek, sending shivers down her spine as he whispered in her ear. 'We're going to do the corniest thing possible in Singapore.'

She sat back and looked at him with a mix of interest and suspicion. 'Should I be scared?'

He laughed. 'Oh, no, definitely not scared. You might even like it.'

She settled back and slid her hand into his, liking the way it felt to be connected to someone. They chatted easily as the smooth train continued and after a short time Fletch gave her a look and leaned forward. 'This is us.'

Esplanade station had seven exits, and as Fletch steered her towards exit E her heart started to miss a few beats. 'Are you serious?' she asked.

Fletch kept his face entirely straight as they walked a few yards from the exit and stood underneath the famous bright white towering façade, with red roof. 'Raffles?' She grinned.

It was one of the most famous hotels in the world. She put her hand on her hip. 'You did say we were doing the corniest thing possible.' She licked her lips and put her hands around his neck. 'And I can't wait.'

Fletch was steadily losing every nerve he'd ever had. He'd always thought of himself as a cool guy. His friends joked about it—as did his exes. He was the guy that never panicked, never flapped, always kept a cool head, and even temper. But around Madison, he felt anything but cool. He felt like a nervous wreck who was turning temporarily into a simmering volcano that could erupt at any second. It was like being an excitable teenager again—and nobody wanted that, least of all him.

'Ready to get a drink?' he asked, knowing there was a glint in his eye.

Madison was beaming. He loved when she looked like this. Ready to take on the world.

Right now, Madison didn't look like a woman who'd

been widowed. She didn't look like the mum to two small kids, one of whom kept her awake most nights. Right now, Madison Koh looked as if she were ready to take on and conquer the world—albeit in a very sexy way.

She sashayed as she walked up the steps to the lobby of Raffles hotel, nodding at the doorman and taking a deep breath as they walked in. The lobby was spectacular, bright white, with floor-to-ceiling Victorian pillars and black wrought-iron railings on the floor above. The sense of space was immense. In the middle was the biggest chandelier Fletch had ever seen and the beautiful flower displays around them gave the place a splash of colour.

'Would you care to visit the Long Bar?' he asked.

'I absolutely would.' She grinned back as her high heels resounded off the tiled floor.

They walked through to the iconic Long Bar. The bar was highly polished with a set of high chairs along its length. A variety of tables and chairs filled the rest of the space, and a barman gestured to them both to have a seat.

Madison headed for the traditional leather bar chair, hitching her dress a little to climb up. Fletch joined her and the barman set down coasters and a bowl of peanuts in front of them. 'What will it be, sir? Madam?'

They glanced at each other and echoed the words that Fletch was quite sure the barman never wanted to hear again in his life.

'Singapore Slings.' Both of them started to laugh, and, to his credit, the barman was completely nonplussed and smiled graciously. They both watched, transfixed as he made the gin-based cocktail for them both, setting down the chilled glasses with the pink mixture inside.

They clinked their drinks together and took a sip. Delicious.

'How often have you done this?' Fletch asked her.

'Twice,' she said, then paused. 'No, maybe three times. I think I came here as part of a very expensive hen dinner once. But it may be blanked from my mind.'

Her hen do? Fletch was almost scared to ask. 'You can't leave it like that. You have to tell me.'

She bent her head low. 'It was the friend of a friend. And she was very late. We'd been sitting at dinner for more than an hour before she showed, and, in that time, we'd had a few cocktails. By the time she arrived, she was hysterical, screaming the wedding was off, as she'd seen her groom with someone else.'

'What? No way?'

Madison gave a quiet laugh. 'Oh, it gets worse. The bride normally wore glasses, but she'd got contacts for her wedding and wasn't really used to them yet, or particularly good at getting them in or out.'

Fletch put his head in his hands. 'No, she didn't.'

Madison nodded. 'Oh, she did. She hadn't put her contacts in properly. In fact, it ended up as a hospital visit since she'd managed to lose one in her eye somehow. But she'd phoned her father to call the wedding off. Phoned the groom's mother to shout at her. And, of course, she'd mistaken some other guy for her own fiancé. It was a bit of a mess.' She nodded slowly. 'But more importantly, we never got dinner because of all the fiasco, which meant the cocktails went straight to my head, I'm not sure if I had a Singapore Sling or not, and I ended up home, in my bed.'

He tapped the bar. 'But you didn't tell the best bit. Did the wedding go ahead?'

She raised her eyebrows. 'What's your guess?'

He held up his hands, then leaned his chin on one. 'I have no idea. But I won't be able to sleep tonight if you don't tell me.'

He loved this. He loved this chat about nonsense. The chance to see the fun side of Madison and leave all the other stuff to one side. Their jobs. Their past lives. And just to be two people, on a date, flirting, and having fun.

The bartender appeared again and Fletch realised their glasses were empty. 'Same again?'

Madison shook her head. 'I'll have a Negroni this time, please.'

'And I'll have a Sazerac, please.'

The bartender disappeared with a nod.

It was early evening and the place was starting to fill up. All the other clientele were discreet, sitting quietly at their tables or the bar and chatting. 'Wonder what it will be like in here later,' mused Madison. 'It's such a classy place.'

'Well, it sounds like you and your friends managed to get all hen parties barred from coming to Raffles a few years ago.'

'At least ten,' she said as she thought. 'And to be honest, I remember being surprised that they'd taken the booking in the first place. I'm sure her mother or sister must have lied and said it was a family dinner.'

As the bartender set down their fresh coasters, glasses and a small dish of olives, Fletch touched her hand.

'I meant it. You need to tell me the end of that story.'

'Ah,' said Madison carefully, tapping her fingers on the bar. 'About that...' She let her voice tail off.

'Yes?' he asked.

'Well, it got even more complicated. Her father had immediately cancelled the venue. His mother had gone around to the bride's house in a rage. A huge fight ensued, and the poor groom came home completely bewildered by everything that was going on. By this point, the bride had realised it was all her mistake and was hysterical. The groom's mother had flounced off and said she'd had enough of everything. And the bride's mother was too busy ranting about how all this had caused her embarrassment and made her lose face with her friends.'

Fletch held up one hand. 'Okay, stop. This is turning into a story that my auntie Mary tells me when I ask one question, and I'm still waiting to get it answered ten minutes later.'

Madison gave him her best conspiratorial look. 'I swear, even if I let you have a thousand guesses you would never get what happened next!'

Fletch, never one to resist a challenge, held up one hand and started counting off. 'They lived happily ever after. They never spoke to each other again. One, or the other, just used the wedding as a giant party, so things didn't go to waste.'

Madison shook her head smugly.

'Okay, let me go for thriller-writer mode, then—one went on the honeymoon and ended up dead?'

Madison raised her eyebrows.

'I've got it,' said Fletch triumphantly. 'One caught an extremely rare, non-identifiable disease—that originated

in the ice age and came from the melting polar ice caps—
and is currently in a top-secret facility somewhere.'

She narrowed her gaze and gave a half-smile. 'I'm beginning to wonder if I should have second thoughts about
you. I really wonder what goes on in that head of yours.'

'Only second thoughts?' he teased. 'I thought we'd be
at least third or fourth by this stage.'

She kept her elbows leaning on the bar and gave him
a hard stare.

'Okay,' he relented. 'I give up. What is it?'

Madison crossed her legs again, and couldn't help but
notice his gaze landing on her bare skin. She stayed quiet
for a second until his eyes rose again to meet hers.

'Busted,' he murmured good-naturedly.

'You want to know?' she asked again.

He nodded.

'Then you picked the wrong theme. Thriller wasn't
what you were looking for—or sci-fi. You should have
stuck with romance. It turned out the bride's father met
the groom's mother in amongst the fights and cancella-
tions. Love blossomed, and they married the next year.'

'No way.' He was frowning. He shot her a sideways
glance. 'I take it the bride and groom weren't too happy?'

She raised her glass to him and finished her cocktail. 'It's very safe to say that they were not. But by that
point—' she grinned '—nobody cared!'

He laughed and shook his head, taking another glance
around at their opulent surroundings. 'You sure know
how to spin a story.'

'But isn't it fun?' She held up one hand, 'And just think
of the history of this building. Think of the amount of
stories that are actually held in this place.'

She couldn't hide her enthusiasm or the wonder she was feeling right now. It had been so long since she'd let her hair down like this, had a few drinks with a handsome man, forgot about life and its responsibilities for a few hours.

'I should bring you out more often,' said Fletch, his head resting on his hand and his eyes full of admiration, and something else.

Madison stretched out her arms. 'I'm a very expensive date. Then, a very troublesome one. You'll get bored of me quickly.'

'I don't think so.' He smiled as he shook his head. 'What do you want to do next? Some dinner again?'

'How about something different?'

'What?'

'Marina Bay. The light show. It's been a few years since I've seen it.'

Fletch stood up instantly and checked his watch. 'It's on at eight and nine. Think we'll make the nine o'clock show?'

She looked down at her multicoloured heels. 'I refuse to take these off to run. The MRT will get us there in plenty of time. The Bayfront station is only a short walk from the viewing deck.'

'Let's go, then.'

They left the beauty of Raffles hotel, and descended back onto the smooth-running MRT, alighting at Bayfront station and taking the walk to the viewing deck for the water, light and music show.

The deck was already crowded with a mixture of tourists and locals. The show was performed twice a night usually, with an extra ten o'clock show on a Friday and Saturday night.

A trombone was playing loudly at a nearby bar restaurant as they watched everyone adjust their positions for the show. As soon as the background music for the light and water show started, the trombone halted, allowing everyone to be entranced by the display.

It was dazzling. It started softly. The colours muted, the water shooting up in bright jets of light in perfect time. But things started to build. The tempo increased, the colours darkened, deep purples and blue, with whirling pinks that shot out brilliantly. Greens and oranges lit the sky as the fountain spurts grew larger. Yellow circular displays appeared like giant suns. What had started in quite a small, concentrated space filled the whole area in front of them, with water spurting from parts that had previously been dry, much to the delight of some of the crowd who were hit by tiny spots of backlash water.

Things grew to a crescendo, with a rainbow of coordinated colours appearing at once, alongside the vibrant music and perfectly directed water fountains.

Madison rested back against Fletch. His arms wrapped around her waist and settled across her stomach. His head positioned behind her head and shoulders. It was the most relaxed she'd felt in the last three years. She felt…safe.

Before she had time to focus on those thoughts, Fletch's lips were trailing along the side of her face. She leaned back into him more, giving him access to the skin at her neck as she tipped her head back. It was easy to flip around, wrap her hands around his neck and meet him head-on.

The lights and water were still erupting around them as if the whole display had been put on entirely for them. At least, that was how it felt.

And that fed into the wave of sensations she was feeling right now. The wall that she had between her and Fletch was gradually eroding. She was doing her best to keep it in place, but it didn't help when he touched her like this. When his lips made her lose focus and struggle to breathe.

A tiny part of her brain moved into panic mode. In a few years' time would Fletch refer to her as his Singapore fling? Would he leave when his contract ended without a second glance, and with Madison on his phone as one of his many friends? Because she didn't want to be his friend.

She wanted more than that. And that realisation was causing her momentary panic.

She pulled back, and spun around so he couldn't see her shocked face. She was already breathless, so her racing heart didn't really matter.

He was a serial dater. She was a mother with twins. Her kids had to be her priority. She wondered how other women did this. Not just those who were widowed, but those who had divorced, had a failed relationship behind them, or had chosen to have children on their own. How did they navigate the dating world? And how would she feel if the shoe were on the other foot? If Fletch were widowed with twins, and she had happily dated one guy after another, with no permanency and no bad feelings.

Putting the shoe on the other foot was illuminating in a way she didn't particularly like.

Would she consider taking on someone else's children and loving them just as much as if they were her own? She wasn't naïve. Of course, she had friends both male and female who'd found themselves in this position. But she'd never actually sat down and asked them the questions that now circled around her brain—because part of her knew she would be heartbroken if she didn't like the answers.

She tried to concentrate. To think about her friends who'd met a partner who already had children. Madison's trouble was, the people she could think about were all shining examples of things working well. Of embracing their new life, and, after a few hiccups, becoming a real integrated family.

Was it wrong that she wished for that too?

She thought back to her chats as a teenager. Being convinced that there would only ever be one great love in her life. Then meeting Jason, and thinking she was set for life.

She still had friends who were single. Who had never met their Ms or Mr Right. Was it too much to wish for two such people in her life?

'Hey,' came the low voice in her ear. 'Where are you? I think I've lost you.'

She jerked just as a cool breeze swept past them. 'Sorry,' she said automatically. 'Thinking about work.'

There was a flash of puzzlement on his face, and she wanted to cringe at her unlikely untruth. The rest of the people around them had started to leave, the light show finished.

'Food?' he asked again, and he seemed hopeful. But

her stomach was unsettled. She wasn't sure she could cope with food.

'Actually, I'm feeling kind of tired. Can you take me home?'

She saw the fleeting disappointment on his face and let it sink in. In an imaginary world he'd take her back to Raffles and check into a thousand-pounds-a-night suite. They'd spend all night in bed and wake up in luxury with no worries at all.

But Madison didn't live in that world. She lived in this one.

Fletch was gracious and put his arm around her shoulder, walking back to the MRT and stopping to buy them coffee on the way. He didn't seem worried that the rest of world was only just starting their Saturday nights, while theirs was being cut short.

It had started so magically and full of fun and Madison couldn't explain what had come over her. All of a sudden she was hit with so many doubts.

And she knew exactly why. Whether Fletch knew it or not, this relationship was taking a turn for her. She'd been happy to keep things private and just go along for the ride to begin with to test her dating wings again.

It had been nice to have adult conversations and feel special again. But she couldn't trust herself. If she let herself truly buy into this, she could end up with a whole host of hurt. Even though she liked to act invincible and sassy, her outer shell wasn't as hard as she'd like it to be. And her insides? They were just a mixed-up pool of melted chocolate and giant brownies.

They rode in silence, sipping coffee. He still had his

arm around her shoulder, and she was leaning into him as if she'd been born to do it.

'Madison?' The heavily accented voice brought her sharply to her senses. Fletch jerked right alongside her and removed his arm from her shoulder.

Koreen Choi appeared in front of Madison. As usual, the childhood friend of Jason was stylishly dressed in bright colours. With her sharp pixie cut and small figure she could have graced the cover of any of the high-fashion magazines. She couldn't hide the curious glance towards Fletch, before leaning forward and kissing Madison on one cheek, and then the other.

'How are you? How are my babies?'

Madison tried to pretend that this was the most normal thing in the world, and she wasn't entirely in shock. Of course, there was always a chance that she was going to come across a friend of hers and Jason's, or a colleague from work anywhere in Singapore. It didn't matter that it was a place of more than five million people.

'Justin and Mia are good. They spent some time with my mum and dad in Scotland just over a month ago, and I'm just trying to get them back into a routine.' She gave Koreen a big smile. 'You should give me a call and come and visit us some time. They'd be happy to see you.'

Madison was totally aware that every part of her body was tense, while she gave the pretence this was a normal everyday conversation. She was aware when Koreen's eyes drifted back to Fletch. She couldn't avoid this. She wouldn't be rude to someone who had always been friendly and supportive. 'Koreen, this is Fletch. He's a new paediatrician working with us at St David's.'

There was a gleam of curiosity in Koreen's eyes, but

she held out her hand instantly towards Fletch. 'It's so nice to meet you. I'm an old-time friend of Madison and the family. Are you enjoying St David's?'

Fletch nodded amiably, but Madison knew that he, too, was tense. 'I am. I've worked in Singapore before and was delighted to come back.'

'Back for good?'

He hesitated. 'I have a two-year contract right now. I'll wait and see.'

Madison's insides coiled in a way they had absolutely no right to. Her brain was telling her she knew this. Her brain was talking in a very firm voice saying that she was nowhere near the point she could have that conversation with Fletch about staying for longer. She had no right.

But her body was listening. Her body was protesting. Her scary cynical gene was yelling at her, saying he never cracked a joke about maybe being 'back for good'.

Madison was always amazed by just how many sensations and thoughts could spring through the mind in the literal blink of an eye.

Sometimes she wished her brain would fixate on bouncing sheep, unicorns, rainbows—even the latest kids' TV show. But no, her brain wanted to torture her on a daily basis with doubts and uncertainties.

'Well, good luck,' Koreen said cheerily before focusing back on Madison with eyes that already sized up exactly what was going on. 'Here's my stop. I'll give you a call, gorgeous, and pop up and see my favourites.'

She gave Madison a wink and made her way back down the carriage to the door. Stepping out as they arrived at the station, her bright pink coat disappearing into the crowd.

Madison swallowed. Her skin was cold and her heart was racing. The dress and shoes now seemed like over-kill.

'Who was that?' asked Fletch quietly.

'A friend of Jason's family.'

'Are you worried about what she might say?'

It was a perfectly reasonable question, and she knew that. But in one sense it seemed like a criticism, and in another it made her want to defend herself.

In the end, she sagged back against the chair. 'I haven't told anyone about us.'

'I know.'

She turned to face him, feeling a bit surprised.

'You said at the beginning you didn't want people at work to know. I respect that.'

'But you haven't told anyone else?' She was thinking of his myriad exes that he texted all the time. Did no one know she actually existed?

'No. Do you think Koreen will say something to Jason's family?'

There they were. The words that made her heart feel as if a giant spear had just pierced it. 'I don't know. I don't think so. She's not like that. Not malicious, I mean.' Madison's hand went automatically to her hair, twisting it around one finger. 'I just haven't mentioned anything to Jason's parents, or his sister. I mean, I'm sure they'll expect me to date again at some point. I just don't know if they'll expect that point to be now.'

Fletch's eyes were fixed on her in a steady stare. 'I think, no matter what the timescale, it might be hard to have that conversation.'

There he was. Being all reasonable again.

'I know that.' She sighed. 'I just want them to be okay about it. I don't want them to hate me. Or to think I've forgotten about Jason.'

He didn't try and placate her with words. He just put his hand over hers. 'You won't know until you have that conversation. And you shouldn't have that conversation until you're ready.'

She closed her eyes for a second. 'But there's the kids as well. What if they mention you've been to the apartment?'

Fletch shrugged. 'That's up to you. You either say I'm Justin's doctor, or that I'm your friend.' He paused for a second. 'Or, that we're dating. Your call.'

She hated that. She hated that he made it all seem so uncomplicated.

'Kids don't keep secrets. We know that. They don't really understand the concept, and in lots of ways that's a good thing. Just do what you think is best.'

'What is best?' she asked.

Fletch looked surprised. But not as much as she was. She hadn't expected to say those words out loud. Maybe this was because they'd kept their relationship secret. She hadn't had anyone to talk to about it. Now the only person it made sense to talk to was him.

There was a long pause. 'I can't tell you that. Maybe it's time for us to reconsider.'

She could swear a chill breeze blew over her skin. 'What do you mean?'

Was that her voice? There was an edge of panic in it. Definitely not cool. She was so out of practice with all this stuff.

He leaned a little closer. 'I mean, is it time to tell

people? Is it time to let colleagues at work know that we are dating?'

Relief flooded through her. She'd thought he was going to suggest they call things quits.

She wrinkled her nose. 'Do we tell people at work before I tell Jason's family—or my own?'

'Your own family is in Scotland. You can tell them whenever you like. Does Jason's family have friends that work in the hospital—would they hear if we started letting people know we were dating?' He held up his hands. 'If they won't, then telling our colleagues might give you some idea as to how Jason's old workmates will act. If you think it could get back, you might want to talk to his family and just mention that you're considering dating again.'

'What if I break their hearts?'

He shook his head and closed both hands over hers. 'Madison, their hearts were broken three years ago when their son died. Nothing changes that.' His voice was low and calm. 'I don't know these people at all. But I hope that they love you and the kids as much as you love them— and it sounds like it. Maybe they'll feel a bit sensitive to it. Maybe, they'll think that it's time. To be honest, I have no idea. But the most important thing is that you do this when you're ready. These people are family for you and the kids. I can't give you an opinion on this.'

She breathed slowly, trying to still her thoughts. The night had started so well, dressing up for fun cocktails. Watching the beautiful fountains and lights. But something had halted her enjoyment, and she was wise enough to know this was all about her, and not about Fletch.

She was racked by self-doubts. And she hated herself for it.

The train drew into their station and they climbed out. She'd left him at her doorway before. And she was going to do it again.

But Fletch seemed to know. He hesitated at the elevator in her apartment and kissed her on the cheek. 'Need some time to think?'

She nodded, blinking back tears she really, really didn't want him to see.

'Thank you,' she whispered, then pressed the button quickly before she could see him walk away.

Because somehow, she knew, that vision would imprint on her brain.

CHAPTER NINE

FLETCH WAS DOING his best to play it cool.

This was it. This was his time to decide if it was make or break.

He'd been at this point at several times in his life. And it had always been break.

Break was the lesser of two evils. Or at least, that was how he'd always felt before.

Because his heart had never really been involved before. And this time it was right in the middle of things. No one woman had ever had the effect that Madison had on him.

And because of that, this time was the first time he hadn't wanted to break. This time he wanted to make it.

And it was driving him crazy, because he wasn't sure that Madison felt the same.

He got that. She had more at stake. She could risk family fallouts, losing support systems she'd had in place for the last three years. Maybe that was just being dramatic, but it was still a potential risk.

What was his risk? Nothing. He had a time-limited contract.

But was his risk nothing, or did he just prefer to tell himself that? Otherwise, he might have to admit to having his heart broken for the first time. And that had never happened to Fletch before. He'd never been the one exposed before. He'd never invested himself so much in one person before.

Chills. That actually gave him chills. If he wanted to think long term with Madison, he would have to take on board the fact he would become a father figure to two ready-made kids. He liked Mia and Justin. But was he ready to go the full way? Was this the life he could see himself living?

He would have to step back from being Justin's doctor and he wasn't sure how Madison would feel about that.

It actually made every part of his brain switch on.

He had to face facts. It had been two weeks since Madison had brought Justin to see him. He'd ruled out a number of possible causes, but still nothing jumped out at him.

But if being Justin's doctor could stand in the way of moving forward, maybe that was what he should concentrate on. Once he had a diagnosis for Justin, it would be reasonable to move his care over to another paediatrician.

And if he was concentrating on Justin, he wouldn't be contemplating the fact that Madison might decide this wasn't all worth it—that she wasn't quite ready to do this—and she wasn't as invested in Fletch as he was in her.

He couldn't believe how much that terrified him. That Madison might decide it wasn't worth it. *He* wasn't worth it. What if she thought Jason's family might dislike him? Or think it was too soon? What if all her friends and family just thought that Fletch wasn't the right person for her?

There were so many outside influences. So many things outside his control. And at the centre of it all was Maddie.

He was staring out over Singapore from the darkness of his apartment. He'd realised the vibe had changed between them tonight, and thought she was backing off. It hadn't helped when they'd met her friend Koreen.

He could almost see her unravelling in front of him. If he was immature he'd be offended that she was worried about being seen with him. But he wasn't that pathetic. At least he hoped he wasn't.

He was trying to focus. He moved over to his laptop and flicked it open, starting to go through every possible condition, disease, virus, infection he could think of. When he'd finished with them, he went back through prenatal issues that could cause issues in children at a later date. When he'd finished all those, he looked at environmental issues, and unusually transmitted diseases. By four in the morning, he was exhausted, frustrated and very, very bad-tempered.

His fingers hovered over the keyboard again. Tomorrow, Madison might tell him she'd thought about it, and decided not to move forward. He'd have to gracefully accept that and step aside.

But he didn't want to. He wanted to stay and fight. But what was he fighting for? A chance just to keep dating her, or a chance to consider a future?

He liked her. He more than liked her. He thought about her all the time. He wanted to text her halfway through the night, then again when he was at work and had seen her only minutes before.

Sometimes, when he held her brown gaze, he just

wanted to reach out and hug her. Even when they were at work.

All of these emotions were new for him. All of them made him over the moon one second, and lower than the belly of a snake the next. Fletch was used to coasting. This roller coaster of emotions had taken him unawares and he was unprepared for the effects it was having on him. And it wasn't just Madison he thought about.

He liked spending time with the kids. Yes, Justin was still under the weather. But he was a good kid. Madison had made sure her children were polite, inquisitive and fun. Mia could run circles around him, and everyone else in a room. She was probably going to end up as a world leader at some point.

But could he realistically consider fitting into that family unit? What if the feelings he had right now for Madison slowly disappeared? Lots of people started re- lationships with enthusiasm that waned over a period of time. Some of his previous ones certainly had.

But, from the moment he'd met Madison, this whole thing had been different. It didn't matter he couldn't give a reason why. It was just something, deep down.

If he wanted to make this work, he had to try and per- suade Madison that he was a good option. But how ex- actly did he do that?

His eyes went back to the screen. Justin. He had to start with Justin, and his unknown ailment. Solve the first problem, and hope the rest would roll away.

Madison was walking on proverbial eggshells. It had been a week, and nothing had been said between them about Saturday night. But Fletch had seen Justin twice more at hospital, and twice more when he'd suggested a reason for them all to spend time together.

She was trying to relax again. And she wondered about telling some of her colleagues she was dating Fletch. Would anyone actually care, or was she just overthinking things?

The range of tests on Justin was getting longer and longer. Thankfully, Fletch had arranged for the majority to be painless. The bloods he'd had taken at the beginning had been used for a number of other screens, but although Justin showed mild signs of inflammation and a small rise in white blood cells there wasn't anything else significant.

Now, they were focusing on background history. Everything he'd done or eaten in the last seven weeks. Part of this was hard, as Justin and Mia had been in Scotland with her parents for two weeks. But Madison's parents were very traditional people. They had relatively plain tastes when it came to food and hadn't taken the children anywhere unusual.

Madison already knew that her children would have frequented every tea shop in the village as her parents proudly showed them off to their friends, and would have spent hours in the local children's playground.

Her doorbell rang, and she answered, Justin already in her arms as he was cranky again. Fletch was standing in front of her holding up a bag.

'Ice cream?' he asked.

He hadn't told her he was coming over, and it was a shock to see his large frame and smiling face in the doorway. But what struck her most was how thankful she was to see him.

She swung open her door and waved him in, shouting over her shoulder. 'Mia, Fletch is here. He brought ice cream.'

The tiny figure dashed through, eyes shining. 'What kind?'

It was like an accusation rather than a question, and Fletch pretended to baulk. 'I have four, I'm sure you'll like one.'

'Don't count on it,' murmured Madison with a wry grin as she closed the door. She was wearing jeans and a T-shirt that was likely covered in stains and her hair was in a ponytail. She couldn't remember if she'd taken her make-up off or not, but was glad that Fletch hadn't given so much as a second glance to her dishevelled appearance.

'Want me to swap?' he asked, holding out his hands for Justin.

She hesitated. But Justin looked as if he was considering things, before finally holding his arms out towards Fletch.

Madison tried not to show her surprise. Justin was picky. He liked his crèche workers, Jason's family and a few select friends. But he'd obviously taken to Fletch.

Maybe it was his manner or his voice. Lots of kids on the wards reacted well to him. Fletch settled Justin on his hip and moved over to the kitchen table, gesturing to Mia to follow him. 'Why don't we sit down and let Mummy open the ice cream? Then we can decide what ones you like.'

Madison took the bag with a murmur of thanks and got four bowls and a variety of spoons from the cupboard. She set out the bowls, then put the ice-cream containers in the middle of the table, opening all the lids.

'Okay, we've got chocolate, vanilla, mint choc chip and strawberry.'

Madison was glad. Singapore had some of the fanciest ice creams and gelatos known to man, with flavours that adults would favour. She was relieved that Fletch had opted for the kids' kind of stuff.

Justin pointed to the vanilla. 'Is there sauce?'

Madison was about to say no. But Fletch nodded back over to the bag. 'Just some small ones.'

She double-checked and pulled out sachets of chocolate, caramel and raspberry.

'Sprinkles?' asked Mia hopefully.

'We have sprinkles,' said Madison and pulled them from the cupboard. She walked back over with the rest of the items. 'Right, is everyone happy? Can I sit back down?'

Two children nodded and she sat back down. The next half-hour was a mess of ice cream, sauce and sprinkles and the children had a ball. Fletch was so chilled around them, laughing and joking and asking questions about their favourite TV cartoon. He told them about one he'd watched as a kid, pulled it up on the Internet, where it was instantly dismissed by both of them.

Justin moved over from Fletch and back around to his mother, which meant he was getting tired again. As soon as he moved, Fletch picked up the bowls, wiped down the table and binned the containers. He nodded to Madison. 'Will I play a game with Mia?' and she gave a grateful smile as she took Justin off for a nap.

By the time she came back out, Mia and Fletch were on the floor in the living room doing a giant jigsaw together. Her heart melted a little. She knew he was making an effort and she appreciated it.

Before long they were sagged on the sofa together. Mia was sitting at the kids' table in the living room, colouring in. The whole afternoon had been impromptu, but she'd liked it. There hadn't been time to overthink things and get herself tied in knots. He didn't even blink when she flicked the TV and stuck on *Star Wars*.

It was so easy just to nestle into his arms and relax. 'I've been thinking,' she said after a while. 'Maybe it is time to start dropping some hints at the hospital.'

'You think?'

She licked her lips, wondering if he wanted to disagree with her. 'It just makes sense. I don't want to have to pretend about this when there are other people round. Or tell any lies. I think it would be okay if people knew we were dating.'

He gave a gentle nod. 'What about your family, and Jason's family? Do you think it's time to say anything to them?'

She tensed a little, knowing this was the hardest part. 'I was thinking of telling them this weekend that I was considering dating again, and that I'd been asked out.'

Her stomach was clenched, because it wasn't entirely the whole story. She wasn't going to give them Fletch's details and say who he was, but hopefully it would give them some time to get used to the idea before she would have to do introductions.

There was a slight pause, then Fletch shifted a little. 'How do you think that will go down?'

She sighed, her hand resting on his chest. 'I honestly

don't know. I think if anything, they might be more worried about the kids being introduced to someone new, rather than me. And I'd be fine with that.'

'I get you wanting to tread carefully. But this is still your life to lead. You can't live it in hiding.'

'And I won't,' she said quickly. 'But I haven't had to do this before, and I want to be sensitive.' Her eyes went to the corridor that led to Justin's room. 'I'm trying to think about it from their perspective.'

Fletch nodded. 'No parent should outlive their child. I get that. And I hate being on the other side of that as a physician. So, I understand. Let's just not be in the same position at a later date.'

There was no timescale attached, and her heart catapulted straight up. Fletch was here for two years—less than that now. But even saying a 'later date' meant he wasn't planning on bailing on her any time soon.

As his fingers traced small circles at the base of her neck she gave a pleasant shudder. This was nice. This was how she wanted things to be. She'd almost forgotten what the quiet moments were like. And now she'd had a few, she wanted them all the time.

She lifted her head slightly, and Fletch's lips were inches from hers. But instead of meetings her lips, he glanced in Mia's direction, and kissed Madison's forehead instead.

She almost laughed but instead she just settled back down to watch the movie. Was this what life could be like now?

She couldn't help but hope she was making the right decision.

* * *

Fletch was getting agitated. He'd had a number of cases over the years that had him stumped, but he hadn't expected to be stumped over a child he knew.

He'd been spending more and more time around Justin. He was developing a real understanding of this little boy's frustration. That horrible sensation of not feeling well, but not having the vocabulary to express it. The way he got impatient and tired easily. It was affecting his learning, and his ability to develop good social relationships with other children.

Fletch had noticed over the last few days, when he passed the crèche, that Justin was often isolated from the other children. Sometimes it was deliberate, and Justin was too tired to get involved in their games. But other times, the children were excluding Justin, maybe finding his behaviour difficult to understand and negotiate at the young age. As an adult, Fletch could see the staff trying their best to intervene, but it was difficult when Justin himself could prove reluctant.

Whatever was wrong was going to affect his long-term development, which made Fletch more determined to get to the bottom of it.

He even had a chart with everything he'd ruled out, and had discussed Justin casually with a number of other paediatricians he knew and trusted across the globe.

'I think you need to switch your brain off, and go with your gut,' said Darren, a friend from Ireland. 'Even if you can't find evidence of it, it can still be there.'

'Take the opposite approach from what you usually do,' urged Jules, a fellow paediatrician at a previous hospital he'd worked in. 'What if an adult presented to you with all these complaints and symptoms. Where would your brain go for them?'

Fletch took deep breaths and ran through the things he'd already considered. What did his gut tell him?

He started scribbling, doing a timeline. With children, things could be difficult. If children had an underlying developmental delay, it often didn't become apparent until this age, when children were more interactive and differences could be more noticeable.

He didn't compare Justin to Mia at all. Two entirely different children.

But two children who'd been brought up in the same environment, been exposed to the same things, and had similar experiences.

He was sitting in his office at work. Madison was by his side, flicking through her phone as she waited on a call back about taking one of her patients for a test.

The news of them dating had filtered out amongst the staff. Madison had told Rui, the ward sister, first. She'd been surprised, but hadn't made things awkward. A few people who'd been courteous to Fletch to begin with were now being a bit friendlier, asking him more questions. Were they making the effort because he was dating Madison? That was what it seemed like.

There had been a few hostile glares, and a few interested ones down in Radiology—the place that had been Justin's space. He was glad because he got the impression people were just getting on with their lives, instead of obsessing over him and Madison. And that was just perfect.

'The latest test results are back for Justin.' He scanned them and gave a sigh. 'I can't see anything of concern.'

The phone rang and he answered quickly. 'Dr Fletcher.'

The words had barely left his lips as he stood up, the chair falling behind him. He gripped Madison's shoulder. 'Of course, I'll come down. His mother is with me now. I'll bring her with me.'

Madison's face instantly paled. 'What is it?'

'Justin. That was the crèche. They said he's taken quite unwell. They'd phoned down to physio but couldn't get you.'

The two of them jogged down the corridor, lifting hands to other members of staff, so they didn't think there was an emergency on the ward.

It took only a few minutes to reach the crèche, where one of the workers was standing with Justin in her arms. She strode quickly over to meet them. 'He just became very lethargic, and he's quite breathless. He complained of pain in his chest, started crying and then became limp.'

Fletch assessed things quickly and lifted Justin up onto his shoulder, 'Back upstairs,' he said to Madison. He tried not to run as they moved through the corridors and back onto the ward in long strides.

'Sister Lee,' Fletch said sharply as they entered, 'can I have some assistance, please?'

He laid Justin on a free bed as Madison pulled the curtains around, clearly trying not to panic.

Rui Lee appeared swiftly, and demonstrated her years of experience. Unhooking the wires from the nearby cardiac monitor, clipping them onto Justin's chest and slipping a probe onto his finger. She glanced at the results and lifted the oxygen mask from the wall, turning it on in one simultaneous move. 'Fletch,' she said under her breath.

He looked at the reading as he unwound his stethoscope and spoke in a low voice. 'Justin, it's Fletch. I'm just going to listen to your chest.'

He placed his stethoscope on Justin's small chest and instantly heard something he didn't want to. He manoeuvred Justin forward and listened to his back too. 'I need an ECG, a chest X-ray and an echocardiogram.'

'What is it?' Madison's hand was on his arm.

'I'm hearing a pericardial rub. I suspect Justin has developed pericarditis. We'll do some further tests and arrange treatment.'

'Temp's fine,' said Rui after inserting an ear thermometer in Justin's ear. She arranged Justin propped up against some pillows, clearly knowing that children with pericarditis weren't comfortable being flat.

Fletch nodded and pulled up an electric prescribing tablet. 'Let's start with some steroids while we await the rest of the tests.'

Justin curled up onto his side, and Fletch gave Madison a sign. 'Do you want to get up on the bed with him?' She nodded and gratefully climbed up, hugging her son close.

Fletch could sense the frustration building inside him. What on earth was wrong with Justin?

As Madison curled around her son, her phone slipped from her pocket and landed on the floor.

Fletch bent to pick it up and froze at the picture on the screen. It was a screensaver of Justin and Mia, in long grass with—what must be their Scottish grandparents. He tilted his head to the side as something came into his head.

'Ticks,' he said.

'What?' asked Madison.

He turned the screen to her. 'Scotland. There are ticks in Scotland. What about the area that your parents stay in? Are there any around there?'

Madison frowned. 'Well, yes, I guess so. But ticks?' She was shaking her head.

Fletch pointed to the long grass. 'Ticks carry Lyme disease. It's a long shot. But maybe that's what's wrong with Justin. Could he have been bitten?'

'Yes, I suppose so. But my mum and dad would have noticed that. Don't ticks leave a big mark?'

He held up his hands, 'Some tick bites leave a red ring called erythema migrans—a rash like a bullseye, but it can also just be a rash. It can appear anything between three days and three months.'

'We didn't see anything on his skin before.'

He nodded. 'I know. But we can check again.' He took a breath. 'So, if an adult presented with joint pains, tiredness, irritation, and gave a history of travel somewhere, we might ask them if they had been bitten.'

'What if my parents don't remember?'

'Not everyone knows they've been bitten by a tick. There's a blood test we can try, but it doesn't always show positive.'

Madison bottom lip started to tremble. 'So, what does this mean for Justin? Long term?'

Fletch held up his hand. 'Let's take this slow. Let's check his body again first. Everywhere, including all the creases. Then, I'll phone and organise the ELISA test. We can also consider starting him on antibiotics.'

'Even though he doesn't have a temperature.'

Fletch nodded. 'If the first test comes back positive,

we would start him on the antibiotics, while we wait for the second test.'

'How long does it take?'

'That's the hard part. It can take several days to two weeks to get the results. If we work on the assumption that Justin was bitten when he was with your parents, it could be at least seven weeks since the disease entered his system. There is a chance that he will have formed antibodies because it's been more than a few weeks. We could also test Justin's cerebrospinal fluid, but we'd need to do a lumbar puncture and I'm not sure he would tolerate that right now.'

'If we can avoid it at all, I'd rather do that.'

'What about Mia?' Fletch asked. 'I think I would like to check her over, just to be cautious and take some blood from her too. Now, she's had no symptoms, nothing that gives me concern. But let's just be sure.'

Madison gave a tearful nod. 'Okay.' She looked around and then shook her head. 'I can't go and get her from crèche right now.'

'I'll go,' Fletch said.

Madison was starting to think straighter now. 'I'll need to speak to my parents, and Jason's. I need to let them know what's happened.'

Rui Lee came back with some pyjamas for Justin and a soft blanket. She nodded to Madison. 'Swap places with me, and go over there and make your calls.'

Madison gave a nod, and Fletch let her walk over to the window, glancing at the other faces in the room. Even though people knew about them now, they'd been very careful at not being affectionate around each other in their workplace setting. It was unprofessional, and they didn't want anyone to think their relationship might impact on their jobs.

And while Fletch knew that, and believed in all those fundamentals, at a time like this he couldn't leave Madison when she looked so distressed. He walked over and circled his arms around her, holding her tight. She sagged into him and, for a few moments, started to sob.

He held her. Just held her, until she'd finally sobbed herself out. Then he could feel her shuddering as she caught her breath. He stroked her hair for a few moments longer before catching Rui's eye.

Rui nodded to him, giving him an appreciative smile. And the smile was like a seal of approval he'd been waiting for.

He gave Madison another few moments to gather herself, and then moved to get back to Justin, speaking quietly to him as he inserted a cannula and gave him some intravenous steroids. He half wanted to climb up onto the bed himself and cuddle him, but he'd promised to collect Mia and check her over too.

His colleague Dr Zhang, another of the paediatricians, appeared and Fletch spoke rapidly to him, handing over Justin's care while he left to pick up Mia.

The crèche staff were all over him as soon as he arrived, asking how Justin was. He explained as best he could, letting them know he'd been admitted to the ward, and that he was there to pick up Mia and take her back to Madison.

Mia was clearly quite confused and upset. It was a different view of the normally confident little girl he was used to. He spoke calmly to her, and told her she could see Justin and then they were going to do some checks on her, once her mother was with her.

'Is Rui there?' asked the little voice.

He understood that. This little girl was reaching out for some familiarity. 'Yes, Rui's there. She's helping look after Justin.'

'Is Justin sleeping again?'

Fletch looked at Mia. She understood more than she probably should. 'He might be. He's very tired. But we hope we know what's wrong with him, and can make him better.'

He was already full of self-doubts. Firstly, about himself. He'd known right from the start that the twins had been in Scotland, but ticks and Lyme disease had never once entered his head until he'd seen the children's smiling faces in the long grass. He was kicking himself.

And what if this was the wrong diagnosis? Lyme disease was tricky to diagnose with the actual known presence of a tick, or the distinguishable rash. There was likely a whole host of adults in the world who had a range of symptoms caused by Lyme disease that had never been diagnosed properly.

He didn't even want to think about the amount of people bitten as a child, unnoticed, who then had a lifetime of symptoms that affected their life.

But what if it was something else?

He was sure about the pericarditis. He'd heard the rub. By the time he reached the ward, the cardiac technician had appeared and the ECG was complete and the echocardiogram under way. Madison was instantly relieved to see Mia and hugged her too, still holding onto Justin's hand as he got his echocardiogram. Rui was on his other side, talking quietly to him.

Fletch's eyes turned to the screen, and he leaned forward and spoke softly to the technician. She pointed to a few parts on the grey screen that showed the inflamed sac surrounding the heart, along with some extra fluid. In some cases, the fluid could be drained, but, in Justin's case, they would put him on steroids and antibiotics first, to see if they made any difference. He might also need some pain relief.

Fletch was clear. This was new. When he'd examined Justin before, there had been no signs of pericarditis. It made him more confident in the potential Lyme disease diagnosis, because of the length of time from potential infection, and the subsequent inflammation that could have occurred in Justin's body.

He looked over to Madison. 'We've confirmed the diagnosis of pericarditis and we'll treat Justin for this meantime. The blood test is ordered too, and, because of the pericarditis, and the fact that Justin has complained of joint pains, I think there is a chance that the ELISA may be positive. If it is, we move to the next stage.'

Madison turned her phone around. She'd obviously been doing an Internet search. 'The list is incredible, severe fatigue, insomnia, headaches, impaired concentration, inability to sustain attention, difficulty thinking and expressing, joint pains, brain fog.' She held up her phone, her arm shaking. 'How could I not even think of this?'

He reached up and pulled down her arm. 'Madison, have you even heard of Lyme disease before?'

She shook her head in frustration. 'I don't know. I can't remember.'

'Then how are you supposed to know about it? It's easy when someone tells you, but figuring out for yourself is hard.' He took a breath. 'Did you get your parents?'

She nodded and started to cry. 'They don't remember Justin being bitten by a tick. The kids did play in the grass, just about every day, and Mum bathed them both every night. She thinks Justin had a tiny rash under his arm that disappeared when she put some cream on it. She didn't mention it because she thought it was just a sweat rash. Just nothing. She's beside herself. She wants to come over. She and Dad are looking for flights.'

Fletch swallowed. 'And what about Jason's family?'

'They're on their way. His mum got really agitated. She doesn't really understand ticks and Lyme disease. She kept asking about dogs. I couldn't really answer the questions that she had.'

Fletch touched her arm. 'I can do that. I can answer their questions.' He nodded to Rui. 'Are we able to cope on the ward if Justin has more visitors?'

Rui was usually strict about there being only two visitors at a time for children, and only the carer allowed to stay overnight. She was conscious that so many children had sensory or neurological disorders, and the hospital environment itself was overwhelming, without adding lots more people into the mix.

'Rui is going to swap Justin into another room. There are two children in this room who are going to Theatre tomorrow and she wants to keep things calm for them.'

Fletch glanced around. 'Okay, I'll give her a hand, but then we need to check Mia over. Okay?'

It took longer than he thought to get Justin moved to another room on the ward. Another patient became un-

well and he had to deal with them first. By the time they'd
finally got Justin settled into another room, he'd sipped
some fluids and fallen asleep again, Madison looked as
if she'd run a marathon.

He picked up Mia in his arms and reached over and
touched Madison's cheek. 'Let's check our girl over. Then
I'll go and get you some things from home so you can
stay tonight.'

'But what about Mia? What will I do with her?'

'I can stay with Mia. If the ward stays like this, she
can sleep in the bed next to Justin.'

A voice came from behind them. 'Madison?' It was a
mixture of panic, and a very big question. Fletch dropped
his hand, but not before he'd met the angry eyes of an
older Singapore man.

Madison literally crumpled beneath his eyes. She became a crying, blubbering parent, trying to say too many
words all at once, with none of them coming out coher-
ently.

The man marched across the room, glared at Fletch
and took Madison into his arms as a slim woman rushed
into the room, to Justin's side.

Rui Lee started speaking calmly to them both in a
mixture of Malaysian and English. Mia was upset. She
could see both of her grandparents and her mother, and
knew that they were all upset, so she started crying too.
Fletch tried to shush her and rock her, but the grandmother came over and took her off him.

He was left standing in the middle of the floor as a
family drama he was very much not part of, unfolded in
front of him. Talk about feeling awkward.

He let himself stay calm, and moved into doctor mode.

He was joined by Dr Zhang, and, between them, they explained about Justin's condition and potential diagnosis. Fletch noticed that both grandparents shot most of their questions to his colleague—almost as if he weren't there. Madison seemed numb. It was as if, now that other people were here to take over, she'd finally shut down in the way her body and mind had probably wanted to do when she'd realised what was wrong with her son.

He got that. She spent so much of her life holding things together. No one could do that indefinitely. Not even the amazing resilient woman that he was growing to love.

The reality hit him like a slap in the face. He loved her. He'd known from the first moment he met Madison that there was something different about her, and the connection he felt, and now he recognised it for what it was.

He loved this woman. He wished he could wave a magic wand and make things better for her. For her, and for Justin.

The thoughts overwhelmed him. And it wasn't the time, or the place. Fletch knew that.

He could have time to have this conversation with Madison at any point in the future. No matter how he felt at this moment, he had to be the best doctor possible for Justin. That was how he could do the most for Maddie now.

He swallowed, trying to gather his thoughts and keep them away from the situation.

But he couldn't. And he knew the first impression he'd made with Jason's family wouldn't help. These people were so important to Madison and her children, and he had to try and keep things as stable as possible for her.

Fletch kept everything professional and let them know that he still had to take some time to examine Mia. Madison was on the bed holding Justin, so he asked Mrs Koh if she would accompany Mia while he examined her.

Mrs Koh looked reluctant to begin with, but when Dr Zhang agreed and encouraged her that it could happen in the room next door, and wouldn't take long, she finally relented.

Fletch was his normal self with Mia. He chatted as he examined her, checking her skin, looking for any sign of a rash, and listening to her heart and lungs. He asked her to do some jumps and bends, asking if anything was sore or hurting. He knew she'd been eating and drinking well—he'd seen that for himself. And there was nothing in her demeanour that gave him any cause for concern.

As he went along, he explained to Mrs Koh about the symptoms Justin had been having and how they could possibly relate to the diagnosis of Lyme disease. He reassured her that Mia showed no signs of anything similar, and, although she remained guarded with him the whole time, she was polite.

When Mia was dressed again, she climbed up onto Fletch's lap instead of her grandmother's and leaned into him. 'Is Justin going to be okay?'

Fletch's brain did that split-second thing of weighing up all possibilities. If he seemed overfamiliar with this child, Jason's mother would know there was more to his and Madison's relationship. If he set her down on the floor, without comforting her, he could upset Mia. There wasn't really a choice.

He stroked her hair and spoke in a low voice to her. 'Justin needs to stay in hospital tonight. And so does

Mummy. But if he stays tonight, and maybe tomorrow, he'll start to feel better soon. I hope we can find a way to stop him feeling so tired all the time.'

'Then he'll play more?' she asked brightly.

A child's perspective and very Mia, straight to the point.

'I hope he will,' answered Fletch, 'but it might take a little time for him to feel better again.'

He could almost feel Mrs Koh's cool gaze on him, but he wasn't letting himself be awkward around Mia. It wasn't fair on her, and she wouldn't understand.

Mia turned back to and put her arms out towards Mrs Koh, murmuring, 'Nenek,' and Fletch handed her back over. He gave a nod to Mrs Koh. 'Let's tell Madison that there's nothing to worry about regarding Mia.'

The woman gave him the briefest nod and carried Mia on her hip as they walked back through.

Madison was still upset, and Justin looked plain exhausted. Fletch caught Rui's gaze and as he opened his mouth to stay something that would make him even more unpopular, Rui got there before him.

'Mrs Koh, do you want a few moments with Justin? I really need some peaceful time for him, so he can sleep, and hopefully the medicines will start to take effect. Could you and Mr Koh then take Mia down to the staff canteen and get her something to drink?'

Rui had a manner that meant no one would ever argue. Fletch saw something flash in Mr Koh's eyes as if he was contemplating it for a second. But he looked around the rest of his room, his scowl saved solely for Fletch, and gave a nod of his head. He touched Madison's arm, but Rui spoke again. 'Please take Madison with you too. She needs a few minutes away from the ward, and a chance to talk to Mia.'

Mr Koh was slightly surprised by these added words, but bent to kiss his grandson, then wrapped his arm around Madison in a fatherly way and led her out of the room.

Fletch felt useless.

Madison looked broken. He wanted to be with her. Help her. Stay alongside her every step of the way.

But Rui stepped in front of him.

'She's in shock. She needs time out. She's held things together for so long since Jason died, and this—this is the thing that's tipped her.'

Fletch took a long slow breath. 'I want to help her.'

'I know you do. But the best way to help Madison right now is to look after her son.'

He looked back at little Justin and his heart ached. 'I've let Justin down too. I should have thought of Lyme disease earlier.'

'Why? We don't have it in Singapore. It's extremely rare. Why would you consider it?'

He was angry with himself. 'Because the children were in Scotland. I *knew* that. And I didn't make the connection.'

'But Lyme disease is still quite rare there too. You can't second-guess yourself here, Fletch. Another paediatrician might not have made the connection that you did.'

He sat down next to Justin and stroked his hand. 'I hate seeing him like this.'

Rui gave him a knowing smile. 'That's because you've formed an attachment.'

He opened his mouth to deny it automatically, then

realised there was no point. 'Yes, I have.' He sighed and looked at her. 'Madison was going to tell Jason's parents about us, but it's clear she's not done that. Maybe she's changed her mind about us.'

As he said the words out loud, he finally understood the kind of impact this had on him. He'd spent the last few weeks fretting about taking the next step. Worrying if he was ready. Wondering what would happen if things didn't work out, instead of just committing to the family that he'd found and clearly loved.

Was it any wonder that Madison had doubts too? He wondered what life had been really like for her for the last three years. Being widowed and left with two babies, only months old. Twins were notoriously hard on any parents, but on a single parent, who was also grieving? And while she'd had a support system when she'd asked for help—he somehow knew that he could likely count on one hand the amount of times Madison had actually done so.

Even now, when she wasn't getting a full night's sleep due to Justin's insomnia, she still turned up to work every day with a smile on her face, and commitment to her patients and her colleagues.

And, in amongst all that, she'd tried to make some time for him. Some time for herself, to try and get a little of her life back. He had nothing but admiration for this woman.

He gave a sad smile to Rui. 'Some people would tell me I was punching above my weight.'

'Some people would be right,' she added without hesitation, then put her hand on his shoulder. 'But you're not so bad, Fletch. I'm just waiting to see how you shape up.'

'I'm not entirely sure I'm going to get the chance. I don't think Jason's family like me.'

'They don't know you. And Madison should have warned them she was seeing someone else. They just dashed here after finding out their grandson was very sick. That's the thing that's front and centre in their mind right now—not you,' she said simply, clearly putting him back in his box for a while.

Fletch could not remember a time that he'd wanted people to like him so much. It was so outside his normal range of thought. He really needed to get some perspective.

He needed a chance to make sure that Madison was okay. But didn't want to make things worse for her. Rui seemed to read his mind. 'Patience,' she said simply. 'I'm going to get Dr Zhang to review some of our other patients while you stay with Justin.' She glanced down at the fragile sleeping child. 'I think he'll be happy that you're there with him,' she said as she walked out of the room.

Fletch looked down at the little chest rising and falling and the ticking on the monitor. If he had only one wish right now, it was to have found the correct diagnosis for Justin, and for him to get better.

The wish wouldn't be for him, nor for Madison. It would be for this tiny little boy next to him, who deserved a lifetime of good health.

CHAPTER TEN

SHE'D BLINKED AND her life had folded in on itself. That was the only thing she could think.

So much had happened so quickly that there simply wasn't time to process any of it.

First and forefront in her mind was Justin. Her son was sick.

Yes, she'd known for a few weeks that something was wrong, but she'd never expected this. The call from the crèche had been a bolt from the blue. And seeing Fletch carrying her limp child had just about been the end of her.

After that, things had just kind of disappeared into a cloud.

This wasn't her. This wasn't her at all. Madison had always been calm in a crisis. She'd prided herself on that fact. But now? She didn't even know what time it was. She was conscious of Mia in her lap, her arms around her, and the fact she was rocking back and forward.

Even when she'd got the news about Jason's accident, life hadn't been like this.

She'd had a few moments of disbelief. Of horror. And complete shock. But then her survival skills had kicked in.

She'd had babies to care for, a funeral to organise and

mourning to do. People had been around her. Food had appeared at her door. Family members had been there to hold her hand on the day of the funeral. The amount of paperwork had taken more than a year to sort out. Wills, bank accounts, insurance, medical records—some of the apparently simple things, like switching names on utility bills, had been the most frustrating of all.

Letters still occasionally arrived with Jason's name on them. Usually from nondescript companies where his name and address had been sold to some mailing list. But she'd got there. She'd managed all that. Jason had been a fellow adult. And while he'd been her husband and she'd loved him, her brain had managed to accept that sometimes accidents happened—even though it seemed immensely unfair.

She hadn't been out on a mission of vengeance. The Singapore authorities had investigated the incident and charged someone with reckless driving. It had been a first-time offence. The person had been temporarily blinded by the sun for a few seconds. It was honestly and truly an accident, and Madison and Jason's family had all accepted that.

But this? This couldn't even compute. This was their child. A part of them. Of course, the kids had been sick before. But not like this. Not with something that could be serious. Lyme disease could have lasting effects on those affected. Pericarditis could have unexpected implications.

It could be irregular heartbeats, or require more serious interventions like surgery. And with surgery, there were always further risks.

Because Madison worked in a hospital, her brain automatically went to the worst-case scenario. She could lose her child. Unthinkable. The words that Fletch had said to her at one point stuck in her head. *'No parent should outlive their child.'* And all of a sudden she was ready to be sick.

She pushed Mia towards her grandparents and dashed to the hospital toilets. Her whole body was shaking, and after she retched, she splashed her face with cold water, and leaned against the tiled wall, thankful for the coolness seeping through her scrubs.

She had to get back to Justin. She had to be by his side. Why was she even down here? Panic gripped her again and as she rushed back out of the door Jason's father was waiting for her. He was calm. Just as she should be.

He put a hand on either side of her shoulder. 'Stop, Madison, just breathe.'

She blinked as tears rolled down her face. 'I have to get back to Justin.'

'You will, just not like this.'

She knew he made sense, but she still didn't like the words. They were keeping her from her son.

'Justin is being looked after.'

His lips tightened at the words, and she knew exactly what he was thinking. *By that man.* The man who had been touching her cheek when Mr and Mrs Koh had come into the room, and clearly been shocked.

The man she'd promised that she would start the conversation with Jason's parents around dating again.

Something she hadn't done. Because she hadn't been brave enough.

She'd seen the reaction. Fletch clearly knew that she'd given them no warning because it had been blatantly obvious. Jason's parents were unfailingly polite and she'd put them in a terrible position. It was bad enough that their grandson was sick, without simultaneously throwing a potential new relationship into the mix. It was disrespectful, and she'd never, ever wanted to do that to them.

'I... I'm sorry,' she started. 'I should explain. The doctor...'

Mr Koh held up his hand. It was as if a mask had appeared over his face. 'You don't need to tell us. And it's not the time.'

He was right. On both counts. But she wanted to tell him, she didn't want to keep things from her in-laws.

'Everything is new,' she said quietly, as she felt tears come to her eyes again. 'I just wasn't sure I was ready.'

'And are you?' It was the tone of the words. She knew this man. She'd known him for more than ten years. This wasn't him. But he'd never been in this position before, and neither had she. Neither of them was handling this well. The answer to the question was stuck on her lips.

Her heart squeezed inside her chest. She didn't want to hurt her in-laws. She loved them and she needed them. And her brain was so confused right now. She needed to focus on her son, and only her son, until they could get through all this.

'N...no,' she breathed.

There was a noise to her right. It was Fletch. He'd come looking for her. Probably because she'd been so upset when she left the ward.

But his face was made of stone. He'd heard. He blinked, and he turned on his heel and walked away.

* * *

Fletch was numb.

He wouldn't think about this. He wouldn't. But he'd heard her truth. She'd said she wasn't ready.

And against all hope his heart was truly broken.

It wasn't as if she hadn't warned him at the beginning. And it was kind of ridiculous that he'd needed to witness this to finally get the message. He should have grasped it a few hours earlier when he'd realised that she hadn't told her in-laws she was dating again. The two things went hand in hand.

Now, he had to put his feelings aside and do his job. Likely under the scrutiny of all his colleagues, who would know exactly what was happening.

But that was the thing. He didn't actually care about his colleagues' thoughts. He didn't want to concentrate on that at all.

He wanted to walk back in and plead with Madison to rethink. To think about spending the rest of her life with Fletch and their children.

His skin prickled and he swallowed, his throat achingly dry. This was so not the time for thoughts like these. He had a child to take care of. Test results to wait for, and likely further tests to do. Whatever else happened, and no matter how much Mr and Mrs Koh disapproved of him, he had a duty of care to that little boy to give him the best outcome possible.

He'd always known at some point he'd get his heart broken. Maybe he deserved this? Maybe his own break-ups in the past hadn't been as amicable as he'd thought. Just because he'd been honest, didn't mean that his exes hadn't been hurt. Had he been naïve all along?

Was this why he always held back? Was this why he never wanted to commit—because he couldn't deal with a broken heart? But no one had felt like Madison to him. No one had given him such strong vibes and good connections. No one had made his heart sing as she did. No one else's smile could light the day as hers could.

Was it worth it? Was it worth feeling that connection only to have it ripped away again? Because right now he just wasn't sure.

He breathed slowly. This was a hospital. His personal feelings had to be set aside here, in order for him to do the job he was supposed to do. But it was hard. Harder than he could ever have imagined.

He tilted his chin and clenched his fists, urging his body to let him hide these emotions and play the ultimate professional, just as he should.

As he made his way back to the ward his mind was set. He was a doctor. That was what he was. And all he would concentrate on the for the near future.

CHAPTER ELEVEN

LIFE HAD COLLAPSED around her like a house of cards.

One minute she'd been on the brink of starting something new and exciting, the next, her kid was sick, her life upside down, and her relationship with her in-laws at risk because she hadn't treated them with the respect they deserved.

Could she have got things any more wrong?

Well, yes. The look in Fletch's eyes when he'd heard her say she wasn't ready had been enough to pierce her heart.

She hadn't meant it. She really hadn't. But she just couldn't say something different to Jason's dad.

And she should have. She should have been honest. But did the fact she couldn't be honest mean her brain was telling her she wasn't ready?

Madison had never been so confused in her life.

She was living her life in a bubble right now. Her parents had arrived, guilt-stricken and worried sick over Justin.

His ELISA test had come back positive, and now they were doing a Western blot test. If it was also positive, then, along with Justin's other symptoms, he would be diagnosed with Lyme disease.

His condition had started to pick up. The steroids had helped his pericarditis and he'd also been started on antibiotics. Her little boy was still tired, but starting to seem more like himself again.

Mia had been a whirlwind of activity, going between two sets of grandparents who were all delighted to spend time with her. She was living her best life.

As for Fletch? He barely met Madison's gaze.

He was still doing his job. He was attentive and kind to Justin. He'd spent more than an hour with her parents from Scotland, explaining the disease and reassuring them that lots of people got bitten by ticks, developed Lyme disease and didn't remember the bite. It waylaid their fears that they'd been neglectful with their grandchildren and Justin's illness was their fault.

She could still see her mum's hands kneading together on her lap, and knew that no words would probably really placate them, but Fletch had tried his best and she was grateful for that.

At times, she tried to catch him, to try and get a few moments to apologise for what he'd witnessed. But he'd clearly made his mind up that the conversation between them was not going to happen.

Rui kept giving her careful glances, obviously realising how anxious she was, but not able to have that conversation with her either, because of all the people around.

Finally, as Justin perked up day by day, Dr Zhang and Fletch decided he could be discharged. She wept with relief. It had been the longest ten days of her life.

His pericarditis was gone—for now—and he would continue to be monitored for any other symptoms connected to Lyme disease meantime. It was hoped that the antibiotics would fight off the effects and lessen the chance of any further symptoms.

When she finally walked through the doors of her apartment again, she gave a huge sigh of relief. Her mum and dad were staying, and luggage was everywhere.

She was just so glad to be home again.

As she tried to find some kind of routine, feeding and bathing the children, then getting them to bed, her eyes kept drifting to the sofa. The sofa where she'd sat on a few occasions with Fletch. It seemed empty without him, and she wondered how the space in the apartment would feel once her parents were gone again.

'What's wrong?' her mother asked when she finally sat down.

'Oh, nothing, and everything.' She sighed.

'What do you mean?'

Madison ran her hands through her hair. When was the last time she'd washed it?

She stared out over the view she loved. Although her parents had invited her to come back and stay in Scotland on numerous occasions, she'd never felt the pull. Her home was Singapore, she wanted to stay here, and was worried that anything she might say might just make them pressure her to move home again.

'What would you say if I told you that I'd met someone else?'

Her mother's mouth fell open for a second. 'Oh, well… I guess I'd ask who it is.'

'You've met him,' said Madison, before she lost her courage.

'It's been three years,' said her father's reasonable

voice. 'We've never expected you to spend the rest of your life alone.'

'But is it too soon?' She turned to face him.

'Only you can answer that,' he replied, ever the diplomat.

'What about Mia and Justin?' asked her mother. 'Have they met this person?'

Madison nodded. 'Yes, and they like him. And he likes them. Everything seemed…to be going well…' Her voice drifted off.

'So, what changed?' asked her father.

'All this,' she said in exasperation.

'Well, if they can't stay around for the hard stuff, are they really the right person for you?' asked her mother. It was a reasonable observation, but Madison couldn't let it lie.

'I pushed him away,' she said as the full realisation swept over her. 'Things were just so complicated with Jason's parents there, and they didn't know I was dating anyone, and they saw him touch me, and I got upset— because I didn't want to upset them, and…' Her shoulders started to shake.

'It's Justin's doctor, isn't it?' asked her dad.

Madison's head shot up.

He gave her a half-smile. 'I noticed things. The way the children related to him, the way he looked at you.'

She sagged her head into her hands. 'I meant to tell Jason's parents I was thinking about dating again. No, I meant to tell them I *was* dating again. But I just couldn't find the words. I can see Jason in both of their faces. I didn't want them to think I had forgotten. That I had moved on without considering how they would feel.'

She shook her head. 'I've made a whole mess of this. I got in a jumble. Mr Koh saw Fletch touching me. I think he was angry. And with Justin so sick… I just told him I wasn't ready and Fletch heard that.'

'It's a misunderstanding,' said her dad. 'You were under a lot of stress.'

She lifted her gaze. 'But I hurt him.'

Her mother looked at her. 'You did. But you know it. And you need to be big enough to have that conversation. How do you feel about him?'

The question from her mother hit home. And she was almost glad her mother had put her on the spot, to make her say the words out loud.

'I love him.' The words were sure. Because that was exactly how she felt.

She took a deep breath. 'But I haven't told him that. Not yet.' She blinked back tears. 'But I hope that he knows. We did talk. We talked about being together.' Her lip trembled. 'Since Jason died, I never thought I would feel like this about anyone else. I never thought I would really find love again.' The more she spoke, the more she realised exactly how much this all meant to her. Exactly how much was at stake. 'I don't want to mess this up.' Her voice broke and her mother reached over and put her arm around her daughter's shoulders.

'Then don't.' Her mother smiled. She gave her a squeeze. 'We want you to be happy, you and the kids. Find your happiness, Madison, and hold on tight.'

CHAPTER TWELVE

HE LOVED SINGAPORE. He wanted to stay here. But he couldn't imagine seeing Madison on a daily basis and not being with her. The thought made every bone in his body ache. So, he started looking at other jobs, other places to be.

He was considering one in Missouri when Rui came into the office. Astute as ever, she saw the job advert straight away.

'You're not leaving. I thought your contract was for two years.'

'It is.' He sighed. 'But I'm not sure I can stay any longer.'

'I'm not sure you deserve to,' she quipped back.

He turned around his chair incredulously. 'What?'

She folded her arms.

He shook his head. 'Madison told her in-laws that she wasn't ready to move on. The message was clear. I just don't think I can spend the rest of my time here without having mixed emotions. This is her permanent job, her permanent home. I don't want things to be awkward for her. She loves her work, and I don't want to get in the way.'

'So, the easiest solution is to walk away?'

'It seems like the kindest thing to do.'

Rui snorted. 'Kind? If you walk away you'll break her heart!'

'How can you possibly say that?'

She walked over to him. 'Tell me this. Do you really think she could answer that question honestly, when she was under so much pressure? You saw her up here. She'd unravelled, completely. Okay, so she hadn't told her in-laws yet about you. And yes, she should have. But she's walking a fine line, of balancing her relationship with them and creating a new one with you. If she'd told them downstairs in the canteen that, yes, she was ready to move on, and with the new doctor who was treating their grandchild, don't you think that would have been a blow like a hammerhead?'

He sat back. 'Maybe, well…yes. But what if it also gave her the opportunity to be truthful to herself that she wasn't ready? Maybe I pushed her when I shouldn't have. This might have been a soft way out for her.'

'You really believe that?' The scepticism in her voice was heavy. Rui folded her arms. 'Let me tell you something. Madison is a coper. That's what she's done ever since Jason died. She's coped. These last few weeks were the first time I saw some sparkle in her eyes again, some real life about her. I caught the way she was looking at you—long before either of you admitted something was going on. I've watched you with those children. They adore you. And you're great with them. Sure, it's only been a few months, but there is time here, Fletch. There's a real chance for you both, and you'd be a fool to throw that away.'

His insides twisted. He so wanted all of this to be true. He shook his head. 'I know what I want, but I don't know if it's what Madison wants. And what about Jason's parents? It is quite clear they don't like me. She has a good relationship with them. I don't want to ruin that for her.'

Rui gave a slow nod. 'It's not about picking a side. It's about being honest. They walked into a scene they didn't bank on seeing, at a time of crisis in their family life.' Her mouth pressed together. 'These are good people, Fletch. They will never get their son back, and, long term, they will want the absolute best for Madison and the kids. You just need to persuade them that the best—is you.'

He straightened in his chair and gave her a smile. It was the first time he'd felt hopeful in the last ten days. 'You realise this could all go horribly wrong, and I could make a fool of myself?'

She shrugged her shoulders in an amused way and nodded.

He grinned. 'But she's worth it. *They're* worth it.'

'Of course, they are,' she agreed.

And without another second of hesitation, Fletch picked up his jacket and walked out.

He kept telling himself he was doing the right thing, even though his stomach seemed to clench and release at regular intervals. By the time he'd crossed the city and reached the quieter street it seemed as though he was the only person around. He checked the address again and walked up to the door before he could change his mind.

He rang the bell and waited, hearing footsteps inside before Mrs Koh opened the door. Her eyes widened slightly in surprise. He gave a small bow. 'Mrs Koh, I wonder if I could have a moment of your time, please?'

She paused for a second before opening the door and gesturing him inside, calling to her husband. As she invited him to sit on a cream chair, her husband came through. The surprise was evident on his face. 'What is this?' he asked, before quickly asking, 'Justin?'

Fletch raised his hand. 'Justin is fine. He is at home with his mother, and his other grandparents.'

The Kohs looked at each other and gave a nod before sitting opposite Fletch, with their hands folded in their laps.

It was like being called to the headmaster's office, and Fletch had to remind himself he'd chosen to do this.

'Thank you for speaking to me. I wanted to talk to you both and Madison, and Mia and Justin. First of all, I wanted to apologise for how you found us in the hospital. I've become very close to Madison and the children since I came to Singapore, and was trying to comfort Madison when you arrived.'

Mrs Koh shifted a little uncomfortably, and Mr Koh's face remained fixed.

He continued, 'I want you to know that I love Madison. I love Justin and Mia too. They are wonderful, and I feel very lucky to have found them.' He paused, taking a deep breath, wondering if this was where everything would go wrong.

'So, I wanted to ask your approval to be involved in their lives. Madison loves you both so much. And I realise that you will be protective over your daughter-in-law, and your grandchildren. I want to promise you that I will love and protect them to the best of my ability.' He swallowed and licked his lips, before breaking into a smile. 'They are very, very special.'

'They are,' agreed Mrs Koh, her gaze cautious.

There was a very long silence. 'Why did you come here?' asked Mr Koh.

Fletch relaxed his tense shoulders. 'Because I wanted to be honest with you. I love Madison. I won't let her go without a fight. I'm sorry if the thought of her moving on is hurtful to you both. I can only promise you that I'm sincere. And if I'm to become part of Madison and the children's lives, I hope I can become part of yours too.'

He held his breath. Wondering if he'd just taken a step too far.

After the longest time, Mr Koh stood up. He took a few steps towards Fletch and held out his hand. Fletch breathed the biggest sigh of relief and stood up to shake it.

'Thank you for coming to see us,' said Mr Koh.

Mrs Koh gave a small nod of her head.

'Thank you,' said Fletch, not trying to hide his smile. 'Now I guess I have to go and speak to Madison.'

'You came here first?' asked Mr Koh, his eyebrows raised.

'I did.'

Mr Koh tilted his head slightly in question. 'And if I'd told you no?'

Fletch gave him a smile. 'I would have respectfully told you that Madison and the kids were worth fighting for, and that I would still try.'

Mr Koh gave an amused smile. 'Well, I'm glad we've come to an understanding.'

'So am I.'

This time as he walked down the street it seemed brighter and full of life. Now, all he had to do was con-

vince the woman that he loved that they were worth fighting for.

And he knew exactly how to do it.

CHAPTER THIRTEEN

MADISON LOOKED AT the text on her phone again.

Meet me at the bandstand at eleven a.m. Fletch x.

Her eyes kept going back to the kiss. That had to be good, right? And the fact he was asking to meet her must mean he was ready to talk.

She'd been nervous when she received the text this morning, and had spent more than an hour deciding what to wear. Finally, she settled on a pink shirt and white skirt and a pair of flat shoes.

It wasn't high heels. But she wasn't sure if it was a high heels kind of day. She knew exactly what she wanted to say. She wanted to tell him that she loved him. She wanted to tell him how sorry she was that she'd said those words in the hospital, and could only hope that he might forgive her. She wanted to start her life over, and she wanted to do that with Fletch.

She was sure there would still be mistakes, still be misunderstandings. But she could live with that. They could work through them. Only she hoped they could.

What if this was something else entirely? What if he wanted to say they would be best being friends and just leave it at that? He'd done that in previous relationships in the past, and it might be her actions had made him think that she didn't really care about him.

Her nerves were jittery as she approached the bandstand in the Botanical Gardens. At first, she thought he wasn't there. But as she drew closer, she saw that he was. He just wasn't standing at the railing, he was sitting down inside.

Her heart felt as if it hiccupped. She put her hand on the railing. 'Fletch?' she said in a quiet voice.

His dark head lifted. His gaze was cautious. 'Hey.'

She moved inside the bandstand, looked around, then sat down next to him. 'What are we doing in here?'

'I wanted to come somewhere we had good memories.'

She gulped, worried about how this might go. 'I want to say sorry. For what I said in the hospital. I was put on the spot and I just didn't know what to do. I hadn't got around to having the conversation I wanted to, then, in the middle of all that, I felt as if I couldn't say it out loud.'

Fletch gave a nod of his head. 'I wonder if that means more than you think it does.'

She shook her head, but Fletch put his hand on her arm.

'Madison, I know how I feel. I know how I feel about you and the kids. But, if things start, I want them to start the right way. And I wonder if your brain, or your heart, was telling you something that you hadn't quite faced yourself.'

She was stunned at his words, and tried to digest them. Could they possibly be true?

She took a deep breath and put her hand on her chest. 'My heart and brain are quite sure how they feel. I was just a distressed mum under pressure, that didn't handle things well. That's all it was.'

She could feel him take a shaky breath next to her. 'I need you to be sure, Maddie. Because I'm sure. I'm sure that I love you and the kids and I want to be part of your lives. I'm so sure, I went to see Mr and Mrs Koh today.'

Her mouth fell open and she turned to face him. 'What?'

He nodded. 'We met under the wrong circumstances, and I'm partly to blame for that. I wanted them to know that I'm serious about you and the kids. I wanted them to know that I love their daughter-in-law. I'm not some fly-by-night kind of guy. I also told them that I'd like to get to know them better too.'

Tears started to stream down her face. He'd done that. He'd done that for her, for Mia and for Justin. 'What did they say?'

'Mr Koh was quiet to begin with, but when I told him I wanted their approval he seemed to realise I was serious.'

She gave a surprised laugh. 'Isn't it my dad's approval you're meant to ask?'

Fletch looked her right in the eye. 'This is a different, and unique, set of circumstances. I thought this might be the best way to start with them.'

She wiped her tears away. 'And did they give it?'

He smiled. 'He asked me what I'd do if he said no.'

Her eyes widened. 'He never.'

'Oh, he did. I get the impression Mr Koh might be a bit of an old rogue. But anyway, I told him if he said no, you were still worth fighting for, and—he agreed.'

He intertwined his fingers with hers. 'So, what do you say?'

She reached up with her other hand and touched his cheek. 'I say thank you. Thank you for being understanding. Thank you for going out on a limb for us. And thank you for making the extra effort with Jason's family.'

His gaze was steady on hers. 'But that's not the part I really want to know.'

She smiled and leaned towards him. 'I love you, Arthur Fletcher. And even though you've told me you've never wanted to do this before, I'm prepared to take a chance on you.' Her voice had a joking tone.

'You are?' His other hand slid into her hair as he pulled her face towards his. He kept his voice low. 'Then you might be interested in the present I bought you.'

She pulled back. 'You bought me a present?'

He nodded his head to the other side of the bandstand where a white shoe box had blended into the surroundings. Her brow wrinkled with curiosity and she moved to pick it up, before sitting back down next to him.

'You bought me shoes?' she queried as she lifted the lid, wondering what on earth he had done.

It only took a few seconds for the realisation to hit. She lifted out a white designer high heel. But it was no ordinary high heel. It was special. It was embellished with tiny white pearls and diamantés. She let out a gasp.

'Think you could find a reason to wear these in the next year some time?'

She couldn't stop grinning as she put the shoe back in the box, and shifted onto his lap, wrapping her arms around his neck. 'Oh, I think I might be able to find a reason,' she teased. 'But you'll need to kiss me first before I decide.'

And so, he did.

EPILOGUE

'I'M FIRST,' SAID JUSTIN, elbowing Mia.

'No, I'm first,' she shot back, pushing him right back.

'Why don't you both go together?' whispered Fletch, as he set them down the path towards the bandstand, lined with friends and family.

They were almost five now, and he couldn't love them more if he tried. They both took a few steps, looked at each, then practically sprinted towards the bandstand in their race to be first.

Friends and family were all laughing, Jason's family members the most.

Fletch's father gave him a nudge. 'I like how they keep you on your toes.' He smiled.

Fletch grasped his father's hand. 'You have no idea.' He beamed.

Asking his father to be his best man and having him by his side had been a no-brainer for Fletch. His father's recovery had continued to progress well, he'd had no further strokes and he'd visited Fletch and Madison frequently in the last few years.

They walked down the path together, nodding at friends, shaking a few hands and climbing the steps to the bandstand.

Rui Lee walked down after them as Madison's matron of honour, dressed in an elegant dark blue gown.

Then the music changed, and Madison appeared in the flowered archway with her father at her side. She was wearing a traditional bridal dress, but it was simple. Pale cream satin, with some beading at the bodice, and a bouquet filled with heather and tartan ribbons. Her hair was loose and she wore no veil, but had some flowers pinned in her hair.

Fletch's breath hitched in his throat. This was it. This was the moment he'd been waiting his whole life for, and it was everything he'd hoped for.

His bride was the most beautiful woman on the planet and she couldn't hide the smile on her face as she walked towards him.

The road had been smoother than they'd thought it would be. Jason's family had been gracious and taken their time to get to know Fletch and welcome him as part of the family. Fletch's position had been made permanent, and he and Madison had bought a new house in the outskirts of the heart of Singapore.

'Hey, you,' she said as she climbed the steps of the bandstand towards him.

'Hey, you,' he replied, taking her hand and holding it close to his chest. 'Has anyone told you that you're the most beautiful bride in the world?' he said.

'I have!' shouted Mia from beneath them.

They both laughed and Madison leaned closer. 'I take it all back,' she whispered.

'About what?'

'Inviting exes to weddings. Monique, Viv and Indira are the nicest women I've ever met.'

He looked out over their friends. Monique was heavily pregnant, and with her husband. Viv had her baby on her hip, and Indira was getting married in a few months. All had been delighted to come to the wedding of the friend they'd dubbed the eternal bachelor.

The messages he'd received back had ranged from *Finally!* to, *Can't wait to meet her!* and *Let's give this lady an award!*

'I'm assuming you'll all gang up against me?' he joked.

'Already done.' Madison smiled, reaching her hand up and touching his cheek. 'Are you ready for this?'

'Been waiting all my life,' Fletch replied without a second of hesitation.

The celebrant gave them both a nod. 'Can we get started?'

Fletch held up his hand. 'Give me one second.' He bent down and picked up Mia in one arm and Justin in the other, resting them both on his hips.

He kissed Madison's cheek. 'We're a team,' he said, 'and now we're ready.'

She looked up into the eyes of the man she loved and kissed him back. 'Yes, we are.'

* * * * *

FINDING FOREVER WITH THE SINGLE DAD

BECKY WICKS

MILLS & BOON

CHAPTER ONE

'LUCIE HENDERSON? Is that really you?'

Lucie's feet found their way to the chocolate shop doorway. Gramma May's good friend Cynthia hugged her warmly to her bosom. 'Oh, my goodness, duck…it's been so long. I thought you were off saving the world! What brings you back to Yorkshire?'

'Oh, you know…' Lucie shrugged.

If she told Cynthia she was here not only to fill a temporary role at the Brookborough general practice, but to recuperate after a tragedy that had plagued her dreams ever since it had happened, she might as well announce it on a megaphone to the entire village. Brookborough was the place where secrecy came to die. Everyone knew everyone else's business on this side of the North Yorkshire Moors. The last thing she needed was for people to start looking at her in sympathy.

'Tell me what I've missed, Cynthia. When did I last see you? I think I was eighteen…'

Soon, the fragrant chocolate shop had her trapped in its cosy interior. She sampled white bon-bons and cinnamon swirls while Cynthia shared the highlights of what she'd missed. The cannon fire of questions she fired wasn't so easy to swallow.

'What was it like, working in Nepal?'

'How are things there now, after the tragedy?'

'How are you, really?'

Lucie was polite, but the barrage of questions was enough to shake her back into a state she hadn't been in since the earthquake. She was so far away from where she was needed...

Cynthia had that look in her eyes now. Narrowed, pensive, a little scared that she might hear or say something that made them both feel uncomfortable. Obviously Gramma May must have told her oldest friend a few things about her specialism in mental health, her international placements with the Medicine Relief Operatives out in distant disaster zones, but how much did anyone know about what had happened to her colleague Jorge that day at the school on the mountain road in Nepal?

'Wow, this is good,' she heard herself say.

The chocolate was demanding full custody of her attention now, forcing her to acknowledge the taste of her childhood. She might as well have taken a bite of Austin Johnstone too, she thought. This used to be their number one Saturday morning activity.

It wasn't hard to recall standing with her best friend on the steps of the Grade Two listed All Saints' Church on the night of the Scarecrow Festival. Austin Johnstone—better known as AJ to everyone around here—would always buy her one chocolate and dare her to make it last all day. She could never do it. The chocolates were just too good.

'Just made 'em this morning, pet.' Cynthia rustled a paper bag and popped more chocolates into it. 'Take a couple home for May, why don't you? Bert used to buy her these, and I know she loves them.'

I won't eat it, I won't eat it...not like AJ would have done.

The scent of the sweet chocolate gift for Gramma, in honour of Lucie's late Grampa Bert, tempted her from her handbag as she walked on.

Stopping at the bottom of the hill, she saw All Saints' Church peering down at her like a weathered, wise brown owl. Her gaze ran over the gravestones protruding from the grassy knoll where AJ had once set up a séance. He'd planned for them to reach the spirit of the Black Knight of the North, who supposedly rested there. They'd done all kinds of stupid things in those days, them and their friends, making their own entertainment in a place the size of a postage stamp.

Until AJ had ruined everything, by hooking up with Claire Bainbridge.

Lucie scowled as she walked on. Of course he'd charge into her brain like that pushy Black Knight. Even the streams that flowed alongside the honey-coloured stone cottages with their picture-postcard pantile roofs couldn't force the memories away. Thank goodness their paths wouldn't cross while she was here.

Gramma May had told her that he'd moved to London. She'd said nothing else—just that he'd moved there and was a very well-respected psychiatrist. Lucie had made the mistake of asking about him years ago and had discovered he'd got married and had two kids. Twins, no less. That had *not* been a good day. Whenever she'd thought about looking him up online after that she'd chickened out. She knew she'd only find photos of him and Claire, all happily married, nesting with their beautiful twin babies.

Nope. No, thanks.

So, the blond-haired, blue-eyed former Mr Popularity was a psychiatrist. It made sense. He always had been the caring kind. Well, until he'd hooked up with Claire, she thought, wrinkling up her nose.

She'd never forgotten the bone-deep hurt and mortification she'd felt that night she'd stood outside his bedroom door, listening to him in there, laughing with Claire about her! Claire had been teasing him for the way 'little lost Lucie' always followed him around like a puppy dog, and he'd said nothing. Absolutely nothing to defend Lucie, who was supposed to be his best friend.

It didn't seem to matter how many time zones and disaster areas she'd found herself in since—she could still be back there in a flash. Eighteen years old, secretly, hopelessly in love with the most popular guy in Brookborough, and listening to Claire telling him, *'Lucie is seriously cramping your style, AJ. How about you let me show you some things little lost Lucie never could?'*

The devastation. The total humiliation of hearing him betray their friendship like that. She'd fallen for him hard. He'd been her rock since he'd found her crying, back when she'd been nine and the new girl in town. Everyone had been whispering about her at school, calling her 'the American orphan'. He'd stood up for her—a real-life hero. She'd barely been able to find the words to tell him about the fire on a campsite that had killed her parents while she'd been watching illicit horror films with her babysitter in Denver. Or her busy, travel-obsessed Aunt Lina, who'd taken her in for a while, but who ultimately hadn't much wanted to be tied down with a grieving child, and had consequently flown her from Colorado to the UK, to be raised by her paternal grandparents instead.

AJ had always been there for her—as a friend, nothing more. He hadn't left her side for a month after Grampa Bert's death. She'd been fourteen then. He hadn't agreed when she'd told him it was her fault. But of course it was her fault. Grampa had been forced to go back to work after she'd arrived, instead of retiring as he'd planned, so they could afford to look after her. He'd worked so hard he'd had a heart attack and died way too young.

'Lucie? Lucie Henderson?'

Flora McNally bustled out onto the street from the gift shop, all smiles.

'Hi, Flora, you look well.'

'What a lovely surprise! May did say you were coming home for a while. How long do we have you for, Little Lu?'

Little Lu. Wow… No one had called her that when she was standing on stages, establishing civic engagement alliances, advocating for reducing disaster risks… It would have made her smile if it hadn't reminded her of Claire's snide comments all over again.

White-haired Flora had crossed her arms. Lucie smoothed her fringe, shook her hair behind her shoulders. Did her thirty-four-year-old self appear so very different from the teenager with a pixie cut who'd switched this place for America?

'I'll be here a couple of months, give or take.'

'May's so very proud of you, pet,' Flora cooed, and her eyes shone with the same look Lucie had seen on Cynthia's face in the chocolate shop. 'What you must have gone through… It was all over the news. I heard you pulled some kids out of the rubble in Nepal? You're lucky to be alive…well done, you.'

Lucie thanked her, eyeing the ground. It didn't take much to make the memories come raging back. The school walls collapsing on Jorge. The creaking cascade of concrete and steel. The water tank toppling from its perch… They'd said it was a thousand gallons. She'd pulled the others out—the three kids had *had* to come first—as soon as the rumble had begun. Brie and Jero from her team had followed after, cut up and bloodied, but fine. They'd called it a miracle that she'd got out uninjured, but she hadn't been able to save Jorge.

They'd given her a medal after that. She'd felt like a total fake, accepting it.

Lucie edged along the pathway as Flora talked. How many more people was she failing just by being *here*? Sure, she had nightmares about Nepal sometimes—but it was nothing really. Not when there were still people out there she could be helping with Medicine Relief Operatives. This hiatus was going to be good for her—a nice, cosy locum GP position to take her mind off things for a bit, and a chance to spend more time with Gramma May. But the sooner she could get back out there, where she belonged, the better.

'Are you OK, pet? You've gone a bit pale.' Flora caught her arm.

'I'm fine. I have to be on my way, but it's nice to see you, Flora.'

Hitting a left at the pub, she took the path along the stream back to Gramma's. It seemed as good a path as any, going past the storybook Beck Isle Cottage. The gentle sound of the babbling water was always better than any CD.

This had always been her favourite part of the village and today every lungful of cool early-March air was a balm. AJ had kissed her here, aged ten and a bit, on the little bridge that boasted a world-famous chocolate-box view. If her memories were correct, she'd dared him to do it a couple of weeks after a dance in the school gym. He'd bought her a chocolate bar that night. She'd thought at the time that his gift had meant something. Clearly, it hadn't.

The way he'd swiped at his mouth afterwards, as if kissing a girl was the equivalent of eating cat food, had not done wonders for her self-esteem. Neither had seeing him with a steady stream of girls after that, while *she* had remained firmly in the friend zone. *Ugh.*

She'd never expected Claire, though. She'd hightailed it back down his stairs and out through the door as fast as a lightning bolt after hearing them together in his room, before she'd been forced to hear anything worse. As if the only reason she'd run to him in the first place hadn't been bad enough... She'd just heard Gramma May admit to Cynthia that she and Grampa Bert had always wanted to travel in their retirement, and that Lucie had stopped them!

Well, not in those words exactly. She knew her grandparents loved her. But she was the reason they hadn't been able to travel as they'd planned before Grampa died.

Cynthia had said that maybe May could travel alone, without Grampa, once Lucie had gone away to university. But May had replied that she probably would not. She would wait, because Lucie would be home frequently for holidays.

She had concluded from that that she was *still* stopping Gramma from living the life she'd wanted before they'd been forced to take her in!

She'd wanted to tell AJ how Aunt Lina had emailed her, offering to pay for her medical training if she agreed to go back to the US and get to know her and her American roots. Apparently, Lina felt pretty bad for being too young and busy and grieving to keep her in America after her sister's death.

She'd hoped that maybe AJ would say she didn't have to go, and that after nine years her home was there. That had been her hope. But after hearing what she'd heard—first Gramma and Cynthia's conversation, and then AJ and Claire's—she'd run home, opened her laptop and taken her aunt up on the offer instead, chasing her dream of becoming a doctor.

She'd never even said goodbye to AJ. He probably hadn't missed her always following him around like a puppy dog, cramping his style, anyway.

Lucie took the little path along the stream, breathing in the spring scent of the trees. She was still failing to shove the memories of AJ from her head when something huge, dark and furry seemed to launch at her from nowhere.

She shrieked, just as a man's panicked warning was hollered at her from a distance.

What the...?

Before she could gather her thoughts, her feet were scrambling for solid ground. The man sprinted towards her, still yelling.

Too late.

Lucie lost her balance and toppled off the grassy bank straight into the icy stream.

CHAPTER TWO

LUCIE WAS MORE mortified than cold, flailing like an octopus in the water, her feet struggling for a grip on the mossy bottom. No sooner had she managed to sort of half-stand, her hair slapped in sodden streaks to her face, than a broad-shouldered man came into view, wading towards her.

'Here, take my hand!'

Lucie blinked, trying to bring him into focus. Leaves and twigs were twirling around her ankles in a frozen serenade. The icy water sloshed at the bank, where a dark brown Labrador paced the path, barking an alert. So *that* was what had forced her into the water!

'I've got you!' The man was behind her now. He looped his arms under her shoulders, bringing her to a fully standing position. 'You're OK!'

She slumped against him, catching her breath. Her red-heeled boots were stuck between stones and fallen branches— her poor boots…they'd take *weeks* to dry.

'Wrong kind of shoes for fly fishing, I see,' he said. 'Hold still.'

That voice.

Her stomach shot to her throat, just as she found herself lifted fully into the man's arms. Five feet in the air, with water pouring from the tops of her boots, she found there were no words to say as two familiar almond-shaped eyes met hers close up, and then grew so wide she thought he was going to drop her straight back into the water.

Here he was. Austin Johnstone. *AJ*. Thick caramel-blond hair, blue-grey eyes that could undo you...holding her up in a stream.

'Lucie?'

She blinked, aghast, feeling butterflies going bonkers in her stomach, then made to break free. He held her even tighter against his impressively muscular chest.

'Put me down!'

Really?

Trust the man who'd waded in after her to be AJ, of all the people in this town. She flailed her arms against him in a pathetic twisty motion, trying to break free of him, but he held tighter still, as if she was nothing but a bag of weightless balloons that might just float away.

'I said put me down, AJ!'

'OK... OK.'

A look of something like annoyance pushed all amusement from his face. He strode with her back to the bank, where he deposited her carefully onto the grass.

'It's nice to see you, too, Lucie,' he said dryly, as his hair flopped damply over his forehead. 'There's a leaf in your hair, by the way.'

She growled and tore off her waterlogged jacket, wringing it out. AJ stepped up beside her as she swiped at her hair, sending the leaf into the air, before all six feet of him straightened before her, commanding her full attention. His hard chest... those broad shoulders that had supported her head for so many train and bus rides...the trace of a beard he'd definitely never had before. He looked good with a beard, actually. Very good. Better looking than ever.

But of course he would be.

Her boots were *destroyed*.

'What are you doing here?' she spluttered.

'I could ask you the same thing.'

Her cheeks flamed hot—an old giveaway. She looked away, so her eyes wouldn't doubly betray her and reveal the burning fire in her belly.

He'd taken his shoes off. His maroon sweater was only wet around the chest and arms, but he pulled it off anyway, revealing a white T-shirt that clung to his washboard muscles. She did a double take as he offered his jumper to her, but no way was she accepting.

'Just take it,' he implored, holding it out.

'I'm fine,' she said tightly, resisting the urge to grab it and smell it. He'd always used to smell so good. His clothes had fallen off her slim frame, but she'd still borrowed his T-shirts all the time anyway. 'I'm heading to Gramma's.'

The Labrador had finally ceased its barking. It lay panting in a patch of leaves on the grass under the trees, as if butter wouldn't melt.

'You need to control your dog,' she scolded. 'Does it always throw innocent people into streams?'

She'd said it mostly to fill the awkward silence while her mind spun. This might have been the right moment to storm away with what was left of her dignity, but somehow her feet refused to move—and not just because her poor boots were still sloshing. What was he doing here, anyway? Visiting family and friends with Claire and the kids?

Ugh... She didn't even want to know.

'Jetson doesn't usually do this,' AJ told her apologetically, pushing the thick mop of hair from his forehead.

It was darker than she remembered.

Antagonised, she huffed. 'Well, he's done it now! Since when do you like dogs, anyway?'

'I always liked dogs. I just never had one till I started working with them.'

Working with them? Wasn't he a psychiatrist?

'Anyway…' He bit back a laugh, no doubt at the look on her face. 'It's bizarre, honestly. He never does that—do you, buddy?'

The dog laid its head on its paws and heaved a sigh. Lucie stared at it warily. Maybe the dog had sensed a connection between them—some lingering, thinning thread that used to tie their two souls together. Dogs were clever. Weird, but clever.

No. She was *annoyed*. Not *amused*. There was no chance she was smiling at him or his goofy dog, now or ever. Not after he'd failed to defend her, and their friendship, to Claire. It had cut her to the quick.

God, would you listen to yourself? That was years ago. You need to let it go.

AJ was still grinning at her. His familiar eyes traced along her body while water trickled down her back into her underwear. Why was he looking at her like that?

'I have to go,' she announced weakly, finally getting her feet to move in the opposite direction, back towards the main road. It was all she could do not to waddle like a deformed penguin.

'Lucie?'

She paused. His voice behind her held the gut-twisting tone of the boy she'd worshipped since the age of nine, plus some small hint of a plea that should have been satisfying after all this time, but only seemed to twist the key in a door she'd firmly bolted shut.

Her heart was back to racing like a freight train.

'What?'

'Will you let me make this up to you?'

Scraping back her bedraggled hair, she turned again, clocking the bulging biceps as he fished for sunglasses in his pockets. Even soaking wet, he was delicious. Why couldn't the sight of him repulse her? Instead it was igniting a million memories, all of them from before the time she'd heard solid proof of her love for him being unrequited, loud and clear through his bedroom door.

Not that he knew she'd heard anything—even though they were always walking in and out of each other's houses back then.

'Dinner tonight?' He slid his feet back into his shoes, which somehow he managed to make look sexy. 'I'll pick you up.'

She scanned his blue-grey eyes. Dammit, he was looking hotter with every passing second. All grown up. A man now, not a teenager.

'How do you know where I'm staying?'

He stared her down. 'You literally just said you were going to May's.'

Lucie frowned. This was all so strange…but so familiar at the same time. Maybe a part of her *did* want to know what he'd been up to the whole time she'd refused to accept him as a friend or follower on every single one of her social media accounts.

'Fine,' she heard herself saying. 'You *do* owe me, AJ.'

For a lot of things, she added silently.

'About that,' he said now, slinging his sweater over his shoulders like a model on a Yorkshire postcard. 'No one calls me AJ any more. It's Austin Johnstone.'

'Well, *I'm* back now,' she sniped, battling a fresh, unwelcome surge of longing. *God, he was hot.* 'And you'll always be AJ to me.'

A smile of something like admiration flickered in his eyes. She would not wait around for it to reach his mouth. Her heart was already in her throat and there was no way she was letting on how his presence was affecting her.

'Pick me up at seven,' she instructed, and turned on her soaking wet heels.

It was tough not to squelch as she made her undignified exit. And she felt his eyes burning into her back the whole way to the bridge.

CHAPTER THREE

'WHERE ARE YOU GOING, Dad?'

The twins cast their blue-eyed gazes up at him from their chairs. 'You smell nice,' Ruby observed.

'Out with an old friend,' he told them quickly, loading their dinner bowls haphazardly into the dishwasher.

'That's right...an old *friend*.'

Belle's voice was mocking, in the good-natured way his sister always spoke, as she left her chair, shooing him away from the dishwasher.

'You'd better go—you'll be late. I've got this.'

Jetson padded in from the lounge area, as if sensing that it was his turn now to help keep watch.

Josiah threw a plastic car in the direction of the blaring TV.

'Josiah, don't throw things at the TV. If you don't like what's on, turn it off. Jetson, fetch the toy.'

At Belle's instructions, Josiah marched to the TV while the dog went straight for the car. He placed the toy at his sister's feet.

'Nice work, sis!' Austin was impressed.

Belle was learning a few things about dogs from him, and as Chief Nursing Officer in the local nursing home she'd also been the hugest supporter of Thera Pups since he'd launched the company. She'd hooked him up with many regular visits to Lavender Springs.

Belle loved the people in that nursing home. Almost as

much as everyone loved the dogs he sent there to keep them company twice a week. There was a lot to be said for animal-assisted intervention, and more benefits still to discover. Her championing him in every aspect of his life was something he could never be thankful enough for. And she was so good at distracting the twins when he held his online evening seminars, too.

There were many people he'd inspired to set up similar canine assistance companies all over the country. Especially since he'd started sharing the fact that his research—soon to be shared fully, in the paper he was writing—showed the potential for dogs to detect cancer in humans.

Jetson had already perfected the ability to detect impending migraines and low blood sugar in people and signal them to AJ. But they were still developing the disease detection training programme. More volunteers wanted to be involved all the time—which was the reason he was so damn busy now.

He hovered in the doorway and feigned a sigh that implied more concern about his sister's impending departure than he wanted to show. 'What will I do without you living here with us, Belle?'

'You'll be just fine.' She smiled warmly at him. 'It's been long enough, Austin. You're doing OK now. Ebby would be proud of you.'

A lump wedged in his throat. Sometimes he pictured Ebby, looking down on himself and the kids. Her tight, springy curls had used to bounce in a certain way when she shook her head in loving disapproval, and they'd be bouncing all the time now, if she saw the way he did things sometimes.

Over five years without her now. Over five years since Josiah and Ruby were born.

It *was* easier to smile these days, though. The days when he'd hardly been able to get out of bed and put the cornflake box on the table were behind him.

It had felt right at the time, selling their London place and buying the family home in Brookborough from Mum and Dad after they'd gone to live abroad for his mum's health. Ebby's life insurance, plus the money from the London house, had meant he didn't have to work for a while, and he'd been able to concentrate on making sure the twins were OK, while living in the place where people knew him best. Belle had done more than enough, too, moving in here with him, making herself a saint as well as a live-in nanny.

But now her engagement ring from Bryce sparkled like a diamond-encrusted ice cube on her finger. They'd all miss her when she moved to Leeds. He'd been thinking of selling this house, too. Getting something smaller he could manage on his own, as well as dealing with the mountain of work he kept piling on himself.

'Why are you still standing there? Go!' Belle told him, as she rooted in the freezer and tossed choc ices to Ruby and Josiah.

They clawed at the wrappers like ravenous birds, despite the stew he'd just served them.

Belle called out behind him. 'Give Lucie my love, and tell her I want a date with her of my own soon!'

'It's not a date,' he said, with one hand on the door. 'She's just back visiting May. This is my attempt at being civil.'

As if Lucie would want a date with him. This was the girl who'd left for America without even saying goodbye to him, before blocking him from any contact with her. It had been as if, after being his friend all those years, she'd suddenly wanted to erase him altogether from her world.

It had taken him months, maybe *years* to get over that, seeing as he'd been tethered to her since childhood. He never had understood what he'd done to make her push him away like that.

Austin took the familiar road past the green and its old stocks, where people had used to throw rotten fruit at miscreants. They'd been the miscreants back then—him and Lucie.

She'd been so much his sidekick for all those years that he'd never been able to get up the courage to put everything on the line and tell her how he really felt about her.

It was probably a good thing, though. Clearly she'd never carried the same torch for him.

After she'd left, she'd still been everywhere he looked in this town. He hadn't been able to leave for university fast enough.

He knew practically nothing about her now, except that she'd won a bravery award for saving some children from a school after an earthquake in Nepal. Everyone here had talked about that for months. Why was she back in Brookborough now?

Earlier, when he'd realised it was her in that stream, he'd almost dropped her in shock. Even when she was angry, she was mesmerising. Once she'd been a lost little girl with an American accent. He'd often found her on the steps of Gramma May's house. She'd used to cry a lot. But then she'd grown up—fast.

There had been something indefinable about her that he'd never been able to pinpoint. A kind of inner fire…a defiance that had him itching to be around her, to hear her next plan or ambition. He'd never been able to keep up.

Then she'd left to study medicine in America without even telling him. He'd had to hear it from Gramma May. And Lucie had blocked him…ceased to need him. All on her terms.

Love. *Hate*. Love. *Hate*.

He'd felt both for her—equally fiercely. Which was why he was here tonight. Maybe he'd finally get some answers…

A familiar shadow drifted towards the door behind the glass. Gramma May answered the buzzer, nodded at him knowingly. 'She's upstairs. How are you doing, pet?'

'You know…'

He could tell his indifferent shrug didn't fool her. His neck prickled hot under his scarf as he looked over May's shoulder to the staircase.

'And how are Josiah and Ruby…?'

Austin barely heard her. Lucie had appeared from her old room on the landing. She glided down the staircase, finding his eyes from under a blunt ragdoll fringe. Her brown eyes were unreadable, but the hallway slipped away. This was definitely not the drenched unfortunate he'd pulled from the stream earlier. This was a grown-up Lucie. Still a force to be reckoned with, a beautiful tornado as always, sending him spinning.

His throat felt scratchy. 'You look nice.' He rubbed his neck as Gramma May spun around.

'Oh, you do. Where are you going on your date?'

'It's not a date,' they both chorused.

Lucie rolled her eyes at him, just like she used to. He half laughed at their secret code for *adults know nothing*. It lifted the tension a little.

'Well, you kids have fun now.'

May suppressed a smile. She had the same look on her face he'd just seen on Belle's—as if they were both plotting something. They knew he and Lucie had only ever been friends. But they also suspected he'd always had a crush on her—and knew that he hadn't dated anyone since Ebby died.

'Well, where are you taking me?'

Lucie slipped on a pair of flats as May closed the living room door behind her. The TV flickered through the glass door. They'd used to watch cartoons and make the cat climb homemade ladders made from cardboard boxes in there…and later he'd almost kissed her, but had chickened out. Again.

'The Old Ram Inn,' he responded.

Although she was a little overdressed for the sandstone corner pub. They'd used to meet there every Friday with the gang. Maybe he should've gone to more effort and booked the Thai place on the edge of town. But he'd got back late from his last appointment in Pickering.

'Ooh! The Old Ram Inn. Do they still have that steak and ale pie with those lovely big fat chips?'

'Of course.' He grinned. She looked like a kid again, asking that.

'And the old red carpet that looks like something from an eighties casino?'

'The one and only,' he confirmed.

Lucie nodded, as if checking off something from a list she might've made on the plane here from... Nepal?

'Good, I've missed it. Lead the way.'

He watched Lucie drumming her nails against the salt shaker while they waited for their dinner. The pub was as busy as ever. But despite the background noise of clanging cutlery and laughter, an uncomfortable tension was drifting up between them.

'So...' Austin started, searching his brain.

Lucie tossed her shiny hair over her shoulder and fiddled with the collar on her blazer. 'So...' she echoed, letting her gaze wander, as if she was looking for an escape route already.

'You made the front page of the local paper. Your heroic rescue and award. Everyone was talking about it. I would have congratulated you myself if you hadn't blocked me from every single angle. There was no way for me to contact you.'

Lucie bristled.

His words had come out before he'd had time to curb them, but she must have seen them coming.

Their pies arrived. Lucie stared at the steaming plate of steak and ale as a bowl of chips was placed between them. The waitress eyed them with interest as she poured the gravy. *Everyone* here was looking at them. To those who didn't know Lucie it must *look* as if he was on a date.

AJ squared his shoulders. Lucie jabbed her fork into a chip and twisted it.

'We're not going to talk about all that, are we?' she said finally, meeting his eyes.

The warning in her tone riled him up. 'Why did you block me, Lucie?'

She glared. 'I didn't think you'd even notice.'

'What? Why would you say that? You treated me like I tried to strangle you in the street or something! What did I do that was so wrong?'

Lucie huffed through her nose. 'It doesn't matter now, AJ. It was years ago. Is that why you brought me here? To dredge up the past?'

Austin sucked air through his nostrils till the vinegar on his chips burned his throat. Old Nigel—the Saturday market fruit and veg guy—was staring at them from the bar. Something about sitting opposite Lucie had him acting like a teenager again. He made an effort to calm down.

'We spent *all* our time together,' he hissed under his breath. 'Then you just…left. Without a word, Lucie. It just doesn't add up.'

'Why don't you ask Claire Bainbridge?'

Austin racked his brains, drawing a blank. What did Belle's friend Claire have to do with anything? 'I literally have *no* idea what you—'

'I told you…it doesn't matter now, does it?' she clipped, but the fire behind her eyes was raging.

For the life of him he couldn't imagine what she meant.

'Let's talk about you, *Austin Johnstone*. I hear you're married now, living in London. I guess you're here visiting your parents. How are they?'

Now it was his turn to clam up. Didn't she know? Hadn't Gramma May told her?

The way she was looking between him and her dinner told him that, no, she knew nothing.

'My wife passed away,' he said quietly. 'It's just me and the twins now. We moved back here from London a few years ago. I bought Mum and Dad's house when they moved to the Italian coast for Mum's asthma.'

Lucie's eyes grew round. She pushed her plate aside and reached across the table, almost sending the chips to the carpet, clasping his hands tightly. Her eyes flooded with horror and grief. It swept him up till he felt like a surfer trying to ride a tsunami.

'AJ... I'm so very sorry...poor Claire."

Claire?

He pulled his hands back. 'What is it with you and Claire? I wasn't married to Claire! Her name was Ebony—Ebby. We called her Ebby.'

Lucie's face was ghost-white. 'Ebby...?'

Austin's chest felt too small for his heavy heartbeat. 'Did May tell you nothing?'

'I told her not to,' she said in a small voice, tearing at a napkin. 'I wanted a clean break from Yorkshire, else I would have been too homesick. I wanted to focus on my studies. All I knew was that you practised psychiatry and had a wife and children...' She trailed off. 'But that's beside the point. I'm *so* sorry for your loss, AJ.'

His head reeled as she frowned in consternation, as if something else was just sinking in. 'Did you say you bought your parents' house?'

CHAPTER FOUR

LUCIE BATTLED WITH surging emotions that may have included something as annoying as envy as AJ described his son and daughter. Josiah was the loud one, the cheeky one, who always had something to say. Ruby was the quiet, thoughtful one. She cared deeply, beyond her five and a bit years, about everything and everyone. She adored her outspoken brother.

AJ was a besotted father. That much was apparent.

It wasn't hard to imagine what they looked like. They were probably beautiful. Maybe they had blue eyes and blond hair, like he'd used to have before he got this hot and toned and manly. Or maybe they looked like Ebby. Whoever Ebby was.

This was just...unreal. All this time she'd assumed he'd married Claire Bainbridge! Maybe that *was* a bit of a ridiculous assumption, now that she thought about it—they were only eighteen when she'd left—but her jealous imagination had filled in all the blanks while she'd blocked him, in case her stupid, desolate heart was forced to take another hit. Of course she wasn't about to admit how she'd came to make that assumption in the first place—sneaking in, eavesdropping, her heart thrumming with a puppy dog love he would never return... But here he was a widower, a single father.

Poor AJ.

'How did she die, if you don't mind me asking?' she dared.

The waitress took away their half-eaten pies.

It must've been something bad, and sudden.

She'd left young twins behind.

'She was out with friends,' he said finally. 'Her first night out since the babies were born. But she wanted to come home early—you know how new mothers are.'

Lucie murmured in sympathy. Though how would she know? The concept of motherhood, of an actual home, a family who needed and wanted her around, was alien to her. She'd lived out of a suitcase for years and loved it.

Most of the time.

'When she didn't come home, hours after she was meant to, I got worried, drove around looking for her. Then the police called. She hadn't even made it back to her car.'

He paused, twirled his pint glass between them, eyed her over it.

'The two lads who hit her in their Land Rover had been drinking for thirteen hours straight. She died on the way to the hospital.'

Lucie's hands flew over her mouth. What the hell could she say to that, except reiterate how deeply sorry she was? Her apologies for his loss sounded hollow to her own ears. She'd never even met the woman, but she must have been something truly special if AJ had married her.

He told her some more about how he'd come back home, bought the family house after his parents had moved to Italy. This was the best place to bring up the twins, he said.

God, just the thought of losing a life partner...someone you'd built a new world with, made *children* with...how was he still standing?

Losing her parents had been a life-altering tragedy, but she'd been nine, almost too young for it to sink in at the time. It was the consequences she'd felt most, as the years had crept on without them. A sense of incompletion and inadequacy around those who *hadn't* been abandoned and sent away. A need to do things for herself, first and foremost, because people left, or died, and nothing lasted for ever.

'So, how long are you in town for?'

AJ took another swig of his drink. Obviously he wanted to change the subject—and who could blame him?

The wobble in her voice when she spoke made his eyebrows rise. 'I…um…took the locum position at the Brookborough Surgery. It's a two-month contract. I thought I'd take a break from Medicine Relief Operatives for a while…'

She tailed off. He was leaning closer now over the table, and his eyes were all-seeing. The boy who'd asked her so many times why she was crying had never pushed her. Instead he'd made her laugh, made her feel she hadn't quite lost *everything*.

'I have these dreams sometimes. Since the earthquake, you know? I watched a good friend die right in front of me. Yes, they gave me a medal for getting those children out, but I was the one who led Jorge into that school in the first place…'

'You led him in?'

'The earthquake happened after we'd stepped inside.'

She took a sip of wine. The sour taste scored her throat, while sympathy shone in his eyes. They had nothing in common—not where death was concerned. He had no idea how much she blamed herself for Jorge. First her Grampa Bert, then Jorge…

'Yes. Anyway, MRO offered me some time off between projects. Auntie Lina has moved to a condo in Miami, which isn't exactly peaceful, and I thought Gramma May could do with the company here. She's come out to America a couple of times to see me, in between projects, but it just seemed like a good time for me to come back to Brookborough.'

She crossed her legs uncomfortably. What on earth was making her tell AJ all this about herself?

The fact that you loved him once. And part of you always wished you were Claire…or, as it turns out, Ebby.

'So, you're still recuperating from trauma to some extent,' he said, thoughtfully.

His look shot her back to the time he'd homed in on her

mouth in Gramma May's living room, when she'd been heavy with grief over Grampa Bert's passing. That one time when she'd seriously thought he might be about to kiss her of his own volition then didn't.

'I suppose we'll be seeing each other around,' he continued. The pub chatter fell away as he searched her eyes.

No matter what had passed between them, what he'd endured without her knowing, there was something about him she'd never been able to forget. His absolute openness and honesty…his heart of gold. Whenever AJ looked at you, you felt like the only person in his universe.

It was exactly why the thing with Claire Bainbridge had shocked her so much. It had been just so *unlike* him to go for someone like her. Claire hadn't even been his type.

'You know what helped me with my dreams after Ebby died?' he said now.

She cocked her head. He'd had bad dreams, too? Did he still have them? It would feel invasive, asking him any more questions now—like how they'd met, how he'd proposed, how he was coping alone, being a single dad with twins. Instead, she asked, 'What?'

'The dogs,' he answered. 'Remember Jamesy Abbot? The kid with ADD who used to jump out of the window in French class when Mrs De Ville wasn't looking and walk back in through the front door?'

She laughed at the memory. 'Our poor teacher…she was always so confused.'

'Right! Well, he asked me to look after his Golden Retriever, Star Lord, a couple of years after Ebby died. His therapy dog. He was helping him with his focus issues, helping him stick to a job after years of getting regularly fired…'

'Star Lord?' She couldn't suppress a chuckle.

AJ barely noticed.

'I didn't want to do it. I had enough on my plate. But the sitter cancelled on him. Anyway, long story short, that dog pulled me out of the hole I was in. Suddenly I was sleeping through the night again. Walking him three times a day forced me to start interacting with people too—dogs will make you do that. It took my mind off my grief a little. Ruby and Josiah loved him too. By the time Jamesy came back I was already looking up how to incorporate canine assistance into my own work. Then came Jetson. He took to his mission as if he knew his purpose from the start. We soon figured out how to help him communicate his findings: low blood sugar, narcolepsy, fear and stress... Dogs can pick up on tiny changes in the human body, from small shifts in our hormones to volatile organic compounds released by cancer cells. That one we're still working on. It's so varied, you know?'

Lucie realised she'd been watching his mouth throughout his whole speech, absorbing not just his words, but his energy. The same energy that had pulled *her* out of a hole, once.

She was so busy admiring him, and how nice he looked with a beard, that she missed his next words. 'Sorry, what?'

'I said, have *you* considered canine assistance? It might help you.'

'I'm not one of your patients, AJ.'

Ugh. Telling him she had nightmares had been a bad move. It wasn't as if they were even that bad. People had far bigger problems. People *she* should be out there with...helping.

'I started Thera Pups to help detect all kinds of things, as well as to help people cope.'

'I'm coping just fine,' she said stiffly.

He cocked an eyebrow. She felt bad.

'So, are many people invested in this?'

Lucie listened in awe as AJ told her as humbly as he could how his company was already hugely successful and sparking others into the same line of work. As well as running seminars and organising conferences on the benefits of canine therapy, he had a growing number of volunteers who took dogs into nursing homes, special needs schools, hospitals…wherever they were needed.

'I've seen real healing come about because of them. Sometimes we can even arrange live-in dogs.'

'That's great,' she said, rubbing at her neck.

How the heck did a single dad with twins find time to do all of this? Was he Superman?

'But I don't need a dog—live-in or otherwise.'

AJ did not look convinced.

'I'm totally fine, really,' she pressed, flattening her palms to the table. Her skin felt clammy under his scrutiny. 'It's just the odd bad dream.'

'Well, if you change your mind, you know where I am.'

'Yes, I do,' she said, looking around for the waitress.

She offered to pay when the bill came, but AJ waved her off, swiping his card before she had time to argue.

Soon, the night air breezed around them as they walked along the silent, dark street towards the village green. AJ stopped and dropped to the wooden bench by the old stocks.

The heat rose up to her collar as he patted the seat beside him.

'Why did you think I was married to Claire?' he asked quietly, turning his face to the sky.

She stared, transfixed by his ruggedly handsome face. So different. But the familiarity of her friend from all those years ago was still there, still having the same effect on her heart.

'I guess I saw you around together,' she lied, embarrassed now. She'd been such an idiot to assume. 'I put the pieces together.'

'The wrong pieces.'

'Well, I know that now.'

AJ draped a lazy arm along the back of the bench. 'She's Belle's friend. I mean, I guess she had a crush on me a long time ago, but that's it.' He sniffed, kicked at a stone on the ground. 'I was kind of messed up, you know? When you left for America and then blocked me.'

Lucie's throat constricted. Her heart thundered in her chest. She'd messed up—abandoned him without even thinking of his wellbeing. He'd missed her, his friend, and she'd snatched her friendship away from him just because she wasn't able to have *more*. So selfish of her.

She stood quickly, shame filling her heart. What if it was showing in her eyes—the fact that she had always wanted more than his friendship? She glanced away, just in case.

'You were meant to meet Ebby, have your twins, start your business—'

'I know,' he cut in, clearing his throat, standing up. 'Obviously I know that.'

'And *I* was meant to go back to Colorado to qualify as a doctor, and then take this job with the Medicine Relief Operatives. I've never stayed in one place very long. I don't really enjoy that...'

'I know.'

They were standing inches apart under the streetlight. AJ's gaze rose from the grass up to her eyes, and she wondered if they were thinking the same thing now: *What if...? What if...? What if...?*

Every nerve in her body was shot to pieces. A compelling need came over her to lie down and close her eyes and process all this. Alone. Her emotions were piling up on top of one another, threatening to spill over.

'Well, this has been great... Thank you for inviting me, Austin,' she managed.

'So, *now* I'm Austin?' A muscle flickered in his cheek.

Lucie hugged herself. 'I'll see you around, I guess?'

'I guess you will,' she heard him mumble as she turned. 'Good that we've cleared things up.'

'Yup, absolutely. Very good.'

Cringing, she hurried on. Maybe it was hearing about Ebby,

the nostalgia of the Old Ram Inn, and the village green, seeing those lips and eyes up close again, all getting to her all at once, but if she didn't move quickly—very quickly—she might turn back and kiss him.

CHAPTER FIVE

IT WAS THE weekend before Austin saw Lucie again. He knew she'd been busy working, but with her specialism in mental health he'd half expected to bump into her on his rounds at the care home. The GP practice was just steps from the hospital, too. But so far he'd not seen as much as her shadow.

Until now.

Here she was right now, studying the fresh eggs on a market stall as if they might hold the secrets of the universe.

The twins were picking out apples from the fruit stall next to him. He knew the market was busy enough that he could slip away quickly without her seeing him if he hurried them on, but...

Nope. Too late.

'Austin! Ruby, Josiah... What a day, huh? Blue sky that matches your eyes and your cooking lesson to look forward to later—am I right?'

Old Nigel, the trader behind the fruit and veg stall, had the loudest voice known to man. Lucie's head turned in their direction.

'Hi...' she said to him, putting the box of eggs down.

Adrenaline buzzed through his belly as she crossed to him, glancing at the twins. Nigel was entertaining them with an apple juggling act. Jetson was lying under the stall, keeping guard as usual, awaiting his next command.

'Hi,' he replied. 'Long time, no see.'

'Long time…' She shifted her basket, laden with daffodils and tulips. Her gaze was directed to the twins.

'Daddy! Dad, look at Ruby!'

Austin spun around. Ruby was attempting to juggle like Nigel. When two apples plonked to the floor, he ran to try and catch one, but Jetson caught it instead. When he stood up he bumped straight into Lucie, who'd bent to grab the other one.

'Sorry,' they said at the same time, clutching their foreheads, laughing.

There she was—his Lucie. As if she'd never left.

It was obvious why he'd wanted to run just now. Just sharing the same postcode with her had him wondering things, questioning things. Feeling guilty, actually. What would people say if they knew how quickly all those unrequited feelings for Lucie had raced back in? He'd fallen for her long before he'd ever met Ebby…

'Here.' She broke his gaze, handed him the other apple, and a moment passed where he didn't quite know what to do or say.

'I recognise you from the pub the other night,' Nigel said, shaking Lucie's hand. 'Good of you to take this one on a date. It's been a while, hey, old son?'

Austin huffed a laugh he didn't mean, avoiding Lucie's eyes. He threw fruit in a bag while they all chatted, aware of Lucie's position, how her red blouse matched her lipstick almost exactly, how hot she looked in her tight jeans.

How she kept throwing glances his way.

When a new person showed up in the village, it was all anyone talked about. Not everyone knew Lucie from before. Nigel didn't. Their history was written in their body language, though. It must be. He wasn't the same around her…he just couldn't be. Even if they'd never been more than friends, he couldn't help wondering if it was obvious how much he'd been thinking about her this past week.

Lucie carried an air of importance. She was someone people respected and admired. She'd left here to make her mark.

But there was something burdened about her now—a heaviness clear to him, yet indistinct. No wonder, after what she'd seen. Her eyes looked tired as she talked with Nigel. Did she have those nightmares she'd mentioned often? Did she wake up lost and frightened, wondering if she'd ever feel normal again, like *he'd* used to…?

Nigel was called away to weigh some bananas and Ruby appeared at his side. 'Who's this, Daddy?'

A loaded question, if ever there was one.

Lucie bent down to her height and held out her hand. 'I'm Lucie. I'm an old friend of your daddy's.' She smiled warmly. 'And you must be Ruby?'

'Yes, and that's my brother Josiah.' Ruby jabbed a finger towards Josiah, who was now trying and failing to juggle apples.

'He always has to be involved in everything,' Austin explained as his mind churned with how strange it was that Lucie Henderson was here, petting his dog, talking to Ruby, who was now telling Lucie all about her plans to help him make an apple pie later, or maybe apple crumble.

'Gramma May makes the best apple crumble,' Lucie responded. 'Remember that, AJ… Austin?'

He nodded, raising an eyebrow. *Austin.*

It was almost as if her using his actual name was a new means for her to put some distance between them. Old versus new. Best friends versus almost-strangers.

Fine by him. Things *were* different now. He was a single dad. Busy. So damn busy. His schedule was rammed…and she was not here to stay.

'You know Gramma May?' Ruby frowned, trying to put the pieces together.

Austin found himself explaining the relationship between Lucie and May, and how Lucie had been away, saving lives overseas.

'*Trying* to save lives,' Lucie reminded him quietly.

Frowning, he struggled to compute the self-deprecation in

her tone. A thousand lives must have been saved by her and her team over the years. The horrors she must have seen sent him cold. Since the other night he'd been thinking far too much about Lucie, and everything he'd felt compelled to let pour out of his mouth about Ebby.

It had always been pretty easy to share things with Lucie. Maybe that was why he'd told her how Ebby had died, in detail. She'd wriggled so far under his skin when he was younger that her absence had almost destroyed him...like getting a vital organ sucked out of him.

From time to time over the years he'd wondered if maybe he'd plucked up the courage and actually told her how he'd really felt about her back then, she wouldn't have moved to America... But trust her to show up now, like an upgrade, a new version of the girl who'd disappeared from his life without a backward glance.

She still had that voice that skittered along his nerve-endings, those ripe berry lips and a dusting of freckles across her nose that he hoped no make-up would ever hide. She'd had a pixie haircut when she'd left. Now her hair was long and sleek, like liquid silk. He could picture it tousled upon a pillow...

Why was he thinking about her in bed?

'Do you want to come and make apple pie with us later?' Ruby asked, and the question was loaded with hope.

What?

'Can she, Daddy? Gramma May could come too.'

Austin stared at his daughter, feeling Lucie's eyes on him. Ruby knew most people in the village. And as Lucie had cut him off, she probably had no idea what a rock May had been for them all after Ebby died.

'I'm sure Lucie and Gramma May are both very busy, sweetie. It's a Saturday,' he told Ruby diplomatically.

But then the old, familiar, unfortunate urge to make Lucie happy forced the next words from his mouth.

'Unless...unless you do find yourself at a loose end later,

Lucie? Belle will be there at some point, after her shift at Lavender Springs. I know she'd love to see you. Both of you.'

'May has plans,' Lucie replied, fiddling with the tulips in her basket. 'She has more of a social life than me, you know. I've been away too long.'

'Then come by yourself. We usually start around four p.m.,' he said, cursing the kid inside him, still trying to comfort a wounded bird.

Why was he inviting her? Let alone to something he'd been doing privately in his kitchen with his kids and his sister for the years since Ebby had passed. Cooking was a kind of reset for them all…a chance to bond and talk. Just them. He'd never asked anyone to join them before.

'I guess I'll come for a bit, then,' Lucie said slowly. 'Thanks for the invite, Ruby.'

With plans made for her to call round later, Austin gathered the twins and did his best to resume what was usually the best if the most hectic time of the week. Time away from clients and meetings and seminars to spend with the twins.

But Lucie played in his head the whole time, like a song.

The past should be water under the bridge now they were grown adults. They *needed* to be OK if they were going to be bumping into each other like this, at least till she left Brookborough to work abroad again.

Lucie would never stay in one place. She loved her job too much for that. And he definitely wouldn't ever let her get close enough for another departure to faze him. But…

But what? What was the big deal in her coming over to help make a pie? It wasn't like it was a date—just like the last time hadn't been a date. Why would he want a date with Lucie, anyway?

What the hell are you doing…literally inviting the first girl to break your heart back into your life?

CHAPTER SIX

'Now, *THAT* IS how you roll pastry—love your work, Ruby-Roo!'

Lucie was struck by the love in this kitchen. The way AJ interacted with his kids was beyond cute. He was patient, encouraging, he made everything fun...and he looked damn fine in an apron.

Crayon and pencil drawings covered the whole fridge, stuck on with alphabet magnets. One was of a scruffy out-of-proportion dog, signed by Ruby. She remembered AJ's drawings had been stuck up there once.

AJ was barefoot, in jeans and a white T-shirt with *Jetson's Human* written on it, under a photo of the dog. He looked like Father of the Year in an apron, complete with floury handprints all over the front. She'd always liked him barefoot...

A couple of hours into their apple pie making session, her heart still vaulted to her throat every time he looked at her. This was weird—like living in two different worlds. The past and the present would not align in her mind.

'Taste this,' AJ said now, holding out a spoon to her over the counter.

His floury fingers clasped hers as she put them around the spoon. His eyes on her lips made the apple mixture taste strange, and the children's chatter blur into white noise. She was back by the church, the night she'd turned fourteen, pressing her finger to his in a blood oath that they'd spend every birthday together for ever. That was after Auntie Lina had forgotten her birthday.

Drawing her eyes away, she busied her hands with rolling out more pastry. They were making several pies today, with the intention of delivering some of them to the care home. At least AJ was.

She caught him sneaking glances at her. Was this weird for him too?

Ebby was here. She could hardly ignore the fact that Ebby was here, even if she'd never lived here. She was in most of the photos on the wall in the hall. The first thing Lucie had seen when she'd walked in. All curly raven hair and smiling eyes, slender arms wrapped around AJ. He'd caught her looking at the pictures for far too long. But she'd never pictured him with anyone other than herself and Claire Bainbridge.

What he must have gone through, losing Ebby...

'So, tell me more about the dogs,' she said to him, when the pies were browning nicely in the oven and the twins had been instructed to go and wash their hands.

AJ pulled out a chair at the dining table, put a cup of tea down in front of her.

'You still take extra milk, right?' he said. 'You used to like it like that—more milk than tea.'

'Still do,' she said, unable to hide her smile.

AJ slid into the chair opposite hers, sending a cloud of flour whirling around them.

'The dogs...' he said. 'Yes, I don't know what I would've done if I hadn't set up Thera Pups.'

Jetson padded out from under the table and headed for the stairs. He was responding to a playful squeal from the upstairs bathroom.

'Since the news about the disease detection programme we're developing went out, it's been full on.'

'Does it really work?' she asked, intrigued. 'I mean, can they really do that?'

'If we train them properly. I'm working on a research paper about modifying these techniques all the time, so we can pass them on. We still don't know exactly which chemical compounds for different types of cancers the dogs are sensing, for example. We can only narrow it down in time.'

'It's incredible,' she told him, feeling pride flushing through to her face as he nodded humbly, as if it wasn't even that big a deal.

'We have a long way to go, still. Did you think any more about taking on a dog while you're here, by the way?'

'Not really,' she admitted, even as her heart skittered.

Had he been serious before, about assigning her a therapy dog? Did he think she was broken because of the accident with Jorge and the dreams? Surely she didn't come off that way? Then again, he *knew* her.

But other people around here knew her, too. They cared.

What was it Gramma May had said this morning, when Lucie had joked about how nice it was to be around people who'd known her for years and liked her anyway?

'It is nice, isn't it? You can't build a community like Brook-borough around you if you always have one foot out through the door.'

Gramma had a point. Lucie had missed all this a lot over the years, whenever she'd allowed herself to really think about it.

'And how are the dreams now you've been back here a while? Any less intense?'

AJ's blue-grey eyes seemed to scan her very soul, in a hundred shades of empathy. She found herself pressing her thumb to her forefinger, over the place she'd once bled into his bloodstream.

'They don't happen that often any more,' she lied.

He frowned, pressed a hand to hers, and it was hard to know whether to be touched by his kindness or offended that he clearly still thought she needed canine therapy. Even so, his concern for her forced a new road through the blocks around her heart. She hadn't let anyone in for a long time. It was surface level interactions for the most part when it came to talking about the things that really tore at her. It was better that way, for someone like her who was always on the move.

Don't go deep, don't get attached.

'What are the dreams like?' he asked quietly. 'When you do have them, I mean.'

A long moment passed between them in silence.

'Awful,' she admitted eventually, suddenly so moved by his concern and the thought of her terrible dreams that she had to blink back the moisture from her eyes.

He wouldn't *want* her to describe them even if she could.

'I know what it's like, Lucie. There were moments after Ebby died when I just—'

The key turned in the front door, cutting him off. A chorus of 'Auntie Belle!' erupted from upstairs, followed by the clattering of little footsteps.

AJ sprang from his seat. He flipped the kettle back to boil, and Lucie swiped at her face as Belle entered the kitchen.

'Lucie, hi!'

Belle hugged her, and she returned the embrace, thankful for the interruption. That had got tense so fast. How did AJ still manage to move her and open her up like a tin can? She always had get lost in his eyes. And he'd been about to confide in her something about Ebby. What?

Maybe she didn't want to know.

'It's so nice to see you! How are you?'

Belle looked the same, blonde hair swinging round her shoulders, blue-eyed and smiley, with the trademark Johnstone cheekbones Lucie would have killed for. His mum Pamela had them too. She'd loved his mum, growing up. She'd loved all of them.

'I'm great,' Lucie lied on autopilot.

AJ raised his eyebrows.

'Belle was at Lavender Springs today,' he explained next,

sticking a teabag into a cup for his sister. 'She's Chief Nursing Officer there. She lets me know which patients might appreciate some time with the dogs.'

'Speaking of which,' Belle said, sinking into a chair, kicking off her shoes. 'Jack Granger had a bad day again today. He's had a stroke and now he can't use his left arm. He's a little quiet. I've a feeling his confidence has taken a knock... you can see it in his eyes...'

Lucie listened as Belle talked about the people in the care home while simultaneously fussing over the kids. They clearly worked well as a unit. But AJ was going to be here alone with the twins when Belle moved out and got married. That must be a weight on his mind. Also...what had he been about to tell her about Ebby?

Maybe she *did* want to know.

She was thinking about him far too much. Maybe it had been a mistake to come here today. If she couldn't accept even now that friendship was all he could offer her, why put her heart on the line again like this?

'What do you think?'

'Huh?'

Belle was looking at her, head cocked, biting into a slice of uncooked apple.

'I was saying, if you're free tomorrow, you should help Austin bring some pies over to the care home and check out our boy Jetson in action. I've discovered Jack had a German Shepherd once, who used to lie under his desk at work and fart all the time. I think he'd get a kick out of Jetson. Mind you, he doesn't say much. He always goes into these monologues, then shuts down, like he's worried he's taking up too much space. Apparently he lost his...'

She trailed off and Lucie drew a sharp breath. Belle had been going to say *wife*. But she had stopped herself.

The kids were still laughing at the word 'fart', tittering behind their hands. At the mention of his name Jetson had padded back into the room and promptly rested his big soft head on AJ's knee, gazing at him beguilingly. AJ stared into space.

Lucie bit hard on her cheek. 'I promised May I would take some things to the charity shop for her tomorrow,' she said.

'That won't take you all day, will it?' Belle challenged.

'Don't pressure her, Belle, she didn't come home for this,' AJ said when she didn't reply.

Josiah wandered in from the lounge, waving a book, saying something about it being time to read to Jetson, and Belle went with him. Soon she and AJ were alone again, breathing in apple fumes in silence.

'They love reading to that dog,' he said to her eventually. 'It helps them, actually. They're advanced for their age.'

Then he shook his head, lowered his voice.

'Sorry about Belle. She's just really proud of the programme and everything Thera Pups does at the care home, you know. Wants to show everyone. You really don't have to go—'

'What were you going to tell me before?' she cut in, surprised at how badly she wanted to know. 'You said there were moments after Ebby died...'

'Oh.' AJ leaned against the counter. He pushed his hair back from his forehead, and the fine lines of time and grief etched on his skin made her want to go to him even before he spoke.

'I don't know... I was caught up in the moment. I shouldn't be telling you things about...all that.'

Her stomach dropped. 'Why not?'

AJ shrugged and turned away, rooting in the fridge for something. He shut the fridge without retrieving anything at all, and sighed again, yanking off the apron.

'Because it's not your problem.'

Ugh. Friends were supposed to confide in each other. But then, she'd cut him off for the sake of her own stupid lovesick heart, hadn't she?

'What is my problem?' she ventured.

Surely enough water had sloshed under the bridge now for

her to be his friend while she was here? It wasn't as if she'd be around for long.

'I don't want to bring you down, Lucie. You still have healing of your own to do, rather than worrying about me. It's been five whole years since Ebby died. I'm totally fine.'

She crossed to him, magnetised by his pain, and put her hand in his. He paused on the tiled floor, still holding the apron. Sparks shot right up the length of her arm.

'I don't think you can ever be totally fine, AJ,' she whispered, despite her galloping heart. 'You can start feeling better, sure...in time...but I hope you don't think it's not OK to... well, to not be OK.'

'I'm OK.'

'This is *me* you're talking to.'

It came out harsher than she'd meant it to. He stared at her for a moment, then at her hand in his, squeezing it before letting go. The lack of warmth left her cold.

'Look at us.'

He huffed a laugh she could tell he didn't mean, before draping the apron on a hook by the door and answering a call from the twins for a glass of milk.

She took a seat at the table again, defeated. *Us.* There was no 'us'. There never had been, really—not in the way she'd wanted. He probably had a hundred people to talk to in this community, so why should he want to talk to her all of a sudden? They were so far beyond being an 'us' now, it wasn't even funny—but whose fault was that? She was the one who'd pushed *him* away all these years.

It hadn't been her intention to get heavy again. It was just so easy to talk to him, and she'd stupidly assumed he felt the same. It was hard to hear about Ebby, but she wanted him to think he could talk to her.

This was so confusing.

By the time she left for Gramma May's house, full of apple pie and stories about therapy dogs, Lucie had decided it was better for both of them if she stayed away from AJ while she was here. All she'd done was complicate things for herself.

They'd be friends, maybe, while she was here. Not *close* friends. More like acquaintances. The kind of acquaintances who nodded on passing but didn't really hang out. The kind whose blood no longer ran in each other's veins.

Only that night, infuriatingly, when the dreams forced her awake in a cold sweat at three a.m., it was AJ's face, and the image of him petting Jetson, with the twins giggling in the background, that she found herself homing in on in order to calm down.

CHAPTER SEVEN

AUSTIN SETTLED ON the edge of the huge leather chair. The carpeted lounge smelled like coffee and air freshener, and in the background a nursing assistant was doing the rounds with a plate of biscuits. Jack Granger, the eighty-nine-year-old stroke victim, was sitting up rigidly in the chair opposite, watching Jetson roll a ball around the floor. Jack refused a biscuit when offered. His long, drawn face and sad, hooded eyes told Austin he was still grieving the loss of his wife as well as the use of his arm.

Belle had mentioned last week, when he'd come into Lavender Springs with the apple pies, that Jack had taken a while to warm up to her, but Austin had hoped that bringing Jetson back again today might scored him bonus points with the man.

No such luck. This was Austin's second visit to Jack, and he'd had barely a peep out of him. He'd hoped Lucie might have taken Belle up on her offer to visit last week too, but she hadn't. He hadn't seen her since, but he'd seen the car she'd hired around.

'How's your arm doing today?' he asked Jack now, before he could dwell on the fact that she wasn't going to go out of her way to be around him—not after all these years. She had better things to do with her time than hang out with a single dad and his dogs.

Jack sighed dejectedly at his question. 'Same as every day. Useless. Can't even tie my own shoes.'

Austin glanced at the old man's feet. 'You're wearing slippers.'

Jack's thin mouth twitched. 'Doesn't mean I wouldn't wear lace-ups if I could. Can you train a dog to tie shoelaces?'

'Not yet...but let me work on that.'

Austin threw the ball for Jetson, who promptly retrieved it and placed it at Jack's feet, panting hopefully. A wistful look crossed his deeply lined face now, almost as if a memory of a better time was playing out in his head...something he didn't want to voice out loud.

They sat in silence for a while. The ball went untouched. Then Austin said, 'I hear you had a German Shepherd once?'

Jack nodded. 'Shadow,' he croaked. 'She went everywhere with me. That was years ago. Before I met my Alice. Never could replace that dog.'

Austin threw the ball for Jetson again. This wasn't about him, but anyone who'd lost his wife had his full sympathy. 'Didn't Alice like dogs?'

'She did. But she didn't want anything to compete for my attention,' Jack replied. 'Later, she said the more she got to know me, the more she wanted to get a dog after all. I never did know quite how to take that.'

Austin couldn't help a chuckle, which Jack seemed to reciprocate behind a weathered hand. To his surprise, when Jetson deposited the ball back at his feet Jack reached for it with his good arm and threw it across the room.

Jetson raced after it, tail wagging, causing one lady in another chair to lift her legs and laugh. Austin stood up to apologise, right as someone tapped him on the shoulder from behind his chair.

'Belle!'

'Hey, little brother, look who I found.'

His sister was all smiles in her pale pink uniform, no doubt impressed by this tiny bit of dog-influenced progress on Jack's part. And there was someone with her.

'Lucie,' he said, blinking back the shock of her sudden appearance.

Lucie was wearing the hell out of a fitted black pencil skirt and a high-necked blouse, and the same blazer she'd worn that night to the Old Ram Inn. Pink lipstick and pink blusher, hair styled and straightened…she was already catching attention in the care home. Maybe they thought she was a celebrity.

Jetson sat before them, waiting to be allowed to greet them, and Austin watched as Lucie patted his head, somewhat awkwardly at first, then with more enthusiasm.

'I didn't know you'd be here with Jack today,' she told him, holding her hand out to Jack, who took it.

Jack looked a little taken aback by her, so immaculately dressed and beautiful. He took off his glasses to study her.

Lucie introduced herself. She was obviously here for an assessment. Jack was registered with the GP practice, of course.

Austin pulled up another chair for her, wishing his heart-rate hadn't skyrocketed through the care home's ceiling. Some warning might have been nice, he thought, as the back of his neck prickled with heat under his shirt collar.

Belle excused herself and hurried back towards Reception.

Lucie cleared her throat, eyeing Austin's lanyard with a small smirk.

Jack looked between them with interest. 'You two know each other?'

'A little,' Lucie admitted.

'I'd wager more than just a little,' Jack said, and smirked.

Austin crossed his arms and Lucie mirrored him, then caught herself and pressed her hands back to her sides.

'What makes you say that?' she asked.

'I can just tell. Your eyes lit up when you saw her,' he said to Austin. 'My arm might not work, but my eyes do.'

'We used to be friends,' Austin said.

Lucie squared her shoulders. He couldn't read her face as she took her seat, but he sensed annoyance radiating from her. He should probably take his leave, let her do her thing, but Jetson had sat obediently at her feet, as if he, too, wanted to know what came next. This was more than Jack had spoken before, ever, which was one good thing, he supposed.

'Right, then…' Austin clapped his hands together and looked around for some other topic of conversation that wouldn't put them both on the spot. He couldn't seem to find one.

His eyes had *not* lit up. Had they?

It was just that his mind had somehow spun him back to that time when she'd appeared from nowhere at the dance when they were ten—just shown up in the school gym under the balloons, the most gorgeous girl he'd ever seen. That was the moment he'd realised he had feelings for a girl.

He'd stood on her toes more than once that night, but he'd bought her a bar of chocolate and she'd pretended not to care. That had been two weeks before they'd kissed on the bridge. He'd known then that she wasn't like the other girls. Lucie had made things wake up inside him. He'd never told her. What if she'd laughed at him? Or wanted nothing more to do with him?

That had been the start of him hiding his feelings from her, keeping their friendship sacred above everything else.

'We knew each other a long time ago,' Lucie said carefully. 'I used to live near here, actually. I've just come back to Brookborough for a while, and I thought I'd see what crazy stuff you're all getting up to at Lavender Springs.'

She went on to explain how her late grandfather had been a resident here, prior to his death, how *he'd* never had any visits from dogs, and how much her family had always loved dogs yet she'd never had one.

Austin felt a flush of pride as she added that she'd been encouraged to read more about canine assistance over the last week or so because of *him*.

She didn't mention her nightmares. Were they still torturing her? Was *that* what had brought her here, finally? The hope that there might be something out there to help aside from some time spent at Gramma May's?

He'd thought a lot about what might be haunting Lucie's dreams—someone close to her had died right in front of her. What had she seen, exactly? The way she dressed… It was almost as if she was trying to be someone else now—someone who hadn't seen all that tragedy.

Soon, it seemed that Jack had clean forgotten Austin was there at all. Somehow Lucie had got him talking more about his German Shepherd, Shadow. He watched her as she listened, assessing his mind, seeing how it worked, what he did and didn't react and respond to. But the whole time Austin found himself trying to decipher what was really going on in *her* mind. He'd used to know her so well and now…whether his eyes lit up around her or not…they were strangers.

He'd pulled away, he supposed. On purpose that time at the house, when she'd asked him about Ebby. Well, it wouldn't exactly be fair to load all his issues on her when she had enough of her own problems, but she'd kept away ever since, and he'd convinced himself she wanted nothing more to do with him.

Maybe he'd scared her off…inviting her to a house filled with photos of Ebby. Lucie had used to view that house as being as much her own as his, and now it was a shrine to a person she'd never even met.

Hang on. As if that was *his* fault.

He prickled, noting how, not for the first time since her return, he was wondering how his life might have played out if he'd told her how he'd felt about her. Would she never have left? Would he not have wound up with Ebby? The thought caused his insides to itch. With just his thoughts alone he was betraying Ebby. The mother of his children.

Jack was asking her why he'd never seen her around before.

'I'm a locum. I'm on a bit of a break from my regular job.'

'Why?' Jack asked.

Lucie paused.

Austin jumped in. 'She'll be back at it soon enough, don't you worry, Jack. Lives on the other side of the world, this one. We can't keep her here. I doubt anyone can.'

Lucie forced a smile, but her eyes narrowed. 'No one ever *tried* to keep me here,' she said coolly.

Austin fiddled with his collar as Jack cocked his head in interest.

Maybe she was right. But even if he *had* told her his real feelings, nothing would have stopped Lucie Henderson from doing what she wanted to do.

Why was he so annoyed with her all over again simply for being *Lucie*? The past was history. It wasn't as if she was trying to insert herself into his life again, only to mess him up a second time. He *knew* she was leaving again—and so did she—and he was totally one hundred percent fine with that. They'd hardly seen each other anyway, since she'd got here.

Yeah, but you've been thinking about her... And just knowing she's around is enough to rock your foundations. That's why you're being snarky.

'Well...' Jack sniffed. 'God bless the work you both do with people like me. Rest of the world might've given up, but...' He winced as he tried to move his arm.

Austin was out of his seat in a flash, arranging a cushion to rest on his lap. Jetson took the chance to lick Jack's hand in moral support, while Lucie tucked a blanket over his knees. Austin's hand caught her fingers across the soft fabric and she pulled her fingers away as if he'd stung her, and tossed the ball for Jetson a little too hard across the floor.

OK. She was clearly annoyed with him for that last comment. He could feel it. He'd have to apologise now.

CHAPTER EIGHT

'WHAT HAPPENED IN THERE?' Lucie faced him the second they were standing in the oak-panelled corridor. Her smile had been convincing enough for Jack—probably—but AJ's words had been pretty loaded back there.

'We can't keep her here. I doubt anyone can.'

It was true, she supposed, but hearing him say it had struck a nerve.

'I don't know why I said that,' he admitted straight away, to his credit. 'I'm sorry for how that came out. I suppose I felt a little put out that I haven't heard from you or seen you since you came to my house last week.'

Lucie sucked in a breath. A woman rolled past in a wheel-chair with her carer and both of them patted Jetson's head. She and AJ forced a smile in their direction.

'Well, I'm sorry for being distant,' she whispered when they'd gone. 'I didn't really know if I should be initiating these…what are they? Meet-ups? You're busy with the twins, and all *this*, and I'm busy at the practice…'

'It's not that, though, is it?' he said.

Her stomach bucked.

'It's weird,' he went on. 'For both of us. Being around each other again. We might as well admit it. I thought the pie-making session would be nice, but…'

'It *was* nice.'

'But it freaked you out…seeing me as a dad, being in that house again.'

Lucie pursed her lips. 'OK, fine. Seeing you as a dad was a little weird. Not *bad*, just…'

'Not what you expected to come home to?' he offered.

Smoothing the seams of her pencil skirt, she avoided his eyes, waiting for him to continue. She had felt strange around him in a house full of Ebby's pictures—especially when her feelings were bubbling up all over again. Feelings for an ex best friend and now widower she could never have. But she wasn't going to admit that part. And, anyway, why should he feel weird around her? Hadn't he got happily married and forgotten all about her?

'I can't just forget that you left without even telling me— without even saying goodbye or discussing that offer from your aunt to go to America.'

He cast his eyes to hers, squared his shoulders. She held her breath.

'What happened?' he asked.

'I was always relying on you, AJ. I had to do something for myself. Things got busy…and you know what it's like when you're eighteen. It's all about yourself at that age.'

Her smile felt brittle, even to herself. Her excuse sounded weak and heartless, but better to keep his mind from jumping on the fact that she'd been deluded back then, thinking he might ask her to stay. Even if he hadn't hooked up with Claire, he'd never have been hers. He'd only ever seen her as a friend.

'I do know what it's like being eighteen,' he said now. 'I spent the year wondering where the hell you were.'

'I'm sorry,' she managed.

She really was. And deeply ashamed to have been such a terrible friend.

'Well, I'm sure you were a great success in America,' he said next. 'And I don't just mean professionally.'

He looked at her askance. Was he was waiting for her to divulge intel on her dating life?

Lucie pulled a face. As if she'd tell him that she'd had just two relationships in her life—both with team members out in the field, neither of which had lasted. Probably because she'd packed her suitcase and said, 'See ya later,' the second they'd hinted that they might want to leave the MRO and 'settle down and have kids some day' with her.

This was getting awkward. He knew something was off because he knew *her*. But it would be even more awkward if she admitted she'd had a giant stinking crush on him once. He might even think she wanted to start something up with him now.

He was a father, for goodness' sake! And *she* had the itchiest feet on earth. Also, no fixed address to speak of. That was hardly the recipe for a stable, doting mother figure, was it? If there was one thing she knew about parenting, it was that she knew nothing at all. How *could* she, having been raised by her grandparents? Stable, devoted, and loving as they'd been, they hadn't been her mum and dad.

They'd barely talked about her parents—as if they'd been afraid it might upset her, and consequently *them*. And as for Aunt Lina—well, there was a woman with even itchier feet than hers. For all her good intentions and generous financial support, Lina had always been more like a busy older sister, who'd invite you to things, then forget she'd ever asked and leave without you.

'I'm not here to drag up the past, AJ. My past here or anywhere else,' she told him measuredly, trying not to bristle as her own maternal impairments and misgivings seemed to rain down upon her head like waste from a space station.

She was probably everything AJ did not need in his life right now. Josiah and Ruby needed stability. Someone they could count on.

'OK, but, I was hoping we could be friends again,' he said in response. 'Start afresh?'

'I'd love it if we could be friends again,' she said, before she could think about it too much.

He took her stuck-out hand and shook it in an exaggerated manner that left her wondering if he remembered the blood oath they'd made. *'You'll always be in my blood, Lucie.'* That was what he'd said.

'So what's your verdict on Jack?' he asked her, changing the subject as he led her to another door along the corridor.

She caught the North Yorkshire Moors and Yorkshire Dales Dark Skies Festival posters along the way, all the framed photos and platitudes that accentuated the caring vibe. It was nice in here. But growing old alone, with no one to visit you or care for you... She shuddered at the thought.

'You can't build a community like Brookborough around you if you always have one foot out through the door.'

Composing herself, she forced this new 'friendship' idea to settle, as if it was a disobedient puppy, bouncing around between them.

'Well, he's still grieving. That will slow his physical healing. But I can see the dog is helping. Like I said, I've been reading about canine assistance...'

'And how it might help your dreams?'

'I wouldn't go that far.'

Of course he knows.

'OK, fine...' She sighed. 'I'd rather have Freddy Kreuger slip into my dreams than the stuff I see sometimes when I close my eyes. I thought maybe if I dipped a toe into your world—' She caught herself, catching his eyes. 'Your world of *dogs*,' she asserted, 'and how they can help with mental health in various capacities, I might at least learn something new while I keep myself busy in this role. You don't mind, do you, if I schedule some of my appointments at the same time as yours? Shadow you sometimes?'

'That depends.'

Here we go.

'On what?'

'Whether you're good with dogs.'

He nudged her. She rubbed her shoulder, stepping away and hesitating before responding. 'I guess I'll find out.'

Why was she feeling so nervous? AJ's gaze held hers, and for a moment she felt he could see right through her, and she through him. Was there something there, between them?

Don't be stupid. It's just wishful thinking...a throwback emotion from your childhood.

She bit her cheek as he offered to come with her to her next patient and bring Jetson along, seeing as he had an hour between appointments. She agreed, of course. Starting again as friends was the only way they could work together, and even though it was slightly uncomfortable, it did feel good to clear the air somewhat.

And maybe there really were a few things to learn from having him around for some of her appointments and vice versa. As long as they kept it strictly work-related, she reminded herself. No more visiting his house or hanging out with his kids—as if they'd want to hang out with her anyway. They'd probably forgotten her already.

She'd have to take a little gift for them next time...

Wait... What? There wasn't going to be a next time!

Lucie's next patient was seventy-seven-year-old Phyllis. She was sitting rather dejectedly in a soft pink high-backed chair when Lucie took a seat, offering her a kind smile. Phyllis was suffering with Parkinson's disease, and as a result often felt anxious and depressed. Her eyes moved quickly to Jetson, however, when AJ and the Labrador padded in after her.

'Who is this?' Phyllis asked.

AJ stuck out his hand. Phyllis's own hand trembled as she

took it, but Lucie didn't miss how her eyes had lit up the second they entered the room.

'I'm Austin, and this is Dr Jetson,' he told her.

Lucie bit back a smile as Phyllis raised a grey eyebrow, seemingly amused. Jetson jumped onto his hind legs and placed his two front paws on the arm of her chair, as if to introduce himself.

'Did you bring my daughter with you?' Phyllis asked the dog with a smile, and then continued to have a sweet one-sided conversation with Jetson, patting his head with a shaky hand. 'You can tell I miss my grandchildren, can't you, boy? Oh, you have such a soft head…like my grandson. Just look at you…'

AJ beamed and Lucie couldn't help but smile. His enthusiasm for helping people through their bond with dogs was palpable, and she felt her heart expand another few inches, just watching him with her patient.

'We're here to talk about how we can help you, Phyllis,' Lucie said softly. 'Dr Johnstone has a special interest in dog-assisted therapy, and he has some ideas on how to incorporate it into your treatment.'

Phyllis nodded, but seemed unsure. 'I don't have time to walk a dog,' she said, as Jetson got back into a sitting position at her feet, panting lightly.

'Oh, don't you worry about that—Dr Johnstone does all the walking,' Lucie told her, and AJ performed a mock salute. Lucie leaned forward, touched Phyllis's arm lightly. 'I was thinking it could be beneficial for all of us to have some kind of collaborative treatment plan…working together with Jetson around here. He could do with some help that doesn't require walking. He really likes being read to.'

She glanced at AJ, who was mirroring her stance, resting his elbows on his knees, looking at her in something like awe or amusement. She'd already told him how Phyllis had used to love reading but was now finding it hard to focus due to her anxiety and her physical ailments. Something about hearing him say how the twins were better at reading thanks to their reading to Jetson had started her thinking. Maybe it would help Phyllis regain some of her focus and get her confidence back, too.

'What kind of things do you like to read, Jetson?' Phyllis asked now, with a slight smirk.

She motioned to AJ to hand her a couple of books from the stack by her head, which he did on command. Within minutes Lucie and AJ were both watching in fascination as Phyllis recited a page from *Moby Dick* to a bright-eyed Jetson, without faltering once.

'Some people think animals can communicate better than humans with people with dementia and Parkinson's,' AJ told her later, when a nurse came in for a quick check on Phyllis's lunch order. 'Animals rely more on body language than verbal communication.'

Lucie nodded. 'I can see that.'

She was beyond thrilled to see Phyllis responding so well to Jetson. The elderly woman was really starting to open up, and they'd both listened intently, taking notes and making suggestions as a team. Strangely, it felt natural working so closely with AJ.

As the session progressed, Phyllis began to relax slowly but surely, so much so that even her hands had less of a tremble—Lucie was sure of it.

It hadn't been planned, but somehow she knew this was the right way to go, the best way to help Phyllis. Her mental health depended on her keeping her autonomy and independence, and knowing a dog appreciated her company was somehow almost as remedial as having her grandson and her daughter there.

As for AJ—the man had the patience of a saint. He was looking impossibly handsome today, in a green woollen sweater and smart black jeans. As for her own pencil skirt and heels... She was probably overdressed, but it was imperative that she was seen as someone who was well put together—at least on the outside.

Watching him pick up the conversation with Phyllis now, she took a deep breath to calm her thoughts. His body language wasn't out of the ordinary around her. Although there were still moments when he stood too close, then corrected himself. Jack had definitely noticed something was up. Had AJ's eyes really lit up when he'd seen her? She hadn't noticed—she'd been too busy maintaining an air of indifference at seeing *him*. But then, when they were kids, he'd always seemed pretty happy being around her. Maybe she'd forgotten that... too busy being offended over something he hadn't even done with Claire!

Lucie studied AJ's every movement now—the way he interacted so kindly and patiently with Phyllis, and with Jetson, and with her.

When she went with him to his next two appointments, he introduced her as a friend.

It was what she'd wanted, after all.

He pressed some dog treats into her hand at one point, and taught her how to command Jetson to roll over, and as they laughed at the dog's antics she could see with her own eyes how Jetson's presence eased the mood. It was the same in every room.

If only he could ease hers.

It *was* what she'd wanted.

Something else was niggling at her. The look on AJ's face, when he'd suggested she must've had a boyfriend or ten over the years.

That *one* look had told her the thought of those other boyfriends affected him somehow.

Not that it should matter, she reminded herself quickly.

It was definitely best to keep this professional and not spend any more time with him than necessary, she decided, listening to him explaining to another elderly patient how Josiah and Ruby made homemade dog treats for Jetson from sweet potato and minced meat.

God, he really was Father of the Year.

Damn him for turning out so perfect. In a way, it might've been better if he *had* hooked up with Claire-bloody-Bainbridge—at least then she could still be angry with him instead of impossibly attracted.

Every time AJ caught her eye he looked away quickly, as if he'd been caught doing something illicit. It made her blood race. Maybe she wasn't imagining it. Maybe there was something there.

No...stop doing this to yourself, Lucie!

She had to stop telling herself that she and Austin Johnstone could be something more than friends. It would only lead to heartache, and that was the last thing she'd come here looking for.

CHAPTER NINE

AUSTIN CALLED THE twins to the kitchen counter, scooping cornflakes into two bowls. 'Get your own spoons. I'm late!'

In seconds the kitchen resounded with the crunch of cereal and talk about the mummies in the book they'd read last night, while Jetson waited patiently for whoever dropped a cornflake to the floor first.

Where was Gramma May? She was supposed to be here by now to look after the twins. She helped him out sometimes on Sunday mornings. Belle was off doing wedding-related things with Bryce—their Halloween wedding seemed ages away to him, but Belle insisted it would come around fast—and he had a meeting with the volunteers about the upcoming Paws Under the Stars event. He was supposed to be heading it up himself. Starting now.

The doorbell rang. *Thank goodness*. Yanking it open, he swiped up his car keys, ready to dash, but it wasn't Gramma May.

'Lucie?'

She straightened and dashed a manicured hand through the ponytail slung over her left shoulder. Her hair disappeared into the folds of a soft white scarf peppered with roses that matched her red down jacket and navy-blue jeans.

'Gramma May's sick,' she explained. 'Nothing serious, just a cold, but she should stay at home. I offered to cover.'

Austin pulled his eyes from her scarf. Her perfume consumed him, throwing him off. 'Are you sure?'

The twins had run to the door now, in a chorus of, 'Lucie, Lucie, come and see our fort upstairs!'

And while Lucie agreed and smiled, and patted Jetson happily in front of them, he knew better.

Why would she want to stay in his house all morning? She hadn't been over since the time they'd made apple pies. They'd done nothing together that hadn't been at the care home or the hospital for a week. Which was fine by him. But he couldn't exactly turn her away, for the twins' sake. They'd think it was weird—they liked her. Only yesterday Ruby had asked when they'd be seeing Lucie again.

'I have a better idea,' he said, before he could change his mind. 'Why don't we all go?'

Twenty minutes later they were climbing out of the car at Newman's Farm in Malton. He watched Lucie take a lungful of the cool morning air, soaking up the views.

'It's beautiful! I forgot how magical everything looks in this light.'

He watched the sun glinting temptingly off her lip gloss. The taste of her lips would no doubt drive him wild if he ever kissed her. He'd kissed her once, he remembered, but he'd been so young he hadn't even known what to do with the feelings such intimacy had elicited.

'This is halfway to where the event will be held at Gilling Castle,' he said, locking the car. 'One of my volunteers runs the tearoom here, and the dogs can run free.'

The twins ran ahead with Jetson, towards the children's farm area, while he walked with Lucie after them. Her eyes shone with nostalgia as she took it all in: the dogs running around, the clucking chickens, the thatched roof farmhouse, the organic vegetable gardens, the weeping willow trees lining the paddocks of sheep and horses.

'Bit different to Nepal' he said.

She looked to the ground. He kicked himself for saying that. It had probably cast a downer on her train of thought, dragging her mind back to the earthquake.

The kids were already knee-deep in hay. They were making a fuss over their favourite goat as he leaned on the fence at the side of the pen with Lucie.

'I'll stay with them while you go and meet the others,' she offered.

OK... It wasn't as if he'd be putting her out. There wasn't much for her to do really, except stand there looking gorgeous and untouchable with the sun in her hair.

Her foot landed in a pile of goat poop the second she stepped into the pen. Darting in, Austin steadied her by her elbow, watching the look of torture in her eyes at both the contact and the poop, before she cursed under her breath and made the twins snort.

'Shi... Shoot!' She grimaced, scraping her boot on a fence post.

The twins just cracked up even more.

'Now *you* both have to stand in some poop, so I'm not the only one,' she joked at them, eyeing Austin sideways.

Ruby and Josiah took it literally and stomped in the hay in their welly boots, shouting, *'Poop dance!'*

'They don't care what they stand in,' he told her.

Lucie looked at them, aghast, then at him, before breaking out into laughter. The sound of it drew him in like a warm fire.

He was still holding her elbow.

Realising it at the same time, she broke apart from him.

Something sad shuddered through him. A memory he'd long forgotten. Lucie had used to cry a lot, back when she'd first arrived in Brookborough. Sometimes she'd cry in the middle of laughing and hide her face. She'd never said why. She'd always denied it afterwards, acted tough, but he'd been drawn to that inner flame. Like a moth tapping on a window…trying to get to the light.

'Daddy!'

Ruby's shriek pierced his skull. He spun to her. 'Oh, Ruby, what have you done?'

Her braid had somehow got caught on the fence. Before he could even act Lucie was at her side, kneeling in the hay, oblivious to the filth.

She worked it out with her fingers, hushing her till Ruby stilled, soothed by her calm conviction. His own redundancy should have stung, but the scene of motherly care moved him. Lucie had patiently detangled Ruby's hair and smoothed it down, told her she was fine, that she'd just done too much enthusiastic 'poop dancing'.

'Thank you,' he said to her, thinking, *Ebby would have done that.*

Why was he busy putting halos around Lucie's head when he should be thinking of Ebby? Guilt-ridden thoughts like this had messed his head up ever since he'd carried Lucie out of that stream. Ebby had been his world, but a tiny part of him recognised that he'd loved Lucie harder, with more of himself.

If Lucie had never left, he might not have even met Ebby. Maybe his feelings would have got the better of him eventually, and he'd have told Lucie he'd been in love with her in silence for years. Maybe she would've rejected him outright. But he was starting to wonder if maybe she wouldn't…

'I know what it's like to get your hair caught,' she replied now, biting back a smile, brushing the hay and dirt from her jeans. 'Once I got mine stuck, climbing through a briar patch to rescue a koala after a flood. You don't want to mess with the brambles in Western Australia. The koala had rescued itself by the time I was free.'

Austin stared at her. She was from a whole other world now.

'I'll watch them now—you guys go.'

Sarah, the sister of one of his volunteers, had brought two

kids of her own. Austin nodded his thanks as the four kids acted out the dramatic, long-winded handshake they'd memorised last time they'd met, sending the chickens scattering.

'Be good,' he told the twins, and turned to Lucie.

'You're off the hook with the children.'

He couldn't help his hand on her lower back as they both walked away, though he removed it as they neared the cluster of people congregating outside the tearoom.

'I didn't mind being on it,' she told him absently, still cleaning her boots in the grass.

He wanted to tell her his kids thought she was hilarious. But for the same reason he'd moved his hand, he kept his mouth shut.

They were doing OK at being friends again after all these years of estrangement, and they'd been working well as a team with Jetson at the care home and the hospital all week, but it was all a lie. He was pretending he could be close to her without stirring up memories of how she'd used to look at him as a girl. Maybe he'd missed something back then, when he'd been all teenage gangly limbs and libido and ego. She was the one girl he'd sworn never to touch, never to ruin. She'd been through enough already. So he'd busied himself with other girls to try and stop himself wanting *her*.

Much as he was still doing now.

There were lines you shouldn't cross with someone who was just passing through, he reminded himself. No way was he getting left again like Ebby had left him, standing at the window, wondering when she'd come home. *If* she'd come home.

But it *was* kind of nice to know he could feel things for someone after Ebby. Before Lucie had showed up again, it had felt as if he never would.

CHAPTER TEN

AJ's VOLUNTEER GROUP were a smiley-looking bunch—mostly women from the surrounding towns and villages.

Lucie was introduced as his friend again. Fine. It was the right thing now—although he was saying it a little too much, if she was honest. If she didn't know better she'd think he was trying to convince himself of something more than anyone else. Maybe he still hadn't quite forgiven her for walking out on their friendship with no explanation.

Before, his eyes had been fully on her when she was with Ruby. Suddenly she hoped she hadn't crossed some kind of line, putting herself in the position of a mother figure...

The not-so-secret stares from him were a new thing too. He'd been doing it all week. Admittedly, she'd been shooting him a few of her own—sizing him up, trying to force her brain to create a new impression of him, one without all the memories of her lusting over him attached. It was still amazing to her that he was a father and a widower and a much-loved member of the community...and even fitter than he had been before.

Stupid, really. He'd just grown up and built a life, like she had, but their two worlds were colliding in her mind. It was hard to separate the boy she'd loved from the man who'd never love her back. Maybe if she hadn't overheard him with Claire she might have someday gathered up the courage to tell him how she felt. Show him, perhaps?

Oh, who was she kidding? The thought of his rejection had always been crippling. Much like now, actually.

She'd almost refused to come here with him. Was it too intimate? Going on an outing with him and the twins?

Ugh...whatever. It wasn't as if they'd planned it. She'd rather this than staying at the house with images of his dead wife everywhere. And the twins were growing on her. They were funny. Interesting, she mused, how amusing kids could be without even trying.

The group were now gathered in the cosy oak-beamed tearoom, chatting amongst themselves. Some of the dogs were sitting quietly and patiently at their owners' feet, while others were sniffing around chair-legs.

One dog bounded straight up to her and sat promptly at her feet, awaiting a pat: a sandy-brown Retriever called Maple.

Her owner laughed in surprise, getting up to greet Lucie. 'She doesn't usually do that.' The striking black woman's raven bob cut swayed around her jaw as she spoke. 'She must like you.'

'She's adorable!'

'Shame I can't keep her much longer,' the other woman said ruefully, placing a hand to the Retriever's soft head. 'My daughter's coming back from university soon, and she's allergic. We'll need to find a new foster home for her. I was only meant to keep her till now, but I've grown so attached.'

'Oh, no, poor Maple...' Lucie pouted. 'And poor you. I hope you can find someone locally, so you can still see each other.'

'So do I.'

The dog placed a fuzzy padded paw into Lucie's hand, stared up at her and stuck her tongue out. She saw AJ smile. His hand found her lower back for just a fraction of a second as he leaned in. His scent caught her off guard. He smelled like the house and fresh linen...and a little bit like goats now too. She swallowed.

'I think she's trying to ask you something,' he whispered into the shell of her ear.

Lucie couldn't look away from the dog's big brown eyes. She was beautiful, and AJ's proximity was throwing her for a loop.

'No,' she said to him firmly, coming to her senses.

'No, what?'

'I know what you're thinking. I'm not fostering a dog.'

'Lucie Henderson?'

Lucie spun around at the sound of her name, and AJ stopped his chuckling.

'Jamesy Abbot?' she cried, taking in the boy she'd known from school, still with the same blond streaked hair. His Golden Retriever, Star Lord, sniffed butts with Maple as they hugged briefly. He was obviously one of the volunteers.

Jamesy looked curiously between her and AJ. 'He said you were back. It's good to see you two together again.'

He grinned as he emphasised 'together', and Lucie looked to the floor. Typical Jamesy, stirring things up—some things never changed. He'd teased her once, about following AJ around, pointing out her crush. Had he ever asked AJ if he thought she had a crush on him?

As if it matters.

AJ excused himself, leaving her standing awkwardly between Maple's owner Iris, Jamesy, and a doting Maple, while he faced the group. He was quick to get down to business, taking the lead, commanding attention with one clap of his hands.

They were apparently sorting out the order of things for something called the Paws Under the Stars event. He was planning the evening as part of the Spring Gala.

The volunteers were going to dress their dogs in LED lights and fantastical costumes and get them to complete an assault course and perform various tricks. Lots of dog-related merchandise was here on display, from dog harnesses to food bowls, to printed T-shirts with the Thera Pups logo on them.

'We have everything but the new calendar good to go,' AJ explained. 'We need to organise that soon, as people always ask for them early. Sometimes I think they just like to look at the photos for longer.'

It was all being done to raise money for some of the establishments they visited, and for some of the volunteers who needed a little support in caring for their animals. Some of them were only fostering, like Iris was doing with Maple.

They were deep into enthusiastic discussion when several of the dogs towards the back of the room began to whine. Lucie exchanged a curious glance with AJ, who looked only mildly concerned. Maybe they were bored, or hungry, she mused.

Then, out of nowhere, there was a thud at the back of the room.

'John!' someone yelled.

Some of the dogs were barking now, others still whining. Lucie hurried over to the collapsed man, now grappling to hold on to a chair-leg on the tiled floor.

'He just said he didn't feel well,' said the woman who'd yelled his name. 'He has seizures. He's on meds for them, but...'

'John, can you hear me?' AJ said beside her, as the rest of the crowd stood around, hands over their mouths in shock.

John was pulsating on the floor now, cold to the touch. Looking to AJ, Lucie brought the man's head onto her lap, blocking out the rest of the room. AJ was already rummaging through John's bag for his medication and she knew they'd have to administer it right away—John's eyes were having trouble staying open.

'We've got you, John,' she soothed, hoping she was right as AJ readied the needle and passed it to her.

The man's body loosened up almost instantly. He stopped convulsing and the crowd let out thankful moans as AJ stood, ushering them back to give John space.

Someone handed her some blankets and she gently laid

them over John, watching the colour seeping slowly back into his pale cheeks. He was drifting in and out of consciousness and complaining of dizziness now. At least he could speak.

She'd never been so grateful for AJ's calming presence.

Gramma May called AJ when they were halfway home.

'Gramma May is calling *you*?' she said in surprise.

He ignored her. 'I guess you heard about John?' he said into the speakerphone, and Lucie listened as the two discussed the event, and how John had thankfully been able to walk away not even twenty minutes later, thanks to AJ's quick actions.

Gramma May thanked them both, in fact, for helping her friend. She knew John and his wife from church.

'And how are *you* feeling now?' AJ asked her.

The kids called out, 'Hi, Gramma May!' from the back seat.

Gramma May insisted it was just the sniffles and not to worry.

How sweet, Lucie thought, that she'd called AJ like this, to thank him, before even calling her. They must be closer than he'd let on...closer than Gramma May had let on all these years.

Community. She'd really missed this.

She caught him as they exited the car and the kids ran ahead with the house key.

'AJ...' she said quietly.

It was hitting her now, just how out of her depth she was, coming back here. He scanned her eyes, and the intensity in them turned her stomach over. She wanted to apologise for asking Gramma May not to tell her anything about him. It must have been so hard for her to keep silent. But something stopped her. She'd been a burden to poor Gramma May even *after* she'd left home and given her her freedom, which wasn't something she was proud of—it would be best to apologise to Gramma herself.

'That was… Well, I'm glad you were there,' she told him instead.

'I'm glad you were there too,' he replied.

The intensity of the moment had her feeling awkward, and he was chewing the side of his lip.

'The twins want to know if you want to come in for a cup of tea,' he said.

For a second she considered that maybe *he* wanted her to come in, more than the twins. Torn, she gave a little sigh. It was probably best if she didn't go into the house and be reminded of all the times she'd watched him while she was meant to be watching a movie, wishing he would kiss her. Or, she reasoned, she could just act like the adult she was and have a simple cup of tea.

She ended up staying all afternoon.

Leaving was near impossible.

Every time she got up, the twins had something else to show her: Ruby's puzzle collection, the way AJ had an ongoing skipping rope competition going with Josiah in the living room. It was sexy as hell, that one, watching him jump just to make his kids laugh.

When she finally had the tiniest moment alone with AJ inside the fort, made of cotton sheets in all the colours AJ wouldn't put on the bed, her knee brushed his for a thousandth of a second . She could have launched herself on him.

'Sorry,' she said instead.

His breath warmed her neck when he laughed, and a groan lingered in her throat that she had to swallow back.

AJ hugged his knees.

She almost…*almost* asked him if he'd ever considered asking her out all those years ago. He'd asked all those other girls out—why not her, ever? But that wasn't like her. That was way too needy, wasn't it? And neediness was not her thing. She'd leave that to the dogs. Instead, she asked him how on earth the dogs had seemed to know what was about to happen to John earlier, before anyone had seen the signs.

Why look for ways to attach herself to him and these two delightful little energy balls he'd somehow raised without his wife? she thought, admiring his mouth, and the passion with which he answered her about dogs' infinite intelligence and potential, and the paper he was writing.

He'd done so much—buried his roots so far into the ground here. While she was still a bird, aiming for the mountaintops. Literally. She was probably just feeling emotional after what had happened today, that was all. She'd never be the kind of woman he needed now—not even if she tried.

Somehow, that hurt more than she wanted to admit.

CHAPTER ELEVEN

THE BLOND-HAIRED BOY'S eyes widened anxiously when Austin entered the room with Jetson. He'd decided to involve him for his second attempted Autism Spectrum Disorder assessment on eleven-year-old Jake, who had refused all attempts to so much as question him till now.

'You brought a dog?' he said suspiciously, folding his arms across the desk he was sitting behind in the quiet room at the GP practice that doubled as Austin's office for appointments like this.

His mother was already on her feet, patting Jetson, encouraging Jake to do the same. 'Come on, Jake... Look how cute he is!'

Jake, who had a severe lack in social skills, according to his parents and teachers, shook his head grumpily and sat back further in his chair. His body language spoke volumes. Austin pictured his sweet, bubbly Josiah as an older child. What lay ahead for him? Would he be a good father, handling their teenage years by himself?

Funny...just before he'd met Lucie again Belle had got in his ear about setting up an online dating profile and he'd actually considered it. It was time he at least thought about opening himself up to the prospect of having *someone* in his life at some point in the future.

Not that he could think about that now, because...well, Lucie.

He pulled out the card game he'd brought with him, placing it on the table between them. 'I thought we'd try playing a game again,' he said.

Jake looked even more suspicious. But AJ had found interacting using a game sometimes shifted the focus in situations like this, and allowed his patients to open up more easily, with less intensity, so he could analyse their behaviour, symptoms, strengths and weaknesses. Last time, however, Jake had not played along.

This time, with his mother in the room, he seemed a little more willing, but it was still grunts and one-word answers when it came to his responses to AJ's questions. He did, however, keep glancing at Jetson, until Jetson seemed to get the message and laid a soft head on the boy's knee under the table.

'Hope you don't mind if I join you? Maple just got dropped off, by the way, AJ.'

They all turned as Lucie appeared in the doorway, with Maple. He knew she'd just finished an appointment down the hall. In fact, he'd asked her to join them afterwards if she was free. Maybe she would be able to help shed some light on how best to open Jake up, if he still didn't respond to him. She seemed to have a knack for bringing people out of themselves—especially his male patients. It was a feminine touch he certainly did not possess.

Jake's mother looked delighted as the second dog padded in. Jake just shrugged, but AJ didn't miss the way he was patting Jetson now, and how he'd welcomed Maple, too. The boy seemed a lot more relaxed as Lucie pulled up a chair, pondering the cards on the table.

She looked tired, but as well put together as ever. She was wearing navy fitted trousers and a matching jacket and a white blouse. Her hair was styled immaculately. She caught his eye, somehow sending him back to the fort the other day, in the twins' room, when he'd struggled not to kiss her.

'Your dog is beautiful,' Jake's mum enthused.

'Well, she's not exactly my dog,' Lucie replied, just as Maple snuffled her nose against Lucie's knee, eager for an invitation from her new temporary handler to prove herself at something useful. 'She'll be staying with AJ for a few days.'

'Looks like your dog to me.'

Lucie kept a straight face, but AJ didn't miss her glance of silent acquiescence. Maple was in his care, that was true, as he was helping Iris out, but Lucie clearly adored the dog. He caught her eye again, biting back a smile. Her being so close, so invested, did things to his insides—a certain kind of twisting and tangling that no one else had ever inspired in him. Not even Ebby.

Which was exactly his problem. That afternoon at the house, he'd wondered...what if she'd never left? What if he'd told her how he felt back then and she'd actually felt the same? Enough to have stayed? Maybe they'd have got serious...got married...

The guilt when he let his thoughts go down that road made him feel cold.

Helping John the way she had the other day...he would always be grateful she'd been there. So calm, collected, even when everyone else around them had panicked. It had just made him burn for her more, admire her more, wanting the best for her. She didn't speak about her dreams, but he knew she was still suffering just from seeing her tired eyes. That was why he wouldn't give up on convincing her to take on Maple while she was here. Maple would help her, he knew.

Not long after Lucie and Maple came in Jake had softened enough not only to answer his standard assessment questions, sneaked as usual into the act of playing the game, but to engross himself in a conversation Lucie started about his travel plans for the year.

It began when she told him, 'You look like the kind of boy who'd be on a swimming team or in a hiking group. Do either of those activities sound good to you?'

Jake's answers surprised him. Rather than being horrified

when Lucie recounted how she'd once hiked up a mountain in flip-flops after a surprise tsunami in Thailand, he threw no end of questions at her, and seemed keen to explore the world, with friends, or maybe even solo 'like Bear Grylls'.

Not so closed off and reclusive as AJ had first assumed, then. In fact, thanks to Lucie's input and both dogs' calming presence, he now almost had enough to provide a diagnosis and a comprehensive treatment plan.

'Can I walk Jetson and Maple sometime?' Jake asked, on his way out.

AJ met his mother's eyes and felt both proud and relieved by the joy he saw in them.

'I think that can be arranged,' Lucie said.

But when she asked if they'd both be at the Paws Under the Stars event AJ was planning Lucie paused, and almost looked sad for a moment.

'I don't think so,' she replied cautiously. 'I'm just a locum here. I'll probably be gone by then.'

Austin's mood plummeted on the spot, and he averted his gaze, looking at Jetson, his tail wagging at the boy's enthusiastic goodbyes. In his head, he'd started to think she was always going to be here. The twins had asked if she would be. They were both talking about her more and more.

He would have to try harder not to let his work with her blend into their private lives, he decided, new resolve pounding through him. Even if that would be almost impossible in a village this size.

But when she asked if he wouldn't mind dropping her at her next home visit, seeing as her rental car was having some issues, he found himself agreeing, of course.

'Gramma May's feeling much better now,' Lucie told AJ, on the road towards Whitby. 'She told me to thank you and the twins for the flowers.'

'She thanked me herself, with a text message,' he replied, looking to the road ahead.

Lucie bit her lip as they sped past a road sign pointing to the ruined Gothic Whitby Abbey—Bram Stoker's inspiration for *Dracula*.

Of course she'd thanked him herself already, she thought. Gramma May was clearly a huge part of their lives, and every time she remembered how she'd asked her sweet, selfless grandma not to talk about AJ over the years she felt terrible. She'd apologised, of course, for asking Gramma to keep quiet about one of the people in the community she really cared about.

Gramma May had just said, 'It's fine. I understand.' Followed by something under her breath about how she knew she'd see the light eventually.

Lucie had left it there. Sometimes she had the distinct feeling that Gramma had long been rooting for her to come home and get together with Austin Johnstone, but Gramma May had never been one to talk about that kind of thing. And obviously there was no point stoking that fire. Had she not said just now that she'd be gone before the Spring Gala and the Paws Under the Stars event?

AJ hadn't even tried to change her mind.

'Want me to wait here with the dogs?' he asked her now, switching off the car engine.

She almost said yes, but her patient Constance was opening the door to her house already, and waving. Then she spotted the dogs.

Constance was bone-thin, dressed in a black shirt and a skirt that hung off her hips as she welcomed them all inside.

'I'm a huge dog fan—therapy dogs or otherwise,' she said, smiling, running her hands over Maple's soft ears as she ushered them through to the living room.

This was Lucie's first home visit to the fifty-seven-year-old, and immediately her appearance was striking alarm bells. She was pale, gaunt, hollow-cheeked, despite being so beautiful.

'I just don't know what's wrong, Doctor,' she explained with a sigh, sinking down into an olive-green sofa.'

A huge blown-up wedding photo obviously taken years ago took up almost all of one wall. The dogs took the space beside her on a chair, as if they owned the place.

She seemed to have trouble walking, Lucie noticed, and her every breath was long and drawn out. She wasn't eating well, Constance said, and she wasn't really able to exercise.

The dark circles around her eyes spoke of worry and sleepless nights—and, oh, Lucie knew that look well. It stared back at her from the mirror often enough. She probably looked exhausted herself right now, she thought, thanks to being up since three o'clock. Last night, in her dream, the water tank that had taken Jorge, took AJ too. The state she'd woken up in was almost unbearable to think about.

Her knee brushed AJ's as she sat on the other sofa. There was nowhere to move away from the friction. She could hardly have asked him to wait in the car after he'd driven her here, and after Constance had been so delighted by the dogs.

'I can't seem to use the bathroom properly,' Constance admitted now, somewhat bashfully. 'Nothing stays in me. It's almost like my body is rejecting food from all angles. And I'm just so tired all the time. Thanks for coming here... I'm not sure I could have made it to the surgery.'

AJ met Lucie's glance as she took the woman's blood pressure. She was just about to suggest a blood test, and request a stool sample, when Jetson started doing something strange.

'What's he doing?' Lucie asked AJ.

AJ stood up. He was trying not to show it, she could tell, but he looked deeply concerned. Jetson was rolling on the floor, over and over. He did it three times in a row before stopping and offering AJ his paw. AJ's eyes grew wide. He hadn't commanded the dog to do anything.

Constance stroked Maple's ears, watching in amusement, but the look on AJ's face had Lucie on edge. Something was going on...but what? Gosh, she was so tired.

He sat down again next to her and squeezed her knee. 'I need to talk to you outside,' he whispered.

Her heart bucked and leapt like a rabbit in her chest at the contact, and at the gravity of his tone. Constance was staring at them now. She nudged his hand away.

'My dear, you do look tired,' Constance commented suddenly.

Lucie shifted uncomfortably on the too-small seat. Rain had started pattering at the windows outside. 'Do I? I guess I didn't sleep much last night.'

'Nightmares again?' AJ probed.

Lucie nodded, defeated. Why lie?

'Constance, we should probably...'

Constance leaned towards her, put a feather-light hand over hers and cut her off. 'I know what that's like. My ex-husband haunts me...well, he did for years. Until I met my new one. That's him.' She bobbed her head at the wedding photo. 'That's why I made the photo so big. Cancels out the ex, somehow.'

Lucie huffed out a laugh.

But then Constance added, 'I don't see a ring on your finger. Is this man looking after you right?' A smile hovered on her pale lips. She looked between them where they sat on the tiny sofa.

'Lucie and I are just friends,' AJ explained bluntly, standing up again. He still looked distracted, and had started looking at something on his phone, bashing out a message.

'Nightmares about what, may I ask?' Constance looked interested.

'I was involved in an accident, of sorts, in Nepal,' she heard herself explaining, as she glanced at AJ. 'A building collapsed on my friend. I was too late to get him out...' She tailed off. Exhaustion was making her loose-lipped.

'But she saved other people, Constance. Children,' AJ said suddenly, shoving his phone back into his pocket and calling to Jetson.

Lucie frowned at him.

'Well, you did, Lucie,' he insisted. 'You went through more out there than most people can imagine. We're all proud of you. And you're going to be OK.'

Such conviction…

For a second, she didn't quite know what to say. She wanted to run to him, feel the comfort of his arms as well as his words. Thank goodness Constance was there. Lucie wasn't here to talk about what had happened to her—especially not in front of AJ. He'd been through enough on his own.

Maybe she was scared to talk about it for selfish reasons, she thought as she measured Constance's height and weight. In case she got addicted to his listening ear. It was just a countdown, really, till she was out of here—and she *was* going to leave.

'If you don't have a man, dear,' Constance went on, 'you should at least have a dog. I hear Maple will need a new foster home soon.'

Here we go.

Lucie packed up her things up Constance sang Maple's praises, saying how she'd have the dog herself if she didn't spend so much time at her daughter's place and the hospital.

Maple's big loving eyes seemed to plead with her. It was highly likely she was reading too much into this, but Maple did seem to have her own way of asking her if she'd be her new foster mum.

OK, yes, it was tempting. The benefits of a furry sidekick were clear: dogs were calming, funny, and a distraction from everyday woes. But it was already going to be hard enough leaving Gramma May, AJ and the twins.

Especially AJ…

There was absolutely no chance a live-in dog would be

getting under her skin, too. Besides, she didn't need one. The nightmares would stop eventually. She would be OK.

'It's raining pretty hard now.'

AJ still looked troubled. She blinked, zipping up her bag, realising he'd been watching her.

'We should get going before it gets worse. The road back can be a nightmare at this hour…especially when it rains.'

CHAPTER TWELVE

THE SEAGULLS SQUAWKED a welcome to the Whitby seaside. The smell of fish and chips assaulted Austin's nose: the scent of their weekends as kids in this very place. Sure enough, the road home had been jammed, and because there were still a couple of hours before he needed to relieve Belle of the twins, who'd be doing homework anyway, they'd come here. The dogs needed to run.

'Are you sure you don't mind the beach?' he asked Lucie.

A gust of wind tugged at her fur-lined hood and blew her fringe back from her face. She squinted ahead.

'I don't mind a bit of rain.'

To her credit, she was not complaining, even though her immaculate look was being severely tested by the Yorkshire weather. He bit back a smile at the way she battled in vain with her hair the whole way from the seafront, down the steps and onto the vast yellow stretch of sand.

'Listen…' he said. Now that they had some open space around them, he could process what had just happened. 'I might be getting ahead of myself, but I'm pretty sure Jetson just picked up on something with Constance.'

Lucie stopped, looked at him aghast. 'Cancer?'

'He gave me the signs,' he said into her wide-eyed gaze. He still couldn't quite believe it himself. 'I think you should…'

'Schedule a colonoscopy. I was thinking the same thing anyway,' she replied, shaking her head.

Austin's heart was racing. 'Lucie, if Jetson's right, we could have proof that the training works.'

She was still staring at him, seemingly lost in thought. 'I don't know what to say. That would be… Well, not great for Constance.'

'So we move fast. Push the tests through. She can get the help she needs as quickly as possible.'

The dogs sprinted ahead towards the surf, tails wagging in joy, and they watched them. He hoped he hadn't stepped on her toes, but this was everything he'd hoped Jetson would be able to do and more. His heart thrummed with adrenaline as he told her more about the signals Jetson had learned so far in the cancer detection training, and he barely noticed the weather. Unlike Lucie, who was still battling with her hair.

'You've probably done more challenging things in worse conditions,' he said, changing the topic, gesturing to her hair.

Lucie grimaced. 'You don't want to be in the Himalayas in a cyclone.'

He waited for her to go on, but she didn't. She stopped walking, crouched down for a pebble.

'Thank you, for what you said earlier…about being proud of me,' she told him suddenly, down on her haunches.

His stomach vaulted. He'd worried he'd sounded patronising—especially in front of Constance. 'I am proud of you,' he said stiltedly. 'The patients adore you…the dogs adore you.'

He stopped short of saying he adored her, too. There were too many ghosts in the wind who might judge him more than he could ever judge himself for the way he'd been feeling around her lately. And she'd moved his hand off her knee a little too fast back there. Almost as if she was afraid to show just how much his touch affected her. Maybe he *hadn't* been imagining something between them the other day, as they'd sat shoulder to shoulder in the kids' fort. Although he knew he wasn't imagining Lucie's insistence on leaving when her time here was up.

'I'm getting a lot out of spending all this time with…with the dogs.' She pressed her lips together, scanning his eyes. He knew she meant with *him*, as well as the dogs, but she wasn't going to say it. That was probably for the best. Because she wasn't going to stay here…

The twins were going to be gutted when she left.

The sea air was colder than he'd anticipated as they walked along the sand, but at least the rain had turned down a notch. Lucie hugged herself, her eyes on Maple. Should he bring up again the fact that she could take Maple home if she wanted, or would that be pushing it? The dog would at least be a good companion for the next few weeks if she woke up in the night.

'So, have you ever dated anyone, since Ebby?' she asked him now, stopping him in his tracks where the escarpment of the layered sea wall provided a sought-after sunbathing spot in the summer.

He faltered. He hadn't been expecting that. 'Um…no,' he admitted.

'You've never wanted to?'

He studied her, wondering how best to reply—and why she was even asking. He could admit that, yes, he wanted to now that she was here, but he wasn't going to admit that when she'd literally just reminded him, that morning, that she wouldn't even be here long enough to see the Spring Gala.

'Forget I said anything,' she muttered, clicking her tongue when he didn't reply.

The jagged rocks seemed an appropriate leaning post—uncomfortable, like the situation. He tossed a stone. Together they watched the seagulls swirling and squawking over the craggy cliffs ahead. She'd been chipping away at him bit by bit, whether she knew it or not, and now here he was, having to face a landslide.

'I feel bad that I think about Ebby less when I'm with you, Lucie.'

There. He'd said it.

Cold, spiderlike fingers scuttled up and down his spine as she turned to him. The dogs were specks in the distance, up towards the headlands, and he'd have done anything for their speed and agility, their ability to run a mile in a heartbeat—away from *this*.

'She was the mother of my children.'

Lucie pressed her back to the craggy wall beside him. 'I don't mean any disrespect. You know that... You know me. You and I are just friends. I know you loved her in a very different way...'

Austin's jaw clenched. She had no idea. 'What do *you* know? I'm betraying her memory right now.'

She pushed away from the wall and faced him, her hair blowing in tendrils around her face. 'We're not doing anything, AJ.'

'But I want to.' The words were torn from somewhere deep inside him.

Lucie sucked in a breath but she didn't move, didn't speak. Her eyes were full of questions, fear, trepidation...desire?

Then she said. 'Why now, AJ?' Her voice was so soft her words were almost imperceptible.

'I never did kiss you properly back then,' he said, stepping closer, his own fierce longing for her propelling him further than his common sense should've allowed.

Lucie swallowed, frowning through her fringe. 'I didn't think you wanted to.'

'Did *you* want me to?' he tested, finding her eyes in her whirling hair.

For a long moment, her gaze roved over his mouth.

'Tell me, Luce. Was there ever a moment, before you left, that you thought about it? Even for one second?'

Her eyes flooded with emotion—right before she squeezed them shut.

He could have kissed her. She'd have been putty in his hands—he could just tell. Suddenly he could see, as if someone had ripped the blinkers off him. She'd looked at him like this before, when she'd seen him making out with Tina…or had it been Sasha…at his seventeenth birthday party.

'Well?' he pressed. He needed to hear her say it.

'No. We were only ever friends, AJ,' she said. 'Like we are now.'

He bit down hard on his cheek. So that was how she wanted to play it.

Tearing his eyes away, he carried on up the beach. He shouldn't have said anything. Stupid…*stupid*.

'AJ,' she said, hurrying after him. 'I didn't mean for this to get complicated for you. I know we're getting all tied up together, because of the dogs and everything, but if I take Maple we can make the rounds separately…'

'Don't be ridiculous!'

He spun around. That was out of the question—especially now Jetson had picked up on something with Constance.

'I mean, yes, you can take Maple. Great idea. But how do you *really* feel, Lucie? This isn't just about protecting me from *complications*!'

Lucie's gaze froze on his. The dogs sprinted back to them, circling them, asking to play. For once, they both ignored them.

'Isn't it getting complicated for you, too?' he said. 'Seeing everything that's changed? Building something here for yourself again?'

'Of *course* it is.' Her eyes clouded over.

He cupped her face, impulsively drawing her closer with one hand, forcing her eyes to his. She pressed her cheek into his palm.

'Do you like being friends with me, Lucie? Tell me the truth.'

The longest, most agonised breath escaped her flaring nostrils. '*You* wanted to be friends.'

'That wasn't my question.'

The warmth of her seeped into him. Her lips parted temptingly…an invitation. He leaned closer, dragged a thumb along her lower lip.

Looking up at him again through lowered lashes, she whispered, 'You were only ever my best friend.'

'Yes. I was. Do you like making *friends* like me and then running away into disaster zones? Does it make you happy? Because you don't seem happy.'

'That's not fair, AJ.'

Her lips brushed over the skin of his palm as she spoke, shooting blood straight to his groin.

'I'll get better—you said it yourself. And my work makes me happy. I *want* to get back to working overseas. It's where I belong.'

Uncertainty flickered in her eyes—just the briefest flash—and he tucked the silent insight away in his mind, dropping his hand from her face. 'You keep telling yourself that.'

'I love my work,' she asserted, squaring her shoulders. 'And I'd love it if we could be friends without all…*this*.' She wiggled her hand between them, as if shooing some kind of annoying pest away.

A slow boil started in his blood, but he kept his face neutral as he turned back the way they'd come. He changed the subject to the dogs, and of course she went with it. No point talking about anything that actually meant anything—not when it sparked the need either to kiss or fight.

At least they were on the same page. Wanting someone else was confusing as hell, but *this* was exactly why he wouldn't do *anything* with Lucie Henderson—even if she admitted she wanted to…which she clearly was not going to do.

This need she seemed to have to prove herself—hadn't she proved enough? What she did was meaningful, but what about her *own* mental health? No one could do the kind of work she did for ever and not be affected…for ever. And now he'd just picture her out there, her beautiful mind and body dancing with all that danger, *another* woman he couldn't keep from being claimed by something out of his control.

Let it go, Austin.

She was going back to it, whatever he did or said. That was just what Lucie did. His heart didn't need this torture and neither did his children. They'd been through enough.

If only every inch of his body and soul didn't still burn to protect her. Like it had when he'd first caught her crying as a helpless little kid.

CHAPTER THIRTEEN

LUCIE FORCED HERSELF AWAKE. Sitting up in bed, she felt the sweat slide down her back, sticking her shirt to her skin. Three a.m. It was always three a.m. now.

Oh, God.

The rumbling aftershock in her dream... Jorge's face melting like butter into AJ's. Jorge had become AJ stuck between trembling walls, broken glass and twisted steel.

'Run!' he'd yelled at her loudly, his face distorted in panic.

But she'd grabbed him and pressed herself hard against him, holding on tightly. Moving hadn't even been an option. She wasn't letting go of him...wasn't going anywhere.

Then the wall tumbled down on both of them.

Lucie fumbled for her water, letting the huge glugs wet her parched throat. Her breath still hadn't quite found her when Maple padded in. The Retriever leapt onto the bed, dropped to her side and pressed a soft, furry face to her belly through the duvet.

I'm here, she seemed to say.

Lucie stroked her soft fur, seeking solace in the steady warmth of the dog's presence. Her big brown eyes gleamed with a certain knowledge in the faint light from the hall.

Calm, Maple seemed to say. *Relax, I'm here. You've got this.*

Lucie's breathing slowed. She closed her eyes again, allowing herself to drift, her hand still locked in Maple's fur, the rhythm of the dog's breathing a soothing lullaby.

Maple didn't move for the rest of the night. And Lucie didn't wake till nine-thirty a.m.

'You look well rested,' Gramma May observed when she wandered into the kitchen, dazed by the morning light streaming through the windows. Usually it was still dark when she dragged herself out of her nightmares and down the stairs.

'I feel rested,' she admitted, reaching for the coffee.

But the dream was still fresh in her mind's eye. Why did Jorge always turn into AJ now?

He was getting under her skin as she'd known he would.

And the conversation on the beach had hardly helped… The look in his eyes when he'd said, *'I feel bad that I think about Ebby less when I'm with you, Lucie.'*

He'd finally opened the door to at least discussing what might have happened between them back then, and she'd slammed it shut in his face. But what was she supposed to say? She was leaving again soon, and he felt bad enough already for liking her…maybe for liking her before he'd even met Ebby?

She'd humiliated him, probably, by pushing him away. But he had no idea that even now she could still hear Claire laughing with him, teasing him about how 'little lost Lucie' followed him around like a puppy dog. She could still hear the silence that had followed from him. It was why she'd run right out of his life. Why hadn't he defended her? She'd always figured he'd been too busy eyeing up Claire, who'd been 'showing him things' that Lucie couldn't. Now, no matter what he said or how he looked at her, it was too late for them.

The doorbell rang. Maple barked.

Oh, no…

'Gramma, wait!'

But Gramma May was already heading for the door. Lucie barely had time to belt up her dressing gown before AJ was stepping into the kitchen, all six foot of him, bringing with him the leafy fresh air and a spicy waft of cologne.

Jetson padded in behind him and greeted Maple with a bum-sniff.

'Did you only just wake up?' He suppressed a smile as she struggled to separate him from the version of AJ she'd clung to in her dream.

God, did she have pillow creases across her cheeks? She let her hair hide her face.

'I thought I told you I have the rental car back?' She gestured to it through the window, parked outside on the street. 'You don't have to drive me anywhere today.'

He stared her down, and the lump in her throat grew golf-ball-sized. They'd both made things a little awkward yesterday. Well, OK, *she'd* made it worse by going into denial mode.

'I thought I'd give you this,' he said, pressing a stack of papers down on the table. 'It's the research I have so far...what I've gathered from the dogs involved in cancer detection.'

'Oh...' She pulled her gown around her tighter. 'Thanks. I've pushed for Constance's colonoscopy this afternoon.'

'Good,' he said.

Then he frowned at her, as if he was seeing straight through her robe. She still couldn't get yesterday out of her head...the way his eyes had burned into hers on the beach.

'I can wait while you get dressed,' he said now.

She blinked at him.

'You wanted to see Samuel get his new therapy dog? He's obsessed with Maple, too.'

'That's the boy in hospital with severe diabetes, right?' she said, looking around for her phone.

His attention on her made her knees as weak as her resolve as she swept past him. How could she ever forget the intensity in his eyes when he'd asked: *'Do you like being friends with me, Lucie? Tell me the truth.'*

Gramma May pulled a coffee cup out for him and patted his head affectionately as she put it down. He beamed up at her. 'Glad you're feeling better, Gramma May,' he said, helping himself to coffee and a biscuit from a plate on the table.

'I'm better now that Lucie's doing better,' she replied. 'She slept so well with Maple last night. I'm guessing that was your idea, Austin?'

'Both of us had the idea,' Lucie corrected, lifting up a pile of magazines. 'But it's only for a few days, till we can find another foster home for Maple. Honestly…where *is* my phone?'

'Lucie.' Austin's tone caught her off guard. He grabbed her phone up from the counter by the kettle and strode to her, holding it out of her reach when she tried to take it.

'What's wrong? Tell me.' He was whispering, although suddenly it was only them in the room.

'I had another dream,' she said. Well, that was half of the reason why she was so flustered in his presence. 'It wasn't as awful once Maple came in, but…'

'So she's helping you already?'

He smiled, and she almost melted. He looked so hot in his leather jacket, and those jeans made his bum look pert and perfect. But that was not for her to contemplate. She'd done the right thing, throwing him off the scent about her real feelings.

'You don't have to do all this with Maple,' he whispered to her now, his back still to Gramma May. 'If it's too much I can take Maple back. I can—'

'No,' she said to his muscular chest as he shielded her from the room. 'I want to do this.'

A moment passed, then he nodded, scanning her face thoughtfully.

The voice in her head was taunting her. *You are the last thing he needs. He's just distracted because he's been single for so long. Stay away...*

'But I told you. I don't want to make things difficult for you.'

His jaw clenched and regret dashed through his eyes. 'About what I said yesterday,' he told her, keeping his voice low. 'I was out of line. You were right. We *should* try to be…'

He stopped short of saying it. But it hovered in the space between their lips.

Friends.

A current of hot white energy bolted through her veins at his steadfast gaze. Maybe he *had* felt something for her back then…back before she tore everything apart.

No, Lucie. He's just confused. Because you're here now and he hasn't dated anyone since Ebby!

'What are you two whispering about?' Gramma May looked just a little bit amused as she rolled her eyes.

'Give me ten minutes,' Lucie said, taking the phone from his hands and hurrying upstairs.

Whatever was going on, the least she could do was show up for Thera Pups—the second most important thing in the world for AJ aside from the twins. The funny thing was, it was starting to mean just as much to her, too.

Lucie's ten-year-old insulin-dependent diabetic patient Samuel had been in and out of the surgery and the hospital since Lucie's arrival in the village, following several scary episodes of unconsciousness—one of them happening at school. It had freaked out a lot of the other kids and left him feeling a deep sense of shame, along with terror that it might happen again.

He wasn't doing so well when they reached the hospital.

'We've had some setbacks,' a student nurse whispered on their way in. 'That last attack really shook him up. I explained that's why you've kept him in, Dr Henderson, but he wants to go home.'

'Is that right?' AJ asked the boy, taking over as the nurse left them to it. 'Is it the jelly they're feeding you?' he whispered, moving the IV aside so he could take his seat beside the boy.

Samuel's mouth twitched. 'No, that's the best part. Even though it's sugar-free.'

'Do they have strawberry flavour?' Lucie followed up. 'That's Maple's favourite.'

'Dogs don't eat jelly!'

Using the hand command she'd learned from AJ, she directed Maple to place her two front paws on the bed by Samuel's head, and without further command the dog obliged, and graced his cheek with a lick for good measure.

'That's her way of telling you you're right and I was wrong,' Lucie said. 'But who knows what your *own* dog will like eating, huh?'

She threw AJ a conspiratorial look.

The little boy frowned. 'I don't have a dog of my own.'

'Well…you *didn't* have a dog,' AJ said, signalling to the nurse standing by the door. 'But Dr Henderson and I were kind of hoping you might like to look after Bingo?'

The door opened.

Samuel's squeal almost deafened them.

One of the ladies Lucie had met that time at the farm walked in, with a cream and brown beagle on a blue lead. She watched Maple do a ballet dancer spin on the floor by way of greeting Bingo, and couldn't help laughing. Gosh, this dog was a star. So beautiful…almost a mind-reader, too. Maybe Maple could take the disease detection training too, she found herself thinking. Like this beagle had.

'Bingo is a very special dog,' AJ said now, running a hand over the dog's long, floppy ears. 'He's specially trained to help people like you who have diabetes. He knows hown to alert you when your blood sugar level is dropping or spiking.'

Samuel's eyes widened. He hugged the dog close, obviously attached already.

'These dogs undergo extensive training to be able to do what they do,' Lucie said, feeling AJ's eyes dart to her.

She'd read everything he'd written over the past week. It was fascinating.

Samuel's mother poked her head in and took a seat as Lucie continued.

'He can detect isoprene—that's a common natural chemical found in human breath. It increases, the lower your blood sugar is—'

'So, keep Bingo close,' AJ cut in.

The new dog had been placed on the bed now, and was licking Samuel's face.

Samuel's mother was wiping tears of joy from her face. 'I can't thank you and Thera Pups enough, Dr Johnstone.'

When Lucie looked up again, AJ was smiling at her, and her blood raced, remembering how she'd clung to him in her dream. This felt so good, she'd almost forgotten how at odds they were.

Clamming up on him yesterday hadn't been her finest moment. Pretending she felt nothing? So selfish! The truth was, she'd panicked. What if she let him in, let herself fall the way she'd always wanted to with him, and *then* he said he wasn't ready after all? Or that he needed more for his son and daughter than some itchy-footed traveller with no real roots and no history of settling down?

You still have no intention of settling down, she reminded herself.

Although it *was* getting tiring, moving around all the time, always trying to outrun the next disaster…

'What do you think, Lucie?'

'Huh?' She'd zoned out, her eyes on AJ…thinking about AJ. Again.

'Should I bring Bingo to Paws Under the Stars?' Samuel asked hopefully. 'I can dress him up…'

'If you're well enough,' AJ said gently. He turned to Lucie. 'We're organising a little outing for several kids who've spent time on the ward this year the night of the event.'

'I want to see them in their costumes, with all the lights!' Samuel grinned, stroking a hand across Bingo's soft head and receiving another lick in response.

He looked delighted at the prospect, and Lucie smiled as AJ's phone rang. She watched him step into the hall with it.

It was awe-inspiring, how much AJ's organisation was helping people heal, each one in a different way, all because of these dogs.

'I want to see them in their costumes too,' Lucie heard herself say, before she could even remind herself that she wouldn't be around for it. She'd be somewhere else by then…somewhere far away.

AJ was back. The look on his face made her adrenaline spike. Something was up.

She threw him a questioning look. He shook his head.

'Do you mind taking the dogs?' he asked her. 'Something's come up. I'll catch up with you in an hour or so if I can.' He paused, lowered his voice. 'And if I can't, call me when you know Constance's colonoscopy results?'

Her mind swam. 'I will. Is it the twins?'

'Yes, but they're OK… I think.

AJ looked frazzled. With a quick goodbye to Samuel, he darted back towards the door.

CHAPTER FOURTEEN

'DAD, WE NEED more tissues!'

Austin suppressed a harried sigh from the kitchen, where he'd just realised they were out of canned food. Belle wasn't exactly responsible for keeping the cupboards stocked, but she'd used to do it anyway. Now, with all her wedding planning, she was spending more time away. He was gradually having to do more and more to keep the big house in order. Which was, as it emerged, quite a lot for one person.

'You're doing OK now, Austin. You've got this!'

He repeated his sister's words in his head, trying to believe they were true.

'Dad, can I have some hot chocolate?'

'Um… I'm not sure that's what you should be having. Chocolate doesn't cure colds, guys.'

'Yes, it definitely does,' Ruby insisted from the other room.

Ruby and Josiah were both sick. They had the same bug that was striking everyone down lately. After the school had called, and he'd left the hospital to collect them, he'd bundled the two sniffling children up, deposited them on the couch with a cartoon show, and tried to ignore the mountain of work he was supposed to be doing.

The kids came first, but what was he supposed to feed them now? He scanned the pantry. Nothing of use but some pasta, and there wasn't any sauce. They couldn't exactly live on hot chocolate.

Or could they?

The doorbell irritated him, but he forced his face into some semblance of calm as he opened it.

'Hi,' Lucie said. 'Am I interrupting?'

He blinked, looking over her shoulder for the dogs. She'd texted to say she'd take them home, and he'd been too distracted to reply with anything other than a thumbs-up emoji.

'They're with Gramma May,' she explained, reading his mind. 'They're fine. She'll look after them for as long as we need. She asked me to bring you this.'

Lucie held out a Tupperware box and he grinned. Wafts of deliciousness sang to his nose and his stomach grumbled.

'That woman is a godsend,' he groaned, standing aside to let her in.

'I also brought you these. I dare you to make one last all day.' She held out a tiny box of chocolates from Cynthia's shop and he took them, touched. He'd used to buy one for her at a time and dare her the same thing.

She remembered that?

Minutes later, Lucie was ladling steaming soup into bowls, which she had somehow located herself, along with spoons, while he bashed out an email to a client that he'd been meaning to write for hours. She took two bowls to the twins, who accepted them gleefully and asked her to fetch some more tissues—which she did, without complaint.

Sending the email, he sat back in his chair, the warmth of his own bowl of soup already calming him.

'Anything else I can do?' she enquired. 'I noticed your cupboards are bare.'

She folded her arms, leaned back on the counter.

Why was she being so nice? He'd pretty much abandoned her back at the hospital, with no explanation. Of course one of the school staff would have told someone, who'd have told someone else about the twins—which was no doubt how

Gramma May had found out in time to make them soup. Everyone knew everything around here.

He ran a hand across his head. Would it be wrong to ask Lucie to get some groceries? He had so much work to do, and he'd already cancelled two clients today.

But she was already grabbing the shopping bag from the hook by the door. 'Don't worry,' she said gently. 'I can see you're busy. Take some time for yourself, AJ. Enjoy the chocolates.'

'I already have,' he admitted, and she snorted.

'I knew you wouldn't make them last!'

He'd been so in love with her laugh. One time when he'd caught her crying, he'd attempted his first cartwheel just to make her laugh. Three hours later he'd been laid up in A&E with a sprained wrist.

Thrown now, he fought the urge to refuse her help. She shouldn't have come here, really. His kids were sick. It was his issue to deal with, not hers. Lucie didn't need to be involved.

Not when they'd end up liking her even more than they did already. And not when he might, too.

'Lucie, come and watch this bit!' Josiah called out. 'It's so funny!'

'We can rewind it later,' she called back. 'Try not to laugh too much without me.'

'Can we have hot chocolate when you get back?' Ruby called out. 'Dad says it will cure us.'

'I did not say that!' Austin said.

With a squeeze of his shoulder, Lucie made her exit, and he listened to the door shut behind her, the crunch of her feet on the gravel driveway. This was what a community did. But Lucie wasn't really a part of it. He'd assumed she didn't want to be. Maybe she was warming to the way things were around here? Perhaps a little trip down memory lane was getting her nostalgic?

It was all just a bit weird, though, especially after what had happened on the beach. He'd given her every chance to confess she might have liked him too, back then, and to admit that she might want more now, but she'd brushed him off.

Maybe this was her way of trying to get their friendship back on track?

He should probably just accept it, he thought. He'd done enough to make things awkward.

An hour passed. Then another one. He managed to straighten out the house, send more emails, and rearrange his schedule in case the twins were sick for a few more days. His heart thudded wildly as he found himself removing the paperwork from the estate agents from the sideboard drawer and studying his house valuation for the thousandth time.

Stop assuming Belle will always be here when you know the clock is ticking, he told himself. *All this space will be too much.*

Still, when it came to calling the estate agent, he couldn't do it.

And Lucie wouldn't leave his head.

He'd told himself to keep away from her—had left her this morning without involving her, short of leaving both dogs in her care. But here she was again. And here he was…letting her in.

This had to change, he decided, abandoning the paperwork on the kitchen table and sighing. When she got back here with the shopping he'd insist she go straight home and not come back.

'I got the results of Constance's colonoscopy!'

Lucie burst past him with bulging bags of shopping the second he opened the door. She dropped them to the counter so hard that three oranges rolled out, and then turned to him, holding out her phone.

'AJ, Jetson was right. Look.'

Mind reeling, he took the phone from her, studied the report and scans.

'The tumour is tiny…in the lining of the bowel. Treatable with surgery, of course. It hasn't spread…' She tailed off.

He didn't know what to say. She didn't give him the chance to speak—she just threw her arms around him.

He hugged her back, stunned into silence, still trying to get his head around the news. Jetson had picked up on this cancer before they had. This was huge. They could analyse the chemical compounds in the cancer he'd sniffed out and put another piece of the puzzle together.

'This is massive, AJ.' Lucie still held his shoulders, elated. 'Your dog is so smart. And you are amazing for training him.'

Her eyes were shining with pride and awe and, caught in the moment, he almost kissed her. Almost.

Quickly, he stepped back—just as she did the same, flushing.

He helped her unpack the shopping, discussing with her what this meant for Constance, for his research. They were both so excited he almost forgot that things had been so tense between them before.

Four hours later, Lucie was still there. She and the kids were deep into a programme on the mysteries of Ancient Egypt—Josiah's new fascination—and Ruby had painted Lucie's nails. If it wasn't for the occasional sneeze and foghorn blow into a tissue, he might have assumed no one was sick at all…

'Daddy, can Lucie sleep over?' Ruby asked from the sofa cushions, where she was huddled against Lucie. Josiah, on her other side, was lost in a book.

Lucie bit back a smile. 'I don't think so, sweetie. You need to get better.'

'And you don't want to make Lucie sick too, do you?' Austin followed up from the adjacent armchair, even while his chest hollowed out.

It was late already—gone seven p.m.—but the twins were clinging on to Lucie like glue, and he had been able to do a few things around the house that he'd been planning to do, thanks to her looking out for them.

If he was planning to sell the house he'd have a lot *more* to do, he thought as his insides twisted.

When Josiah started yawning he stood, ordering them both up the stairs. They protested, of course, but Lucie offered to read from his favourite book about Egypt.

Austin shot her a questioning look as he scooped Ruby up in his arms, and she shrugged. 'I like Egypt,' she offered. 'I got stuck in a pyramid once, in Cairo. They almost closed it up with me inside it...like a mummy.'

'Are you going to be *our* mummy?' Ruby interjected sleepily.

Austin froze. Lucie's face flushed red.

'That's not what she meant, honey,' he said quickly, motioning Josiah to follow him up the stairs—but not before catching the look in Lucie's eyes. There it was: a hint of sadness and confusion where he'd expected to see laughter.

What did she really want? Certainly not to be anyone's mummy—although she'd make a better one than she thought she would, judging by how she'd been acting around the twins. But she couldn't give up the thrill of running round disaster zones, surely.

Lucie followed close behind Josiah, letting him lead. She was quiet while he got the kids changed, fetched them more tissues, and glasses of water in case they got dry throats in the night. He perched on the edge of Josiah's bed while Lucie took a chair and read from the book between their beds. The soft lull of her voice almost sent him to sleep, too.

He studied Lucie's profile in the night light and shadows. He was a ship on a rocky ocean...sailing right into a sinkhole opening up in the seabed. Her being here now was great, but it wouldn't feel great when he was forced to miss her again. Another woman gone in a flash, almost as fast as she'd arrived.

'Are you going to be our mummy?'

The kids craved a mother figure in their life—especially Ruby. Belle could only do so much, he thought. But this little unit of three he was cultivating alone would be a lot for any woman to take on. Especially a woman with one foot already out through the door, like Lucie…

'Let me get you that box before you go,' he said pointedly when they were back downstairs.

She followed him into the kitchen and stayed quiet while he washed and dried Gramma May's Tupperware. Too quiet. It made him feel nervous, as if the walls were closing in, trying to force them together when she should leave without the twins begging her not to go.

He turned around. She was looking at him, holding the house valuation papers in her hands. His stomach plummeted into his shoes.

'You're selling the house?' she said, her voice thick and unsteady.

'I don't know… Maybe.'

Dropping to a chair at the table, she stared at him, then at the papers, as if trying to convince herself it was real.

He took the seat opposite. 'I think I have to,' he explained. 'Belle's moving in with her fiancé, soon to be husband, shortly…'

'But this house has been in your family for years! Generations!'

'Well…' He struggled for the right thing to say. The truth was the truth. 'I can't manage all this on my own, Luce. It's too big for just the three of us.'

Lucie drummed her nails on the table, looking between him and the paperwork. 'I understand. But, honestly, I don't know what I'm feeling about this. I know I don't actually have any right to feel anything.'

'Of course you do,' he said, as the hurt on her face tore at him. 'You practically grew up here with me.'

He bit hard on his cheeks. He and Ebby had never lived here together, but he and Lucie… Well, Lucie had used to walk in here just as if it was her own house, without even ringing the bell!

Lucie blew air through her lips. She wasn't wearing as much make-up today. It made her eyes seem lighter, her skin paler. She looked younger—more like the girl who'd turned his life upside down by leaving with no explanation at all.

She still hadn't really given him a good reason for that— she'd said she hadn't wanted to miss him, or anyone here? It didn't make sense… But she hated him dragging it up and he didn't particularly want to antagonise her.

He found her hand on the table, as if he might comfort her for stomping on some precious part of her own past. She let him this time, just for a second, before standing up and facing him, folding her arms again.

Her shoulders were tight and he waited. Whatever she was about to say was going to be important. He braced himself— but a sudden flash of lightning cut her off. She shot to the window as the thunder crashed in quick succession, groaning as the rain that had been a light drizzle all afternoon turned into a thunderous shower, the strength of which could probably cause whiplash.

'Are you kidding me? This has got to be the wettest spring on record,' he said, walking up behind her.

She was inches from his face. Her eyes bored into his like a drill through to his brain, and he stopped short of asking if she was still going to walk home.

Of course she shouldn't walk home in this, Austin. You're supposed to be a gentleman.

'It'll stop soon enough…come through to the lounge. I'm sure there's an episode or two that you haven't seen about Ancient Egypt,' he offered, and though she looked conflicted, she agreed.

A cloud of white-hot tension popped straight back into the room and followed them both to the sofa.

CHAPTER FIFTEEN

THE AFTERSHOCK WAS almost as bad as the earthquake—only this time Lucie was at ground zero. Gripping the doorframe, she struggled for breath as the dust gripped her throat in a choke-hold. Jorge had ushered the kids towards her, but now he was turning back, looking for something.

'Where are you going?'

'She wants her backpack…there's a photo of her mother in it! She's lost her mother, Lucie.'

'It's too dangerous, Jorge. Come with us.'

'Take them outside. I'll only be two seconds.'

The kids were screaming, crying in terror. They came first—that was the agreement. The kids came first.

Dread pooled in her stomach. They were in a tiny village school halfway up a mountain road that had already been semi blocked by fallen trees. It had taken ages just to get there.

'Jorge, it's not safe!'

No sooner had the words left her mouth than another tremor shook the ground so hard that they were all thrown sideways.

Somehow she'd made it to the door with the kids, pushing them through into the open. *'Go! Go!'*

Behind her, Jorge screamed an agonising scream as a steel cabinet crashed down across his leg, trapping him.

'Jorge, no!'

She hurried back, shoved it with all her strength, but it

wasn't budging. It would have fallen on the kids if she hadn't got them out.

He was gasping for breath. Blood rushed through his jeans below the knee.

'You're going to be OK,' she soothed as the red stickiness seeped ominously through his clothing.

The blood was all over her as she locked her hands under his shoulders and tried to hoist him up. He wouldn't move. He was well and truly stuck.

'Go! Just go, Lucie!'

'No, I'm not leaving you!'

The light fixtures swung overhead. A chilling, creaking sound froze her to the bone. It was happening again. She stood there, torn, as the walls began to crumble and she was blinded by yet more dust. Jorge had gone eerily silent. Lucie fought the giant sob welling in her throat—right before the thousand-gallon water tank crashed down from its steel perch, smothering him completely.

'No! Jorge, no! No...'

'Lucie! Lucie, wake up!'

AJ's voice dragged her from the dream. She started awake, hot, sweating.

'What? What happened?'

AJ was crouched on the carpet beside the sofa, his shirt open, unbuttoned, as if he'd pulled it on in a hurry. A blanket that must have fallen off her lay crumpled by his knees.

'You fell asleep…you had a nightmare. God, is this what happens to you every time you have one of these dreams?'

He pressed a cool hand to her cheek and she sucked in a breath, scrambling to sit up.

'I'm so sorry.' She blinked beneath her fringe. 'How loudly did I scream? Did I wake the twins?'

'They're fine…' He frowned, moving beside her on the cushions, urging her against his shoulder.

She slumped against him, defenceless, comforted by the

bulk and naked warmth of his exposed chest. It lasted hardly any time at all before his unexpected presence caused all her other emotions to pile up and spill out. Her arms snaked around him impulsively, her hands clutching fistfuls of his hair and open shirt as she cried.

'I had no idea,' he growled, rubbing her shoulder, smoothing her hair back.

Relief had her sobbing like she'd never sobbed before. She'd never let it out. She'd bottled it up. Too afraid of her dreams getting worse if she uncorked all those emotions. But AJ was here. He was here, and she felt better already, with each sob into his chest. She could let it all out into him—he would take it and keep her safe, like he always had. It felt so good, finally, to be safe in his arms again.

Eventually, embarrassed, she pulled her head away, pressed the heels of her palms to her eyes. Not only had she passed out from exhaustion on his sofa, in front of the TV, she'd gone and shown him how deeply messed up she was.

'What you must have seen...' he said gruffly.

When she turned he was looking at her in fierce defiance. He looked angry, for what she'd been through, and sleepy too. Had she drawn him downstairs with her screams? It was bad enough that he'd left her here instead of waking her up.

'Why didn't you wake me up when I first dropped off?'

'It was raining, and you needed sleep! I told Gramma May you were safe, don't worry.'

He swept stray strands of damp hair back behind her ears and drew a thumb across her cheek. She wanted to sink deeper into him, into the comfort. The look in his eyes was undoing her again. Just like it had on the beach.

'I should go,' she managed.

But she was still shaking. Her legs would have buckled beneath her if she hadn't already been sitting down.

'You don't have to go anywhere,' he said gently.

'You have enough to deal with. What if the twins wake up feeling sick? I don't want to cause any trouble.'

'Lucie—damn it, just stop. You're not causing me any trouble. They're fast asleep.'

AJ fetched her a glass of water. He ran his hand up and down her back as she drank it and she realised she was still trembling, both with adrenaline and humiliation.

'Did I…did I shout your name?' she asked weakly, wiping at her face.

'*My* name?' He frowned.

She hid her eyes from him behind her hair.

Great, why not drop yourself in it a bit more, Lucie?

'Why would you have shouted *my* name? You don't dream of *me* in a landslide, or a hurricane, or whatever else you're trying to get away from in these nightmares, do you?'

She closed her eyes, breathed deep and hard. 'Sometimes my dreams get crazy, if you can believe that.'

'Can you talk to me about it?' he asked, pulling the blanket back up around her.

She stared at it, at his familiar eyes. It wasn't exactly what she'd come here to do. But his eyes were so kind, and his mouth was set in *I'll listen but won't speak* mode. Trusting him was second nature.

And so it all poured out of her. How she'd watched the water tank fall, how she'd had to escort the kids to the mountain road, willing herself to find strength as they wound around fallen debris to the sounds of distant screams. They'd gone there to talk with the kids, some of whom had lost parents, friends, siblings… Everything.

She told him how she'd had to direct the rescue team to where Jorge was buried and had watched him being carried out in a white body bag…how she'd made the call to his wife—the call no wife ever wanted to receive.

AJ must have suffered the same kind of shock, she realised. He would have heard the same gut-wrenching sobs coming from himself after finding out Ebby was gone. She shouldn't be telling him all this, she thought in dismay.

But he wasn't making it about him. And AJ's arm around her shoulders was the steady kind of certainty she hadn't felt in years.

The way he listened without comment or judgement made her tell him more. Jorge had had two kids, an expat wife in Cusco who'd moved there for him, built a life with him. It should've been *Lucie* who had died in the Kathmandu Valley that day, not him. It wasn't as if *she* had any significant others...no kids, not even any parents left.

'I should never have taken him there!'

AJ held her closer, as if he knew he was holding her together. And just as her heart rate started to calm he said, 'Don't go back to that job, Lucie. I'm begging you.'

Oh, God.

Patting her eyes, she struggled to regain her composure.

But he wasn't done. 'Even if you *can* go back to that kind of placement, Lucie, do you even want to? Surely there's a limit to how much one person can take?'

She shook her head. 'I need to go out there again. I promised myself I would carry on doing what Jorge can't...'

'Lucie...' He swivelled her round to face him. His face had that same look she'd seen on the beach: the serious AJ.

'I don't know what else I would do if I didn't go back.'

'You could stay here...in Brookborough.'

He held her stare. How was it possible for him to convey so much emotion with just a glance? she thought, leaning closer, suspended in the moment, magnetised. It was as if she could feel his soul now, and he could feel hers—as if every part of each of them was reaching out and connecting to the other. They were so close their breath mingled and the heat from his body radiated off him, calling to her. He wanted to kiss her. And she wanted the same...so badly...

No.

With difficulty, she pulled her hands back, drew the blanket tighter around her.

AJ stood, raked his hands through his hair.

'I can't stay in Brookborough, AJ.'

She'd promised herself she wouldn't let Jorge down. Besides, AJ knew she wasn't and could never be Ebby, or anything *like* the kind of woman he needed. She wasn't mother material, for a start! If she stayed, he'd figure that out soon enough.

Aunt Lina was back in her brain now. *'Kids are burdens,'* she'd always said. *'So are men, if you must know.'*

Lucie's teenage self had come to believe that. Lina was a successful, perpetually single woman who'd done everything by and for herself and thrived.

Her advice had always been, *'You can only rely on yourself in this life, Lucie!'*

Ostensibly she belonged nowhere, to no one, and that was working out just fine. Or had she just been telling herself that this whole time? In order to give Gramma space to live her retirement years in peace? To get away from being AJ's helpless little puppy dog shadow?

'You should try and get some sleep,' he said, cutting into her uncomfortable thoughts. 'I'll walk you home when the sun's up,' he said, coolly.

The moment was ruined.

To her dismay, he turned and made his way back up the stairs.

Lucie made sure to sneak out before the sun came up.

CHAPTER SIXTEEN

AUSTIN PULLED THE car into the sweeping driveway of the Mayflower Care Home just outside Staithes. A flock of birds darted like arrows from the willow trees and Jetson's ears pointed skywards in the passenger seat. Being well-trained, he didn't try to run for any birds when Austin let him out of the car, but he wanted to. A feeling Austin knew well.

Heading for the entrance, he saw the late-afternoon sun send dapples across the white stone walls of the stately home turned care facility. In the distance, boats formed tiny black dots on a molten golden sea. Was Lucie here yet?

They were meeting one of Lucie's patients together. It would be the first time they'd been together since their discussion at his house. Lucie had called him, said she needed him and Jetson for this one. Her invitation had come as a bit of a surprise, as she'd taken to going it alone with Maple lately.

He'd shot her brief texts from time to time, and she'd given him brief replies. Yes, she was fine, thanks. Yes, Constance's surgery had gone very well. And, yes, it was OK for her to keep Maple a while longer. Blunt. Brief. The way she was when she didn't want to deal with her emotions.

His fists clenched around the dog's lead as he walked into the building and a sweet old lady with a walking frame asked him something about Jetson. He replied on autopilot, distracted, wondering where Lucie was.

His eyes shot up to see her coming through the door behind

him. Rising to attention, he raised a hand, hating how he forgave her lateness and everything else the second he saw her.

'Sorry, sorry… I was with Constance. She'll be out of the hospital soon, but we lost track of time discussing…'

She trailed off as he stood there, as if just seeing him had thrown her brain off track. He bit back a smile.

'You look good,' he told her, greeting Maple, straightening his shirt. He should have worn his other jeans, but Josiah had dropped yogurt on them before he'd even pulled them from the drying rack…

'You sound surprised,' she quipped. Her teeth caught her lower lip as she flicked her eyes to him. 'Maple's been helping me a lot.'

'No more nightmares, then?'

She hesitated. 'Like I said, she's been helping.'

Austin nodded, eyebrows raised at her. *Little victories*, he thought as they shared a moment that took him back to the sofa. Holding her. Hearing her cry.

There was nothing he could have done then to make her laugh. They weren't kids…he couldn't cartwheel now any better than he'd been able to back then. So he'd tried to fix it another way…asking her not to go back to all that. Almost kissing her.

She'd almost kissed him too. He'd had the distinct impression it was more than just her job and her need to leave the village that had stopped her, but he'd been trying not to dwell on it too much.

What did it matter now? She was going back, regardless of what he said.

'We're so excited you're here, Doctors,' a chatty nurse enthused, walking them through a sunlit corridor.

Paintings lined the walls: flowers, a windmill, a toad in welly boots. Mayflower was smaller and more exclusive than Lavender Springs. It had a kind of cosy wildlife theme going on that was a bit unusual. But Gramma May had a couple of friends in here, and his volunteers had brought dogs here before.

One lady with narcolepsy had used to keep one full time until she'd passed away—her cocker spaniel, Rigby, had proven to be the best way to detect an oncoming attack. Rigby had even learned to stand across her lap, to prevent her falling out of her wheelchair.

Austin admired Lucie's tight blue trousers and heeled boots, listening to her make amicable conversation with the nurse while her daffodil-yellow scarf wafted more perfume back his way. Everything about Lucie seemed designed to lure him in.

She really did seem to be looking better too, he noticed. Not as tired, and way more energetic. One step closer to getting back on the road? he thought, picturing Ruby's face. The twins were asking for her. Was it better to let them see her, or not? These were questions he was not equipped to answer.

'I take it you know all about Sundown Syndrome?' Lucie asked him, as they came to a stop by some floor-to-ceiling patio doors.

'Of course,' he said. 'Dementia can make people upset in the early evenings. It's a restless time. They get confused, and some of them wander about—'

'I know walking and talking helps,' she interjected. 'My patient here, Ethel, is a new arrival. She's a little lost at the best of times lately, but I thought we could try her with the dogs. She used to have one, I think.'

He knew what she was getting at. Maybe the dogs would distract this lady and help her to remember a few things.

'Talking helps,' he repeated, and he raised his eyebrows pointedly.

Talking with him at the house that night must have helped Lucie in some way. She probably didn't let those kinds of debilitating thoughts or feelings out to many people. At least she knew she could always talk to him—even if she'd never say what he wanted to hear.

The sea glimmered in the distance as he, Lucie and Ethel took to the gardens. Shrubs and flowers lined the concrete paths, and a bubbling water feature caught streaks of late sunshine in its ripples.

He walked with Ethel on his arm. She was beaming beneath a mop of wiry grey hair as if she'd won the lottery. Lucie walked at her other side.

'This is such a beautiful garden! You are so lucky you get to see all these flowers blooming, Ethel.'

Lucie seemed genuinely awed by the garden, and he caught himself smiling at her. She returned the smile at full wattage and the hint of tension lifted from between them.

They made light conversation on their walk around the rose bushes. Ethel kept stopping, looking around in confusion, her brow more wrinkled than it should have been. The dogs were playing and chasing each other, but Maple came back on command as Lucie stopped by the fountain. She'd noticed Ethel needed a distraction, as had he.

As they gathered around the fountain, Ethel's eyes soon moved to the dogs again. Sure enough, she started talking about the dog her husband had brought home once. 'It often came with us to a lovely pub in Staithes !'

'Did you go there a lot with your husband?' Lucie asked.

Austin followed with more questions, most of which Ethel answered quite articulately.

A nurse came to check all was well and raised her eyebrows on hearing Ethel talking, before leaving them to it.

Ethel told them all about her stint in the restaurant at the pub, when she'd waitressed there. She regaled them with the story of the day of a great storm that blew in and washed the seafront away.

'My husband was a fisherman. But that day he was plucking bottles of wine and beer from the water after the pub got flooded. The dog, too. Great at catching full beer bottles, he was.'

'Sounds like a smart dog. What was his name?' Lucie asked.

Ethel frowned. She got lost again for a moment.

'What colour was he?' Austin encouraged.

'Brown, of course.'

Lucie put a hand to her arm gently. 'What year was the storm, Ethel?'

'1953,' she said, without a beat.

Austin could barely suppress his grin. 'She's right,' he said, and Lucie laughed.

She blushed slightly as he touched a hand to her back before she stood up.

Another small, shared victory, and it felt like everything in that moment.

'Ethel's communicating more clearly than she has in days,' the nurse said later, hands on hips, impressed.

She bent to pat Maple, and Austin watched the pride flicker in Lucie's eyes, feeling it as if it were his own. It wasn't just Maple and Jetson who'd opened her up. Lucie's calming presence had been key. She was good at getting people to talk, even if she wasn't so good at it herself, he mused. Not about the truth behind her need to keep running, anyway. He knew there was more to it than their failed friendship, and more than her just not liking Brookborough. It shouldn't still get to him after all this time, but it did.

'We should walk the dogs before we go back,' Lucie suggested, as they made their way to the exit with a promise to stay longer next time. 'Unless you have to get back to the twins?'

'They're with Belle,' he replied.

It was impossible in that moment for him to concoct an excuse not to walk the dogs with her. And in minutes she was steering her car behind his on the narrow country road towards Staithes.

CHAPTER SEVENTEEN

PARKING WASN'T ALLOWED in the old town, due to the narrow streets. So Lucie parked her hire car by AJ's in the public car park near the station and they walked the winding lanes with the dogs towards the pub that Ethel had remembered—the Cod and Lobster.

They let the dogs run on the sand beneath the pub, and Lucie resisted bringing up that night at his house…the promise of a kiss that had shimmered between them but never eventuated. He probably regretted even thinking about it. *Ugh*, the humiliation.

She'd woken him up with her screaming, so he'd probably just been tired and confused. It was best not to say anything, she decided. Her own growing feelings were highly inconvenient, and she should do absolutely nothing to stir this pot any further.

Even being next to him again was excruciating. His snuggly knitted sweater was just the kind she'd have huddled into against the wind if she hadn't been trying her best to ignore their undeniable attraction and not make things harder for them both. Obviously until she'd called on him and the dogs to help Ethel out of her slump he'd been trying to keep his distance in light of her leaving, and she was going to respect that.

'Are you hungry?' he asked, breaking the silence.

Without either of them saying it, Lucie knew they would be heading back to the Cod and Lobster.

They ordered battered cod and mushy peas and chips. While the dogs salivated, Lucie wondered if there would ever be a time when she would look at AJ and *not* find him the sexiest guy on earth. So different from the boy she'd once known.

'Remember your crab races?' she said, recalling the buckets of the snappy creatures he'd used to collect from the rock pools.

'Remember the first time we found fool's gold?'

He grinned, and she sat back in her seat as a flood of the best kind of memories washed over her. A sense of belonging was slowly creeping in. She wrestled with it, but it kept on winning. It felt kind of nice. More than nice.

'I tried to convince everyone at school that my gold was real,' AJ said, smiling.

They'd both been fascinated by those shiny little nuggets of iron pyrite that looked so much like the real thing.

'If only it *had* been real...' She sighed.

'What would you do with all the gold in the world?' he asked her.

His warm blue eyes twinkled in the firelight from the open hearth. It was dark outside now.

'Buy your house,' she replied without a beat. 'And give it to you.'

He bit his cheek. 'It's paid off,' he admitted, omitting the information that Ebby's life insurance had covered most of it. 'I told you—it's just too big. We need something smaller now Belle's moving in with Bryce.'

'I'm sure you could fill it,' she said, serious now.

It had been playing on her mind for days—the house he loved going up for sale. It didn't feel right. Probably because she loved it, too, and also because she knew the twins would be moving from the only place they remembered living in.

A feeling of displacement threatened her calm. She should know how to be a rock for a family who'd lost so much. She'd pretty much walked her childhood in their shoes.

'Aren't there a few more dogs you could adopt?' she asked. Maybe she could help them find a solution.

He shrugged. 'Let me guess... That sounds like your worst nightmare? A house full of kids and dogs...'

Lucie bristled, glancing at the sleeping dogs. 'I've had worse nightmares—as you well know.'

'But fewer, lately?' he probed. 'Since you talked to me?'

'Since I got Maple.' She winced. 'OK...*and* since I talked to you.'

She bit her lip. How did he know?

She hadn't exactly admitted it before now, but he was right. She shrugged. So what if she'd slept better since talking to him? It didn't mean she'd be relying on him for anything else. The only person she could count on was herself, she reminded herself. Though somehow it didn't quite ring as true as it had used to.

'As for having a house full of kids and dogs,' she continued, 'I don't think I've ever really let myself think beyond the next place I might unpack a suitcase.'

'Why not? Why do you always have to keep going? All on your own?'

'I'm not on my own. I have my team.'

'You know what I mean, Lucie.'

She paused, open-mouthed, ready to make a biting remark in self-defence. Then she realised she didn't really have one.

AJ eyed her thoughtfully. 'It's OK to want to stay in one place, you know,' he said. 'You don't have to keep putting your own life in danger just because you couldn't save your teammate—which wasn't your fault, by the way.'

'Who died and made you my therapist?' she snapped, taking a gulp of water.

AJ sat back in his seat. 'Sorry,' he said to the bobbing boats outside the windows.

He wasn't sorry though. And she knew he had the right to

give her his brutal honesty. Their history had given him that right long ago and there was nothing she could do about it.

'I just don't think you should go back to something just because you feel guilty, Lucie.'

'Is that the only reason you don't want me to go back?' she shot back, surprised at her own courage.

Silence.

She continued, 'I wouldn't make a good mother figure, AJ. You know that.'

AJ let out a loud snort of indignation. 'Is that what you think? That I'm trying to replace Ebby with *you*?'

Blood rushed to her cheeks but she kept a straight face. 'I don't know.' She turned her eyes to the view through the big glass windows. 'You almost kissed me that night in your living room, after my dream.'

Her heart was like a hopping rabbit. Of course it would slip out. And now he knew she'd been thinking about it.

AJ cleared his throat. 'I did.'

She swallowed—hard. What exactly was she fishing for here? She'd decided not to go there, and he already regretted it, judging by the look on his face.

'I just don't want you going back out to disaster zones,' he said measuredly. 'That's no secret. I've seen what it's done to you. But I'm not looking to trap you into marriage, if that's what you think. Maybe you've just opened my eyes to some... stuff.'

'Oh, yes?'

Oh, God.

'I can't keep living in the past. I don't want to any more.' He rearranged his napkin on the table, lifted one eyebrow in an imperious arch. 'I kind of feel...guilty about this, you know? But maybe I *am* finally ready to date someone.'

Her heart lurched, but she kept her face in check. 'Someone who'd be good for the kids?' she managed. Nausea ate at her from the inside as the thought of it took her mind hostage. 'Good for you.'

'Of course Ruby and Josiah will come into all my decisions,' he said carefully.

She frowned. 'You should do what's right for *you*, AJ.'

'Ditto.'

'And you don't have to feel guilty about that.'

'Neither should you feel guilty for living your life when your friend lost his.'

'Mmm...'

Lucie played with her phone, pretending to answer an important email. She feigned indifference to the thought of him dating, while her jealous heart roared. Who would he date now that she'd riled him up and made him see he was ready to let someone in? Who would win his heart when she'd disappeared again?

Definitely better not to think about that. Especially if Claire Bainbridge is still single.

'So, it looks like you're enjoying Maple being around,' he said next, signalling for the bill.

Lucie swallowed, and admitted that, yes, the dog was helping her exponentially, actually.

Although the truth was letting it all out onto AJ's shoulders back at the house the other week was what had really put her on the path to healing. He was right about that. It felt so good to have got it all out, to have someone who knew her really *hear* her.

'Hopefully you can find her a new foster home before I leave,' she found herself saying, as he paid the bill.

If only her stomach would stop tying itself into knots.

AJ grunted something indecipherable, pulling on his jacket.

Cringing, she cursed herself. She'd stupidly said that on purpose, to distance herself more. Because the worst had already happened in her head. His marriage to the new amazing woman who'd make all his thoughts about *her* disappear into the ether. There was someone out there just waiting to fire up his bloodstream. He was pulling away from her faster than she could push him.

They were halfway back to the cars with the dogs, in an orange-lit cobbled alleyway, when she realised her tears were causing serious vision impairment. She blinked them away, but it was too late. AJ had seen.

Blinking again, she watched his face come into view, close up, concerned…almost angry. It was suddenly all too much. She had to tell him why she'd left all those years ago.

'AJ…' She felt words piling up on top of themselves in her throat. There was nowhere for them to go any more, other than out. 'You humiliated me, AJ! I trusted you!'

AJ balked. 'What do you mean? What are you talking about? When did I do that?'

'With Claire Bainbridge! I heard you that night, in your room. I came to talk to you about Aunt Lina's offer to pay for my tuition if I went back to Denver…and I heard you and Claire, talking and laughing about me.'

AJ took a step back, but Lucie closed the space between them.

'She said I followed you around like a little lost puppy…that I was cramping your style. And you said nothing to defend me! I thought we were friends, and you let her speak about me like that. You were more interested in sleeping with her—'

'Wait!' He ran his hands across his head and jaw, glowering. 'You overheard that?'

'I didn't mean to! I left before I had to hear you guys having sex.'

'We didn't have sex!' He stared at her now, incredulous. 'So *that's* why you decided never to speak to me again once you went to America? Lucie, I didn't need to defend you to her, or to anyone, because what we had was nobody else's business. If you'd stuck around for long enough, you would have heard me tell her that. I certainly did *not* sleep with her!'

Lucie gaped at him, feeling heat and mortification creep through every bone in her body, turning her legs to jelly. She sank against a brick wall.

He followed her, forcing her into his shadow, towering over her. 'You left Brookborough, and me, because of *that*? Lucie…'

'You were *everything* to me!'

'*You* were everything to *me*.'

She lunged for him with an aching desperation, and their hands and bodies suddenly intertwined in a tangled embrace. He took her hair in his fists and kissed her fiercely, with all of his soul, till she felt as if she was underwater, pulled along by the tide of him, swept away.

'Lucie…' he moaned against her mouth.

She dissolved into a thousand tiny shards of longing as he moaned her name.

AJ pinned her against a shuttered storefront and the streetlight shone in her face, creating a silhouette of him. Her back rasped against the rough wooden door, jingling a tiny bell that she ignored. His hands slid across her body with intent now, stirring a fire in her chest, igniting her flesh under her clothes. He was her everything…he'd been her everything…and she wanted him so badly it hurt.

Their breaths were coming hot and hungry, like a fire finding its way back up from burnt-out embers. When AJ stopped for just a moment, as if to absorb her, she saw his eyes were transformed in the streetlight. A craving she'd never seen before shone back at her.

Arching further into him, she felt her body vibrate with need. Her hips sought his, pressing against him as if she might slip into his skin, and a flood of hot moisture filled her core. If they hadn't been out on the street she might have laid him down and demanded he show her what he'd never shown her before—she would have gladly taken it…she'd waited for ever for this.

It was only when a passing stranger cleared his throat that

they sprang apart. Her mouth was full of the taste of him. It wasn't enough. Ramming her hands through her hair, she caught her breath as AJ adjusted his sweater, then his jeans.

'I didn't mean for that to happen,' she managed, when the stranger had gone.

Her words were futile. Actions spoke far louder. Neither of them could have stopped if they'd tried. Even the dogs looked as if they were judging them.

'We shouldn't have done that...' She tried again, coming to her senses, but he was stepping towards her, determined.

'Neither of us is dating anyone else, are we?'

'Not yet.' She sighed out her frustration, her lips still stinging. 'But I'm no good for you.'

He cupped her face in one hand, drawing her to him firmly. A shuddering exhalation left her throat.

'Why don't you let me decide what's good for me while you're still here?'

'You don't mean that, AJ. This will only get complicated.'

'Maybe it will.'

His determination cancelled out her next string of excuses. He was willing to take the risk if she was. It was written all over his face.

He brought his mouth to hers and she lost herself in him all over again. They could kiss, she supposed. It didn't have to mean anything. Besides, they were good at it. *Very* good at it. His tongue aroused primordial parts of her that felt as if they'd been in hibernation for years. Oh, the places his tongue could go...

They *wouldn't* do anything else, though, she warned herself. No going home with him, or her resolve would be ruined. She had to be strong and let kisses be enough.

CHAPTER EIGHTEEN

THE PROBLEM WITH kissing Lucie, Austin thought, opening the car door for her, was that it wasn't enough. Now he wanted more.

Constance could see it on their faces the second she answered the door—he was sure of it. The two women made small talk like old friends while he made tea and Lucie performed her check-ups. And although Constance was weary, with a lingering loss of appetite after her straightforward surgery to remove the tumour, she fed treats to Maple—her favourite—and asked Lucie about Gramma May.

'So how are things with you?' Constance asked him as they all took their seats in the living room.

The little green sofa felt even smaller than last time, when he'd sat down on it with Lucie. A flyer for the Paws Under the Stars event sat on the coffee table—not long to go now. Maple was going to be Yoda. As for Jetson…he was still waiting for Josiah and Ruby to decide.

'I should be asking you that,' he told Constance, ignoring the little wink she shot him.

Was it obvious to her that something had happened between him and Lucie?

Just a little taste of Lucie before he got back on the dating scene—that was what he'd been telling himself their kiss had been. But all he'd been able to think about since that kiss was Lucie—which was exactly why he *had* to find someone else.

Surely it would be better to have someone lined up to distract him when the crushing absence of her kicked in again?

They hadn't told a soul about that kiss, but everyone seemed to know something was up. Gramma May was giving him looks whenever she saw him and the twins. And Gramma May had told Cynthia something, and Cynthia had told everyone who wandered into the chocolate shop. Even if they only cared about chocolates.

He'd agonised over it—the fact that Lucie had left Brookborough thinking his loyalties lay with Claire Bainbridge instead of her. But even though he'd as good as said she was his world back then, she'd backed off, still convinced she should be somewhere else. Well, he wasn't about to beg her to stay if she didn't want to. She wasn't good for him—she was damn right about that. Not when she was a fleeting ship just passing by this village.

But instead of doing what he should be doing—which was keeping far away, where he couldn't get burnt—he'd arranged to work with her again. They were a good team, after all—the patients loved her, and that *was* why they were here. Clearly he was also a glutton for punishment.

'I just had to see you and Jetson,' Constance told him now, over her teacup. 'You know, you both might have saved my life. How can I ever thank you?'

'Your good health is thanks enough…it's what we're here for,' Austin told her, feeling himself tense as Lucie's eyes rested on his profile.

'All I can think about is how grateful I am for Thera Pups, Dr Johnstone, and I'd like to donate, or help in any way I can. Sponsor a dog, maybe…?'

Lucie reached for her hand as the woman's voice faltered. 'You don't have to do that.'

'I just… I'm going to miss you.'

'We can come and see you for as long as you need.'

'There are plenty of people who need you more—and the dogs.' Constance's hand found Jetson's furry ears, and the dog promptly put his big soft head in her lap.

'Just because other people need us too, it doesn't mean we won't still find time for you,' Lucie assured her.

Until you leave us all, Austin thought begrudgingly, wishing he didn't keep on getting hit so hard by the thought of it. She wouldn't find time for *anyone* here when she was gone again. The sooner he got used to that, the better.

'How much longer do we have you for, Lucie?'

Constance seemed sad at the prospect of losing her, too.

'A few weeks,' she admitted, glancing his way.

The two of them had clearly talked about her 'real' job. A chill coursed up his spine, and he fought the sudden nausea that roiled in his stomach.

'And where do you go on your next mission? I think it's so wonderful what you do. Don't you, Dr Johnstone?'

He nodded mutely, focusing on the dogs, ignoring Lucie's eyes drilling into him. Constance seemed excited for her. But all he could do was stop the resentment from showing on his face as she answered, 'I don't know where I'll be placed just yet.'

She could build her world right here. People would love her and need her just as much as they would in some as yet undetermined but no doubt dangerous location across the globe. But she didn't want to do that.

Lucie's phone buzzed through her jacket. As she pulled it out, her face showed confusion. 'Lavender Springs...' she frowned. 'Belle says Jack Granger has asked for me and Maple.'

Oh, really?

Austin watched as she tapped into the phone. Their elderly stroke patient was obviously having a bad day and he'd directly asked for Lucie. She'd made even more of an impression on people than he had thought. Pride swelled through him—before the dread set in. It wasn't just himself and the twins and Gramma May who'd miss her.

'I should go,' she said.

'And go you must,' Constance said with a good-natured sigh, ruffling Maple's ears.

Austin called to Jetson. Jack had been *his* patient first, and he would be again when Lucie disappeared.

'I'll go with you,' he declared, leaving her absolutely no room to argue.

Belle met them in Reception. 'Thank God you're here!'

She ushered them and the dogs through to a private room, where Jack Granger sat in an armchair, staring with melancholy out of the window.

'He says his heart hurts,' she whispered. 'We haven't seen any immediate signs of cardiovascular issues, but…'

'We'll check him out,' AJ said.

The dogs had already padded over to Jack, who was so far ignoring them.

'Hey, Jack,' Lucie said in concern, crouching beside his chair. 'Your heart hurts? Will you let us take you through to another room, so we can check you out?'

'You won't find anything,' he replied, finally acknowledging them.

'You don't know that,' AJ said.

'Yes, I do. It's just Alice. She has a habit of doing this thing to my heart. She died on this day, you know. I feel her on the day…every year.'

Lucie put a hand to AJ's arm. Both dogs lay at Jack's feet, as if they were perfectly happy to bide their time.

'Silly, I know,' Jack continued. 'But I'd rather be with a dog right now than *any* human.' He glanced at Lucie. 'They listen. They know our hearts. At least, mine always used to.'

Austin caught Lucie's look.

'Something about having a dog keeps me calm, too,' she replied. 'Which, in turn, makes me think about things more rationally.'

Jack nodded.

Lucie went on. 'I think I told you on my last visit that the dogs have helped me so much, since I got back to the village. And they'll always be here to listen to you, too.'

Austin's heartbeat skidded. Was she trying to hammer home the fact that she was almost ready to leave them?

'She would have liked you, my Alice,' Jack said, as his leathery hand reached for Jetson's ear.

His bad arm was still in a sling, but the man had more colour in his cheeks than the last time Austin had seen him, and he seemed to be talking more to Lucie than he ever had to him.

'How long were you married?' he cut in, determined to strike up a rapport.

Jack sighed. 'Over fifty years. I never remarried. Never did find anybody quite like her. She was a dancer...'

They listened as Jack spoke about courting Alice, calmed and encouraged by the dogs' gentle presence. Before half an hour had passed they had him out on a short walk and throwing a ball for the dogs in the garden by the shallow duck pond.

Lucie took Austin aside. 'Are you OK? Hearing this stuff?' she whispered in concern.

'Stuff?' He feigned ignorance.

It should be a good thing that he didn't feel quite as jarred by the subject of losing a spouse as he would have done a few months or even weeks ago. Lucie had a lot to do with that, he supposed. For all the good it would do him when she was gone again.

'I'm OK,' he assured her stiltedly.

'You're allowed to talk about Ebby if you want,' she replied, clearly reading him all wrong. 'It's healthy. Talking about Alice has just helped Jack.'

'I'm not Jack,' he said, frustration making him snap. 'Maybe I just don't want to talk about it, Lucie. Not with you.'

Lucie looked hurt and he squared his shoulders, turning away towards Jack. He felt bad immediately. He shouldn't have snapped at her. But she had no idea that the way he'd felt for his late wife had never matched the extent and depth of his long-hidden love for Lucie. And even now there was nothing he could do to change that.

Belle caught his arm on the way out. 'Austin, are we still on for tonight? I have some great ideas for your new dating profile!'

His stomach plummeted.

Lucie's eyes grew wide. Then she turned and feigned un-interest as Belle winked at him.

'When the twins are in bed we'll go over it,' she said. 'I'm working on making you sound like the most eligible bachelor in town. Not that he isn't—right, Lucie?'

'Sorry…what?' Lucie was stroking Maple, pretending not to listen.

He felt his lips twitch at the look on her face. Sure, Belle was stirring the pot—trying to suss out what was going on with them following the rumours—but poor Lucie was clearly seething inside now, her cheeks red as cherry sorbet under her make-up.

'We're getting this boy back on the market!' Belle grinned, ruffling his hair.

'I'm not some prize bull, Belle,' he told her gruffly, shaking her off, daring another look at Lucie.

Her lips were a thin, jealous line. She was bashing at her phone with furious, stabbing motions, as if she wished it was his face.

It hadn't exactly been his intention to make her jealous. In fact, up until this moment his own pent-up frustration had left a bitter taste in his mouth. He should just get her out of his head *and* his life for good and move on. Why live in the past when he had to focus on the future? Especially when that future wasn't going to involve Ebby *or* Lucie.

But the look on her face! It *was* mildly entertaining, seeing how much she actually cared. Maybe she didn't want to get out of here as much as she liked to think she did?

'You couldn't even wait till I'm gone?' she said coolly, as soon as they were outside.

The spring sunshine infused the air with warmth, and the sky was a vivid blue now the rain seemed to be behind them. The dogs sped on ahead into the garden, towards the pond again, and he followed them—they clearly needed a longer run before getting back in the car.

'Are you jealous?' he dared, unable to stop the grin from spreading across his face.

'I'm not jealous,' she hissed. A couple of geese flapped in a panic, moving away from the oncoming dogs. 'But I know you're just doing this to antagonise me, Austin.'

'You know, you only call me Austin when you're angry,' he teased.

Her hands flew up in the air as she walked across the grass beside him. 'Whatever. I don't care what you do.'

'Yes, you do. And anyway, this is all Belle. I don't know why you're angry with me. She just wants to help me out.'

'So let her. I'm sure she'll line you up with a whole string of dates before the week is out. You can have your pick.'

'Maybe so,' he said, stopping in his tracks by the pond. 'But none of them will be you.'

Lucie sniffed, looked at him askance, then rolled her eyes.

'You're cute when you're jealous,' he said.

A flicker of a smile took over her face, but then she scowled, staring at the ducks. 'I'm not cute.'

'Aha! You just admitted you're jealous.' He prodded her side and she squealed and jumped back, laughing.

'You're such an idiot!'

She pushed him playfully with both hands. His foot slid on the wet grass.

Oh, no!

Before he knew what was happening, he was splashing into the pond, ducks and geese flapping everywhere. The dogs barked furiously, thinking it was a game.

'Oh, my God, AJ!' Lucie's hands flew to her mouth as she ran to the edge. 'I'm so sorry! Here, take my—'

He waded over, took her outstretched hand. But instead of using it to pull himself out he pulled her into the water with him. Lucie screamed and flailed her arms, landing backwards, and he couldn't help it. He cracked up. He could barely stand up in the waist-high water, he was laughing so hard.

'What are you...? AJ, I can't *believe* you!' she gasped, scraping back her wet hair, blinking as mascara streaked her face.

She splashed him, and he reciprocated, until they were sloshing water wildly at each other, laughing hysterically. Deep belly laughs ricocheted through him at the utter ridiculousness of the situation—he hadn't laughed this hard in *years*.

'Was that payback for that day you arrived?' he asked through his tears of laughter.

She waded towards him. Her shirt was totally see-through.

Hot. Damn.

'It was an accident and you know it. *This*, on the other hand, pulling me into the pond, was not an accident. Look at me!'

'It was funny, though,' he said, as his laughter subsided. He found her waist and pulled her close possessively, tracing the outline of her bra through her shirt with his eyes. 'And I am looking at you. Why do you have to be so sexy?' he growled.

Lucie caught her breath. He waited for her to push him away, but she moaned softly, pressed her hips to his under the warm water...an invitation. For a moment they stood there, breathing deeply, forehead to forehead. Excruciating.

Do not kiss her. Do not go there. You'll be a total idiot if you do this again...

It was hard to tell who kissed who first. Lucie gripped the front of his sodden shirt, tugging him closer, opening her mouth to him. The feel of her set a wildfire alight in his veins that should have evaporated every drop of water in the pond.

Then self-deprecation came crashing in too, as they kissed. He shouldn't want her...should not still be doing this. She'd said it herself. She was no good for him...

Except in this moment she was everything.

Their mouths crashed, exploring, tongues twirling, sucking, licking, groaning. Half a decade he'd waited, to feel an ounce of what he was feeling around her. Half a decade. Wasn't that long enough to have let the darkness and rage and helplessness consume all his fire? Wasn't it the point of life? To love, and be loved, even if that love was fleeting?

Lucie pulled back first, breaking their kiss to run her eyes over his face. They told him she was hungry for more of him, but her hands had stopped roving up and down his back and were now resting firmly around his shoulders. She put her forehead back against his. His fingers traced the contours of her beautiful face. She exhaled deeply, as if all the world's problems were escaping her.

'I want you.'

'I guess we should get out of this pond then,' he responded.

Another giggle escaped her mouth.

'I'd actually forgotten we were in the pond,' he admitted, pulling out his shirt, only to find it slapping back, cold and wet against his skin.

She stuck out her tongue as he swept her fringe aside. The deep affection and longing in her eyes struck him to the core before she looked away, hugging herself.

He could still read her after all these years. Leaving him was going to be hard for her—harder than she was letting on. Even harder now. But if this was really all he could have of her, he suddenly wanted all he could get while he could.

'You can expect an invoice for another pair of boots ruined!'

she huffed playfully, wading back to the bank, with him following close behind.

It wasn't till they were standing on the edge, wringing out their clothes and their hair, that he realised several people, including Belle, were standing at the large window of the care home, laughing and clapping in delight.

'And they thought the dogs coming was the most exciting thing to have happened all week,' Lucie said, wiping the mascara from her cheeks and daring a wave.

Grinning, he waved too. 'I think we gave them something to talk about,' he said, trying not to think about the questions Belle would no doubt have for him later.

Luckily she'd be at work for another few hours, and the twins were going on an after-school playdate at a friend's house.

He took Lucie's hand. Her fingers curled around his. They locked eyes.

'There's no one at my place,' he said, cocking an eyebrow.

Lucie closed her eyes and nodded.

Together, still laughing, they hurried back to the car, the dogs sprinting after them. Slamming the door shut, Lucie leaned across the gearstick and pressed her mouth to his.

'Are you sure you want to come back with me?' he asked her, mid-kiss.

Her wandering hands between his legs was the only answer he needed.

CHAPTER NINETEEN

AJ's BREATHING WAS the only sound in the room. It mingled with her own hot gasps at the feel of him, his muscles, his hard lines and sounds and touches. The way he kissed her, with her back pressed to the cool bird's-egg-blue of the bedroom wall. It drove her mad for him.

Downstairs, music sang from the stereo and for a second Lucie feared the twins might come darting up the stairs, demanding something. But they weren't home.

It was just them, and there was no going back now—not after that kiss in the pond. And not after the steamy shower they'd just shared...all the foreplay. He'd tasted parts of her no one had tasted in a while, and he was definitely not the awkward teen she'd first fallen for. Every atom of her being wanted—no, *needed* him—all of the amazing adult AJ. Just once. Just this one time.

He was urging her to the bed, his hands roaming with intent across her sides and back, kissing, stroking, caressing her, and then teasing away the towel he'd given her just seconds before in the bathroom.

'Do you even know how crazy you make me?' he uttered in equal awe and frustration.

Desire was written all over his face as he took her in, naked and sprawled beneath him across the sheets. It didn't cross her mind to feel self-conscious, but an overwhelming flood of emotion threatened to steal the moment as she looked into his eyes.

No. She would not admit how much his honesty moved her—how much this sense of connection and of comfort made her question every solo plan and goal she'd ever made for herself. That would be getting in far too deep.

She didn't know where she was going next. That had never been an issue before…going into the unknown. It was the thought of staying here that got to her, she realised solemnly, as this new-found intimacy threatened to make her cry. God, his mouth, his eyes…she could fall into him and keep falling…

'You're amazing…you know that?' she said, meaning it, stroking his bottom lip with her thumb, memorising every detail of his face.

She was falling already. But what if she let herself go, offered it all up, and then he decided *no.* She'd be broken. She'd have to leave anyway—she owed it to Jorge—but she'd leave with her heart doubly broken. Like after Mum and Dad had died…when she was sent to England.

'I wish I could get inside your brain,' he said, kissing her eyes softly.

He traced the lines of her mouth with his thumb, sending a current through her bloodstream. Suddenly her whole body zinged and burned for him, hot, sticky and ready. This was not a time for emotions.

Get a grip. Just enjoy it.

She dared to nibble on one forefinger, sucking it into her mouth, twirling her tongue around it—a teaser. She smiled at him, taking all of him in, savouring the sound of his deep, throaty moan as he stroked her hair.

AJ didn't want to wait a moment longer and neither did she. But it wasn't good to rush these things, she thought. Not if they were only going to do this once.

Hovering over her, AJ murmured her name against the smooth skin of her ear, brushed her damp hair away to reveal more flesh, whispering how much he wanted her against her lips, and kissing his way down to her inner thighs.

She shuddered as his mouth explored below her hips, and when he leaned across her to fumble in a drawer for protection she kissed her way along his arms, up to the contours of his torso. The familiarity and the mystery of him combined was such a turn-on she couldn't stand it.

Rolling her over to her side, he spooned her, his hardness pressed to her back, and for a moment they slowed.

'Something tells me you like it like this,' he murmured, sending a spark and a thrill of anticipation bolting through her, so delicious it was almost unbearable.

'I do,' she encouraged, arching back into him.

Lucie bit down on her hand to stop her cries of pleasure giving them away to the neighbours as he entered her, rocking slowly at first. She felt herself swelling around him, her body accepting his, welcoming him, expanding and contracting to please him. God…how had she ever left without telling him how much she wanted this? How had she given up without even trying?

They might have made love for thirty minutes or an hour—who could remember? Sometimes their eyes were closed, when they were lost in the moment and each divine sensation. Sometimes they locked eyes, tried new positions, then laughed and tried more. He seemed intent on pleasuring her, making sure he was the best she'd ever had, and all she wanted to do was make him remember her. For ever.

He would think about her when she was gone…when he was filling in that dating profile. Or maybe he wouldn't… This was one afternoon of fun—not love…not something to carry into for ever.

He's never told you he loves you.

She shoved the thought away to deal with it later, letting him worship her. She kissed him for every single moment he'd missed her, when she'd left him to go to America. Kept him close inside her for all the times he'd felt broken and alone. Pressed her hands to his heart and kept to his rhythm, knowing she'd be conjuring up this memory for months and years to come. Wherever she ended up next, she would take this moment with her.

AJ threw himself into her. They were both in the fire now. But it wasn't as if they could help it. He'd decided, as she had, to accept that they were just going to burn…

'Where were you? There's a letter on the sideboard for you,' Gramma May said later, when she finally made her way home.

AJ had made it pretty clear that she needed to be gone before the twins were dropped home after their play date. But walking away from the house had been tough.

And now she was starting to think she might have made a big, fat, stupid mistake, telling herself she could leave permanently again with zero consequences. Her head was still reeling…the taste and smell of him was all over her like a coat she didn't want to take off.

She swiped up the envelope. The handwriting wasn't familiar. Opening it, she felt only half present. She was changed, somehow—different from the woman who'd left for work that morning. While he hadn't exactly said he loved her…he'd never say that…she could have sworn she saw it in his eyes.

Gramma May met her in the kitchen as she poured a glass of water. Her throat was parched.

'You were with Austin all day?'

'I was,' she replied, filling up Maple's water bowl and running her hands through her fur as she lapped at the liquid with her tongue.

Crouched beside Maple, Lucie finally read the letter. Her hand stopped dead in the dog's fur as a small bookmark fluttered out. Her own face beamed up at her, alongside Jorge's. The picture had been taken just weeks before he'd lost his life. The letter was from Jorge's widow, asking when she'd be back in Peru. She had a gift for her: a memorial book she'd had made for all the victims of the earthquake, too heavy to mail.

It was months ago that Lucie had given permission for some of the photos from their operation to be included in it.

Thank you, Lucie, for your continued work for MRO. I bet you can't wait to get back out there!

   Jorge would be so proud of you—as am I.

   I hope you're enjoying your well-deserved break in England.

   Love, Maria

Her hands were shaking.

Gramma May was still talking. 'Cynthia texted me. Her mother was at Lavender Springs, visiting a friend today. She said some couple put on quite a show in the pond, after they fell in. Would you know anything about that?'

'What?'

Lucie barely heard her…her nerves were shot. Just when she'd allowed herself to feel good, maybe even to contemplate staying here longer, to see how things went with AJ, here was yet another reminder that she had a life and responsibilities elsewhere.

Thanks a lot, universe!

'You know what I'm talking about.' Gramma May rolled her eyes, then frowned. 'So, you're back together, are you?'

She pulled hot sheets out of the tumble dryer and loaded them into a basket. Lucie shoved the letter into a kitchen drawer and sprang to her feet to take over the chore.

'We never got together in the first place, Gramma,' she informed her, realising her cheeks were probably flaming red, and her hair was a dishevelled mess.

'You didn't? I thought you must have. I don't know… He always carried a torch for you.'

She was taken aback. 'Did he?'

Gramma May rolled her eyes. 'The two of you belong together. Cynthia said it was the highlight of their day at Lavender, the pair of you in the pond. I quote, "Like something
from a great romance." The residents can't wait to see their favourite couple again. With the dogs, of course. They've never
had such a laugh.'

Lucie swallowed a pang. 'We're not a couple,' she reminded
her.

'Tell that to the ducks in the pond. Sounds like they got a
close-up look at your antics.'

'It was just a kiss...' Lucie trailed off, folding a sheet all
wrong, then starting again.

It had *started* with a kiss, anyway.

'Don't mess with his heart,' Gramma May said suddenly,
and Lucie flinched. 'That poor boy has been through enough.'

The severity of her tone shook her.

Lucie sank to a chair, dropping her head into her hands as
the flood of oxytocin and adrenaline from the amazing sex
with AJ evaporated with a *poof.*

Of course Gramma was right.

'I don't mean to say *you* haven't been through a lot, too,'
Gramma May added kindly, stopping her folding to place a
hand to her arm. 'But he's the one who has to stay here and
lose you all over again when you go.'

'He's a big boy, Gramma, he knows what he's doing,' she
retorted, thinking of the online dating profile Belle would assist him with creating.

The thought of it stole her last remnants of happiness after
the love they'd just made, along with her breath. Gramma May
looked worried now, and Lucie flinched again.

Moments like this, when she felt like such a burden, reminded her of how sad Gramma had sounded, telling Cynthia
she'd never travelled with Grampa Bert and now she never
would—all because of her.

'You don't have to go,' Gramma said, as if sensing her melancholy. 'You know that, don't you, pet? If you have something good here…'

Lucie blinked, struggling to form a thought in her head. Gramma was sweet…always so sweet. And AJ was a very good thing that she had here. But… She didn't have him, exactly. He hadn't so much as hinted that this afternoon wasn't just a one-off, a chance to see what they'd missed out on all those years ago. He was looking for a woman who had experience with young children…

'Did you hear me?'

'Yes…yes, Gramma. And, yes, I know I don't *have* to go back. But it's my job.'

'Get another job.'

'It's not that easy.'

'Yes, it is. You could work with AJ. He's doing some wonderful things.'

'I have to go.'

'Go where, exactly?'

'I don't know yet!'

Gramma May made a *pfft* sound, and mumbled, 'Doesn't sound like a great job to me.'

Lucie's arms trembled in her still-damp shirtsleeves as she made her way upstairs.

That night, when AJ called her, she texted back, saying that she was tired. She wrote Thanks for a fun afternoon and cursed at the moon through the window.

Gramma May was worried for AJ's heart. But *she* was going to be hurt more. AJ would be fine…he was the most eligible bachelor in town! Any woman would be mad not to snap him up, pin him down…just like she'd pinned him down in bed earlier.

Oh, God, that had been so amazing! Better than she'd dreamed it would be—better than they would've been as awkward teenagers together, surely.

But this was just a bubble she was passing through dreamily on a foamy wave, like the remnants of the great storm that Ethel had talked about.

Jorge's face when the walls came down... She would never un-see that. Not until she'd got back out there—back where it had happened, maybe? People were expecting her back, relying on her! She was needed.

Her message had to be clear.

It was really special, AJ, but it can't happen again and you know it.

He replied after some time.

I hate it when you're right.

Turning her phone over, she left it at that.
That night, the nightmares rushed back with a vengeance.

CHAPTER TWENTY

AUSTIN TURNED HIS face to the sky, listening to the soft banter between Ruby and Josiah. They were negotiating turns on the bouncy helicopter ride. The play park in Dalby Forest was busy this Sunday, now it was coming into late April, and this morning's organised dog walk had twenty-three attendees so far. Here was another one now.

The car door swung open and Lucie stepped out into the sunshine with Maple. A silent groan formed in his throat. Trust her to look amazing for a forest walk. Sheer tights showed off her legs under a short skirt. A light denim jacket swung from one hand. She'd been invited by Samuel's mother, who wanted to talk with them both about Bingo, now their live-in beagle.

'Lucie!' The twins rushed to greet her and started patting an enthusiastic Maple through the fence.

Austin fanned himself with his sweater, waiting for the usual cloud of tension to descend from the clear blue sky.

'Hey, guys!' Lucie looked good in pink lipstick as she high-fived the twins over the low play park fence. 'Are you excited for this dog walk your dad's organised? I didn't know you were coming.'

She shot him a telling sideways glance and he shrugged. 'Belle was busy.'

They gabbled on at her and he watched with interest as they interacted. Ruby especially was excited to see Lucie. She couldn't wait to tell her absolutely everything she'd been doing over the last couple of weeks all in one enthusiastic breath.

It wasn't a great feeling. He'd been extra-careful since they'd slept together at the house not to let the twins get close to her. He and Lucie had continued working together, of course. They were adults. They could cope without acting on their attraction. But only just...

It wasn't exactly easy—at least not for him—knowing they'd done that...in his bed...to each other's bodies...after so many years of wondering. And now she was all set to leave again. He knew he probably wouldn't have gone that far with anyone else *but* Lucie—which didn't help his guilt.

The walkers showed up one by one. Some were his volunteers, but not all of them had dogs. Some had kids and relatives who needed a little animal therapy in the fresh air.

'It's so great that Thera Pups does this for everyone,' Lucie said when they'd set off as a group down the wide forest track.

The sunlight dappled her hair through the canopy. Songbirds tweeted their approval of the warm weather.

'Every other weekend...late April through to September,' he told her, noting how Josiah had struck up a conversation with Samuel, up ahead, and was now throwing sticks for Bingo. Samuel's mother was chatting with Tom, who ran the model railway shop.

'They take after you,' Lucie said, looking with affection at Josiah. 'They'll be working for Thera Pups before you know it.'

'Maybe...who knows?' he said. 'I added Jetson's cancer detection in Constance to my latest paper. It's got a lot of people pretty excited.'

She raised her eyebrows in interest. Encouraged, he told her about a few potential investors for a training programme similar to his in the States. In turn, she told him how Ethel had asked for him and Jetson today at the Mayflower Care Home. And then she told him how Cynthia had probed her earlier, in the chocolate shop, about the pond incident at Lavender Springs.

He cleared his throat, not sure what to say. All he'd wanted to do every night since that day was show up and bang on her door. Now, the second she locked eyes with him and blew her fringe away, it was obvious that even in their recent forced indifference it had been playing heavily on her mind too.

'Are you OK?' she asked, lowering her voice to a whisper barely audible over the rustling trees.

'We're pretty good at being professional,' he replied carefully. Then he glanced at her sideways. 'Except around duck ponds.'

'That's not what I meant but…those poor ducks,' she added softly.

He smirked as they crossed the wooden slats of a bridge. His pillows had carried her scent for days afterwards, and he was ashamed to admit he hadn't washed the sheets until he'd absolutely *had* to.

'The twins keep asking about you.'

'I've kind of missed their energy,' she admitted.

Oh, really?

He watched her face for signs that she was just saying that because she thought she should. She seemed genuine, though. His heart began to thud wildly as he held his hand out to help her jump down from the bridge.

He looked around them. No one was looking. The twins were fine. He led her swiftly off the path and pulled her behind a tree, put his hands to her shoulders.

'I've been trying to keep them away from you on purpose.'

'I'm no good for them anyway.'

She scanned his eyes as if she was looking for him to agree with her. The colour around her pupils pulsed in the sun, from sunflower and amber to mahogany. Her sadness was palpable.

His instincts shot to red alert. 'That's just not true, Lucie…'

'Well, I'm not exactly a great role model, am I?' she scoffed self-deprecatingly.

He faltered, tilting her chin up to face him. This wasn't anything he'd heard from her before.

'Not that I'm asking you to fill a role—you know that. But...' An instinctive need to reassure her rose up to his throat. 'But why would you say that?'

'I don't know. I just can't forget how I was—maybe how I still am—because of what happened to Mum and Dad. I missed them so much, and I felt bad about bringing all my drama into Gramma and Grampa's lives—and yours, AJ... And now I'm back here, bringing everything that happened to me in Nepal. The twins must pick up on the fact that I'm not exactly normal...'

He ignored her. 'What drama did you bring to Gramma May? Lucie, she adores you—and so did Bert.'

She chewed on her lip. 'Grampa had to work a lot longer than he should have—for *my* sake,' she said. 'And then he died too soon. Without going with Gramma to see the pyramids of Egypt, or Niagara Falls, or the Great Barrier Reef, or any of the other places they'd planned to go when he retired.'

This was tough to hear. He couldn't help feeling that, for all the years he thought he'd known her, he hadn't actually known much at all.

'They loved you,' he reiterated.

'I know. But it doesn't change the fact that I took something away from them, AJ. And they never talked about my parents with me—ever.'

'Probably because they didn't want you to live in the past, Lucie. They wanted to give you a future. And maybe they were grieving themselves. May loves you so much you don't even know...'

He trailed off. This was not the time to tell her how upset May had been after she'd gone back to the States. But of course the sweet woman hadn't wanted to stand in Lucie's way.

'She told everyone how much she missed you, Luce. *Everyone* here missed you.'

She bit on her lip, as if she hadn't ever thought about that before. 'Well... I felt I had to take Aunt Lina up on her offer,' she said. 'For various reasons.'

He felt his jaw start to twitch. One of those reasons was because of what she thought had happened with him and Claire. If only he'd left his stupid bedroom door open that night, instead of letting Claire close it, he would've seen Lucie appear.

'And it was great,' she continued. 'But Lina wasn't exactly around a lot. She was too independent to change. I guess what I'm saying is, I have no idea how to be a role model for anyone.'

He almost laughed. 'And you think *I* do?'

She winced. 'You're doing so well, AJ. You're the kind of dad who wears out skipping ropes!'

If only she knew the struggles...

'I make it up as I go along, Luce. Trust me—everyone does. Anyway, it's not that I don't want them around you. They love you. I just don't want them to have to miss you.'

He paused as she turned her hands in his, as if she was memorising the feel of them for later. He almost said, *And I don't want to miss you again.* Which was the truth.

But she knew that already. He'd made love to her, hadn't he? He didn't have to say he loved her for her to know...and why should he tell her? She'd only throw his vulnerability right back in his face, then close the door on it again.

He leaned into her, stroked the hair back behind her ears. She narrowed her gaze at the ground as he traced her cheekbone with his thumb, moving it down to her lips. Before he could refrain, he pressed his lips gently to hers. Right now his own feelings didn't matter. He only wanted to kiss away whatever imagined incompetence she might be feeling—no thanks to what she'd gone through as a child.

'I guess all that affected you more than I ever knew—losing your parents, having to move all the way to England, to Yorkshire,' he said, putting a palm to her face.

She leaned into him and he caressed her warm face, forgetting that he shouldn't. It was only just dawning on him: *this* was why Lucie never felt like anywhere in particular was home.

Lucie urged him closer, pulling him by the collar, and kissed him just as softly, then harder. Every thought flew out of the window and it was no one else but them, just like it had been at his house, in his bedroom…

All too soon she pulled away gently, shaking her head. He resisted emitting the growl of frustration building up in his throat. He'd walked right into that.

Why do you keep doing this to yourself, man?

'Gramma May told me not to mess with your heart,' she told him, pressing her fingers to her lips.

He was silent, thoughts reeling. 'I'm sure she did.'

'I have to go back to my job, AJ.'

Austin shoved his hands through his hair so as not to reach for her again. His heart was already hers, whatever she did—sucker that he was. But moving on was ingrained into Lucie. As for him… He was only just getting used to the thought of loving someone after Ebby. Still trying not to feel awful for even *wanting* to love Lucie.

'Do you know when you're going, exactly?' he managed, thinking of Ruby's and Josiah's faces when he told them Lucie wouldn't be around any more.

'I don't know the exact date yet.'

He bit his tongue as they walked back to the path. Asking her to stay wouldn't work. If he kept pushing he'd only push her further away—like last time. And what did he have to offer a global wanderer anyway, except chains?

Maple's sudden barks were manic, deafening.

'What's up, girl?'

Lucie reached out to pat her, but Maple ran halfway back

towards the group, stopped, and then ran back to them, wagging her tail furiously.

He and Lucie exchanged glances.

'She's acting strangely...' Austin scanned the path ahead, then Lucie's face. She was on high alert now, as he was.

'This happened before...when John had his seizure,' she said, clutching his arm.

Just then Jetson bounded back to them and started barking wildly too. His stomach dropped. Then they both hit the ground running.

CHAPTER TWENTY-ONE

THEY REACHED Tom just in time to stop his head from crashing into the ground.

'He's having a heart attack!'

Lucie's heart bucked in her chest as she lowered him down, cushioning his fall.

Austin, already on the phone, went straight for the twins. He guided them to the side of the path before joining her, and they watched, wide-eyed, as she and their dad knelt beside the ashen-faced man on the ground.

His pale cream trousers were streaked with mud where he'd fallen. He must be...what? Sixty? She swallowed the panic that was building in her at the sight of him, clutching his chest in the middle of the forest.

Focus.

How far had they walked from the car park already?

'I'm a doctor,' Lucie said, clearing the bystanders with one quick command.

The dogs barked and yapped wildly, even as people tried to calm them. Had the dogs really tried to warn them again, *before* this had even happened? Jetson was the one who'd spurred AJ into action, but Maple had seemed to know something was up, too.

'It feels like a ten-ton bear is sitting on my chest,' the man croaked.

Discomfort was etched into every line of his face, but he was conscious.

'OK, Tom…' Lucie placed a hand on the man's arm comfortingly, while AJ finished the call he was making to the emergency services. 'When did this start?'

'Just a few minutes ago. I thought it must be heartburn…' He tailed off, wincing, then dropped in her arms.

'His eyes are closing,' she whispered, laying the man down as gently as she could.

He was groaning now, drawing deep, ghastly breaths, as if the atmosphere had been sucked from all around him. 'He's definitely in cardiac arrest.'

AJ was right there, looking to her for guidance. 'What can I do?'

'Help me,' she ordered, unbuttoning his shirt.

The twins were mumbling in panic by the trees, along with the rest of their group. Somewhere, someone was sobbing. The dogs whimpered intermittently, in a spooky soundtrack.

'Stay with us…help is coming,' she told Tom, as AJ used his own jacket as a pillow.

Pressing her hands to his heart, she thought Tom's skin felt strangely cold. His face turned an even whiter shade of pale and he drooped some more. She started chest compressions.

Please, please, please…

AJ's hand on her back told her when to stop. She let him take over the next round, letting his confidence calm her. The knees of his jeans were caked in dirt, but AJ's face showed pure, fierce determination.

'Come on, Tom!'

Lucie cast her eyes to the twins, who were sobbing now, and in the distance she heard sirens wail.

Moments later two paramedics appeared, and AJ half stumbled backwards into her, letting them take over.

'He's breathing—let's get him up!'

The twins rocketed into them both, almost sending them tumbling to the floor as Tom was given an oxygen mask and loaded onto the stretcher.

'Daddy! You saved his life!'

Ruby's face was streaked with tears, and Lucie had only just composed her thoughts when Josiah threw his arms around her middle and hung on tight.

'Lucie saved him, too,' he said loudly, as if this was his proudest moment to date.

He squeezed her so hard with his little arms that he jolted a nervous laugh from her, and in seconds Ruby was hugging her as well, fighting to get more of her in her grasp than her brother.

Jetson and Maple jumped at them too, eager to get in on the attention.

AJ ruffled their hair, thanked Jetson, and as the paramedics hurried off the way they'd come with Tom she realised the crowd of walkers and several other passers-by were clapping and cheering them.

She closed her eyes, feeling awkward and embarrassed. This wasn't what she needed or expected. She'd just been in the right place at the right time...and if it hadn't been for the dogs they might not have got to Tom in time to stop serious injury—he might have been hurt if he'd fallen.

AJ's arm snaked around her. Silencing her thoughts in one fell swoop, he pulled her harder into their group hug. Lucie let her relief and gratitude out into his broad chest, breathing in his comforting scent as her heartrate slowed.

Her face finally broke into a smile, although she was half expecting the squeeze of an enthusiastic child to bring her to her knees.

'Jetson tried to warn us,' AJ said later when, exhausted and hungry, they took the twins back to the house for sandwiches. 'Maple, too.'

Lucie sat back in the couch. 'I know.'

Accepting the glass of water he'd poured her, she looked

for signs of distress in Ruby and Josiah, who were busy making the dogs their dinner.

'I was thinking that. Do you think she's learning from Jetson without even being trained?'

He shrugged thoughtfully. 'Interesting concept. There's so much more research to be done,' he said, brushing down his jeans.

They were still streaked with mud. She pictured the shower upstairs. They shouldn't… The twins were here. They couldn't. Not that she would have anyway, she reminded herself. Gramma had told her not to mess with his heart, and hers had been messed with enough, too.

But, then again, he was the one who'd kissed her back there. *Again*.

'Daddy, when we sell the house, can Jetson still live with us?'

Lucie drew her lips together.

Visibly thrown, AJ sank to the couch beside her, a wall of tension all over again. Her hand found his in support—she couldn't help it.

'Who told you we're selling the house, Rubes?'

Ruby had refused to let Lucie go back to her own house this evening and, all things considered, Lucie had relented. No kid should have to see what they'd watched playing out today. Surprisingly, though, they seemed fine, obsessing on Lucie and AJ being heroes, rather than the tragedy itself. Till now.

Ruby eyed her father beguilingly from her place on the carpet, where she was now brushing Jetson. 'I heard you and Auntie Belle talking about it.'

'We'll talk about it later Ruby-Roo,' he said gently, looking down at Lucie's hand in his before removing it gently.

Lucie cringed inside.

Josiah had wandered in. He plonked a book called *Aliens and the Mysteries of the Universe* onto Lucie's lap. 'What are you talking about?'

'Daddy's selling the house,' Ruby informed him. 'I was asking if Jetson can still live with us.'

Josiah's face fell. 'But where will we go?'

To Lucie's horror, his eyes pooled with tears. Impulsively she drew an arm around him, held him tight.

AJ looked drained.

'Nothing's been decided yet, sweetie,' she said on his behalf, as soothingly as she could, willing AJ to turn around and face them.

Suddenly she was nine years old again herself, being told she had to leave Colorado for a place in England called Brookborough. Lost. Frightened.

AJ stood and paced the living room, stopping by the window. Ruby continued brushing Jetson pensively.

'We can't stay here for ever, guys,' he said with a sigh.

'Why not?' Josiah demanded, through a sob and a sniff.

'We just can't.'

Lucie drummed her hand on her knee. 'Nothing has been decided yet,' she said again, racking her brains for a way she could make this situation better. No child should ever feel forced out of their home.

AJ's shoulders tensed. He eyed her arm around Josiah until she felt as though she shouldn't have hugged him.

'We have to be realistic. Auntie Belle is moving out. It's too big for just us three.'

'Not if Lucie moves in,' Ruby said, matter-of-factly.

Josiah nodded vehemently, wiping at his tears. The look of hope on his face sent her reeling.

'Yes! Lucie can move in! And Maple.'

Lucie scratched at her neck, avoiding AJ's eyes. Kids said the craziest things…but it seemed AJ had been right. For some reason she would never understand, they did really seem to like her.

'Lucie's not staying,' AJ said sternly.

OK…

The seriousness on his face spoke a thousand words. The twins wanting her around was everything he didn't want to happen, and after their conversation earlier it was hardly surprising he'd decided to tell them the truth. She'd pretty much hammered it home that she was definitely going back to work abroad.

So why did she feel so sick?

Because you told him Gramma May warned you not to mess with his heart and he said nothing. His heart seems perfectly fine!

Ruby pouted. 'Where are you going, Lucie?'

'I don't know yet, honey,' she answered.

She was thinking of the bookmark, the memorial book that was waiting for her in Peru. Maybe she'd go to Cusco, to the base there, while she waited for her next position.

Ruby's blue eyes were narrowed in genuine confusion. 'If you don't know where you're going, how will you know when you get there?'

Silence.

Lucie opened her mouth to reply, but a snort of laughter from Josiah cut her off. Then Ruby started giggling, till both children were rolling on the floor with the dogs, laughing hysterically, as if she'd proposed the riddle to end all riddles.

Her mouth twitched in amusement. Kids were insane.

AJ rolled his eyes and dropped back to the couch. 'Welcome to my world,' he sighed, so close to her it made her ear tickle in anticipation.

Today had been crazy, totally unexpected on all accounts, but at least they were laughing. The subject of the house going up for sale was dismissed, at least for now, and she was here. She shouldn't be. But she was. And the rare moment of togetherness curled and swirled inside her, warming her blood.

Yawning, she moved to lean her head against AJ's shoulder.

He stiffened.

Before she'd even touched his shirt he jumped to his feet again, held his hand out to her. 'I'll walk you to the door.'

'Oh, yes…thanks,' she said quickly, as if she'd been about to leave anyway.

Gosh, how mortifying… But what did she expect?

'Say goodbye to Lucie, kids,' AJ told them, and they obliged—but not before Josiah asked for a bedtime story.

Flustered, she told him, 'Not tonight, sweetie.'

At the door, AJ looked at her apologetically.

'You don't have to say it,' she told him, pulling on her jacket. 'I understand.'

'It's just… I can't do it to them, Lucie,' he said. 'Selling the house, you leaving—it's all a lot for them.'

'And for you too?' she said, searching his face.'

He straightened up. A flicker of anger crossed his features. When he spoke, his voice was tight. 'I'll see you before you leave?'

She pursed her lips, ignoring the way he was drawing a line under her imminent departure already. So he wasn't going to talk about the truth of it. That no matter what he said, and whether she left or not, she could never give him half of what Ebby had.

'I guess so,' she said.

He nodded, and lingered for a moment, watching her in a way that made her wish she could read his mind the way she'd always used to feel she could.

'Lucie, thank you for today. You were…' He tailed off, scratched his chin, and she forced a straight face.

Awkward.

She turned around, forcing herself not to look back. She knew he was watching her walk away, and she could literally feel him observing the space between them widening.

CHAPTER TWENTY-TWO

NIGEL REACHED OVER to Lucie from behind a box of bananas, offered her a high five over the market stall, then tossed her an orange.

'Great job Miss Henderson,' he said, throwing a wink at Gramma May, who was inspecting the avocados.

Lucie racked her brains.

'Tom,' Nigel reminded her. 'You and Austin saved that guy from kicking the bucket in the woods. Thank God you were there, yeah? He's a good friend of my wife's sister...runs the model train shop?'

Lucie smiled awkwardly as Gramma May handed Nigel an avocado and some grapes to weigh. No end of people had cornered her over the last week or so, telling her how they all knew Tom, thanking her as if she was their new hero. A reporter had even called the day after it had happened and asked to interview her.

She'd politely declined. She was no hero. If only they knew!

'You've got a good one here, May,' Nigel said, dropping the fruit into a paper bag. 'Do we know if we can keep her yet?'

Lucie cringed, and then told him her locum position was almost up and she'd be leaving soon—which was starting to sound scary even to her own ears. An email from her team had arrived only that morning, and was still sitting unanswered in her inbox. She had drafted a reply, deleted the draft, retyped it and deleted it again more times than she could count.

There was more flooding in Pakistan. Landslides. Buried villages. The team were congregating in Karachi ASAP. They wanted to know if she would join them. Her hotel room would be ready for her, they said.

Guilt raged through her. She'd let her feelings for AJ get in the way of all her promises, but time was quickly ticking down on her now.

Usually she'd have been chomping at the bit to get back out there, but this place and its people had sneaked their way into her heart and tugged at her ventricles like vines. And AJ... All she could think about was him. The way they'd left things, all weird and unfinished.

That was what it was. Unfinished. They'd always be un-finished.

But he hadn't given her any indication at all that he wanted her to stay for anything other than her job as a locum and her friendship.

Maple was waiting patiently for scraps by the fish stand up ahead, but before she could make her way over Gramma May's excited cry echoed Nigel's.

'Pamela!'

AJ's mother.

Lucie froze.

'I didn't know you were visiting from Naples,' May en-thused, dropping a kiss to her cheek.

The two women started chattering at a million miles an hour, and then Pamela's eyes shot to her. A warm smile that looked so much like AJ's spread from ear to ear as she held both hands out.

'My Lucie-Lu. Oh, pet, it's so good to see you!'

Pamela made a fuss of her, told her how lovely she looked, told her how Doug, AJ's dad, had been asking after her. It was a flood of love. Lucie was moved.

Before she quite knew how to put her head up out of the

whirlwind, she'd accepted an invitation for dinner on Friday at the house they were renting for the week in Whitby.

Austin had been catching the pretty research assistant's eyes on him all morning. *Annabel*, according to her name tag. Blonde, blue-eyed...the kind of young, pretty thing he would have gone for before Ebby, probably.

The opposite of Lucie.

'They got it again, Austin,' she said now in excitement, hurrying over to him and patting the golden Retriever, the Labrador and the border collie on her way. 'They all identified the contaminated samples over the clean ones. That's four different bacteria types with over ninety percent accuracy!'

'I had every faith they would,' he said, as his volunteers whispered excitedly amongst themselves and praised their dogs.

This was just one part of the disease detection training they'd been perfecting here at the hospital, in a dedicated research space, getting the dogs to sniff out urinary tract infections from female urine samples. Not the most glamorous of tasks, but still important.

He was going over his notes with Annabel, her warm breath tickling his cheek, when there was a knock at the door. He saw Lucie peering through the glass before she stepped inside, and something made him take a step back from Annabel. But not before he'd caught the look of jealousy in Lucie's expression.

'Hi!' he said, surprised to see her.

'Hi,' she said. 'I thought you'd still be here.'

Her eyes darted to Annabel and he introduced them quickly, not missing the way Lucie looked her up and down as if she was sizing up a rival boxer in a ring. There it was again— the green-eyed monster. Something about seeing it in Lucie tickled him...

'I brought Constance to say hello,' Lucie said now, motioning for her to step in from the corridor. 'We were just running a check-up on her.'

Constance beamed as she took his hand with both of hers, then reached for Annabel's—which seemed to irk Lucie more.

'I got the all-clear,' Constance told them.

'Oh, that's great news,' he said, relieved.

Lucie nodded. 'The biopsy came back clean for cancer cells,' she told him, looking to Annabel again, who still kind of hovered, like she had been all morning. 'Now it's just a check-up every six months and a colonoscopy every few years to make sure no more tumours sneak back in. But we're hoping that's it.'

Constance smoothed down her silk scarf. She already looked less gaunt, and her face had more colour. 'Thank goodness. I mean, I'm still a little weak post-surgery, but I still can't thank you and these dogs enough, Dr Johnstone. Because of them I'm alive.'

'Yes, you are.' He smiled. 'And you'll be happy to know we've just been approved to showcase the new disease detection course at the Global Medicine Conference in Chicago next month. Thera Pups is expanding faster than I could have anticipated.'

'That's so wonderful,' the women chorused, and Annabel clapped her hands together in agreement.

Austin saw Lucie flinch. Was she sad that she wouldn't be around to see it grow on home turf?

Lucie cleared her throat as Annabel touched his arm lightly, drawing his attention back to her. 'I'll be outside, I have some calls to make,' she said, speaking a little too close to his ear. 'Nice to meet you both.'

Lucie's lips were a thin, cross line. Her eyes burned into him. He raised his eyebrows at her as Annabel slipped out. It wasn't his fault if women flirted with him. In fact, he usually barely noticed them doing it. But Lucie had woken something up inside him. Some kind of hormone that spoke on his behalf about craving…wanting…needing.

It was Lucie he craved, obviously—for all the good it was doing him. They'd only seen each other a handful of times since he'd escorted her out of the house, mostly just in passing at the hospital. Watching her go that day, all he'd wanted was to run after her and kiss her, stick his last flag in the sand as a claim on what was his before it flew out of reach. But what good would that have done? Besides, he had to put the kids and their feelings first.

Constance had just bade them both farewell, and he was about to excuse himself from Lucie too, when his phone pinged with a message from his mum.

Is Lucie still a vegetarian? I don't have her number, sorry!

'Has my mother invited you to dinner on Friday as well?' he asked her, as he led her outside into the corridor.

Annabel was on the phone across the hall, but she held her hand up at him in a wave, which he returned—much to Lucie's obvious annoyance.

'You're coming too?' Lucie crossed her arms warily, then moved to block Annabel from his eyeline. 'I thought it was a personal invitation for me and Gramma.'

He blew air through his lips. Of course he was going too. The twins were coming with him. They couldn't get enough of their grandparents whenever they flew over to visit.

'Mum and Dad don't know anything,' he told her now.

Lucie's eyes narrowed. 'What do you mean?'

'About us,' he said, lowering his voice and picturing their faces if he told them how he'd put the twins' happiness in jeopardy all over again, giving them false hope about Lucie sticking around.

Talk about bad parenting.

'There is no us,' she retorted.

Ouch.

'Anyway, do you really think no one's told them about the pond incident?'

He frowned. She had a point. If they didn't know yet, they soon would.

'I'll just tell them something's come up and I can't go, if that's what you think is best,' she offered, glancing at Annabel again.

Austin considered it. The last thing they needed was any drama around the dinner table. Lucie would have to explain yet again that she didn't know where she was going next, and he'd have to bite his damn tongue to stop making a fool of himself, begging her once more not to put her life in danger. As if he had any claim on her, really.

Why did his parents have to ask her to dinner?

'AJ?'

The hurt in her eyes caught him off guard. Maybe he was being a little selfish. She'd used to be pretty close to his mother, who'd always adored her.

'Do you want me to stay away?'

'No, don't be silly—you should come,' he said on a sigh. 'Mum's asking if you're still a vegetarian, by the way.'

'I forgot about that phase.'

She laughed dully, but her heart clearly wasn't in it. She seemed distracted now. Was she thinking about Annabel? Wondering if anything was going on?

So what if she is? She isn't sticking around. This will be both a hello and a goodbye dinner, as far as Mum and Dad are concerned.

'I'll see you on Friday, then? I'll pick you up and we can drive there together.' Even as the words came out, he kicked himself. 'It makes sense…just taking one car. You, me, Gramma May and the twins,' he reasoned aloud.

'I guess so,' she replied.

But he caught the uncertainty in her eyes, and one final glare in Annabel's direction too, before she turned and left.

CHAPTER TWENTY-THREE

THE DRIVE BACK from her last home visit felt as if it took for ever. Lucie only half saw the beauty she was starting to take for granted again. The open pastures with their horses…the endless trees and huge brown barns. Her head kept flitting to tonight's dinner and whether she should actually go.

AJ had been flirting *so* hard the other day at the hospital… or at least that pretty blonde research assistant, Annabel, had been flirting with him. Lucie half expected to find her sitting at the dinner table tonight, engrossed in conversation with Pamela and Doug.

AJ hadn't been in touch at all since they'd discussed whether she should go or not. Maybe he really didn't want her to come and was hoping she would cancel.

She scowled at a scarecrow in a field as she passed it. He was probably wishing she'd already left, so he could just get on with asking Annabel out—and all the other women who'd fall for him after just one scan of his online dating profile.

Yuck.

Flicking the radio on to calm the fresh wave of jealousy that was strangling her brain, she heard another news bulletin blast through the car. The floods in Pakistan were getting worse. She had no real reason to be here, she reminded herself. Her locum position would be pretty much all wrapped up in a matter of days, when the full-time doctor returned.

She'd done the right thing the other day, finally replying to the email that she'd been stewing over. So what if her jealousy over AJ and Annabel's flirting had been the final catalyst? She would've had to do it anyway...she'd just been stalling.

She hadn't told him yet, though. The thought sent a bolt of dread through her innards every time.

The second she'd hit 'send', and confirmed she'd be joining them shortly, a scroll had gone across her brain with the words *Just tell him* on it. She'd picked up her phone, let her finger hover over his name. It would not swipe. It simply would not let her call him.

The thought of it made her feel quite nauseous. The fact that she'd sent the email at all had set some kind of slow-release hand grenade in motion. She'd opened the email up in the 'sent' folder, reread the confidence with which she'd written her reply, trying to make the firm decision sound real. It hadn't really worked. The confidence had been faked to begin with.

She would have to tell AJ now. So he could prepare...if he still cared.

What if he *didn't* care, thought? Oh, God. Hearing the indifference in his voice would be heartbreaking, to say the least. She'd sit on the plane, imagining him out on a date, laughing about little lost Lucie with Annabel...

Oh, stop feeling sorry for yourself, she scorned herself, pulling up at some lights.

It really couldn't wait much longer. Time was ticking.

Her hand lingered over her phone, in its holder on the dashboard. She had to tell him.

Now?

No, she decided, chickening out again. Tonight, after dinner.

Austin stepped out of the car outside Gramma May's, checking himself in the wing mirror. His nerves were shot.

'Hey,' he said, when Lucie opened the door.

She smoothed down her maroon dress and he vaguely registered that the colour of it matched his sweater, as if they'd planned it. Of course, she would look stunning.

Maple greeted him, then sprinted past him to the car, where Jetson was waiting.

'No Gramma May?' he asked, looking over her shoulder.

'She said she'd meet us there. She went shopping in Whitby,' she said.

'OK. Well, the twins are already with Mum and Dad—they picked them up after school.'

Lucie looked flustered, as if she had something on her mind. More than just their impending awkward ride for two to Whitby. It fed his own anxiety. Her time was up at the surgery—just a few more days next week, as a crossover to fill the doctor in, and then she'd be free. But he didn't think she'd booked a flight anywhere yet. She would have told him.

'Shall we go?' he said, touching a hand to her back as she took the steps down from the door.

He held the car door open for her. Maple jumped in first, of course, and the small space closed in on them in the twilight. He'd wrestled with the urge to ask her to stay so many times, just as he wanted to do now, the second he had her to himself... But every time that voice in his head told him he was crazy. She wanted to get back to her adventures. She was only passing through. This was probably the last time he'd drive her anywhere.

'Oh, shoot,' she said suddenly, just as he'd started the ignition. 'The pie! Gramma asked me to bring an apple pie for dessert, and it's on the kitchen counter.'

'Stay with the dogs. I'll run in,' he told her, cutting the engine and taking the door keys from her hands.

In moments he was standing in the cinnamon-scented kitchen. The darkened room was lit only by the screen of a laptop. He recognised it. Lucie's.

Where was the pie...?

He picked it up from the counter, glanced at the laptop again to check the time—Pamela hated it when people were late and her appetisers went cold.

An email was open on the screen. Clutching the pie to his chest, he couldn't help catch the subject line.

Karachi assignment accepted.

Leaning in closer, he read some more. His blood ran cold.

He left the pie where it was and stormed back outside to confront her, fury and humiliation making a storm of his entire mind. She'd arranged all *this* without telling him.

'I'm sorry, AJ,' Lucie said, her eyes wide with shock and guilt. 'I know I should have told you sooner.'

'I can't believe you.'

He turned to her as she scrambled out of the car. Her shoes clicked on the tarmac and the breeze picked up her dress.

'When were you going to tell me?'

'You always knew I was leaving, AJ. The locum position was only for—'

He shook his head. 'I asked you recently for an *exact* date.'

She shrugged. 'I didn't know it till now.'

'You've known for days that you're going to Pakistan and you've made all the arrangements—it was all in the email!'

She reached for his hands, but he pulled them back. 'AJ, look, I just didn't know how to tell you...'

'It's pretty simple, Lucie. You just say it!' he seethed, as the memories crashed back over him of the last time he'd discovered she'd skipped town, with no word to him about why, or where she was going. 'This isn't much better than last time, when you got on that plane and left for America without warning!'

She shook her head, dropped to sit on the stone wall. 'You know why I have to go this time.'

Humiliation clouded his brain. Some part of him knew he

didn't really have the right to be this angry with her, that this had always been going to happen. It was why he'd tried to keep his distance in the first place.

If only he hadn't bombed at it.

For a second words hovered on his lips...the truth.

I love you...don't go again. Don't leave me wondering if you're dead or alive. You are all I want. I would even have chosen you over Ebby if you hadn't left the first time, and the guilt of that's nearly been killing me!

He stopped himself, as if frozen in time, staring at her face. He barely recognised her now. She would seriously just up and leave him all over again? After everything they'd shared? She'd known when she was going, and the fact she hadn't told him... Did she really care that little about him?

'AJ, please...'

She reached for him again but he pulled away, turned for the car. He was already picturing the floodwaters in Pakistan... Lucie losing her footing on some mud bank, sliding away in a monsoon.

Ebby was gone. He'd stomped all over her memory for Lucie. And now he was going to have neither of them.

She followed him to the car, then stopped as he yanked it open. The dogs were whining. 'Are we really going to leave it like this?'

He couldn't even respond. The last time he'd seen Ebby he'd been too distracted at the prospect of staying at home alone with their twin babies even to kiss her goodbye. It had never crossed his mind that it could all just end like that...that she wouldn't ever come home again.

Now it was all he could think about. Him waving Lucie off and waiting. Waiting for the news.

She opened her mouth to speak, but he wouldn't hear her— not one more word that would only haunt him for the rest of his life.

'Just go,' he spat. 'Go! Go and be a hero. But if you do, don't come back here. Because I don't want to see you again. And I don't want my kids to see you either.'

I don't want to have to think about you dying out there.

'AJ...'

'I mean it, Lucie.'

A strange sense of déjà vu settled over him as she pressed her hands to her eyes.

'I never should have made love to you,' he heard himself growl, and Lucie's sobs broke his heart in two.

He sat heavily in the driver's seat, slammed the door and skidded away so hard he knew the asphalt would carry the scars for months.

So what? The separation process started now. This second. On *his* terms this time.

CHAPTER TWENTY-FOUR

LUCIE PRESSED HERSELF against the wall in the busy hotel reception area. The signal here in Karachi was less than reliable for reaching Yorkshire, but Gramma May was asking about Maple's costume for the Paws Under the Stars event. It was happening just one week from now. She'd never felt so far away from where her heart ached to be.

With the costume located, in a bag in the wardrobe, Lucie waved to a passing colleague as Gramma May told her Maple had learned some new tricks under her care, which made her heart swell. Gramma loved the dog so much that she'd adopted her. It was hard not to miss them both.

AJ's words were still a hideous echo in her head.

'I don't want to see you again. And I don't want my kids to see you either.'

'So, where is it you're flying to the day after tomorrow?' Gramma May asked.

'Another of the flood zones,' Lucie said, relaying the name of a village she could barely pronounce, straining to be heard over a Tannoy announcement and a rumbling trolley packed with towels.

She was exhausted already. She and the team had flown to three rural locations and back to their new base here on the outskirts of Karachi over the past two weeks. Keeping busy was key. She'd poured her heart and soul into it—counselling homeless women and kids at schools and community centres, making sure the local dogs were fed.

But AJ was everywhere.

He never left her head.

She was itching to ask Gramma May about him, but no. There was absolutely no point. Instead she let Gramma tell her about Nigel's new market stall cat, and asked about Tom, who was now back in his model train shop, seemingly fit and healthy. Thinking about all the people she'd grown so fond of made her smile.

Then Gramma said, 'Austin's house is on the market. I reckon it'll sell pretty fast.'

Lucie's stomach lurched. She forced a wave at another passing colleague, turned to the wall. So surreal...

'Did you hear me?'

'Uh-huh,' she said, wiping at her face.

It was hot here. Too hot. Uncomfortable in more ways than one. Tiredness was making her bones ache. And the dreams had found her again. Not about floods or earthquakes. Those were over. The nightmares were different now. They were all about AJ shutting doors, calling from the other side of walls. And the worst one...him passionately kissing Annabel, right in front of her.

Somehow, since she'd left and put all this physical space between them, he'd become absorbed even deeper into her bloodstream. He'd felt like home. And now she was here, and everything felt wrong, and they weren't even speaking.

She growled in exasperation. '*Ugh*... I made a mess of things, didn't I, Gramma? You warned me not to hurt him and I did.'

Gramma was silent for a moment. 'I think you're hurting each other,' she said. 'Am I allowed to speak about him this time?'

Lucie frowned as her heart bashed her ribcage. 'Yes,' she

managed, dreading what she might hear. 'But please don't tell me you've seen his dating profile, Gramma.'

'I don't think he wants to date anyone, Lucie.'

She felt sick. 'Yes, he does.'

'He's worried to death that you'll die out there, Lucie! For God's sake, can't you see that?'

Lucie clutched at her stomach, sliding down the wall to the floor.

'He doesn't *want* to love you in case something happens to you—like it did to Ebby.'

Lucie pressed a hand to the phone to hide her sniffle. Gramma sounded so distressed.

'He's already lost you once, Lucie, can you blame him for shutting down? God knows, we all missed you enough the first time, so please...just come home.'

Tears ran down Lucie's face. 'I didn't think you'd miss me very much the first time, Gramma. Not after what I did.'

Gramma was silent a moment. Then, 'What you did?'

Lucie swallowed. 'I forced Grampa to go back to work, so you could afford to care for me. I made you stop living your life after he died. You should have gone travelling, seen the world...'

'Honestly, where is all this coming from? I've done plenty of trips with Cynthia, and we're perfectly fine. I've seen enough of the world through you and your eyes, too. My darling, in no way did you force anyone to do anything—we did it all with love. Grampa wouldn't have swapped raising you for all the pyramids in Egypt!'

Gramma May went on to reassure her that Grampa's early death had been in no way her fault. He'd always kept his dodgy heart a secret. They laughed about the memories they had of him, and cried about a few more. She'd never felt this close to Gramma May, ever, and yet so far away at the same time.

Lucie was so moved and so exhausted when she hung up that she wept on the floor until a passing stranger had to hand her a tissue.

Hours later, she was still processing Gramma's words, alone in a tiny, dimly lit restaurant that had none of the charm of Brookborough's Old Ram Inn. AJ didn't want to love her in case he lost her. He might feel terrible for having moved on from Ebby with her—but he did love her, and he was hurting now she'd left.

She cursed her own idiocy and her stubborn pride, picturing Ruby and Josiah. There wasn't a day that dawned when she didn't think of them and how they'd bonded, against all the odds. No wonder AJ had tried to keep her away from the twins…from himself. He'd been protecting himself and them from another disaster.

A stray dog loitered at the restaurant door. She stood up with some scraps of meat she'd saved, making a new friend in an instant. The dog walked her back to the hotel, and she fought tears the whole way.

It was almost ironic, how much of a disaster she was. She'd given it a good shot, but AJ was right. All this stupid guilt had piled up on her. Guilt for shutting out what was left of her family, and for living her life when Jorge had lost his.

But that guilt was no good to anyone! Her heart was at home, where she was loved unconditionally.

'How could I have been so stupid?' she said to the dog.

Maybe it wasn't too late.

Austin stood in the corner of the kitchen, watching the couple opening his cupboards, taking measurements along his windowsills. It was so strange, watching other people planning a life in his home.

Belle saw the look on his face and took him aside. 'You

don't have to do this, you know,' she whispered. 'Nothing's been signed yet.'

'It's fine, Belle,' he said, forcing himself to believe it.

Belle wasn't buying it. She stepped backwards onto a stray plastic puzzle piece and her yelp made the couple turn in surprise.

One of them mumbled something like, 'Thank God we won't have kids in this house!' and they chuckled between them.

Belle looked infuriated. 'It's not fine, Austin, it's wrong,' she hissed. 'Lucie should be here with you. You both love this house and you love each other! I don't know how this has gone so wrong.' Belle hopped around the hallway, holding her foot. 'You had the girl of your dreams right here and you let her go. Again!'

'Don't make a scene,' he told his sister quietly.

She didn't know about the open ticket to Karachi, burning a hole through his drawer upstairs, but she was right. He had let Lucie go. He'd practically ordered her away from him and now nothing made much sense any more.

But...

There was always a but.

'It's been five years, AJ!' Belle simmered, kicking the puzzle piece out of view under the stairs. 'Are you seriously still telling yourself you're not supposed to be moving on? Ebby would want you to be happy, you know!'

Austin dropped to the bottom step of the stairs, his eyes on the couple who were now making a wide circle around Jetson as if he might suddenly attack them, or eat the shoes from their feet. They clearly weren't fans of dogs, either.

He scrubbed at his face. Regret and shame had coated his bones since the second he'd sped from that driveway, and it wasn't just Belle reminding him of his glaring faults lately. Everyone in this village had hammered it home over the past few weeks, in their own special ways.

'*Where's Lucie? We love Lucie.*'

'*Lucie is one of those rare special ones, pet.*'

'*Oh? What do you mean she's left again already?*'

In his head he'd boarded that plane a thousand times already, followed Gramma May's instructions to find the hotel in Karachi, told Lucie everything that had stopped him begging her not to go when she'd been standing here right in front of him.

But the house sale…the kids…his patients…

What if you get there and she still doesn't want to come home?

The woman in the pea-green coat dragged a finger along the top of the fridge. She grimaced at what she saw, and then she moved Ruby's dog drawing from under its alphabet magnet, where it had been for three whole years.

It was the final straw. He was losing his mind. This house was his, and it had always been Lucie's too.

Family.

He hadn't tried hard enough before to keep her here. But this time…

'Belle,' he said, interrupting her mid-rant, 'can you please look after the twins till I get back?'

'Wait—what? Where are you going?' she called out in confusion.

He was already sprinting up the stairs.

CHAPTER TWENTY-FIVE

LUCIE WHEELED HER bags out of the elevator into the bright hotel reception area, clutching the giant memorial book. Jorge's widow had done his memory proud. Her colleagues had flown it out here to Karachi for her. She just prayed it wasn't too big for her carry-on.

It was raining outside. Would she even be able to get a taxi to the airport at this hour?

Now that she'd made her mind up, and her team had been informed that she was leaving, she'd expected a sense of excitement to find its way to her. It hadn't reached her yet. All she felt was nerves.

What if she got all the way back to Brookborough and AJ still didn't want to see her?

At least she would know she'd tried, she supposed. At least she wouldn't have let her panic over another rejection stand in the way of what she really wanted.

Maybe she'd imagined most of it, all these years. People hadn't always left her out in the cold… If anything, she'd been the one to leave them.

'Taxi, please?' she asked the receptionist.

'Maybe I can drive you. Where are you trying to get to?' came a voice from behind her.

'I'd rather get an official cab, thank you,' she said, flustered, turning around.

A man in a raincoat shoved the hood back from his face.

Lucie dropped the memorial book to the floor with a thud. *Oh, my God.*

'AJ...?' She blinked, fully expecting the mirage to melt away into a puddle of rain.

He picked up the book, put it on the counter and took her hands. His blue eyes brimmed with intense regret and determination, and she flung herself straight into his arms.

'What are you doing here?' Her voice came out as a croak as his big arms looped around her, tightly and possessively. She'd never been this glad to see *anyone.*

'I didn't come to get you once before, when I should have. Lucie, you have to forgive me for what I said last time I saw you. I wasn't thinking straight.'

'I can't believe you're here...' It was all she could manage.

His warmth, his familiar smell...he was even wearing the cable knit sweater that made her want to curl up against his chest, where she was safe.

'You came all the way *here*...'

'I know you have to work, and I know it's what you want, but you're in my blood, my Lucie. I couldn't let you go again without telling you how much I love you.'

The receptionist wiped a tear from her eye, and then pretended she wasn't watching and listening to all this.

Lucie pulled Austin down to the couch. 'My God, AJ, this is crazy. I was about to go to the airport...to come home.'

'So you *do* know where home is?'

His voice was pure relief, and her heart skidded as he stroked his thumbs across her hands, then reached for her face again. Lucie melted into his fierce kiss there on the tiny hotel couch. She'd already forgotten completely where she was, or that she'd made possibly the biggest decision of her life without even knowing he was already on his way here.

Gramma must have told him where she was. But he'd made this decision on his own. He wouldn't have done anything like this unless he was one hundred percent serious about wanting her in his life, in the twins' lives.

'I've quit,' she said quietly. 'You were right. I don't need to do this—not full-time anyway. Maybe a few weeks of the year, in some less dangerous places, so you're not worried about me. You could even come with me if you wanted to…' She tailed off and he laughed.

'That I could deal with. But, you know, there's a vital position opening up with Thera Pups and the research clinic. I know people. I could put a word in.'

'They all know me already—no thanks to a certain incident in a pond that almost made the local news.'

He kissed her again, and she scruffed up his damp hair with her hands, thanking whatever god was looking out for her that she hadn't lost him.

'I love you. I don't want you to worry about me leaving you, AJ—ever,' she said quickly. 'I'm not going anywhere. You're my home. And Ruby, and Josiah, and Gramma—all of you.'

'I almost sold the house,' he said, grinning against her forehead. 'But I couldn't do it. The couple hate dogs. And kids, apparently.'

'Well, that's no good!' She laughed, breathing him in… her lifeblood.

Maybe she had met her soulmate when she was nine years old. If only she hadn't just given her room up she'd have dragged him into it.

'It's your house too,' he said, seriously. 'If you want it. With me.'

'I do.' She bit her lip, then kissed him yet again…and again. She kissed him pretty much all the way home.

Austin glanced around the gleaming gardens. A sense of pride settled on his shoulders along with the late-afternoon sun, just from looking around at his volunteers—and Lucie. She'd been up since seven o'clock that morning, helping him lug boxes of Thera Pups calendars and branded hats and harnesses into their spot in the castle grounds. The Paws Under the Stars event was sold out.

Gilling Castle's gardens were stunning right now, surmounted by carved lions and lined with blossoming flowers. To their credit, the twins had been good as gold all day, running about with their friends. They couldn't wait to see the dogs all lit up later, and to start their stargazing safari.

'The dogs look so great!' Constance squealed, greeting Jetson as he bounded up to her in his costume. 'Is he a hot dog?' she asked, taking in the squishy fabric bread rolls either side of him, and the fake mustard blob tied around his head.

Lucie came up beside him in a long red dress, slipping her hand into his. 'He is. And Maple is... Where is my little Yoda?'

Austin squeezed her hand. Just her being here beside him was still unreal to him. The fact that she'd moved into the house the same night he'd brought her home even more so. Words could not describe how good it had felt...the two of them ripping the *For Sale* sign from the daffodil patch and tossing it onto the bonfire.

He spotted Maple. 'There she is. Maple! Come here, girl!'

Maple padded over from her place with Gramma May, Flora McNally from the gift shop and Cynthia, who'd kindly donated special dog-shaped sweets from the chocolate shop. *The coven*, he called them. They waved at him from the merchandise stall and brandished the new calendar excitedly.

He put a finger to his lips. Lucie hadn't seen it yet.

The second Maple reached an adoring Constance she was immediately called away again, by young Samuel, who was making Bingo the beagle perform an impressive jump and spin move. Everyone was here.

'Maple has so many friends!' Lucie smiled, looking around at all the people she'd got to know in recent months.

'So do you,' he added, and she pressed her lips to his, sighing in satisfaction.

The private moment between them, in a not so private place, sent a tidal wave of love and longing through him. He pulled her against his chest, holding her tight until she squealed and laughed, and then he silenced her with more kisses. He could never get enough of kissing her, and although the twins pretended it disgusted them he could tell it didn't. They loved her nearly as much as he did.

'Get a room!' someone called.

Lucie shrugged and stuck her tongue out. Gramma May told her off, but even she was laughing.

The sun was starting to sink behind the trees. On the stage by the castle the live band began a rendition of a song he knew, and Ruby called out, 'Can we dance, Daddy?'

He turned to Lucie. There was stuff still to do…like making sure all the dogs' lights had working batteries for the great moment when they'd turn them on for the parade.

She must have read his mind. 'One dance won't hurt,' she said.

Ruby took both their hands and led them on to the dance floor. He'd never seen his daughter so happy as she'd been all this week. Having Lucie around was probably her dream come true, but he was being careful, still, not to push any parental duties on her. Everything she did must come from her own heart, and she'd already promised to help Ruby paint her bedroom.

'Come and dance with us,' she said now, pulling Josiah in with them.

The next thing Austin knew, the four of them were spinning in circles, dizzy, laughing so hard he thought he would burst.

'You call that dancing?' someone called out from the sidelines.

'Jack Granger!'

Lucie raced to get him, pushing him straight onto the dance floor in his wheelchair. Austin half expected the old grouch to complain and protest, but he let the kids push him around, a smile hovering and growing bigger and bigger by the second on his thin lips.

In the middle of the chaos, he took Lucie's hand with his good arm, beckoned her closer, and whispered something in her ear.

Lucie frowned, shook her head. 'No... No, I couldn't.'

Jack was pressing something into her hands. Lucie tried to hand it back, but Jack waved her off, then wheeled his chair back towards their event space, as if he wouldn't take no for an answer.

'What did he give you?' Austin asked, following her off the dance floor.

The twins skipped off towards Belle and Bryce.

'A necklace,' she said, stunned, holding it out to him. 'He said Alice would have wanted me to have it.'

Wow.

He swept her hair aside and fastened the sparkling necklace around her neck.

She pressed a hand to it in awe. 'It's gorgeous. Are these... real diamonds?'

'See? You do have more friends here than just Maple,' he told her, smiling away the mild disappointment that old Jack Granger had possibly outdone the gift he himself had planned.

Lucie knew she should be looking at the stars, but she couldn't tear her eyes away from AJ and the way his smile stretched his handsome face every time Ruby and Josiah got excited about a new constellation.

'That's Ursa Major,' he was saying now, whilst slipping an arm around her shoulders.

She leaned into him. The night air was warm, and it smelled like honeysuckle and all the goods from the food marquees.

While her thoughts sometimes flickered to her colleagues out in Pakistan, she didn't feel guilty any more for being here instead of there. They were happy for her, had told her how Jorge would be looking down on her, wishing her happiness. She liked to think Ebby would be wishing the same for AJ.

'Lucie, look—what's that one?'

Ruby turned the telescope towards her and she pressed her eye to the cool rim. The northern star flickered brightly, as if on cue, and she smiled, picturing Jorge's face. Weird timing...

'Make a wish,' she said to the twins.

They stared up at the sky in deep concentration, as if they couldn't decide which wish might be the most important, and AJ sneaked in a kiss to her cheek.

'I've already got my wish,' he said, nudging her.

She laughed, nudging him back.

Secretly, it turned her on. All his stupid dad jokes did, too. They reminded her that she was part of a family—one huge extended family—who wanted and needed her as much as she did them.

Maple and Jetson were stars in their own right tonight. They'd got the crowds roaring just now, doing their little tricks in their silly costumes, all lit up under the sky. Hopefully they'd raised a lot of money for Thera Pups, so they could really get AJ's venture on the map.

Now that she could help him full time, she was brimming with ideas. She and Constance were already thinking up more fundraising events. Maybe she *had* made more friends than her dog, she considered, touching a hand to the necklace.

Seeing the twins were now busy with Belle, AJ pulled her over to the merchandise stall. Most of the items were sold out already. He handed her a calendar.

'What's this?' She frowned. The Thera Pups logo and a huge photo of Jetson with his tongue out took up the front page.

'You haven't seen April yet,' he said.

His blue eyes shone with mischief and she chuckled. He

looked the cutest like this, as if the young boy she'd met all those years ago had come back to play.

Intrigued, she flipped through the months. There were Samuel and Bingo, standing together with another volunteer and a basset hound. There was Jack for March, looking less than impressed while Jetson stood on his back paws by his chair. So many gorgeous photos. And then… April.

Lucy let out an excited *Eek!* at the photo of her and Maple with Constance. 'I didn't even know you'd taken that,' she said, touched.

It had been a moment in her new friend's living room, with the giant black and white photo of her happy wedding day behind them, and Maple's paw in Constance's hand. Lucie was laughing at something behind them.

'It was a pretty sweet moment,' he told her, sweeping her hair back.

She pressed a hand to her heart, kissed him. 'I shouldn't tell you this…but I like it as much as my necklace.'

'I won't tell Jack.' He grinned, glancing at the twins, still gabbling to his sister. 'I just thought…you know… You're part of this, Luce, and you always were. I hope you believe that now?'

'I do.' She smiled.

'Good—and to make sure you don't forget it, we'll put ten of these up in the living room.'

She pretended to whack him with the calendar. 'I told you… I'm not going anywhere!'

He looked serious suddenly, and she felt a nervous flutter around her heart. Until he swept her face into her hands.

'Lucie, *you* are my home.'

'And you're mine.'

All she could think was how she couldn't wait to get him back to the house and into his bedroom, where she would make love to him all night. Even if another nightmare tore her from sleep she wouldn't care. She would just roll into his arms and hold him tight.

October

'Austin, how could you do this to me on my wedding week-end?'

Belle pouted playfully at him as he entered the room, undoing two buttons on the shirt under his *Beetlejuice* jacket.

Lucie did a double-take, and a swell of pride puffed out his chest as the twins clapped their hands in glee.

'Daddy, you look so good in a stripey suit! But what's with the green hair?'

'I'll show you the movie when you're older,' he told them. 'Do what to you?' he asked Belle.

But one look at Lucie and he knew. She'd told Belle.

The wedding rehearsal was in one hour, downstairs in this sixteenth-century manor house, and Belle, in one of what was probably five or six planned outfits, pretended to cry as she flopped back onto the bed.

He hurried the twins outside and told them to count the Halloween pumpkins and paper ghosts strung up in the corridor.

'I had to tell her—look at me,' Lucie said when they'd gone, pressing both hands to her visible bump. 'I wasn't going to, but my dress doesn't fit. We'll need the dressmaker to alter it...'

'Don't worry about that—I was only joking. We'll fix it.'

Belle jumped back to her feet, sending a glitter shower from her Tinkerbell wings all over the floor. She engulfed them both in a huge bear hug that made Maple and Jetson pad over in interest, wanting to join the excitement.

'I am so, so, *so* thrilled for you both. Lucie, when are you due?'

'April... God, I'll be huge by then.'

She fiddled with the zip on the side of a sweeping ochre-coloured V-necked gown, and Austin bit back a smile at how beautiful a pregnant Morticia Addams she made.

She was definitely bigger already. With *his* child. It had happened so quickly, once Lucie had told him that she might, possibly, if he wasn't completely opposed to the idea, quite like a baby with him.

Why wait? he'd thought.

They had the room, and plenty of money, and more than enough love to spare.

He'd gone about trying to make it happen every night and every morning—in the bath, in the car... It was almost as if the kid had been waiting there for them to say, *'We're ready to meet you...come and join our madhouse, little one.'*

'Well, luckily my crazy sister opted for a themed wedding,' he said, wrapping his arms around her, then pressing his own hands to her bump from behind.

Belle made a gagging sound, but he ignored her, kissing the side of Lucie's neck. She turned her head in its waist-length wig, dropping a kiss to his purple-stained lips.

'Dark colours mean you won't show...as much...' he said, and paused, noticing another rip along the seam of her leg. 'OK, maybe people will guess. I suppose we'll have to tell everyone else now.'

'We should tell the twins first,' she said tentatively, as Belle floated out of the room, mumbling something about them stealing her thunder.

Austin knew she was joking. She couldn't wait to dote on another niece or nephew. Since moving out, Belle had actually been back a lot more than he'd expected her to. She missed the twins, she said. Couldn't wait to have her own children with Bryce.

Austin sat Ruby and Josiah down in the Halloween-themed hall downstairs. He was nervous suddenly, holding Lucie's hand tight. They eyed him in suspicion over their orange-coloured Jack-o'-Lantern lollipops as he tried to find the words.

It was Lucie who found them first.

'Listen, you two. Your dad has something to tell you. It's

hopefully something you're going to be very, very excited about. As excited as we are!'

She crouched down to their level. An almighty rip from another busted seam made them snort with laughter.

'Oh…well, now we definitely need the dressmaker,' she laughed.

'Lucie, your dress has broken!'

'That must be the baby inside her,' Josiah said, with his toothy grin.

AJ started. Lucie stood, clutching her ripped skirt. They exchanged glances.

'We know there's a baby in your belly,' Josiah added, matter-of-factly.

'We were waiting for you to tell us,' Ruby followed up, giving Lucie a giant hug.

Her little arms only just fitted around the bump. How the…? He would never know. They were smarter than even he gave them credit for.

'Does this mean you're going to stop renewing your wedding vows every two weeks, like a couple of crazy teenagers?' Belle asked, coming up behind them and thoughtfully adjusting the parrot on Ruby's pirate jacket.

Lucie grinned and looked at him sideways. It was true. Ever since their summer wedding Austin had made it a thing to regularly sweep her away somewhere for a night, so they could both renew their connection. She knew it was because he loved letting her know how much she belonged in his world, with him, and she loved him even more for it.

'Let's just enjoy your wedding weekend, shall we?' He smiled. 'The rehearsal's starting!'

He laced his fingers through Lucie's, clutched her hand tight to his side, and walked towards the aisle.

* * * * *

COMING SOON!

We really hope you enjoyed reading this book. If you're looking for more romance be sure to head to the shops when new books are available on

Thursday 28th September

MILLS & BOON®

Coming next month

HER OFF-LIMITS SINGLE DAD
Marion Lennox

This was not sensible—not sensible in the least. There was no need at all for her to stay with Rob for a moment longer. She was this man's tenant and a colleague, and that was all. She lived at the far end of the house. She needed to keep some distance.

But distance had never been Jen's strong suit.

Maybe it was her childhood, absent parents who'd appeared sporadically, causing her to cling fiercely, to take what she could because she'd known they wouldn't be there the next day.

Maybe that was why she'd jumped into all sorts of disastrous relationships—okay, Darren hadn't been the first. Jump first, ask questions later. Take people at face value because looking forward didn't change a thing.

And here it was, happening again. This man had so much baggage—impossible baggage—yet here he was, looking down at her, smiling, and here was that longing again—for closeness, for warmth, for connection.

Her friend Frankie might have poured a bucket of cold water over her, she thought, demanding, "Will you ever learn?" But right now...

Right now Rob was reaching down to help her up. His

hands were strong and warm, and his smile was oh, so lovely.

Maybe this time…

What was she thinking? It was too soon—way, way too soon.

But that smile… She had no hope of fighting the way his smile made her feel.

And he tugged her a little too strongly, or maybe she rose a little too fast, and all of a sudden she was very, very close.

Here comes another catastrophe! She could almost hear Frankie's inevitable warning.

But Rob was right here, and she could feel his warmth, his strength… His lovely hands were steadying her, and he was still smiling.

She was lost.

Here I go again.

She could hear her brain almost sighing in exasperation, but did she care?

Not tonight. Not when he was so close.

So, she thought blindly as she felt the warmth of his chest, felt his hands steady her. Catastrophe, here I come.

Continue reading
HER OFF-LIMITS SINGLE DAD
Marion Lennox

Available next month
www.millsandboon.co.uk

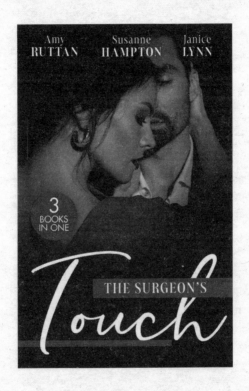

MILLS & BOON

THE HEART OF ROMANCE

A ROMANCE FOR EVERY READER

MODERN

Prepare to be swept off your feet by sophisticated, sexy and seductive heroes, in some of the world's most glamourous and romantic locations, where power and passion collide.

HISTORICAL

Escape with historical heroes from time gone by. Whether your passion is for wicked Regency Rakes, muscled Vikings or rugged Highlanders, awaken the romance of the past.

MEDICAL

Set your pulse racing with dedicated, delectable doctors in the high-pressure world of medicine, where emotions run high and passion, comfort and love are the best medicine.

True Love

Celebrate true love with tender stories of heartfelt romance, from the rush of falling in love to the joy a new baby can bring, and a focus on the emotional heart of a relationship.

Desire

Indulge in secrets and scandal, intense drama and sizzling hot action with heroes who have it all: wealth, status, good looks...everything but the right woman.

HEROES

The excitement of a gripping thriller, with intense romance at its heart. Resourceful, true-to-life women and strong, fearless men face danger and desire - a killer combination!

To see which titles are coming soon, please visit

millsandboon.co.uk/nextmonth